# KING of HEARTS

*The Deuces Wild Series*
*Book 1*

## IRISH WINTERS

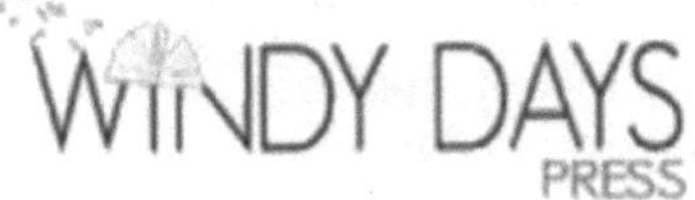

# Praise for Irish Winters' Sniper series

### ALEX, Book 1

"These characters were so well written at times I felt like I was feeling the love, the loss, and the triumph right along with them." *Amazeballs Book Addicts*

### ZACK, Book 3

"This is my first book by Irish Winters and I have to say I'm sold!" *ThePleasureofReadingToday.*

### HARLEY, Book 4

"… one of the sweetest male heroes that I have come across in a long time." *ReadsAllTheBooks*

### CONNOR, Book 5

"Thrilling, suspenseful, heartbreaking and tender - you will not want to put this book down once you start." *Jen M.*

### RORY, Book 6

"Irish Winters' Sniper series is a pure, one hundred percent, five star read!" *LJ Vickery*

### MAVERICK, Book 9

"Irish Winters, you have ruined me with Maverick, ruined me in the very best of ways." *ReadsAllTheBooks*

## ADAM, Book 11

"These books are like potato chips. You read one and you just can't stop. Keep them coming." *Lhill*

## LEE, Book 12

"Irish's BEST EVER!!! Best book I've read in a long time!! Little twist here, little twist there and BAM...She's got you!!" *Kindle customer*

## KY, Book 13

"Home run!" *Melissa Raywood*

# For My Readers

Be sure to go to IrishWinters.com and sign up for my newsletter to receive hot-off-the press, upcoming book release announcements. You'll also receive a link in the newsletter to download *Christmas Hearts* when it's released on November 24th. *Christmas Hearts* is a collection of Christmases spent with Alex Stewart and several of his team.

Don't miss this limited time offer. It's my gift to you!

# DEDICATION

God Bless America

# ACKNOWLEDGMENTS

So here we are, off on another adventure, this time running with the elite paranormal unit in the Federal Bureau of Investigation. After the bitter feud between Alex Stewart's TEAM and the FBI in my Sniper series, this book has been a long time coming. I couldn't ask for a more headstrong alpha male than Tucker Chase to lead what will, *I think,* be a three book series. But then, I never intended the Sniper series to grow to what it is today, thirteen books published and another three primed and ready to go in 2017.

To my faithful fans and good friends the world over, I wouldn't be where I am today without you. You've touched me with your patriotism and dedication to our country. I've heard from so many of you willing to share stories from your military experience, your love of country and spouse, and honestly, that's the best reward of all. You've made me cry at what you've suffered, and how much you love America. I love America, too. Thank you for taking a chance on this new series.

As always, I end with my husband, Bill. My real hero. Because of your patience and understanding, sweetheart, my guys and gals live. Don't go anywhere. The best is yet to be!

# The Dead Man's Hand

Old West lawman, gambler, gunslinger and showman, James "Wild Bill" Hickok, was murdered on August 2, 1876, while playing five-card draw at Nuttal & Mann's Saloon in Deadwood, Dakota Territory. Jack McCall, a disgruntled gambler, approached Hickok from behind and shot him at point-blank range in the back of the head, killing him instantly. McCall was later hanged for the murder, but by then, America had lost one of its premier Wild West heroes.

Legend tells us "Wild Bill" held two pair at the moment of his death, black aces and eights—the *dead man's hand*. The identity of the fifth card has been the subject of conjecture for years. For the purpose of this series, I've chosen a deuce of hearts for that card-in-the-hole, in honor of a little boy named Devlin who loved to play the violin. In honor of a father's undying love for his son.

Some players think wild cards are amateurish and juvenile. Others believe the more wild cards in the game, the greater their chance of winning. I only know that one Deuce and a pair makes three of a kind, and that sounds a lot like a family to me. You be the judge.


*Deuces Wild.*

# Prologue

*I'm on my way.*

Again.

Tucker Chase couldn't get to her house fast enough, but damn, he was tired of the on-again, off-again rollercoaster romance with Melissa McCormack, and the siren call of the temptress he wasn't man enough to resist. He was sick of her mixed signals, too. One minute she was pulling him in for another kiss, the next, pushing him back, not ready to move on. Why not? *He* was ready. Why'd she have to make everything so hard? Why couldn't she find that God-blessed closure she needed?

It was a stupid question, and he got it. Really, he did. A widow needed more time to move on than a divorced man, but how much more time? *To hell with closure.*

He punched the steering wheel of his black Dodge Challenger. He'd been playing this game for over a year, and during that year, he'd been uncharacteristically faithful. He hadn't once looked at another woman, which was not his style. He'd taken it slow with Melissa—also not his style. He'd romanced and dined the hell out of her, he'd bought her more roses than he'd ever bought his ex-wife in their short, explosive marriage, and he'd waited. Oh, how he'd waited.

But every single time he took things a little too far, every time he read her sexy body language and thought she was past regret and ready to give in to him, bam. She drew back and pulled away. Son-of-a-bitch but he was tired of the regret glimmering in her blue eyes. The shadow she seemed to nurse like a long-lost friend. The ghost of her dead husband.

Damn Brady McCormack for being such a stand-up guy. For being her hero. For getting shot to hell in Iraq and coming home a quadriplegic. For dying. And damn Melissa for still being eternally faithful to her first true love. How could a flesh-and-blood guy compete with a marble headstone in Arlington?

Tucker couldn't. He looked both ways before he crossed the busy intersection against the light. Damn it. Despite his intense heartache for Melissa, he wasn't angry with her for loving her husband. Not really. That was actually part of what drew Tucker to Melissa. Her loyalty. Her undying devotion. She was that        once-in-a-lifetime,        too-good-to-be-true, impossible dream girl. From the get-go, she'd been a single ray of sunshine in his solitary world where warriors crossed paths with evil incarnate. She was that first breath of fresh spring air on a chilly March morning. If anything, he was jealous of Brady, and more than a little angry the guy went and got shot up so bad that he'd eventually died. Melissa deserved to be happy again. Tucker wanted to be that guy.

The car to his left blared a warning. He flipped the driver off, hit the gas, peeled rubber, and kept moving. There he was, half-crazy with needing Melissa and running red lights to get to her side before she changed her mind. Dodging slow traffic. And cursing all the way.

Melissa was not like other women. She was a one-man-and-one-man-only kind of gal, and he'd been caught in the same breathless grip ever since. One look into the liquid depths of her ocean blue eyes and he'd fallen like a punch-drunk sailor over his own big feet. Strength swelled in those shimmering windows to her soul, but other things lingered in the shadows. Sadness. Bravery. Her morals.

He cussed the early morning traffic on the Northern Virginia freeway. Tapping his fingernails on the stick shift, he forced a deep breath to calm his need for speed. The last thing he wanted was another ticket, and this souped-up pony would get it for him if he didn't rein it in and take it easy. Melissa wouldn't like *that*, either.

*Sheesh. That woman!*

For now, she lived in a singles-only condo west of Arlington, close to her family and her husband's family. That was another thing. Her parents were good Christians and nice people. Tucker had met them. He liked them, especially her mother. Camille had welcomed him with open arms, a hug and a big smile. But her father? All he'd done was scowl and grumble during Tucker's visit. It took extra patience to get through that night.

Then the McCormacks, Jed and Lois. Where to begin? Brady had been their only child, their pride and joy. When he'd died from complications due to his war injuries, Melissa became their world. If her own parents didn't dote on her, Jed and Lois surely did.

She was everyone's rock star. Tucker was just another groupie hanging around for an autograph. She meant the world to them. He was the proverbial bad boy they hoped she'd grow out of, get over, and leave in the dust when she moved onto someone more socially acceptable. So what if he had a reputation for being a notorious hard-ass around D.C.? What decent FBI agent didn't? They got the dirty jobs done, and they had a lot to be proud of, damn it.

He pulled onto Melissa's street and roared up to the security gate of her condo complex. "Hey," he said smoothly to the up-tight security guard. "I'm back."

"I see that. Slow it down. Five miles per hour, please." The stuffy guy raised the wrought-iron security gate, and Tucker made sure he didn't exceed the pathetically slow speed limit to her door. Melissa waited for him on the sidewalk and double damn if she didn't take his breath away like she always did.

He shoved the stick shift into park and let the sight of her wash over him. His heart swelled. As frustrated as she could make him, Melissa also made him proud. This woman was as strong as she was beautiful, as intelligent as she was kind. She also had a soft streak the size of Texas, and it ran clear to her soul.

He took time to drink in her voluptuous curves. There wasn't a hard line or edge to the woman. "Melissa," he called as he scrambled out of the Challenger, his heart in his throat like always.

*But look at her.* What man could resist? Blond long hair hung in spirals down her back and over her shoulders. Full breasts bounced beneath her pale yellow top. As she walked toward him, curvy hips swayed with a provocative catch-me-if-you-can. Even her lush, sweet lips were turned up into a perfect bow of juicy temptation, the soft Virginia sun bright on her face. The woman had been created to drive him crazy, all lush curves from her plump hips to her full and very soft breasts. He would know. Second base was as far as he'd gotten. She just wouldn't give it up, no matter what he'd tried, and believe him—he'd tried.

"Tucker! Hi!" She smiled, full of vitality and happy to see him. Her fluffy Yorkie, Taz, bounced at her ankles. He looked happy to see Tucker, but what dog wasn't? Dogs were smart enough to recognize a good guy when they saw one.

Tucker closed the distance with long strides, wondering which of them was the bigger fool, her for leading him on or him for letting her. "You called?" he asked as she walked into his arms. He gathered her up, and closed his eyes, inhaling the feminine scent of green apples and vanilla musk. Maybe cinnamon. God, it was happening again. He wanted to rub her over his chest—and other places—just to keep her essence with him all the time. That was what he'd missed—this simple reminder that she really did belong to him. That they were made for each other. That he could be her hero, if she'd just let him in.

The battle for her heart never went away. It hadn't since he'd first seen her, and her scent only made it worse. There he was, as hard as a rock in all the wrong places and ready to try again.

Tilting her chin upward with his thumb, he looked into the sweetest face. Her lips blossomed with a genuine smile, and he succumbed to her invitation. He took her mouth with all the tender love in his heart, running his tongue over her lips and allowing her time to let him in. She always did, and Melissa knew how to kiss. She seemed to pour all of her womanly charm into that sensual contact. She fully engaged, her arms around his neck, her breasts pressed to his chest, and her teeth and tongue actively involved. Nipping. Tugging. Tasting him the same way he tasted her.

Like it or not, Tucker Chase was hooked like a great sea bass off the Atlantic coast. A man could get used to the sensual sweep of her tongue over his, the tango of mint and lipstick. The promise of that elusive more he'd been looking for. The way she sucked his lower lip into her mouth and nibbled. The soft murmurs of a satisfied woman he ached to satisfy even more. Yeah. She wanted him, and God knew he wanted her.

He let his hand sink to the small of her back, his fingertips splayed over the round plump cheek of her ass. He longed for the day she'd let him get a good grip, but he didn't dare tempt fate. Not today. She'd sounded anxious on the phone earlier. He needed to pay attention.

She eased away from his mouth and leaned her cheek to his chest, her head tucked under his chin. See, that was what turned him inside out. She wanted to be close, really close—just not as close as he wanted her to be. And yet she did. He could read it in her eyes, just before she'd push him away. She wanted him as much as he wanted her, but that noble Marine she'd married and buried stood in the way. Every time.

"It came," she said, a tremor of excitement in her tone. "It finally came. I've been selected."

He would've answered, but the seductively warm heat radiating from this woman's sexy body robbed him of all common sense. He cocked his head and waited for the rest of the story. What had come?

She'd accused him of not listening enough, and he knew better than to open his big mouth, insert foot and admit it.

"I'm leaving next week. Remember?"

Tucker needed to see her face for sure then. He eased her back, his thumb under her chin to tip her gaze upward, just enough to read the answer in those lovely eyes. "You're what? Leaving to go where?"

"You didn't hear me, did you?" she asked, that look in her eyes again. *That* look. The one that showed up right before every shove-off and goodbye. "You weren't listening to me last week, were you?"

"I thought I was, babe," he admitted guiltily. "I really do try, but you're so intoxicating. I might have missed something."

The smile faded. *Here we go again.*

"You never listen, Tucker, and don't give me that 'babe' or 'I'm so intoxicating' stuff." She bobbed her head back and forth in a bad imitation of a swagger. "I need you to care about the things I care about. I need you to see me. Really see me."

There it was again, her palm square in the middle of his chest, enforcing her personal space. Like he didn't know what 'no' meant. He didn't mean to snort like he did, but holy shit. This woman drove him nuts ten ways to Sunday. "Where are you going, Melissa? Just spit it out and tell me."

"I've been accepted for a three-month mission with Doctors for Charity. I leave next Tuesday," she said quietly. "I've talked about this with you. It's important work. Tell me you remember."

He scrubbed a hand over his chin. Three months? She might as well have told him to drop dead because his heart sure felt like it had. What was he supposed to do while she gallivanted to the other side of the world on some humanitarian crusade with a bunch of horny doctors? Sit home and wait for her to decide to come back? Write letters? *Shit. Just shit.*

She took a step out of his arms, her eyes narrowed. "You honestly don't remember, do you?"

"Yeah, I remember." Kind of. She had been excited about something a month ago. Maybe he should've listened a little better. *Three months?* "When will you be back?"

Melissa rolled her shoulder, sending a cascade of golden silk flying, the curled ends cupping her breast the way he'd like to. "I just told you. Three months, Tucker. I'll be back the middle of February."

"February what?" He ran a hand over his head and down the back of his neck. That meant she'd be gone over Christmas. Holy hell. There'd be no joy in Whoville and less in his heart.

Melissa peered closer, her nose wrinkled. "What is that thing in your eye, *Tucker Chase*?"

*Oh, oh.* Her tone and use of his full name jerked him back in time to grade school and his ornery third grade teacher, the one who used to smack him to get his attention. He blinked, stalling. "It's nothing. Just an implant to help me see better. Don't worry about it."

She took a step closer and tipped his chin up, her brows joined in a deeply etched and sexy V. She squinted. "You've... you've got a contact? When did you get it? What's wrong with that eye?"

The implant was more than a contact lens. The state-of-the-art mechanized zoom lens was a futuristic FBI option that went along with his cochlear implant, only people weren't supposed to notice it. Especially not Melissa. *Damn.*

Tucker bowed his head, wishing she'd understand the advantage it gave him in the field but knowing that was unlikely. "It's not a contact. It's just an ocular implant, no big deal. It's cool. I can adjust it and... Thursday," he admitted, losing ground. *Two days ago.*

She cocked her head, challenging him. "You had eye surgery, and you didn't think to tell me?"

*Shit. Just shit.*

"You know..." She tugged Taz's bright pink leash, bringing the happy-go-lucky little guy to her side. "Maybe we need to take a time out, maybe figure out what's really going on between us."

"Are you breaking up with me?" he asked, a titch too sharply. Women just didn't do that. Not to him.

"Honestly, I don't know what I'm doing," she said sadly. "You don't let me into your life, Tucker. Like this implant. I should've been there with you when you had the surgery. For that matter, you should've talked this over with me before you took matters into your own hands. But you never do, do you? For heavens sake, one minute you're hot, but the next—"

"Damn it, I'm always hot, Melissa. That's who I am. I'm hotheaded, and I'm hot-blooded, and I want you in every way a man can possibly want a woman, but you never give me the same signal twice!" He took one step away from her before he said anything that would get him into more trouble. "You let me hold you like a lover, but you're not one, are you?"

"Excuse me?" she asked, blinking as if she'd just been slapped.

That wasn't what he'd meant to say. True maybe, but not smart. He took a deep breath and tried again. "Babe, I'm sorry. You know I've got a big mouth, but I lo-lo-l—" *Oh shit.* He snapped his big mouth shut. He'd almost said it, the one word that wasn't in his playbook. Not anymore.

Of course she picked up on that little mistake. "Don't you dare tell me you love me now, Tucker. Don't. You. Dare." She stabbed her index finger into his chest, punctuating his mistake. "Love isn't a cheap pick-up line and it isn't a cure-all when you're too busy to listen. It's not a solves-all blurb for the few moments you're interested, either."

"But I am interested. All the time." *How could she not know that?*

"No, you're not." He loved the spark in her eyes when she got riled up. "Every time we're together, you've got your finger in your ear listening to that voice in your head, that FBI cochlear implant that keeps you up-to-date twenty-four-seven on everything else in the world but me. And now we'll have your bionic eyeball. We'll never have one uninterrupted moment alone, will we? You can't save the whole planet, Tucker. Have you ever once considered that? Do you always have to be the hero?"

He would've told her how stupid that question was—after all, who didn't know that SEALs were always the heroes—but his cell phone buzzed an incoming. Didn't it figure? At least HQ hadn't called the hotline this time. She'd be pissed if he stuck his finger in his ear to better listen to the latest calling-all-cars over her ranting. He'd never hear the end of that.

"Do you?" she asked again. Melissa closed her eyes and took a deep breath. Sweet little Taz whined. He wasn't happy either.

Tucker's heart kicked up a funny thump because he'd forgotten her question. His phone buzzed a second time. *Here we go again.*

She was absolutely right. He needed to take a timeout from his job once in a while, but something big was going down, maybe in D.C. His cell buzzed an incoming. He needed to respond to headquarters before everything blew up.

"Sorry," he mumbled, scooping his vibrating cell phone out of his pants pocket. Her lips pinched into a thin, tight line, but he answered anyway, one eye on her and not the bionic one. "Chase. What's up?"

"Trespassers on the White House grounds," the FBI switchboard informed. "They jumped the fence. Three of them. Wearing hoods. Possibly armed. Metro is engaged now. Requesting FBI backup."

"On my way," he replied, because that was what FBI agents always did. Like SEALs, they showed up every time and they did their job.

"See?" Melissa asked, her smile gone and the sunshine with it. "Each time we get together, this happens. You get some secret message. You take off because you have somewhere better to be. Someone else to save. Someone who isn't me. And to top it off, now you've got your office in your ear talking over anything I say. I'm tired of it, Tuck. You're exhausting. I'll see you in three months, but I want an answer then, and it better not be sex-related. Got it?"

*Hmmm. Sex-related.* He couldn't help but notice that her breasts heaved when she got her dander up. That her nipples peaked beneath that pale yellow T-shirt. That her pretty face flushed with an enticing peach blush that probably matched her petal soft breasts. That she chewed her lower lip. That *he* wanted to chew her lower lip. His tongue slid against his teeth just thinking about the way she tasted. Honey with the sweet, salty hint of caramel apple and—

"Tucker," she growled, another splash of hot-damned sexy on his already hardened manhood. "Are you listening to me? Have you heard anything I said?"

He nodded, but the blood supply train to his brain had jumped tracks and headed south. "Yes. I heard you. Three months. Ninety days. Middle of February. Got it."

"And then what?"

He gave her what he thought she wanted to hear. "You'll be home."

Her lashes went down. She shook her head just enough to let him know he'd gotten it wrong again.

And Melissa walked away.

# Chapter One

Like it or not, Tucker had to put his dilemma with Melissa out of his mind. He had bigger problems. Early the next day, he decisively swallowed his pride and called Alex Stewart, the owner of the most elite covert surveillance company on the East Coast, for help, something he didn't think he'd ever do. Wasn't that a surprise?

More surprising was Stewart's quick comeback. "Sure. I'm open at noon. Can you make it or not?"

"I'll be there," Tucker said, not a little shocked that Stewart had actually made time for him. They hadn't gotten along much in the past. Tucker and Stewart's rivalry went back years to a botched FBI protective order in the little farming town of Spencer, Wisconsin. Stewart and his men had come charging in and set things right. They'd fought hard and they'd saved lives—at the expense of a hard slap in the

Bureau's face. Make that a middle finger, a defiant 'Up yours!'

Good God, the man never backed down from a fight, not once, and he held a wicked grudge over the single civilian death during the op. Several FBI agents had also died, but did he care about them? Hell no. Only the young girl who'd died that day.

But Alex was right. Tucker had held a grudge too.

The field agent in charge of the fiasco, Matt Hartigen, had sorely underestimated their Russian opponents. Tucker would've kept those girls with their parents on their farm instead of splitting them up like Hartigen had insisted, but he was new to the Bureau then. Knowing what he knew now, that Matt was a lying son-of-a-bitch to the deepest dregs of his rotten soul, Tucker would've made sure Hartigen died at the safe house instead of that pretty little Faith Clifton.

*Yeah. If wishes were fishes...*

After teaching an early class of FBI wanna-bees on the how-tos of infil/exfil, and how to get out of Dodge before the tangos cut loose and opened fire, Tucker headed north from Quantico to Alexandria, Virginia. He called Melissa on his in-car phone, but Melissa still wasn't picking up. For the past two days, her cell went instantly to voicemail. Either she was still mad, or she'd really called it quits this time. He didn't blame her. They'd been on and off again for months, and to be truthful, the lack of a clear way forward had worn him out, too.

Maybe this was for the best. A man could only hold on for so long before he tossed in the towel. But the idea that she'd blocked him out of her life, that she wouldn't even talk to him and let him explain, sucked the energy out of him. A heavy darkness hovered over northern Virginia on this November day. Happiness seemed as fleeting as ever. That damned brass ring of a healthy, happy marriage, the one with a loving wife, and the one always a hair's breadth out of reach, taunted him.

The story of his worthless life.

Melissa had honestly felt like his last chance to be a whole man, to finally be happy. Wasn't that a joke? Him? Tucker Chase? A big, tough bruiser of an ex-Navy SEAL, an absolute alpha and one badassed FBI agent, the one Uncle Sam called when he needed someone to knock on Hell's door and kick the Devil's ass, the one all his buddies looked up to, not a real man?

He slapped his steering wheel. Hell, not even half a man, and all because of that divorce decree buried under a stack of junk mail at home.

Nicole, his ex-wife, had done this to him. Then her lawyer had screwed him over. By the time the decree was final, Tucker was not only divorced, he'd lost custody of his only son as well.

There was a thread of truth mixed in with her carefully woven lies. Civilians didn't get it, especially prima donna wives like her. He *did* like who he was—a Navy SEAL. He absolutely loved the adrenaline rush and the fight, but most of all? He loved being with like-minded people who went for broke and kicked butt instead of whining and crying that the world was unfair. *Wah, wah, wah.* It *was* unfair. Get over it! That was why he'd enlisted, to do something about it.

That was why he'd joined the Bureau when he processed out of the Navy, too. There was no tighter group of guys than the ones he'd fought with, kicked ass with, and protected while the hard jobs got done. Nothing in civilian life—*absolutely nothing*—compared to being the toughest dog in the fight. The boss.

Tucker drummed the steering wheel. He loved his Challenger, another bad boy like himself, and possibly the only thing he'd have left to love if Melissa really was done with him. His body ached to the point it was hard to breathe just thinking about her being gone for three months. He couldn't remember. Had she actually said where she was going? *Damn. Damn. Damn.*

She was right. He should have listened better. Everything was his fault.

He'd been a real man until Nicole left with Deuce. What was a guy supposed to do with the rotgut a divorce left behind, huh? How was he supposed to transition from being superman to super deadbeat dad? What did a hero do when he woke up one morning, and he'd been turned into a lousy father and worse—a loser?

Tucker didn't know how to lose. First Deuce. Now Melissa. He clenched the wheel and kept on keeping on, the only thing he knew how to do. Stewart might be able to help get Deuce back. Melisa was another heartache altogether. But Nicole?

The day he had to tell his little guy goodbye rolled back on him. Wouldn't you know? She'd had him served with divorce papers the same day he'd planned to introduce Deuce to the wonderful world of Little League. It would've been the kid's first game, his chance to be part of a winning team instead of te pretentious orchestra Nicole had enrolled him in.

What kid doesn't want to hit a homerun to make his old man proud? Deuce looked good in his blue-and-white striped jersey, his cap on backward, and grinning like he was proud of his team, the Lakeside Chipmunks. He had his very own bat on his shoulder, an Easton Make Youth model, the most expensive one Tucker could find. Nothing was too good for his boy.

There were no words for what happened next. The police showed up. Some guy ducked around the two officers at the door, slapped an envelope in Tucker's hand and said he'd been served. Father and son missed what would have been their one and only Little League practice. Nicole had blindsided them both. Heartbreaking.

Tucker swallowed hard. He could still see his little guy standing there in the entryway, trying to be brave, his roller bag already packed and ready to go. Deuce wasn't a baby, but that morning there were teardrops on his thick, dark eyelashes and wet streaks down his cheeks. He'd tried hard to be tough when he handed his baseball bat over, his lower lip quivering. Tucker choked recalling what happened next.

"Come here, son," he'd said softly, trying to diffuse the pain. It wasn't fair to tear this kid apart like Nicole had done. Tucker had honestly thought he'd see Deuce again.

Deuce plowed into his old man's waist, his head against Tucker's gut. "I don't want to go, Father," he'd cried. The evil she-troll always made him call Tucker that.

But Deuce corrected himself. See? The kid *was* bright. "I love you, Dad. I'll never forget you, and I'll learn all about baseball, and I promise I'll be just like you some day. I will."

Tucker could've bawled as he'd dropped one knee to the floor and cradled his son for what ended up being their last hug. If he could've turned back time and changed every knuckleheaded decision he'd ever made, he would have, right there and then. Instead, he'd sucked it up like the tough guy he was, and he'd refused to shed a tear. He couldn't let his main man see him break down. He couldn't break Deuce's heart the way his was breaking.

But that last hug...

That last armful...

That last nose full of the scent of his son's squeaky-clean hair...

It never went away.

"Shit, who cares but me? It's done," he muttered, sick at heart all over again, mad at himself and his whining. Stewart sure as hell wouldn't have whined. Tucker stepped on the accelerator. Speed was his answer for everything.

Bottom line? He needed Stewart's help since Nicole had left town without any notification, and she'd taken Deuce with her. Tucker hadn't talked with his eleven-year-old son since that last hug. Damn her, she had no right.

By the time Tucker tracked her down via those far-reaching, world-wide FBI networks, she was in Vietnam with her new husband, one Nguyễn Vin Li, an American-born Vietnamese entrepreneur in the textile industry. Didn't it figure? Vinnie was everything Tucker wasn't. Suave. Rich. A sleek Rolls Royce to Tucker's rowdy Dodge Challenger.

It wasn't that Tucker couldn't get into Vietnam, he just couldn't do it without raising the ire of his director, Zachary Strong. An FBI agent on foreign soil was never a good thing, and Tucker couldn't guarantee he'd mind his business once he got there. He was like that—a hothead and quick with his fists, especially when it came to his boy. He would've asked for permission, but Director Strong had made his answer clear. The Bureau didn't need anyone muddying up the international waters like Tucker tended to do. In other words, Tucker couldn't get into Vietnam alone, plain and simple.

But Stewart could.

Tucker parked his car in the visitor's stall of The TEAM's underground parking lot. Didn't it figure? There he was in downtown Alexandria, Virginia, coming to beg an assist from an ex-Marine who'd made good with a two-bit covert surveillance company. A guy who'd been to war and made a decent name for himself despite his demons. How the hell did that work?

*I mean, look at the place.* The guy owned a five-story brick building outright, the lower-level parking garage, too. How did one jarhead get so lucky or so rich?

Tucker opted for a fast run up the stairs instead of an elevator ride to the second floor. He needed to burn off his edge. It wouldn't do to meet Stewart with a chip on his shoulder. At the fire door, he entered ground zero, Stewart's kingdom.

"Hey, Mark." He offered a thumbs-up to Mark Houston, Stewart's second-in-command.

Tall, dark, and built like an ox, Mark shoved away from the customer service desk. An ex- Marine like Stewart, he offered a solid handshake. "Tucker. Good to see you again. Alex said you were stopping by. What's up? Anything I need to be involved in?"

Tucker rolled the knotted tension out of his neck. He knew most of Stewart's men and women in the Alexandria office, a few from the Seattle office, too. He just didn't want them knowing his business. "Just here to talk shop."

Mark chin-nodded toward the hall. "Go on in. He's finished with Senator Yost."

That prominent name piqued Tucker's curiosity and spiked his federal rivalry bone. Yost was the current Speaker of the House up on Capitol Hill. He ruled the roost. What did he need from The TEAM? So what if Stewart had a reputation for working well with ornery politicians. The Bureau was proud to serve. Why hadn't Yost come to the FBI?

"Hey, Tucker!" Ky Winchester called out from his desk. "Good to see you. How's Becker?"

As in Sam Becker, ex-FBI agent turned Secret Service, also a SEAL, and a good buddy. Tucker waved Ky off with a, "Good, as usual. The prick's in Sierra Leone again. Want to guess why?"

"Little Sammie finished his doctorate?"

Tucker nodded with a grin. "Sure did. Sam wanted to be there for his graduation party. Bobby's nearly done with her business degree. It'll be a hot time in Freetown tonight."

"Alex will see you now," Mark said politely.

"Later," Tucker called to the guys and gals he wouldn't mind working with some day. Stewart's men and women were tough professionals. Like him.

Stewart stood stern and formal behind his desk, his arm stretched forward, one palm open for a handshake. "Tucker," he said curtly. Business-like.

"Good morning, Alex." Tucker returned the chilly greeting, but the second he took hold of the man's hand, he met a bone-crunching challenge. Instant assessment flashed between Marine and SEAL, each testing the other's fortitude to see who'd blink first. Was that an ultimatum radiating straight up Tucker's arm from Stewart's firm grip? A dare? It sure felt like it.

Tucker maintained eye contact, his face as expressionless as Stewart's until the handshake ended. Stewart released first, but he hadn't blinked. Tucker acknowledged the standoff for what it was—a simple turf war. He blinked, gave the guy the first round, and took his seat. Mark shut the door and parked his bulky frame in the chair at Stewart's left like his private bouncer.

Tucker got down to business. "I'll be blunt. I need your help finding my son."

"Devlin?" Stewart's brow arched. "Who took him?"

"My ex-wife." Tucker lifted both palms forward to halt the next question. "I know, I know, she's got custody, but here's the thing. She took him out of the country and into Vietnam without my knowledge. That's the first foul."

"Did you contact the local authorities? The police?"

"Of course I did, but they keep telling me they're working on it. I've filed a case with the National Center of Missing and Exploited Children, too. Guess what? I get the same run-around with no results. They're all *working on it.*" He ended on a sarcastic note with air quotes for all the good following the rules did. That was why he needed Stewart. Alex could get the job done.

"I can check with the Federal Office of Children's Issues," Mark suggested. "They're good to help out with cases like this."

"Already done that. *They're working on it.*" Again the air quotes.

"Then why are we here?" Stewart asked sternly.

"Because it's taking too long." Tucker bit his bottom lip to keep from shouting, *'Duh! You morons!'* "And that's not all. She hasn't touched the child support I've deposited in our joint account for months now, and I can't get her to answer any phone calls or emails." He gulped at the note of desperation seeping into his voice. *I'm not going to grovel, damn it.*

Stewart leaned back in his chair. "I can't help you, Chase. Sorry. My company doesn't sanction or assist non-custodial parental kidnappings, nor do we—"

"No, no, no, that's not what I'm asking," Tucker shot back, his fingers raking through his hair. "Shit. I don't sanction traumatizing my kid, either, but I do need to know if Deuce is okay or not. I've got visitation rights. I just need to see him. Can you find him or not?"

"You call him Deuce?" Mark asked, a gentle sting of rebuke in his tone.

"Devlin's a sissy name." Tucker faced the man who had every right to hate him for the grief he'd caused his pretty wife. It was Libby's sister, Faith, who'd died that day in awful Wisconsin.

Mark was no pushover. The guy looked like he could get any physically demanding job done, only Tucker didn't get the I-can-beat-your-ass-any-day-of-the-week vibe from him. Mark Houston was a giant of a man, but a gentle giant. Tucker cooled his jets.

"Just asking." Mark crossed his arms over his broad and very muscular chest. "I just wanted to make sure we were talking about the same little boy."

"I've only got the one kid," Tucker pointed out, searching form common ground with Houston. "You?"

Mark held up three fingers. "Three girls. JayJay, Faith, and Taya."

"Three girls?" For some reason, Tucker assumed Mark had a family of rough-and-tumble linebackers at home, not daughters. *I mean, look at the guy.* Six foot tall. All muscle. Wide in the shoulders, narrow in the hips, the guy was built of more brawn than most NFL players. Tucker found it puzzling, all those daughters. He almost asked Mark if he was trying for a boy—not that it mattered. But still. Didn't every real man want a son in his lineup?

"How long has it been since Nicole left the country?" Stewart kept on track, his steepled fingers to his lips. God, the man had the icy stare of a cold-blooded killer. He might look the part of a dapper businessman, but the soul of a predator lurked beneath that crisply ironed white shirt and navy blue tie. The soul of a brother. Tucker also recognized that Stewart had done his homework. He knew the ex-Mrs. Chase's first name. Deuce's too.

Tucker stared him down, wondering how much more of his personal life Stewart already had at his fingertips. "She took off right after she married Nguyễn Vin Li. Vinnie. And she married him right after our divorce was final. Six months ago."

"And you haven't been able to reach her or speak with your son since?"

"That witch hasn't let me see him since she told me she was leaving. She called once after the wedding, left a voicemail, said she'd moved into Vinnie's place on the Saigon River. She said she was *inescapably happy*, her words, and that life *was so much better in Vietnam than it ever was in America. That people were nicer. Bullshit like that." And all of it aimed at me.*

"You're getting the slow roll from the authorities because you don't have joint custody, Agent Chase. Why don't you?" Mark asked quietly. Diplomatically. It still felt like a shot below the belt because it was, damn it. What kind of a man lost custody of his only kid?

Tucker rolled his eyes. *The kind of a guy who was dumb enough to trust his two-timing wife, that's who. As quickly as she'd remarried, Nicole had to have known Vinnie awhile.*

"It's not hard to figure out, is it?" He didn't need to lie. "You know how it is in the Navy. I was a SEAL.

One of the best. One of the guys who did the impossible every damned day, and I was good at it. I roamed the world, and I got the hard jobs done. I did what I was sent out to do. Didn't you?" He couldn't help it if his voice rapped up higher the more he defended himself.

"And I'll bet you had a girl in every port," Stewart said evenly, his gaze narrowed as if he could see the core of the problem.

"So?" Tucker rolled the bullshit off his shoulders. He didn't need to explain anything to this guy. This was a job, pure and simple. Money in the bank. Stewart could take it or shove it.

"Why exactly do you want to see your son now? What's changed?"

That was the question of the day, wasn't it? Tucker swallowed his pride again. His life was empty, that's what had changed since Deuce disappeared. To be honest, Tucker didn't like what he saw when he looked in the mirror anymore. He'd screwed up big time. Being a hero meant nothing without someone to come home to at the end of a long day or a tough night. He was desperate for the chance to set things right.

"I want to see my kid on a regular basis—is that so much to ask? I'm not going to abduct him, though I'll admit I've thought of it, but no. I just want the right to see him a couple times a year, more if she'll let me." The notion of Nicole holding his leash curdled in his gut. "Shit, Stewart, he's my son, too. You know what it's like to miss your kids. I know you do. That's all. I want a father/son relationship with Deuce. He's a good boy, and I... I miss him." *There. I'm groveling. Are you happy now?*

"You know nothing about me." Stewart threw up the first roadblock even as he offered the barest hint of a smile. "You'll need your director's permission to go into Vietnam. You do realize that, don't you?"

Tucker bowed his head and raked both hands through his hair, letting his too-long-for-government locks drop over his brow. That was the fly in the ointment. Strong and Stewart were bi-polar buddies. Clones. Both hard hitters, but both decent men. Stewart might not like the Bureau, but he damn sure liked the Bureau's current director for some reason.

But that was the last straw.

"You know what? Never mind." Tucker stood, shoving the chair away with the backs of his legs. "Coming here was a waste of time."

"Sit," Stewart commanded softly.

Tucker waved him off, headed for the door and a shot of bourbon for lunch. He'd humbled himself enough for one day. It hadn't worked. No fucking more. In the last six months, he'd gone from a respected ex-Senior Chief SEAL who ruled the FBI world, to a lousy dad who'd lost parental custody and communication with his only kid. Now he'd lost Melissa. His heart had turned into a barren wasteland. He'd paid a hard price, and yeah, he'd had it coming. He knew how to be a hero; he just didn't know how to be a loser. There was no way he'd tell Stewart that.

"Sit down, Agent Chase," Stewart said more firmly. "I can get you into Vietnam. That's no problem. I can even get Strong's approval, but you have to promise me one thing before I'll accept this job."

Tucker looked over his shoulder, not willing to bend more than he already had. Mark leaned his elbows to his knees and his eyes on his boss. Damned if that smart-ass Stewart wasn't smiling. "What?"

"Take extra good care of my newest junior agent while you're in country."

That made no sense. Stewart's agents were all top-notch snipers from one military department or the other, each and every one highly trained. None of them needed oversight. Tucker had to ask, "What?" because he didn't dare ask *'what the hell are you talking about?'*

Stewart nodded while Tucker returned to his seat. "This particular junior agent has never seen combat, but I'm certain he can help you locate Devlin. He's good at finding lost people."

"Deuce," Tucker corrected. "Who is he? Some Air Force flyboy?"

"Mr. Stewart. You wanted to see me?"

Tucker glanced up at the guy peeking into the office, the guy in a red-and-white checkered button-up shirt, pleated black dress slacks, and shiny black loafers. The dark-haired guy with horn-rimmed glasses who looked more kid than man, certainly not SEAL. The guy with dark, black eyes who resembled Clark Kent, a total nerd instead of a reliable operator. *Shit.* Isaiah Zaroyin. The doctor's kid. The son of the madman who'd wreaked havoc on a hundred or so FBI volunteers with his ill-fated drone program and lousy brain implants. *Why him?*

"He's working for you?" Tucker groused in disbelief.

"Actually..." Stewart waved Isaiah in to take the chair next to Mark. "Isaiah's on loan from the Bureau. He's the first FBI/TEAM exchange agent. Didn't Director Strong tell you?"

Tucker had to admit, "Yeah, I heard a rumor. Just didn't think it was true." Isaiah was a level-ten psychic, not a trained covert operator. What help could he be in Vietnam? "Can you shoot?" he asked the kid bluntly. "Diffuse a bomb? HALO jump?" *Any-friggin'-thing?*

Isaiah nodded, his black hair shaved close to his scalp and most of his scars faded. He'd endured a few rounds of torture at the hands of one of his father's more psychotic partners-in-crime. In the end, Ky Winchester and Mark Houston had rescued Isaiah and FBI Agent Eden Stark from the despicable Senator Bick and his demented wife. But did Tucker want to go all the way to Vietnam with the kid? On a real mission? Where someone could get hurt? Stewart's solution was ludicrous with a capital *Hell No.*

Tucker stretched one long leg out in front of him and stuck his shoe under the center of Stewart's elegant desk. Looked like black granite and polished steel, maybe titanium. Man, the man had done well. "What's he going to do? Read his crystal ball while I hunt for Deuce?"

"Not at all," Isaiah spoke up. "I've been in training since I've been here. Agents Cartwright and Lennox have taught me to shoot, field strip, and clean every weapon in the vault. Izza Maher has been teaching me to infiltrate without making a sound." He rolled his eyes. "I have to be good and quiet at that. She busts my chops if I so much as breathe hard. I've even gone on a couple parachute drops with Agent Torrey—low altitude though, not high. I'm not a black operator, but I'm not a liability, either. I'm trained. I'm good enough."

*You're trained, my ass.* Tucker drew in a slow breath. Not being a liability didn't mean a thing, not in a foreign country where anything could go wrong. He lifted his gaze to Stewart. "You expect me to take a FNG with me. That's the best you can do?" *FNG as in fucking new guy.* Military slang for *it sucks to be me.*

"It is," Stewart agreed as if Tucker's snarky question merited a calm answer. "Isaiah will handle communications with my office. He'll keep me and Strong informed. Trust me, Tucker, if anyone can find Devlin, Isaiah can."

"Deuce," Tucker growled. *Get my boy's name right.* He looked to Mark Houston, wondering how much of this was a set-up. A mind game. But Mark didn't blink. Not once.

Isaiah's mental voice filtered through the bad taste in Tucker's mouth and ended inside his head. *"Your wife and Deuce will be at an outdoor concert at the Bến Thành Market in Hồ Chí Minh City in two nights. Do you have a passport? I can get the airline tickets, but can you be ready to travel by three p.m.? We might be able to intercept Nicole there if we leave right away."*

Tucker met the kid with a hard gaze. He'd forgotten Isaiah's psychic talent for mind reading, and he hadn't expected to actually receive a mental message from the kid. That was new. *Hồ Chí Minh City? Three p.m.? Yeah, I can do that,* he thought.

Isaiah nodded, message received. "Good. I'll meet you at the airport at one," he said out loud. The kid's bright-eyed hope and willingness to help breached Tucker's negative opinion, nudging him into action. Maybe this wasn't such a bad idea after all.

*"Wait a minute. Did you just read my mind?"*

The smart-ass had the nerve to smile. *"And you answered me. This is going to be fun. Better yet, Alex and Mark don't know we're talking to each other. Think about it."*

Tucker put both hands on his knees and jumped to his feet, not admitting to anything. He wasn't psychic or psycho, and he hadn't mentally communicated with anyone. Whatever just happened, he and this wannabe agent could figure it out in Vietnam. "Come on, kid. You're with me."

# Chapter Two

Melissa McCormack kept a close watch in Hồ Chí Minh City for her friend, Kim Lành, another volunteer for Doctors for Charity and an especially pretty Vietnamese woman. Kimmie had come into the busy metropolis for three truckloads of medical supplies a couple days earlier, but hadn't returned.

When attempts to reach her by phone went instantly to her voicemail, Dr. Chet Hanks, the manager of the newly established Doctors for Charity clinic west of the city, had no choice. He needed those supplies, but he couldn't get away from the over-loaded clinic, so he'd sent his least medically skilled assistant, Melissa. He'd given her enough Vietnamese dong, paper currency, for a couple of meals and bus fare, and a copy of the invoice.

Melissa had the address of the warehouse near the Tân Sơn Nhất International Airport where the supplies were waiting. Dr. Hanks had assured her the freight company was legitimate, that he knew the owner and drivers. There was nothing to worry about. All she had to do was take the bus there, and the drivers would bring her back to the clinic with them. If she came across Kimmie, good, but the supplies were her first priority.

Kimmie might have changed her mind about working at the clinic, and Melissa couldn't blame her. The work was brutally hard, the tropical climate stifling, hot, and humid. Not to mention the deplorable state of the refugees streaming eastward out of war-torn Cambodia where a bloody coup between rebels and the current prime minister's regime was in process. Aid workers were desperately needed, but more—the medical supplies.

Melissa hurried to the bus stop just outside the clinic, paid her fare, and worked her way to the empty seat in the middle of the bus. She would've preferred not to go into the city alone, but there was no choice. For the moment, her mastery of the Vietnamese language consisted of *xin chào* for hello, *tạm biệt* for goodbye, and her favorite, *ở đây để giúp đỡ* for I am here to help. *Cục kẹo* for candy came in handy for the children, and Melissa never failed to keep a pocketful of peppermints just in case.

Her heart went out to the children in this country. She'd never get used to the horrible cost of conflict. Many smiled, but so many did not. Even now, the young man in the seat across the aisle glanced furtively in her direction. Not smiling. Maybe scared? He seemed frightened, but Melissa clasped the strap of her bag just in case. That was another thing she'd never get used to. The tender age of pickpockets and muggers.

She had yet to be targeted, but she'd seen it happen the day she arrived, and she couldn't risk losing her bag. It held her passport and cell phone, her way back home.

She relaxed, despite the dirty cushion beneath her backside. She'd been in the country for two weeks, thrilled to be needed but bone-tired every single night. She'd no more than closed her eyes when her mind brought up the handsome face of Tucker Chase, complete with his scruffy chin pinched between his thumb and fist, and a world of mischief in those dark, sexy eyes of his.

Ah, that man. He was eye candy, and he knew it. Ego, his greatest asset and his biggest fault. Vanity, his second. Truth be known, she adored him. What woman wouldn't? Tucker was drool-worthy, a man's man with a streak of bad boy a mile wide. Ruggedized. That was what he was. An ex-Navy SEAL, ruggedized from the work of war and proud of it, he challenged anyone who got in his way. And that was the problem.

Tucker had a way about him that made her feel protected, as if he could take on the world with one hand tied behind his back. But she'd been down that same road with Brady, her deceased husband. All that raw masculinity came at a high price. Brady and Tucker were the kind of men who needed to serve, and in doing so, they'd put their lives on the line. Melissa wasn't convinced she could endure another hero in her life and the baggage that came with him.

But mostly, Tucker had a set of two perfectly good ears that didn't seem to pick up the frequency of her voice. Or something. She could look right at him and make eye contact, or at least think she was making contact with the man behind those twinkling eyes. He'd nod, smile, and say all the right things, but she knew he wasn't really listening. Not to her, but always to that cochlear implant in his ear. Darn the FBI for that. What woman could compete with a twenty-four-hour switchboard that lit up her man with the adventure of faraway missions and risky assignments, with other people that desperately needed him? She couldn't.

She stared out the window at the bustling city and its wide array of colors. Men and women were everywhere, their heads under cover of the traditional nón lá, the conical straw hats of most Asian countries. Baskets of brightly colored vegetables beneath arrays of multi-colored umbrellas lined the street, carefully stacked pyramids of melons, oranges, and other fruits. The ever-present smell of fish and spices mingled with smoke and wood, filling the air.

Melissa drank it all in. For whatever reason, this exotic land reminded her of the cocky and incredibly brave man she missed. Since their final words, she hadn't spoken to him, not even to say goodbye before she'd left the States, but now she wished she had. He'd meant well. He did. If only he'd listen once in a while. If only he'd stop trying to impress her with his war stories. If only he'd stop taking risks.

Tucker would have had his arm protectively around her shoulder if he'd been there, and she wouldn't have a care in the world. He'd get the supply trucks, and he'd probably drive one of them back to the clinic if he had his way.

Her cheeks warmed at the thought of him having his way—with her. A trickle of sweat trickled between her breasts. She crossed her legs at that too willing clench at her core. One look into his sexy blue eyes, one thought, and she'd always turned into a silly woman, ready to throw caution to the wind and ride that bad boy to the ground. Or the bed or floor, wherever they ended up.

Nothing had changed since she'd first met him at that ridiculous cult in California she'd gotten tangled up with. Her tongue slid between her lips, savoring the memory of the taste of his mouth. His tongue. The prickly scrape of his whiskers on her chin. In the crook of her sensitive neck. His hot breath in her ear. It really was lust at first sight.

Tucker never failed to show up at her place deliciously fresh from the shower, his black hair still wet, his masculine scent mingled with some exotic blend of mandarin and amber. A hint of gunpowder. Fourth of July fireworks. Sizzle...

She shivered under an assault of goosebumps that chilled her to her bones and prickled her breasts. It had been so long since she'd been intimate, and Tucker was a heart-stopping, sinfully gorgeous real man. And he knew it.

The sight of him and his typical swagger never failed to leave her breathless and more than a little weak-kneed. He knew how to handle a woman, and Melissa definitely enjoyed being handled by him. She just didn't want to end up like that elite rifle he toted, the one he could field strip in his sleep without thought or care. The one he slung over his shoulder with all his other weapons. The one he took for granted...

Intimacy was a big step. Tucker'd been around the world, and he'd been with a lot of women. Not her. Brady McCormack was her one and only, her childhood sweetheart. She might never get that special, love-of-my-life feeling back again, but she needed to be more than just another pretty girl in Tucker's harem.

Hence, her three-month sabbatical from all things Tucker-related. He needed to decide if she was worth giving up his wild lifestyle for, and she needed to decide if she could live without him if he wouldn't. The man was an adrenaline junkie, ready to run into danger the second it winked his way. She wasn't.

The bus swayed through the circular drive to the airport. The terminals gleamed ahead, the sun bright off the massive plate-glass windows. Melissa climbed off at the first stop. Dr. Hanks had told her the warehouse would be easy to spot from a distance with the Trans Air Freight sign over its front dock. With her bag clasped tightly in one hand, she shielded her eyes and searched east of the busy airport.

A breath of relief escaped her. There it was on the other side of the fenced runway. Three rigs backed up to the long, concrete dock. Several workers scurried back and forth with hand trucks and forklifts. It looked to be a mile away, but the day was sunny and cloudless. The walk would do her good, and soon she'd be on her way west with the supplies. Good enough.

The young man from the bus shuffled past her, his head down and a dirty jute bag slung over his right shoulder. He gave her a quick sideways glance, then headed down the same path. She stretched the tension out of her shoulders and followed. Wouldn't it be a coincidence if they both had business at Trans Air Freight? A jetliner rumbled out of the sky and landed, drowning out the traffic behind her. She picked up her pace, anxious to get back to the relative safety of the clinic. The heat and humidity were getting to her.

She lost track of the young man when she entered the warehouse through the office at the far side of the dock. Relieved that her errand was nearly finished, she went straight to the desk and presented the invoice for goods received. "Good morning," she said to the man with the Trans Air Freight logo on his shirt. "I've come for Dr. Hanks' order."

"You must be Mrs. McCormack," he replied with a definite smile. "Chet called earlier. He said you were on your way, and that Kim took off again. I'm Barry Cummings. Good to meet you. I was starting to wonder how long I'd have to park those rigs for the good doctor."

Oh, good. English. She breathed easier. "Hi, Barry. It's good to meet you, too. Has Kim run off before?"

He nodded. "I knew her before she went to work for Chet. She runs with a tough crowd. Sign here and I'll get you on your way."

Melissa signed for the supplies, troubled that Kimmie had dropped the ball. She knew how much Chet depended on her. What could've happened that was more important than the clinic?

"Right this way." Barry ushered Melissa through the busy work bay toward the rear of the warehouse. "The refer rig's the shortest. I imagine Chet wants that more than the others since it's full of pharmaceuticals and other perishables. Don't worry. We've kept everything cold."

"When can we leave?"

"As soon as I get the drivers rounded up. You're welcome to sit in our break area while you wait. It's cooler. Coffee's more like mud, but the fridge is well stocked. We've got sandwiches, some chocolate milk. Help yourself; I won't be long."

"Thanks. I will." She ducked into the small room and selected a turkey and cheese sandwich, and a bottle of apple juice from the refrigerator, thankful for the familiarity of Americans and American food items. Fish, rice, and phở, the traditional noodle soup of most Vietnamese diets, were good, but turkey and cheese? A very welcome change.

Downing the last drops of her juice, she stared out the open rear warehouse bay. Men's voices called out to each other in both English and Vietnamese from the yard, a mixture of camaraderie and typical male banter. Tools bumped and clanked as they dropped to the concrete floor. Another big rig backed to the rear dock, its driver calling for someone to come help him maneuver. Heat waves radiated from the blacktop out back. Only the oscillating fan in the corner of the break room offered a cooling draft amidst the workday world of men.

She must've dozed off when a loud *BAM!* startled her. The table beneath her fingertips shuddered, the massive light fixtures overhead flickered off, and a cloud of gray smoke billowed in from the loading bay. Men shrieked. One screamed. More yelling in English and Vietnamese.

Melissa jumped to her feet. Something must've exploded. They might need her limited medical training. Trembling from the sudden adrenaline rush, she ran toward the noise until—

*Pop. Pop. Pop! Br-r-r-rt.* Another gunshot then… silence. She stopped dead in her tracks.

"Hey pretty lady," a young male voice taunted. "You come with me now."

She spun around, her heart climbing up her throat. It was him. That young man from the bus. Only now he was armed and leering at her as if he owned this part of the world.

*Maybe—he did.*

# Chapter Three

Tucker saw the smoking warehouse from the terminal as he stepped around some kind of welcoming committee blocking the exit from customs. The shindig with its bright red banners and crowd of cheering people had to be for someone mighty important. He'd just landed after a long international flight with his new buddy, Isaiah Zaroyin. He was tired and on his way to a shower and a clean hotel room. Who cared what burned in Vietnam?

Thankfully, Isaiah had kept out of Tucker's head the entire flight over. Isaiah was a good kid; Tucker just didn't want to cut him any slack until he knew how helpful he could be.

An explosion rattled the plate-glass windows along the east terminal wall. Black smoke billowed from one of the industrial warehouses opposite the runway. Tucker kept walking. He dismissed the explosion as just another interesting side note to the mission when his ears detected the rapid-fire of an assault rifle. Things happened on job-sites like the industrial one east of the airport. That was why the Occupational Safety and Health Administration was alive and well in the States.

He stopped walking long enough to scan the corrugated-steel warehouse, now blanketed in flames. Three tractor/trailer rigs fled the scene. A camouflaged pickup, too. He squinted, forcing every last atom in his eyes to see more than was humanly possible. If folks only knew how *meched-up* he was, that the cochlear implant in his ear was nothing compared to the mechanized zoom lens implanted in his eyeball...

He pressed his index finger to his temple, activating the optical zoom, straining to see farther. Better. With sharper acuity.

A gutsy woman rolled out of the moving truck, her arms tucked in tight, her hands cradling her head. At least she knew how to duck and roll. She scrambled to her feet and took off running back toward the warehouse, the wings of the bright yellow scarf covering her head trailing behind her. Tucker dragged Isaiah to the window, his FBI brain on duty and taking in every last detail of the obvious daytime abduction. A guy gave chase. Damned if he wasn't brandishing a pistol, the little prick.

"Maybe we should call the police," Isaiah murmured.

"Shut it," Tucker ordered. "I'm working here."

The kid with the gun lifted both hands and aimed, but another guy raced from the truck waving his arms. The gunman lowered his weapon. By then the other had run past him and tackled the woman. She covered her face when she went down, but he jerked her to her feet, his face in hers, berating her. The bastard hauled off and struck her, knocking her to her hands and knees. A blonde cascade of golden curls fell over her shoulders and—

*Son-of-a-bitch. No.* Tucker's mouth went dry. *Melissa?* That woman couldn't be her. Not here. God, where was that Doctors for Charity clinic she'd been so thrilled about? Could it have been in Vietnam? Had she ever said? Had he been too preoccupied with himself he'd missed something this important?

"Read that woman, damn it," Tucker demanded angrily of his psychic buddy, his fingertip stabbed against the glass window. "Read her. The blonde. Is that Melissa McCormack out there? Tell me!"

"I'm already reaching out to her." Isaiah's brows came down. His eyes narrowed. For a mind reader, he took long enough to say, "Yes, it's Mrs. McCormack. She's scared. I'm picking up six men with her. All armed. They're after the drugs in that refrigerated trailer that just pulled out of there."

Tucker didn't wait for the rest of the story. Not his country. Not his war. But that was his woman. "Keep up with me or get the hell away," he growled at Isaiah, pounding his way out of the airport.

Stewart's agent was smart. He let his boots do the talking.

"Where are they headed?" Tucker asked.

"West. They've got her inside the truck with them, back seat and she's pinging loud and clear. She's terrified, but she's gathering details and landmarks. She wants to remember where they're taking her."

*Good girl. Keep your wits, Melissa. Don't fall apart on me. I'm coming.*

Isaiah kept up, and he kept close. "How are we going to get over there?" he finally asked at the terminal exit. "We don't have a car. Should we call a cab, or—"

"Maybe," Tucker muttered under his breath. *Or borrow that American-made Buick idling at the curb. The one with the fancy chauffeur in the stupid get-up.* A guy just didn't see many American cars like this one in Vietnam.

He double-timed it to the driver's side, and told the flustered man to shut the hell up and get out of the way while Isaiah climbed in, strapped on, and sputtered, "Alex is going to bust my ass for this."

"Not Stewart. He'd do the same thing," Tucker declared, his foot to the pedal as he executed a mean U-turn. "Where is she now? Can you tell?"

"The three diesel rigs are going south into the heart of the city, but she's in the truck headed west. Watch out!"

"I see it," Tucker hissed, dodging the herd of three-wheeled rickshaws and mopeds, since he was going the wrong way on a one-way street. He put his foot on the gas and laid on the horn. Swerving, he tested the Buick's skid control with a mean side drift, his instincts on automatic. Isaiah hung on, both palms braced to the dash. Sirens blared from somewhere close by.

"Turn right," Isaiah ordered. "See the dust cloud? The truck's a half-mile up ahead."

Tucker obeyed, finally on the right side of the road, impressed with Isaiah's talent. He'd only known one other psychic in his life. Isaiah might just be as good as Eden Stark Winchester.

A wispy cloud of red smoke billowed ahead over the steady traffic. Horns blared. Something popped. It sounded like a bomb. These guys were getting desperate if they were blowing explosives on their way out of town.

"Keep to the left shoulder," Isaiah directed. "The guys in that truck are tossing grenades into the shops at the side of the road. Traffic's tied up on the right, but your left shoulder should be clear. Just don't run over anyone."

"Would I do that?" Tucker complied, grinding his teeth at the audacity of those men to abduct Melissa. To slap her. *Damn them all to hell!*

His buddy, the Grim Reaper, lifted up from his soul to ride on his shoulder, a constant reminder of all he'd seen and all he'd done. What he'd become. The justice he'd delivered. The debts he'd collected at the point of a gun. What he meant to do when he caught up with those men.

Darkness shifted at his peripheral, the snaky tendrils of the smoky Armageddon he meant to wreak on those clowns in the pickup. His eagle eyesight drew a bead on the guy sitting beside Melissa. If only Tucker had a mechanized weapon to go along with that futuristic lens implant. He could end this here and now.

"They're six cars ahead of you."

"I see them." Speed was of the essence. Tucker stepped on the gas and passed three cars and one truck, dodging an old man pushing a flower cart, his endgame never wavering. Melissa *would* be safe in his arms tonight.

He'd never loved Nicole the way he loved Melissa, and maybe it was time to tell her. Maybe it was possible. Maybe he wasn't the monster he honestly felt he was. Maybe there was hope for his wicked soul. Melissa certainly seemed to think so. "To hell with her self-righteous morals."

"Excuse me?" Isaiah had the nerve to look shocked.

"What?" Tucker snapped even as he inwardly cringed. *I didn't say that out loud, did I?"*

"Umm, never mind. Punch it," Isaiah prompted, stabbing his index finger forward. "You're going to lose her if you don't get up there now."

Tucker spared his cohort a quick glance. What did Isaiah know that Tucker did not?

*Oh shit. That.*

He slammed on the brakes. He had no choice. An old-fashioned, steam-driven locomotive. That was what Isaiah knew that Tucker didn't. Clear out of the past century, it came chugging out of nowhere from the stacked-up buildings at the right. No horn. No warning. Just an iron wall sprung up between Tucker and Melissa, just a train Tucker could've beat if he'd known it was coming down those tracks.

"Damn it!" He punched the steering wheel and scrambled out, eyeing the train cars while working the probability of an idiot flying between two of them and making it to the other side, preferably alive.

"What then? Steal another car?" Isaiah answered Tucker's unspoken challenge, his dark eyes also locked on the train. "You'll never make it, Agent Chase. Aren't trains over here required to lower their speed inside city limits?"

Tucker couldn't answer. His heart was in that pickup racing west away from him.

Something in the atmosphere shifted. A stiff breeze picked up. The once clear sky darkened with the onset of rain. The change in weather suited his frame of mind. Those men in the truck needed to know that hell was on its way—that Tucker Chase never gave in and he never gave up. That he would kill every last one of them when he caught up. "Can you track her?"

Isaiah nodded. "I'm still in touch with her. She isn't aware of me, though. She's crying."

Tucker flinched at the sucker punch of his woman suffering. He sucked in a gut full of remorse for not getting to her in time. Her pain and her fear was his fault.

"Make sure your seatbelt's tight," he ordered as he dropped back into the car and slammed the door. The end of the train was in sight. "We're going hunting."

"But you're supposed to meet your wife and son tonight," Isaiah reminded him.

"Ex-wife," Tucker clarified. "I will." *Somehow. Maybe.*

Isaiah blew out a controlled breath. "All right then. The trucks are at the edge of the city. Fewer buildings. Less traffic. Once they reach the countryside—"

"Don't lose her!" Tucker punched it just as the last train car cleared the tracks. He would've made it too, if three police cars hadn't just rounded the corner ahead of him and blocked him in, their sirens blasting and their lights flashing.

"Son-of-a-bitch! I don't have time for this," he gritted out as he screeched to a sideways stop, a dozen local yokels descending on him and his stolen car with their weapons drawn.

"You do now," Isaiah mumbled, his hands already up in the air.

*This can't be happening.*

Melissa kept her face to the window, fighting tears and trying to keep track of her surroundings while she did. She wiped her bloody nose on her sleeve. The guy beside her, the one from the bus, still had her purse. He was the youngest of the three. He and the other two spoke angrily and too fast for her limited grasp of the language.

The guy in the front passenger seat seemed to be the most agitated. He hadn't stopped talking since they'd left the warehouse, and he kept looking over his shoulder. She'd never forget his bleached blond hair over black roots. Only after they'd crossed the train tracks and barely missed the train did he slap the driver's shoulder and settle down. He'd grinned at her then, his eyes dark with menace.

Tempted, she glanced back, straining to see if anyone might be following, if anyone was coming to save her. Whoever that guy up front had worried about, police or airport security, the train had effectively cut them off. She was on her own.

Melissa shuddered, truly scared for the first time in her life. These men were soldiers and well-armed. They'd just stolen a couple of months' worth of supplies, amongst them morphine and other drugs. If this was just about the drugs, they might kill her because she could identify them. If they connected her with the world-renowned McCormack Industries, they might want ransom. Either way, she was in big trouble.

She squeezed her eyes shut and sent a silent plea to Virginia and the man she loved. *Tucker. Help.*

# Chapter Four

"You what?!"

Tucker held the phone away from his ear. He knew he'd get his butt chewed by Stewart, but some of the expletives exploding out of the guy's mouth were anatomically impossible, and throwing gasoline on the already raging fire in Tucker's gut didn't help.

He hunkered low, his arm against the jail's concrete wall and his forehead pressed to his wrist. A pansy-assed guard in a pea green military uniform tapped his baton on the same wall, reminding him to hurry it up. Isaiah had grown mute since they'd been apprehended—probably a good thing. Tucker didn't need any more trouble.

"I just got here," he ground out. "Damn it, Stewart. Shut up and listen."

"You let them take her! You lost her!"

"I didn't lose her, I just couldn't catch up to her. It's different. I wasn't prepared to see her getting kidnapped in broad daylight. I didn't even know she was here. Don't worry. I'll find her. I've got your brilliant psychic with me, remember? Wonder boy Isaiah?"

"How the hell are you going to do that from a Hồ Chí Minh City jail cell?"

Damn, the man was dense. Why the hell did he think Tucker had called? "You're going to get me and your agent out of here, that's how."

"I am? Why didn't you call Strong? He's your boss."

Tucker wanted to scream. The Hồ Chí Minh City police hadn't been gentle when they'd taken him and Isaiah down. His head pounded from too many blows from multiple batons similar to the one tapping the wall and aggravating his blood pressure and his patience. Every wasted minute took Melissa farther away. He didn't have time for Stewart's bullheadedness when he knew the guy would help in the long run.

"Can you help or not?" he growled instead of answering. "Jesus Christ, Stewart, I hired you, remember? You work for me. Get me and pretty boy out of here."

"I'll see what I can do," Stewart snapped, and the line went dead before Tucker had the chance to ask Stewart if he'd already known Melissa was in Vietnam, and if he did, why the hell was she there?

Was it that Doctors for Charity bullshit clinic? Better yet, why hadn't he told Tucker? Stewart knew he and Melissa were seeing each other. How big of an ass was the guy? Had he kept that info-byte to himself intentionally? He was in tight with McCormack. Was he trying to drive Tucker off?

Tucker slapped the phone into the cradle, rolled the knot out of his neck, and rejoined Isaiah on the concrete bench in what he hoped was just a holding cell, a dirty, small cut of humanity. Steel bars. Windowless. The cell was surrounded on both sides by other cells, some filled with as many as five men, all dressed in the uniform of the day, a black pajama outfit with Vietnamese script on the back and front. No shoes. Flimsy sandals that barely fit his big, American feet.

The guard growled something as he slammed the cell door, words Tucker didn't understand. Probably a good thing. It was best he didn't speak the language. He'd only open his big mouth if he did. He didn't need more abuse.

"He said you're an ass," Isaiah said softly when the guard walked down the row of cells then disappeared out the metal exit. The door clanged shut behind him.

"I don't care what Stewart thinks."

"I meant the guard. He said you're a rich American ass who thinks you can break laws in his country just because you've got money. He'd like to hit you again, but he can't do it while his supervisor is here. His boss won't let him hit Americans."

Tucker raked his fingers over the swollen knots and tender bruises on his scalp, one on his cheekbone. The day he cared what a guard thought of him was a long way off, but still. Those batons hurt.

"But Alex thinks you're an ass, too, if that's any consolation."

"Tell me something I don't know," Tucker growled.

"I know the letters on your shirt spell 'criminal,' and that Agent Stark decked you with a chunk of ice in Canada when she thought you'd lost your mind."

Tucker slanted an evil eye at his partner. "How'd you find that out?"

"Because I'm the guy who put those suggestions in your head that day. I'm the one who got you to believe Director Strong wanted you to bring my dad down or die trying."

"No shit? You screwed with my head and got me to hear something he never said?" Tucker rubbed the side of his skull where Eden Stark had hit him so hard with a chunk of ice he'd thought she'd knocked his head off. "That wasn't very nice. Stark gave me a concussion. The guys thought I was dead when they found me. I had a migraine for days."

Isaiah shrugged. "I needed you to think your phone was dead, but when Eden took over and put a call through to Director Strong, I had to improvise. She's good. I never could beat her."

"I ought to whip your ass for messing me up."

"Yeah, well, sorry about that, but a guy'll do anything when someone's peeling his skin off with a razor. It could've been worse for both of us."

"Guess so," Tucker muttered and let it go. The Canadian op had been one smoking mirror after another, and behind the scenes was Isaiah Zaroyin. Abducted by the psychotic Senator Bick and his insane wife, Cassandra, Isaiah had been strapped to an autopsy table and tortured to perform mind tricks for the sole intent of tormenting Eden, the only FBI psychic at the time. In a bizarre twist of fate, it ended up being Isaiah who ended Mrs. Bick with a taser, and Ky Winchester who ended the senator. A two-fer from the gods of karma if ever there was one. All was well that ended well. The Bicks were dead, and the FBI now owned two level-ten psychics, Eden and Isaiah. Go figure.

"I also know Mrs. McCormack's nearly at the Cambodian border."

Tucker slanted his gaze at Isaiah, for the first time really seeing him. The poor guy had a puffy, black eye and a scraped chin. His nose wasn't broken, but his nose holes were caked with dried blood. "You can see her? Is she okay?"

"So far." Isaiah put his head down, but kept his gaze on the exit. "I can't see her, Tucker. I'm a mind reader, not a magician."

It seemed like the same thing to Tucker. "Why'd they take her? Does she know? Do they want ransom?" He plunged his fingers through his hair, frustrated enough to tear it out. The McCormack name was money in the bank. Who knew how low these people might go or what they might do with Melissa to get what they wanted.

"Not yet. She speaks Vietnamese as well as you do, which is zero, but she's not as frightened as she was when they first grabbed her. I don't get the feeling this is about ransom, at least not yet."

"That's good, isn't it?" Tucker asked. "She must not believe she's in danger if she's not scared."

"Or they've given her something to keep her quiet," Isaiah shot Tucker down. "But I don't think that's the case. Her thoughts are faint but fairly clear. She's not groggy. I won't be able to keep contact if they keep taking her west, though. There's a limit to my reach sometimes. It depends on the subject I'm following."

"Can you read them?"

Isaiah shook his head. "They're transmitting a mix of euphoria and rage. Nothing useful."

Tucker felt like a yo-yo. One minute, hopeful. The next, edgy with frustrated despair. He punched one fist into his palm. He'd seen the inside of too many cells. They all made him crazy, but this was worse. Melissa was out there and she needed him, but he couldn't get to her. She was in serious trouble while he cooled his heels and waited, not something he was good at.

"Are you okay?" he asked his cell partner.

"Believe me. I've been worse." Isaiah chuckled, his sharp black eyes scanning the aisle between the cell rows. "This is nothing."

"Did you cause Stark's pilot's heart attack? Did you make him crash in Canada?" Dragging up their last operation together calmed Tucker's nerves. A little.

Isaiah shook his head. "Nah. I can't do stuff like that. Neither can my dad. He's brilliant, but not psychic. Bick's the one who came up with those GPS locator implants—the spider implants, too. He wanted absolute control over his drones. That's how he killed Eden's pilot. He used the GPS locator to force a pinpoint crash landing near my dad's medical center, then the spider implant released a toxin into the pilot's brain. It triggered the heart attack. We were all lucky Charlie Sweets was able to crash land as safely as he did. Agent Stark, I mean Winchester, was a lucky woman."

The spider implants Bick had stuck in his drones' heads still creeped Tucker out. Usually inserted behind the ear, they'd dug themselves into the subject's skull, and, via a scary and very illegal hallucinogenic drug, they either influenced the subject to do what Bick wanted or they ended the subject's life. Eden had endured massive migraines until Ky Winchester dug it and the locator out of her. He'd gotten close to Eden during that op, something that still bugged Tucker. Eden Stark was that genius little girl who'd needed a big guy to protect her from creeps like Ky, only she hadn't seen Ky as a creep. By the time those crazy kids were married, neither did Tucker.

He also had a couple of spare parts that rivaled Bick's, but he'd volunteered for them. He'd known exactly what he was getting into. Zaroyin's volunteers hadn't. In the end, Zaroyin and Bick had run a scary black op that nearly killed hundreds of FBI volunteers with his brain implant idea. By then, Zaroyin had a change of heart. He'd redeemed himself when he'd tried to save Eden.

Not Bick. He'd meant to rule the world, but when the implants failed to perform as he'd wanted, all those FBI volunteers were expendable. He'd turned intelligent, hard-working agents, who diligently served their country, into mindless drones, some Tucker had been forced to kill in order to defend Agent Stark. Yeah. Not a nice guy at all. "How's your old man holding out?"

"He's good, but he's still going to do hard time for working with Bick." Isaiah arched his back, stretching it from side to side. "I visited him last week."

"Where's he serving?"

"FPC Montgomery."

Tucker knew it well. The Federal Prison Camp in Alabama, a minimum-security facility. "I thought he'd end up at Leavenworth."

"He still might," Isaiah said thoughtfully. "The trial isn't until next year. What he did is no small thing. I love him, but I can't defend him. Not this time. He deserves what he gets."

"I'm sorry," Tucker admitted. Having to own up to a criminal father was a major downer for any kid. He knew. His old man had served time for armed robbery of a 7-Eleven when Tucker was seventeen. Overnight, he'd gone from being the much-lauded high school quarterback and school hero to the creep with the scumbag father. It had sucked defending his old man, but by hell, he'd done it. Over and over, he'd come home with black eyes and bloody noses until he'd graduated early and joined the Navy.

*Screw high school.* The Navy never cared who his old man was, and by the time he'd had a shot at BUD/S and becoming a SEAL, he knew damned well how to tough out the bad times. He'd never once thought of giving up and ringing that bell, not because the Pacific Ocean was too cold in January or the sand was too hard on his lily-white skin. Uh-uh. By then he was the badass most guys avoided. If they didn't, he made sure they did. And he *was* a hero, damn it.

"She still loves you," Isaiah whispered. "She's thinking about you right now, wondering if you're still mad at her."

"I'm not mad at her," Tucker growled. Frustrated was more like it. Perplexed. Women were so—complicated. Emotional. They needed to think more like men.

"That will never happen," Isaiah muttered, just as quietly. "Women are better than men. They're smarter in so many ways. Don't you know that by now?"

"Damn it, will you stop reading my mind?" Tucker glared at this partner-in-crime. "Stay out of my head."

Isaiah lifted his brows. "Believe me, I wish I could, but it doesn't work that way. You're an angry man, Agent Chase, and you radiate hostility most of the time. Your mind is wide open. Want to or not, I hear everything."

*Hell yeah, I radiate hostility. I want my kid and Melissa back, damn it!* "Focus on Stewart." Tucker brushed Isaiah off, sick and tired of the mental intrusion. "Influence him with all your psychic babble. Make him find a way to get us out of here before noon. Do your job."

Isaiah pursed his lips and closed his eyes. "Alex is out of my range, Agent Chase. We're here. You're stuck with me."

Tucker needed to hit something. A good sparring match and a sixty-second bell would come in handy, but there he was, jammed into a one-man cell with a guy who knew how to use his brain, not his fists. Stewart had better get off his ass and contact the American Embassy in Vietnam. He'd better do something!

"Move your feet."

"Excuse me?" Isaiah's brows slanted into a lop-sided *V*. "Oh. Okay."

Tucker would've explained, but Isaiah had already lifted his feet to the concrete bench and out of Tucker's way. If he could read minds, he didn't need to be told everything. Tucker dropped to the floor and assumed a push-up position. Pounding out fifty took the edge off. By then he was sweating heavily, but still pissed and antsy. He pumped fifty more while Zaroyin sat cross-legged on the bench and watched, the wimp.

Tucker's problem with Isaiah was simple. If he really could read minds, and it seemed that he already had, he knew how Tucker had lost his only kid. He knew what a loser Tucker was. *Shit. He knew everything.*

All those push-ups didn't help. Tucker didn't want to wait for Stewart. He was a man of action. He wanted out!

In between sets, Isaiah tapped his sweaty right shoulder. "The truck stopped moving."

Tucker rolled to his butt, his wrists on his knees and breathing hard. He ran a quick hand over his face to wipe the sweat away, wishing he had a bottle of water and a towel. "Where?"

"She's in the jungle. It's dark. She can't see. I think she's blindfolded."

That made sense. Whoever these guys were, they probably didn't want her to see their hideout. "And?"

Isaiah pressed two fingers to his right temple and shook his head slightly. "That's all I can see. She's frightened again. Blood. I'm smelling blood and human waste." He wrinkled his nose. "Wherever she is, it's not a good place. Lots of people. Wait."

Tucker held his breath. He needed out of this cell!

Isaiah blew out a soft growl through pursed lips. "They're making her kneel. No. Crawl."

Tucker's body clenched at the thought of Melissa on her knees in front of those bastards. That could only mean one thing. Humiliation. Maybe—*God, no.*

He jumped to his feet and rattled the bars, his heart exploding with rage. "Guards! Let me out! I need to make a call!" *I'll break out if I have to!*

Isaiah kept going. "She's crying, but she's not hurt. She doesn't understand what her abductors are saying or what they want. That's why she's crying."

"Not Melissa!" Tucker roared out his frustration. He crouched one knee to the floor, his fists to his temples, willing the ugly scene of Melissa being assaulted out of his head. Of her being raped. *Fuck me! This is my fault, gawddamn me! I did this to her!*

"She's in some place very dark and damp," Isaiah whispered, "but she's not hurt, Tucker. Listen to me, will you? She's not hurt. They're not doing—that—to her."

Tucker could barely think straight, much less quell the rising angst in his body to listen. No guard had answered his demand yet, and maybe that was a good thing, but a few of the other prisoners yelled at him. That was a bad thing. The jail had turned into a noisy zoo full of whistling, grunts, and bellows.

"What's going on, Isaiah? Tell me. Don't spare any of it."

Isaiah nodded. "I will, just don't hit me if it's bad news."

That proved how well Isaiah could read Tucker. Rage lent him incredible energy, and an angry man sometimes forgot who he was and what he was capable of.

The suspense tore him up at what sweet Melissa was going through. His gut burned with his own impotence, that he wasn't there to save her. "Just tell me. Is it bad now?"

"She's in a small wooden box, Tucker," Isaiah said sadly. "I'm sorry. It's cramped. She's sitting with her knees drawn up, and she can feel all four sides. The top. It's old plywood. The layers are old and cracked, coming apart. It's damp and it smells bad, like animals were caged in it. She's... she's praying."

Melissa, scared and praying for her life? Nothing could've hurt Tucker worse. There he was, stuck in his own box with a guy who might be safer in another cell if this nightmare couldn't be resolved soon. That in itself was an arrogant expectation. It took months for the diplomatic wheels of a prisoner release to turn, if the Vietnamese government even entertained the idea. This was a hopeless situation. He might never see Melissa again, and the thought of her praying for her life gutted him. *Damn Stewart. What's taking you so long?*

"I can teach you some relaxation techniques—"

Tucker stuck one palm in Isaiah's face to stop that nonsense. Relaxation was the last thing he needed. He snapped his fingers. "You're going to make a phone call. On your feet. Now. Call the guard. Tell them you're allowed a phone call, the same as me."

"You really think this will work?" Isaiah asked, already on his feet and at the bars. "What do you want me to say? Oh. You want me to call Director Strong now?"

"No, Sally, I want you to call the First Lady. Yes, Strong. Why'd you even ask? Read my mind, and just do it."

Isaiah let out a deep sigh. "It doesn't always work that way, and you need to stop with the name-calling, Tucker. Show some respect. I'm not some dumb kid on his first Boy Scout sleepover. I'm here to help, but you've got to let me."

*Oh, boohoo.* Tucker sucked in a breath, fighting for an ounce of restraint. Isaiah was right. He needed to cool his jets, idle down the throttle, and take his lead foot off the pedal. None of this was Isaiah's fault. He deserved professional respect. "Agreed. Now call the guard."

# Chapter Five

They'd nailed the box closed like she was some kind of an animal.

Melissa sat trembling in the cramped, sweltering darkness, straining to hear what was happening outside of her confinement. She tugged the bag off her head, thankful her hands hadn't been cuffed behind her back. Several harsh male voices vied to be heard over the din of what sounded like a crowd of people. Children and women, dogs too. She wasn't in the city though. These sounds were different, and she smelled campfire smoke. Other things too. Sweat, blood, and a latrine. Maybe something dead. Or someone...

The only vehicle noises came from heavy equipment, maybe the trucks from the warehouse. She couldn't help but feel bad for all the refugees at the clinic. All those supplies wasted. Dr. Hanks would be so disappointed. He needed what was in those trucks more than these rebels.

She stilled and listened intently, an animal in a cage for the moment, but not helpless. Not if she kept her wits. The cuffs at her wrists were tight, but with a little wiggling around and a few contortions, she'd taken stock of her flimsy jail.

It was nothing more than a plywood box with plenty of room between the nail in one side and the door her captors had made her crawl through. She'd expected much worse at their hands when the one guy shoved her to her knees. Maybe he hadn't meant for her to fall, but she did. The smelly bag they'd put over her head the last miles had made it impossible to see, much less catch her balance.

They could've kicked her while she was down, but they hadn't. If anything, they'd seemed glad to be done with her once they'd locked her up.

Four quarter-sized holes in the roof of her wooden prison revealed leafy jungle overhead, but that was most of Vietnam—jungle and trees. No surprise there. She took a deep breath. She'd prayed when she'd first been forced into the box, but the time for prayers and tears had passed. She wanted out.

"*Xin chao,*" she called out, hoping that was correct for hello. How dangerous could one unarmed woman be? Then, in case there were any English-speaking people in the crowd, she called, "Excuse me, is anyone out there?"

Okay. Foolish question. She got that, but it was the only thing she could think of to get attention. She'd always relied on Christian kindness and common courtesy to get her through life and the troubles it had brought her way. It worked before; it would work now.

"Hey, pretty lady." It was him, that young man from the bus again. She couldn't see him, but he'd used the same words. "You hungry or something? Maybe thirsty?" He tapped the top of the box with something hard.

"I'd very much appreciate standing up straight," she replied evenly, her dignity intact despite her circumstances. "I'm not a dog you can keep locked up. It's hot in here."

He chuckled. "You not afraid I hurt you? You promise you not run away?"

Melissa honestly didn't know the answer to that. He had hurt her during the abduction. Her knees and elbows were skinned from rolling on the asphalt, and he had slapped her and knocked her down. She wouldn't give him the benefit of cowering like some frightened female, though. Not anymore. If he meant to kill her, he might as well get it done because she would run for freedom at the first opportunity. That was what Tucker would do.

"I won't run if you're reasonable and treat me right," she compromised. "Do you promise not to hit me again? That was uncalled for. I didn't hurt you, did I?"

He wrenched one of the plywood sides, the nails screeching as he twisted it backward and off. Tall and thin to the point of gaunt, his straight black hair hung over his eyes in bangs. Wispy black whiskers trailed along his jaw, but his teeth were amazingly straight and white, not what she'd expected in a drug runner, or whatever he was. He wasn't a boy, now that she had a better look at him, maybe younger than twenty. "You come out now, pretty lady. Be smart. Do not run away and do not make Simon angry. He may let you live."

"Simon?" she asked as she climbed to her feet, the cuffs making it more difficult than it needed to be. "Who's Simon?"

The young man reached one hand for her cuffs and pulled her into him. Her heart kicked up at the implied threat. He stood a good foot over her, but instead of roughness, he pulled a key from the pocket of his ragged trousers and gently set her free. Stuffing the cuffs in his back pocket, he met her gaze. "Simon is our leader. He teach us plenty good way to live."

She extended a hand in friendship, determined to strike a truce. "My name is Melissa. What's your name?"

He slanted her a suspicious, sideways glance, but allowed a quick handshake. "Tristan."

That was unexpected. "Tristan? But that's not a Vietnamese name."

"My grandmother marry American GI. My mother likes American ways. You like her."

Melissa offered up a sigh of relief at the progress she'd made. After her initial harsh meeting with this young man, his brand of civility calmed her nerves. Maybe this was nothing but a bad misunderstanding she could clear up with a few words with that Simon fellow. "I'd like to meet your boss, if you don't mind."

"Melissa?" Tristan asked as if trying the taste of her name on his tongue. He rubbed one hand over his chin, still looking at her through his bangs. "I think Simon might be ready to meet you, too. Come now. I take you to him."

*At last. Progress.* Melissa stepped to Tristan's side, prepared to give Simon a piece of her mind, but the sight of her surroundings took her breath away. This was no camp. It was a village.

Wooden huts with thatched roofs blended into the jungle at her left, a haphazard parking lot of trucks, the three big rigs, and numerous other vehicles at her right. The group of men in the center of the parking lot stopped arguing to look at her. Some Vietnamese. Some Caucasian. Some darker skinned. Most wore camouflaged pants and shirts, albeit dirty and irregular. Boonie hats and ball caps. Dark glasses. Rugged boots.

One guy stepped away from the group and walked toward her. "Ma'am," he said crisply, his hand extended. "My guys didn't rough you up too bad, did they? They can get a little overzealous."

Sandy haired and clean-shaven, he cut an impressive but stern profile. Tall and broad-shouldered, deeply tanned, his chin shadowed with days' old scruff, he was military in his posture and his language, a definite authority figure. A rifle slung over his shoulder pointed down, but he also packed a long knife in a leather sheath on his hip alongside a holstered pistol. Worry lines etched the corners of his eyes, and the same hard emotion bracketed his mouth.

She returned a solid grip to let him know she meant business, somewhat surprised at finding an American soldier amongst a band of drug runners. "A little overzealous? Is that what they told you? They killed men back at that warehouse. Is that what you call roughed up?"

He nodded one curt nod toward the huts. "I'm Simon Siegel, and frankly, I don't care what they did. Tristan will show you to your bed. He'll see to your needs while you're here."

"While I'm here? You make this sound like a vacation." She stuck her chin at him, her body thrumming with adrenaline. "This is an abduction, clear and simple. I'm not staying. Take me back to the city."

His expression hardened. "You'll stay until we move out or get run off."

"I will not. I'm an American citizen, and I—"

"Will you climb off your bullshit soapbox and shut it?" He ran a palm over the back of his sweaty neck in aggravation. "I'm an American citizen, too. So what?

Nobody cares out here. In case you haven't noticed, we're in Vietnam, not Hollywood."

She tried another tactic. "You do know that you just stole two months' of supplies from a charitable organization, Doctors for Charity, don't you? You'll kill more people if you don't return those supplies."

"Yes, ma'am, I do know that," he said tiredly. "I guess I figured we needed it more since we've got nothing, and your fancy clinic's got doctors and staff and the ability to get more supplies. Never mind, Tristan. I'll handle the tour. Scrounge up some food for our guest, kid. Go tell your mother I need her with the guys. They head out in twenty."

Tristan nodded once and obeyed without a word.

"I'm not your guest," Melissa corrected. "I'm your prisoner."

"Whatever." Simon slapped at the cloud of gnats hovering around his face. "You're here."

"Is Tristan your son?" she asked, running her sweaty palms down her slacks—not like that did any good. The humidity index had to be close to one hundred percent in the shade, and her anxiety level was easily twice that.

"I wish he was, but no. His father died before he was born. All he's got left are his mother and two brothers." Simon nodded toward the huts. "Come this way. I'll show you what I need."

That didn't sound good. "What you need?" she repeated, barely able to keep up with his long strides as he made his way toward the rear of his shantytown. "What about my needs, like a cab back to the city, or my purse, or a bus to the clinic? Is there some place around here where I might freshen up and tend to my scraped knees? What about that?"

She caught up to him, her fingers clenched into fists and her head on straight, fully intending to tell him off until a little tyke ran up to her, giggling and hiding behind her leg while another gave chase in a game of tag. A young woman stepped shyly to her side and lifted the littlest guy into her arms, scolding in her soft language as she hurried away. He waved back over her shoulder, his eyes bright and sparking with mischief.

"It's okay," Melissa tried to explain to the woman. "He wasn't hurting me. I'm fine. Really."

The woman ducked her head and disappeared around the back of one of the huts.

"You've got kids here?" Melissa sniped, a titch of tartness to her question. "Kids and drugs don't mix. They shouldn't be exposed to..." She couldn't find the words to describe Simon's lack of humanity and ended with an indignant, "... all of this."

"You're right. They don't." He cupped her elbow and steered her around some bushes, between two huts and into the center of the village. "But this is where they'll stay until it's safe for them to go home."

Her hackles lifted. She jerked her arm away from his grasp and into her side. This arrogant man had his nerve. She didn't want to go anywhere with a guy who'd sent boys to commit murder while he let children play in his despicable drug camp. She didn't want a thing to do with him until...

*Oh, my God.* Melissa froze in her tracks, the breath knocked out of her at the sight. This was no village. This was a massive hospital zone, the ground littered with makeshift beds, families crammed side by side with women and children squatted alongside their husbands and sons, their fathers and brothers. A definite odor of decay and sickness filled her nose. Tiny little kids scrambled between the cots and beds.

She waved a mist of flies away, needing to understand what she was looking at. "Who are these people?" she asked.

Simon lifted his shirt collar to cover his mouth. "They're Cambodian soldiers and the families of soldiers in the now defunct prime minister's army. If they go back, the rebels will execute them. If they're found here, same deal, only it'll be the Vietnamese Army running the firing squad. Vietnam can't and won't give them safe passage. They won't risk their tentative truce with the new Cambodian leader if this military coup holds."

"They should go to the clinic. They can get help there."

"No, ma'am, they can't. They're afraid that rebel spies will be at the clinic. They'll get caught and sent back to their country."

"You're helping the Cambodian army?"

"No, ma'am. I'm helping men, women, and children who don't have any options left."

"But they can't stay here. Look at them. They're sick. You have to get them decent help."

He pursed his lips and blew out a small breath. "That I do."

The mother and the little boy who had played tag squatted alongside a small girl and an older man, his left leg bandaged and bloody.

"Oh, my," Melissa breathed. Her heart hurt for all these people. She scanned the men and boys on the ground, some on mats, some on rags. Many of their wounds had to be from gunshots. Some looked utterly hopeless. All needed doctoring and a cleaner place to rest and heal.

"What's in the huts?" she asked, her inner Florence Nightingale rising to take charge of the desperate, quiet chaos. Needing to reach out and help. This was why she'd come to Vietnam—to serve in some small measure. She'd learned long ago that she couldn't solve the world's problems, but that even one person could still make a difference.

"More of the same," Simon murmured, rocking on his heels. "I was hoping we'd find mosquito repellant and insecticide in these supply trucks to keep the bugs down. Maybe clean bedding. Netting. Bandages. A living, breathing doctor would've been nice, but I don't suppose they come in a box."

Melissa glanced over her shoulder at the box she'd been forced into upon her arrival. "Like I did?"

Simon's moss green eyes slanted over her. "I won't apologize for helping these people, so you need to back off the piss-and-moan routine, ma'am. You're here, and you're a helluva lot healthier than they are. Deal with it."

She turned the tables on him. If she had to deal with it, he'd have to deal with her. "Do you think you could get some lumber and building supplies without murdering anyone?" she asked haughtily.

He lifted a brow, his lip pinched in disgust. "Why? Do you want me to build you a hotel room so you won't have to look at these people and the squalor while you're here? That's not going to happen."

"No, I need a clinic," she declared evenly, her mind made up and her head lifted high. This was why she'd been created—to help people. "These families need help, and as long as I'm here, they'll get it. Can you do it or not?"

Simon wiped the sweat off his brow and shook it off his hand to the ground, a glimmer of light in his eye. "How big do you want it?"

# Chapter Six

It was going on midnight. The guards hadn't let Isaiah make his call yet. Every guard they'd asked had just sneered in that superior way of guys who knew they had the upper hand.

"You're not going to like this," Isaiah muttered, lifting off the bench as two armed guards approached.

"Why not?" Tucker rolled his bare feet to the floor. He'd been sitting cross-legged on the bench, his sandals kicked off, and dozing because there wasn't much else to do. Despite Isaiah's warning, these two guards actually looked hopeful. Maybe Stewart had more clout than Tucker thought he had. Maybe they were on their way out of jail.

"You," the one guard pointed at Isaiah. "Come. Now." The second guard snapped his rifle on Tucker while the first unlocked the cell and urged Isaiah out.

He slammed the door, locking Tucker behind bars again. "What's going on? Where are you taking him?"

"They're releasing me," Isaiah managed to say before he was jabbed in the back with a baton and yelled at. He lifted his hands in submission.

"Silence!" the first guard ordered. "You go. He stay. No talk."

Didn't that beat all? Tucker caught the perplexed message in Isaiah's raised brows as he was hustled out of the jail and disappeared behind the doors. He didn't know what was going on, either, but the second the door closed, Tucker got a covert earful from Isaiah. *"Keep your head down, Tucker. That asshole with the nightstick is still here. His boss is going home soon."*

Tucker grabbed onto the bars, daring that guard to try anything with his little billy club. Several prisoners bellowed back, but that only raised Tucker's ire all the more.

Letting go of the bars, he paced a tight, worthless round, but gave it up after a couple dozen got him nowhere. He hit the floor again, pumping out a hundred push-ups and growing madder by the second. His angst had no end to it. He needed out of this cell, but no. Isaiah had been set free to go off on his own to do what—think? *Bullshit!*

Sweating up a storm, Tucker rolled to his feet and commenced a hundred-mile run in place, lifting his thighs and knees high to feel the burn. To suffer. To quell the ache in his gut while physical torment inflicted upon every last strand of burning muscle in his body. Let that bully come with his baton. Tucker meant to shove it where the sun didn't shine.

By the time he'd worked up a horrendous sweat, he'd run out of steam, and he knew damned well Stewart had planned it this way. That Stewart saved his own man, but left Tucker to rot in jail until Stewart was good and ready to negotiate a release. Tucker dropped out of high gear to a walk, then dropped to the bench, his body sheathed in one slick layer of aggravation.

*I should've called Strong.*

Tucker dropped his chin to his chest, worn out with jet lag and disgust. Stewart had connections the world over—maybe not as many as Strong, but he could've gotten Tucker out along with Isaiah—if he'd wanted to. Which meant? He didn't want to. Prison for a damned long time. *Damn.*

Tucker was his own worst enemy. If there ever was a dumber man, he didn't know the guy. Melissa had once called him arrogant. Said he always had to know everything. He always had to be right. What man didn't? And yet, his ego hadn't done him much good today.

He stared at the grimy floor between his feet, droplets of sweat dripping off his chin and nose to splatter below. Life shouldn't be this hard. The sun was supposed to shine on a yellow dog's butt once in a while, so why not his? How much could a guy take?

He honestly didn't know. He'd been a world-class whipping boy for months now. Make that years.

He wiped the stinging sweat out of his eyes and brushed his palms to his pants. His head hurt and his stomach growled, but he kept staring at the floor. Thinking. *Deuce. Melissa. Stewart. Nicole.* They were all part of the same puzzle. Tucker just couldn't get them to line up and make sense the way they should. He couldn't make them fit. Now Isaiah was gone, not even sending him one of his spiffy mind messages. What was the kid doing, looking out for himself? On his way to the airport and headed home?

Tucker still had an ornery woman to meet up with in less than twenty-four hours. What would Nicole do when she saw him? Run the other way? Call the police? Or listen to him, for once in her life? Tucker bet Deuce would be glad to see his old man, but Nicole was the key to him and his kid having a semi-normal father/son relationship. He needed to win her over so they could at least talk civilly about their son's welfare. So he could be part of Deuce's life.

And somehow, he needed to rescue Melissa before the personal drama began. He needed her to be safe before he could do what he'd come to Vietnam for. But how?

He closed his eyes, disgusted with his arrogance. Melissa might've been right. Everything that had gone wrong was his fault. He shouldn't have stolen the Buick, and he shouldn't have taken off like a mad man through the city, either. Instead, he should've alerted the proper authorities and waited until they'd shown and told them all he'd seen. He should've let them do their job and...

*Bullshit. No real man sat on his thumbs when his woman was abducted.*

Tucker lifted his head and faced the cell opposite him where three scrawny young men were jailed, all asleep at the moment, one sitting in the corner of the bench, one sprawled on the bench, the other on the floor. All Vietnamese. He studied the cells. Ceiling-to-floor thick, mesh wire. Bars for doors. No give. No way out. Dirty floors. One stainless-steel sink attached to the floor beside one stainless-steel toilet.

He dug deep into his reserves of positivity and willed himself to sleep while he could. He was on his own. Whatever happened next, he needed to rest and reserve his strength. Vietnamese prisons were notorious for human rights violations. Amnesty International had them on their top five as the world's worst. They used persecution and humiliation as a means to an end. Torture, too. It wouldn't matter that he was an American citizen, especially once they found out he worked for the FBI.

He dozed, dreaming of Melissa and Deuce, that they were safe at home waiting for him. Smiling. Happy. His head dropped, when—

*Bam! Bam! Bam!* Tucker looked up into the sneering face of his worst nightmare, the guard with the baton. Mr. Big Stuff. He wrinkled his nose and hit the cell bars again. "You American."

*No shit.* Tucker met his sneering gaze, but kept his mouth shut. A good bar fight was one thing. Being beat to death in a jail cell, something else. The guy kept slapping that shiny black baton of his into his open palm, waiting.

Unexpectedly, he struck the horizontal bar in the door, no doubt thinking that would intimidate his prey. *Guess again, jerk-off.* Tucker Chase didn't so much as flinch. He was no pansy. *Bring it on.*

The guard cocked his head. "You tough guy," he taunted. "You want trouble." He tapped the baton to his chest with a toothy grin. "You found it. My name Trouble. You want some?"

*Interesting. An English-speaking guard.* Tucker had nothing to say that wouldn't get him hit, but he would let this idiot make the mistake of opening that cell door, and—*we'll see who's trouble.*

Damned if the guy didn't unsnap a set of keys from his belt and do just that. Tucker shifted his feet, his muscles flexed and coiled for battle. This POS might get a few good licks in with that baton, but Tucker meant to wipe the floor with him.

The bully swung the door wide and stopped, still slapping that billy club to his palm. He yelled something over his shoulder. By now, all the other prisoners were on their feet. It sounded like they were laying bets, calling to each other, jeering and laughing.

Tucker lifted slowly. He towered over most of these guys, outweighed them, too. And he'd been trained to fight against all odds.

Two more guards shoved through that metal door, batons in hand, and the same sneers on their faces. Mr. Big Stuff cocked his head and offered another jack-o-lantern grin. "I got friends, but you got nobody. You scared? You wanna cry now or later?"

Tucker rolled his neck to the left, then to the right. Scared was not in his vocabulary. Neither was later. He sucked in a deep breath of whoop-ass and clenched his fists into hammers. Their jail. Their rules. But they were going to know who they'd messed with at the end of the day.

He launched himself into the gang of three, swinging with a hard right that garnered a blow to his forearm with Mr. Big Stuff's baton, but still knocked the guy off his feet and broke his jaw. It cracked loud enough. Tucker got a few more good licks in before he went down to his knees, and they tag-teamed him, kicking, screaming, and beating the shit out of him.

More guards blew in as the beating blew up. The prisoners went wild. A screaming siren sounded overhead. In the end, all Tucker could do was duck and cover his face while all those batons pummeled him into submission.

The guards ceased the attack as quickly as they'd begun. Two dragged him into his cell, but Mr. Big Stuff was noticeably absent. Tucker crawled to the bench, spitting blood and wiping his nose. Everything hurt. Every muscle. Every joint. He hadn't been able to protect his skull as much as he'd tried. Blood trickled down his jaw from his ear. He clawed his way onto the bench and leaned against the wall. *God, that hurt.*

And there he was again, Mr. Big Stuff with his baton. Frowning. A large, bloody bandage wrapped around his head, holding his left jaw in place. "You out. Now. Move!"

That hadn't taken long. Tucker waved him off. "No more. You made your point. Let me be."

The guard unlocked the door, jerking his head for Tucker to get out of the cell and do it fast. God, the balls this bastard thought he had just because of that baton. Hadn't he already learned his lesson? Tucker certainly had.

Placing both palms to his throbbing kneecaps, Tucker pushed up from the bench. The cell walls tilted to the left. The grimy floor shifted like waves in the sea. He lurched forward, he grabbed the doorframe and startled the guard enough that he jumped back a step, his baton raised and panic shining in his black eyes. "I kill you next time," he hissed, threateningly.

*Yeah, yeah, yeah.* Tucker nodded. He got the point. "What now?" he asked, subdued for the moment, his hand braced to the cell bars to keep his balance.

One guard was nothing. Tucker knew he could take Mr. Big Stuff and shove that baton up his ass, but all those other guards... they were the problem. Sometimes discretion really was the better part of valor.

The guard pointed at the phone down the narrow aisle by the exit door. "You have phone call," he mumbled while Tucker took satisfaction in knowing he'd gotten a few good licks in. "Five minutes only. Go. Talk."

Tucker shuffled to the phone, wondering who the hell would be calling him in this hellhole now that Isaiah was gone. He lifted the receiver to his tender ear and answered with a croak, his lips split and bleeding, his tongue dry. "Chase"

"Chase?" Oh. Stewart. A shiver of hope rattled up Tucker's sore back. "Are you okay?"

"I'm good," Tucker answered, tasting blood and leaning heavily against the wall. He turned his back on the guard.

"You don't sound good."

*Now you care?* Tucker kept his voice low. "I'm fine. You heard from Isaiah yet? They took him out of here a couple hours ago."

Stewart hissed. "Son-of-a-bitch, if they've hurt you—"

"I said I'm good," Tucker growled back, not as threatening as he'd meant to sound. "Tell me you've got Isaiah. Tell me the kid's safe."

"Yes. He's in a hotel nearby waiting for you. You're next. I had trouble getting them to agree to let you go. You had to steal the mayor's car, didn't you?"

Tucker groaned remembering that noisy welcoming committee at the airport. It could've been for the mayor. No wonder he was still stuck in Hanoi Hilton. "I didn't ask whose car it was. You know how it is when you're trying to save someone. You take chances. You improvise."

"Two minute!" Mr. Big Stuff screeched over what sounded like a mouth full of marbles, cracking that baton of his against the wall, just missing Tucker's forearm.

"You'll be released on one condition, Agent Chase," Stewart said hurriedly. "The Vietnamese government wants you out of their country in twenty-four hours. No excuses. This is not negotiable. You may have enough time to locate your ex before you have to leave, but if not, you *will* be on that jet and on your way home."

"You already made the reservation?" Tucker prickled at Stewart's insistence, but stifled his natural tendency to argue if he had.

"One minute!" The guard just kept badgering.

"I expect you on that plane, Chase. Isaiah has orders to make sure you comply. Don't screw up this one-time good deal."

"What about Melissa?" Tucker ground out. "You expect me to leave her here? What kind of a man do you think I am?"

"One who follows orders! Let me worry about her. I have a team already in transit. They'll track her down. They'll save her. Just get out of Vietnam before you make a bigger mess."

Tucker sucked down his rage at the non-negotiable, asinine plan Stewart was selling him. But what could he do?

"Tucker?" Stewart snapped. "I can't help you if you don't help me."

"Fine," Tucker breathed, his lungs on fire and his legs about to give out. "When?"

An audible sigh of relief filtered through the line—just before Mr. Big Stuff bashed the phone with his baton and cut Stewart off. "Call done. You over. In cell. Now!"

*Shit.* It would've helped to know how many days of hell he had to endure before that twenty-four hours kicked in. Tucker hung up the phone and shuffled back to his cell, enduring a few rude comments and jeers from his fellow prisoners along the way. Like he cared. He was on his way out of there. Soon, he hoped.

Once he was locked up tight again, he slumped to his side and tucked his legs onto the short bench. Stewart hadn't had the chance to spell out the particulars, but he'd sounded genuinely concerned. He might just care.

Tucker lifted his hands to his head, one for a pillow, the other to block the noise from the losers around him. He'd been a SEAL, for God's sake, and now he was one of the Bureau's finest. They did the impossible every damned day. He wouldn't leave

Vietnam without finding Melissa and without at least seeing Deuce.

Alex Stewart could take his one-time good deal and shove it up his ass.

# Chapter Seven

"Quick! Come quick!"

*Mmm. It's too early to have to go back to work...*

Melissa sighed, but rolled her bone-tired body off her mat on the floor of what had become clinic central. She now shared a hut with three families that consisted of eight adult males, four of whom were seriously injured, several women, and a dozen or so children.

"What now?" she asked patiently as she climbed to her feet and slid into her shoes.

The longhaired little girl at the doorway waved for her to hurry with an anxious, "My mama! My mama!"

"Okay, okay. I'm coming." The work never slowed in this out-of-the-way refugee camp. During the twenty-four hours since she'd arrived, Melissa had delivered two babies, cleaned, disinfected, and bandaged as many injuries as she could.

Simon was brusque in his dealings with her, but good for his word. The footings for the new clinic were already dug and the vertical posts planted. Where the lumber and concrete had come from, she had no idea and didn't ask. It was probably stolen, too.

She'd become quite familiar with patient care during her short years with Brady, but she'd had nurses and doctors to rely on then. They were the experts, not her. There in the camp, there was no one but her and the few American soldiers in league with Simon Siegel. She'd met Ralph Jackman, an ex-SEAL. Aaron Neumann, ex-Army. Orlando Schwartz, also ex-Army, nicknamed Oreo because of the blond dye job over his black roots. He'd been the guy in the passenger seat when she'd been kidnapped. These guys had done a decent job taking this impossible challenge on, but some of these wounds were devastating. One poor fellow had been shot and needed his leg amputated. She didn't want to have to learn how to do that.

The girl took off running, and so did Melissa. In her wildest dreams, she'd never imagined herself in such a heartrending predicament. She'd wanted to serve others, but wow. The universe had certainly provided this time.

When the girl dropped to her knees alongside a man in obvious distress, Melissa's heart pitched up her throat. God, not him. Not the poor man with gangrene in his leg.

"No, no, no," the girl sang out. "My mama."

Melissa recognized the mother of that darling boy who'd wanted to play tag amidst all this suffering. "How can I help?"

The mama in question ducked her head into her shoulders, shy and embarrassed, but in obvious pain, her face drawn and her hand tucked inside her shirt. The cute little guy sat on her lap, his head on her chest. It was the little girl who tugged her mother's hand free where Melissa could see it. *Oh my.* She leaned forward and gently took that swollen, red hand into her palm, searching for the reason for this raging infection. Angry red streaks lined the wrist, all five fingers distended and looking more like sausages. The hand was on fire, but there was no laceration that Melissa could see, and she didn't want to cause this poor woman any more pain by unnecessary handling. "How did you do this?"

The woman shook her head and tried to pull her hand back, but Melissa didn't release it. Not yet. "This is serious. You need an antibiotic," she explained, wishing she could breach the language barrier. She lifted the hand to examine the underside of it. "I'll need to open this up and flush the infection once I know where it's coming from. Can you come with me?"

"What's going on?" Simon dropped to one knee at Melissa's side. "Damn. Snake bite." He rattled off a few curt words to the woman. She pointed over her shoulder into the jungle. Simon never gave her a chance to argue. He had his knife out, the blade ready, and in a blink, he'd sliced the heel of her palm just above her wrist. She whimpered, but he only dropped to both knees, lifted her hand to his mouth and sucked the knife wound. He spat a mouthful of blood and saliva into the dirt. "Antidote," he muttered at Melissa as he leaned into the woman's hand again. "Snake bite. Get Oreo. Step on it. He's unloading the supplies. He'll know what you need."

Melissa scrambled to the parking lot, not sure which supply truck. "Oreo," she called out, needing him to be where Simon said.

"Yeah. Over here." Oreo peered around the open back door of one of the supply trucks. His spiked hair actually looked more like feathers than a cookie. "You need me?"

"Snake bite," she gasped, out of breath. "I need the antidote."

He jumped off the ramp where boxes were stacked and ran to a pickup across the way. Ducking his upper body inside the back seat of the king cab, he retrieved a medical kit. "Where?"

"Simon. He's with the man who needs his leg amputated. I don't know his name," Melissa gasped out. "His wife. Hurry."

"That ain't no good," Oreo muttered as he marched between the huts. "What kind of snake? Did Simon say?"

"No. He just said to get you and the antidote."

"Hope I've got the right one," Oreo said, swinging the kit as he hurried. "There's a hundred different kind of snakes in this country and most of 'em are poisonous. Not all antidotes work on all snakes."

Melissa gulped, glancing sideways in case any of those hundred kinds of snakes might be slithering nearby at that moment. Her heart pounded at the thought of that sweet little girl and boy losing their mother.

"What are we looking at?" Oreo called to Simon as he approached.

"Sounds like she got bit by a Malayan pit viper," Simon replied curtly, his hand shackled at the woman's wrist. "We'll know for sure in a minute. I sent some guys into the trees where she said she got bit. If it's a pit, it may still be there."

The woman sat sedately at Simon's knee, her gaze to the ground and her children clinging to her side. "My mama," her daughter cried softly. "You save my mama."

"Don't you worry, Mimi," Simon answered with a smile and a wink. "This little snake bite's nothing. I'll save your mama."

"Are you sure?" Melissa asked quietly, not wanting to give the child or her mother false hope. She found it interesting that some of the children spoke English.

Simon cocked his head at her. "Mostly," he muttered out of the corner of his mouth. "The pit's poisonous and it's nasty tempered, but it's also slow-witted. Chances are it hasn't gone too far from where she ran into it. We'll know in a minute."

A triumphant yell went up from the east side of camp.

"See? They found it. What'd I tell you?" He called to the men, "Bring it in."

A group of three men and two boys ran excitedly into camp, a serpent swinging from the fork of a branch in the one guy's hand. They waved its still wriggling body close enough that Melissa shivered with revulsion. The thing had to be eight feet long. Okay, maybe not. Make that two feet of writhing, vicious snake. It was brown with black-edged triangular blotches along its back. It reared its pointed snout and hissed before it struck out, missing the nearest man's arm.

They laughed. These foolish men laughed like they couldn't get hurt if it bit them. Men! If she lived to be a hundred, Melissa would never understand them.

"That's a pit all right." Oreo unlatched the med-kit and drew out a small vial and an already filled IV bag. He tossed a foil packet at Melissa. "Thirty milliliters of anti-venom, coming right up. Melissa, swipe the inside of her arm. Let's get this antidote going."

She hurried, certain time was of the essence. When she fumbled the antiseptic wipe and it fell into the dirt, Simon cupped her shoulder. "Hey. Slow down. She's not dying. It was just a pit."

"But it's poisonous, and..." Melissa brushed her hair out of her face, all but hyperventilating. This poor family had suffered enough.

Oreo tossed another foil packet at her.

"Pits are nasty, but she'll be okay," Simon reassured her. "We got to her in time. She might get nauseous. She might lose some healthy tissue to a little necrosis, but she won't lose her limb. She'll live."

"How do you know?" Melissa retorted, annoyed at his lackadaisical answer as she barely caught the antiseptic wipe. "What makes you so sure?"

"Because of this." He lifted his arm showing off his bicep. An ugly red scar the diameter of a tennis ball marked the back of his arm above his elbow.

"You were bitten, too?" she asked, amazed at the size of the pockmark that snake had left. She could've sunk two fingertips into the depression if she'd been so inclined. She wasn't, but she could have.

"He's wearing the skin of that devil snake on his boonie hat to prove it," Oreo bragged as he inserted a line into the IV bag. "Simon's a badass."

"When did it happen?" Melissa asked, swiping the woman's arm. "How long have you been in Vietnam?"

A look shifted between Oreo and Simon, one of those looks only guys understood.

"I didn't get it in Vietnam." Simon settled cross-legged on the ground, still holding the woman's wrist while Melissa and Oreo hurried. "I was in Nepal. The snake sneaked into my tent to snuggle one night. Damned scary is what it was—for the snake." He waggled his eyebrows at the little girl, now smiling, and he said something to her in Cambodian. She nodded solemnly, her lashes lowered, her dark eyes shy with the attention.

"Smart girl," Simon said as he turned to Melissa. "I asked her to take good care of her mother, and to be sure to tell me if her mama gets sick to her stomach or has trouble breathing. You might want to watch for those symptoms too, just in case."

"In case we're too late?" Melissa asked, worried.

"Settle down. She's okay, I promise, but she might be allergic to the anti-venom. I don't want to kill her while I'm helping her. I'm just glad her little girl wasn't bit. That'd be a whole different story. We'd be holding a funeral. The pit's venom works faster on little kids."

Melissa shook her head, overwhelmed at the jungle teeming with risk on all sides, but just as aware of this unlikely hero's concern for these people. She'd honestly thought she was going to die at the hands of drug runners when this bizarre adventure began, but seeing this village and the families caught up in the latest Cambodian tragedy, she knew better.

Simon wasn't so bad, either. He seemed to be one of those guys who knew how to lead a beleaguered group of men, women, and children, but also how to protect them. That was what he and his team were doing, standing between that vicious viper and a sweet little girl.

"It's all good, Melissa," Simon insisted again. Just like Tucker would've said if he'd been there. How many times had he admonished her for her compulsory attention to detail in the same laidback way?

Melissa held the IV bag steady while Oreo attached the line to Mimi's mother's arm. "It'd be better if she were prone, but I doubt she'll leave her old man," he said quietly. "This will have to do."

"Move them into my hut," Melissa insisted. "The whole family. There's room, and that way they'll all be off the ground."

"What are we going to do about him?" Oreo's eyes scrolled over to the man on the mat, the one covered in sweat and in obvious pain, then to Simon.

"There's no choice, is there?" Simon muttered under his breath, one brow raised. There was that look again. It was almost as if these men had a secret code between them. "The leg's got to come off."

"I... I don't know how to do that," Melissa whispered, faint at the thought. "Do you?"

Was that why they'd kidnapped her? Had they thought she was a nurse? Was that what that shifty guy-look was about?

Simon nodded. "I do, but I've been holding off to see if we've got any antibiotics strong enough to knock the infection down first. I'd hate to take his leg if there's no need to."

"Are you a doctor?"

"Not exactly."

She gulped past the dry lump in her throat. "He needs to taken to the clinic then. Dr. Hanks will know what to do."

"I won't send a man to his death. Spies will be looking for him there."

She bit her lip and nodded. Simon meant to save these people, and deep down she agreed with his motivation. "When do you want to do it?" she asked reluctantly.

Simon blew out a deep sigh. "Let's get Mimi, Peewee, and their mother settled first. Oreo, you got any painkiller in that truck?"

"You know I do. Morphine. Oxycodone. The usual."

"We still got some of that brandy?" Simon asked, running his hand over his head.

"You'd rather give him liquor than the morphine?" Melissa asked, appalled at the thought.

"The brandy's for me after the surgery. Will you assist, Nurse Melissa?"

He could've knocked her over with a feather. "Me?" she asked, her voice as squeaky and as timid as a mouse's. "I'm not a nurse."

His brows furrowed. "Of course, you. Do you see anyone else around who's smart enough to help me do it?"

She rolled her eyes at that ridiculous compliment. Her? Help him? Amputate? Never.

"You have very pretty eyes," Simon said quietly, "especially when you underestimate yourself and do that silly eye-roll thing. But I can see a different world in there. You're braver than you think. Please say yes. I really need your help."

She had to look at him then, this man with a big attitude about himself and life in general. What did he know about her? Nearly nothing. Still, the light of sincerity glimmered in his soft green eyes, like a jungle pool of calm in the middle of mayhem. Like a man who meant to do what he could as long as he could. Just like Tucker.

Melissa girded up her audacity at the thought of Tucker and determined to be more like him and less like her. "Okay. I'll help."

# Chapter Eight

The rats came out in the Vietnamese jail at night.

*Big rats.*

SEALs called it a blanket party when guys rolled a teammate up in his own blanket and beat the crap out of him. It was a rowdy form of team discipline. He'd seen it once in the Navy where a certain corpsman got taught a rough lesson in personal hygiene. The guy outright refused to shower daily, said it wasn't good for his skin or some other bullshit. His team wouldn't put up with the daily stench anymore, so he got one final hint. A sound thrashing. Problem solved.

But this?

The guy the bully guards were beating wasn't going to live the night. He'd stopped calling out, wasn't even grunting when they hit him with those damned batons. Or whatever those slimy bastards were doing to him. He wasn't the first. The ruthless gang moved from cell to cell, selecting certain prisoners for their night game, leaving others alone.

Certain that he was on their hit list, Tucker hunkered in the shadows with his back to the wall, his head down, and his body coiled and waiting. He should've known better than to be caught in this predicament, but there he was, headed for another beat down. Given how much he was already hurt, his chances for survival were just as slim as that other guy's.

A cell slammed shut. Some guy growled a menacing sort of chuckle, and shit. They all stopped at Tucker's cell. He stuck his chin out, sure as hell not going peacefully into the night. He jumped to his feet, made a production of flexing his muscles and rolling his bruised shoulders, trying like hell to shake off the after-effects of the last beating. These guys wanted a piece of him? Some of them would die trying to get it.

Suddenly, the overhead lights burst on, blinding him and the thugs outside his cell. A stern voice shouted in Vietnamese, and the guards snapped to attention. Not a second too soon. A uniformed officer with brass buttons and medals pinned to his chest marched up to the guards, and stared them down.

Tucker waited, hoping for the best, but prepared for the worst. If this was the joker behind all the rough treatment, things could get ugly real fast.

"Mr. Chase," the leader of the pack said in perfect English, his gaze still riveted on his men's faces. "It is your lucky day. You will follow me, sir."

Tucker blew out a huff through his nostrils, not believing his nightmare was over. Not yet. He tensed for an ambush, a stab in the back the minute he cleared the cell, another lie the instant he foolishly thought he was free. That was when it always happened.

The officer had to cock his head to look up at Tucker, his lips pinched tight while his eyes scrolled over his prisoner's bruised and bloodied face. His broken nose. His split lip and swollen eye. The officer's upper lip twitched right before he hissed, "You Americans."

Whatever that meant. Tucker kept his fists clenched and his one good eye on the bastards behind him while he followed the officer down the narrow aisle and out the exit into another room where he'd been forced to don the black uniform earlier. The officer handed him a woven basket with his clothes and boots and directed him to change.

Tucker still didn't believe. Getting a guy's hopes up was the cruelest form of mental torture of all, and these guys were low enough to do it. He stripped quickly out of the black prison getup while the officer watched. Finally back in his own clothes, jeans and a T-shirt, he dropped to the single chair to put on his socks and boots, wondering how long this game of cat and mouse would last.

If it was a game.

Wearing his own clothes bolstered his confidence. Still... he didn't believe.

The officer retrieved a gray vinyl pouch from the desk at the other side of the room and tossed it at Tucker with a curt, "Your valuables."

Tucker made quick work of examining his passport, something he'd thought he'd never see again. His wallet had been rifled through, his American Express card in its slot, but his US currency gone. "I had cash in here. Where is it?"

The man didn't so much as blink. "I'm sure you are mistaken."

*And I'm sure you're a lying, thieving son-of-a-bitch,* Tucker thought, but he stuffed his things into his pockets. At least his kid's school photo was still in its place.

With his palms on his knees, Tucker was ready to go. He could take this guy, maybe break his skinny neck before anyone was able to intervene, and the guy knew it. He maintained a respectable and safe distance. "Now what?"

"You have important friends, Mr. Chase," the officer murmured, his eyes narrowed to slits, "but make no mistake. There are places in my country where your friends cannot help you, not if they searched for a thousand days."

*Yes, and if not for your army of goons, I could make you disappear in a vat of phở.*

They stared each other down, Tucker still seated on the chair, the officer lording his position of power over his prisoner, one hand on his hip. Until Tucker had enough. He lifted his butt from the chair and stood, amused when the officer was again forced to raise his chin and look upward to maintain eye contact, when this puny little guy finally realized what a bug he was in comparison to the real man in the room.

"Are we done here?" Tucker kept his fingers straight instead of clenched for battle, his tone level instead of threatening while he looked down at the officer.

The man nodded toward the exit. "The next time we meet, I will kill you," he enunciated very clearly, "and I will do it slowly."

Tucker kept his opinion to himself as he did the gentlemanly thing and reached for a handshake. The last rule of negotiation: *Always ask for one more concession.* The first rule of a good SEAL: *Never let an opportunity for one-upmanship slide.*

The officer sneered at what he most likely perceived as a weak American offer of friendship, but he did return a limp handshake.

Then—Tucker believed.

He stuck the keys he'd just stolen into his jeans pockets, rolled the last two days of hell off his shoulders, and turned his back on the man.

The next room was empty, except for an armed guard at the exit and Isaiah. The kid's mouth dropped when he caught sight of Tucker, but he kept quiet. Tucker offered one nod to let his companion agent know he was good. Finally on the street, he blew out a deep breath.

The cool night air felt good. Tucker sucked in a deep lungful and let it slowly escape, but it hurt too. He coughed and rubbed the tender spot under his left arm, stretching his spine and self-diagnosing the multiple complaints registering. He'd had worse, but these were enough for the day.

"What'd they do to you?" Isaiah danced at his side, his eyes bright with concern. "You're bleeding. Your... your eye."

"I'm good. You got any water on you?"

Isaiah produced a bottle from the backpack slung over his shoulder. "Take this. I've got more. They beat you?"

"Don't worry about it." Tucker opened the bottle and drained it in one gulp. He screwed the cap back on and grabbed the second one Isaiah had waiting for him. "Shit, that feels good going down. I'm hungry. Let's find something to eat while we make plans."

"You need to see a doctor. That eye looks bad," Isaiah said quietly, glancing over his shoulder while they walked away from the station.

"This?" Tucker scoffed it off, his fingertips to his swollen eyelid. The thing felt as big as a soft ball, only puffy and twice as tender as he'd expected. *Ouch.* "This ain't nothing. You got wheels?"

Isaiah motioned toward the lime green mini-truck parked at the curb. "It's economical."

Tucker bit back his comment at the clown car. "It'll do."

Isaiah scrambled to the driver's side and climbed in. "I know a place."

Tucker folded his aching, beat up body into the cramped passenger seat. Eating would be good, but better? He jangled the keys he'd stolen in front of Isaiah's nose. "Don't let me forget. Before we leave town, I need to come back and pay my friends a visit."

Isaiah shot him a withering glance while he cranked the engine. "It's not funny, Tucker. They could've killed you. You're not going back. I've been waiting for hours. If I'd known they were mistreating you, I would have—"

"You would've what?"

Isaiah pulled away from the curb. "I would've made them pay. I hate bullies."

Tucker cupped Isaiah's shoulder, for the first time noticing the kid had some muscle on him. "I need a beer."

"You need medical care, but you won't listen to me, will you?"

*Stupid question.*

Isaiah wove through the city streets like a pro, finally stopping at a noodle parlor. "You can't go in looking like that. Wait here. I'll be right back."

He was out of the truck before Tucker could argue—a good thing. He didn't have the strength for it. He collapsed into the small seat, one elbow on the open window, and his head on the headrest. What a godawful day, even for a tough guy like him. He'd seen his share of cruelty, had dispensed some of it himself a time or two, but nothing was better than getting away before the beatings got worse. Those jail guards were as low and as depraved as men could get. They were predators and did what they did for the sick pleasure of degrading another human being.

The night sounds of a city that never slept drifted through the open truck windows. The Hồ Chí Minh City night market came with all sizes of people on bikes or mopeds. Motorcycles. Mini-cars. You name it. Horns honked, squeaked, and dinged. He shielded his tired eyes from the flashing neon lights and willed the vision of something pleasant into his mind.

*Melissa.* He could almost smell her. Vanilla and cinnamon. Apple pie and freedom, that was what she smelled like. She was his true American girl, all the way down to the scent of her sexy body.

A scent of cinnamon drifted on the breeze to his nose. He inhaled deeply, savoring the tender changes Melissa had brought into his life. Yes, her self-control and uppity morals had hurt his ego, but in so many ways that he'd never admit, he liked that she was strong enough to set personal boundaries and make him stick to them.

She posed a unique puzzle in a world gone crazy with sex, prescription drugs, and pornographic selfies. Most women threw themselves at men like him. That kind of vapid attention used to impress him. Not anymore. Melissa wasn't them. She was something above them. She was worth waiting for. Maybe even worth changing for.

*If* he was smart enough to get her back.

Out of nowhere, Isaiah jerked the truck door open, startling Tucker. He climbed inside, his arms full of bags and boxes. "Here, hold this stuff," he said as he offloaded them to Tucker's arms. "Noodles, dumplings, and spiced shrimp. More bottled water. I've got a room ten minutes from here."

"Is it on ground level with an easy exit?"

"Yeah. Sure. Do you think I'm stupid?"

*That had to be one of those rhetorical questions.* "Where's my beer?"

Isaiah frowned. "You didn't really think I was getting alcohol for you, did you? Not with the shape you're in. Sit back and relax. I know what I'm doing."

Tucker shot his junior agent a sideways glance. "Do you?"

The truck lurched into traffic, then stalled to the irate blaring of horns and what Tucker guessed were curse words in the native language. "Depress the clutch, smart guy," he told Isaiah while he worked the stick shift. "It's the middle pedal on a standard transmission, buddy. Not automatic."

Kids these days. None of them knew how cars worked.

Isaiah blew out a quick breath and followed instructions. "I know, I know, I just forgot. Guess we're not in Kansas anymore."

"No, Toto, we're not."

Isaiah took over the stick shift rather well after that. The foreign sights of Hồ Chí Minh City nightlife flew by in a blur. A beer sure as hell would've been nice, though.

Isaiah was as good as his word. The joint was ground level with a sliding glass door where a man could make a quick getaway. His hotel selection left a little to be desired, but Tucker was too spent to worry. He needed a bed to land on—fast.

Tucker flipped up the light switch and surprise, surprise. Isaiah had been a busy boy. "Where the hell did you find M203 grenade launchers?" Tucker asked, his estimation of his junior agent on the rise.

"You'd be amazed what you can get on the streets in this town. I've been busting my butt since I got my get-out-of-jail-free card. Look what else."

Tucker ran a hand over the wooden 5.56x45 NATO ammo boxes, and the matching Colt M4 automatic rifles with ACOG scopes that went with them. Air-cooled. Gas-operated. Magazine-fed carbine. M4s were lighter and a sturdy choice by Army, Navy and Marines alike, a weapon he'd used enough over the years. He had one in his private collection. "These are American-made."

"See this stuff?" Isaiah couldn't have looked prouder when he held up a contraption with det cord, a numerical gauge, and an off-white brick of—*oh hell. C4.* "It's an IED kit. I wasn't sure if we'd need one, but they were fifty percent off, so I bought ten. Really cool, huh?"

Tucker eased the device gently out of his junior agent's excited grip. "Ah, yeah. Let me have that. You do know you're holding enough explosives in your hand to cook this hotel and you along with it, don't you?"

Visions of what had happened to the seventeen sailors onboard the USS Cole when Al-Qa'ida used C-4 to blow a hole in it flashed to Tucker's mind. And Khobar Towers, the military housing complex in Saudi Arabia. Hundreds of suicide car bombings across the world. Holy hell. Some jerk was selling this crap on the streets to imbeciles like Isaiah? *Incredible.*

Tucker set the device flat to the end table beside the bed, his adrenaline spiking. Isaiah knew how to shop, but having money in your pocket didn't equate to shopping smart. *That was close.*

The geek's lower lip dropped open. His brows arched as he stepped away from the *really cool, huh,* bomb. "Even without the detonators?"

Tucker slanted a sharper look at the kid. "You know to keep the detonators separate? Where are they?"

Isaiah pointed to his stack of supplies. "In that paper bag. Stewart's men trained me, remember? I'm not dumb enough to keep wired explosives in a hotel, Tucker. Come here. For feeling so good, you look like shit." Isaiah stuck his chin out. "Now sit down and shut up. Let me do my job, why don'tcha?"

Tucker let Isaiah win that round. He did tend to overreact when he was beat to hell.

Sitting on the end of the nearest bed, he scanned the rest of the room with his good eye. Two double beds. Clean sheets. Decent-looking pillows. Aside from Isaiah's spot-on purchases stacked near the door and the scare of near annihilation by C4, the interior of this two-bit hotel was a definite improvement over the exterior. "Where'd you get the money for all this shit?"

"I have ways," Isaiah said as he knelt at Tucker's right and gently examined the messed up eye, his fingertips peeling the eyelid up. He cringed as he took stock. "I was afraid of this when I left. Those jail guards were waiting for their boss to go home before they jumped you."

"Yeah well, I wasn't the only one they tangled with. You keeping an eye on Melissa?" Tucker stared at the ceiling as best he could, kind of hard when someone was poking around in your eye.

"You know what's odd," Isaiah murmured just before he squirted a heaping shot of molten lava into Tucker's eyeball. "Sorry. Saline solution. Your eye looks like hamburger. That might sting a little."

A little, nothing. A sharp stick couldn't have hurt worse. Tucker shuddered involuntarily, willing the pain back into the shadows where it belonged, where he could deal with it later. He'd learned early in life. *Never let 'em see you cry.*

"What's odd?" he croaked. "Is she okay?"

"You've got a bionic eyeball?" Isaiah asked, breathing on Tucker's chin he was so close. "Is that what I'm seeing? A lens transplant? God, Tucker. Why would you let them do something like this to you? Is this part of my father's drone experiment?"

Tucker shook his head to clear the tears running out of his poor, pummeled eyeball. Isaiah's attempt to help stung like an angry hornet. "I'm not a drone," he bit out. "This was all my doing. My call. The lens helps me see better and farther when I'm on sniper duty. That's all. I never miss a shot now. It's not damaged, is it?" *Because it sure feels like it's turning my eyeball into sushi.*

Isaiah's forehead wrinkled, and his brows dipped as he once again peeled the eyelid open and peered closer. "It's still in one piece, but your entire eyeball's blood red. I have no idea if the lens will work right once the swelling goes down. Can you see any light?"

Tucker nodded. "Yeah. I can see. Everything's just blurry."

Isaiah's lips thinned. "That's good. I was afraid you might have retinal detachment going on, as bad as it looks. Do you have to activate the lens or is it always on?"

"It's always on. Stop worrying about me. Is Melissa okay?"

Isaiah nodded, his eyes grim and his lips tight while he wiped Tucker's tender eyelid with what felt like a rake but was only an antiseptic wipe. *Crap, that stung.* "What's odd is I have no trouble reading Melissa's emotions, but I can't get inside of her head like I can yours. I can't talk to her. You heard me tell you about meeting up with your ex back in Alex's office, didn't you?"

"Yeah, so?" The soothing gel Isaiah had just saturated Tucker's bleary eye with must've had an anesthetic in it. Instant relief. The stabbing pain was gone. His shoulders relaxed. He let out the breath he hadn't realized he'd been holding, and relaxed his clenched fingers. He no longer wanted to kill Isaiah with his bare hands.

"So I can communicate directly with you, but not her. It's like one-way transmission. She has no clue I'm picking up her thoughts. You must have some level psychic ability. With you, it's two-way."

"Bullshit. You were sitting three feet away from me. That's all." He was not psychic. End of story. "How is she?"

Isaiah hummed and hawed, not arguing while he doctored the rest of Tucker's face, cleaning the bruises and dosing two of his cuts with ointment and butterfly bandages. "She seems to be calmer now, more confident, but she's very tired. Several American men are with her. She feels safe with them. You want me to look at your leg? I saw the limp."

"Leave my leg alone. What men? How many?" Tucker would never admit to the pain. Besides, it wasn't his leg. It was a rib or two.

Isaiah repacked the med kit and set it on one of the wooden ammo boxes. "A handful, from what I can tell. Military. The last hint I detected from her had something to do with an amputated leg."

Tucker glared as best he could. "Hers?"

"I don't think so, but her mind was definitely overloaded with anxiety. She's an interesting study. Sweet, but strong-willed. Caring, but independent. I detect a streak of a control freak."

"You have no idea." Tucker made it a statement. Melissa was as confident as an Amazon woman on the hunt and twice as defiant, but saturated with the cream of human kindness. Drizzled with pure honey and a touch of cinnamon and vanilla. A touch of cayenne pepper. That was Melissa, from the crown of her golden locks down to her painted toes. "She's okay?"

"She's still stressed. I'm not able to tell precisely why, but I'll keep checking on her. Then I need to make another call."

"Who do you need to call?"

"Never mind. First..." Isaiah poured a carton of steaming noodles into one of two bowls he'd pulled out of one of his many bags. "Let's eat. Vermicelli and pork. There's a box of eggrolls around here somewhere. Ah, there it is. Here. Chopsticks. Then we'll talk some more." He handed Tucker the first food he'd had since they'd landed in Vietnam.

Tucker stuffed his mouth with a few good-sized helpings before he asked again. "Spill. Who else have you been talking to? Stewart? Strong?"

"Your ex," Isaiah admitted, slurping a heaped mound of rice noodles.

Tucker choked. "Nicole? Why?"

Isaiah stopped playing with his food. "Because we came to Vietnam to locate your son, remember? This trip is supposed to be about Devlin."

"Deuce," Tucker corrected, his Irish up, and his chopsticks clenched like weapons in his fist. "I can't worry about him right now, Toto. I've got to find Melissa first. Then I'll go look up my ex and negotiate custody of my son. What were you thinking?"

"Will you stop calling me names? I located your ex like I was supposed to and I phoned her. It seemed like a good idea. Nicole wasn't too thrilled to hear that you were in the country, but I told her how much it meant for you to see your son. She agreed to meet with you some place where there would be a crowd. What'd you do to her that she's leery of meeting you in person again? Beat her up? Slap her around?"

"No," Tucker shot back at Isaiah, sick of the attitude in Isaiah's voice. The woman had a way of turning everyone against him. "I don't hit women, moron. Didn't you read her mind? Couldn't you tell she was lying?"

"No, but I will if you want me to."

"Then do it," Tucker snapped, pissed that Isaiah thought for one second he'd abuse a woman. There were times he'd come close to slapping Nicole. She'd certainly had it coming with all of her lies. The woman could make the Pope swear, but not once had he laid a hand on her in anger.

Isaiah set his chopsticks across his bowl. "Okay. I'll only be a second." He closed his eyes, two fingers to his temple, then grunted quietly before he peered at Tucker out of one eye. "You're right. I probed deeper. She's a shallow piece of work, isn't she? Sorry. What on earth did you see in her?"

"Man, I wish I'd known you during my divorce," Tucker admitted, genuinely relieved that someone just might believe his side of all the stories Nicole had told. "I wouldn't be stuck in the mess I am today."

"But we wouldn't be here to help Melissa, either," Isaiah reminded. "Everything happens for a reason, which is why I've been stockpiling guns and ammo since I got out of jail. I knew you'd choose to go after her first. I just hoped we could squeeze Devlin into whatever time you have left in country."

"Twenty-four hours," Tucker muttered. "I'm supposed fly the friendly skies out of Vietnam in less than a day, and his name is Deuce, damn it. Get it right, will you?"

Isaiah looked away, and Tucker caught the attempt to avoid eye contact. Maybe he was psychic or something. "You saw something else, didn't you?" he asked, his father's heart climbing up his throat. "With Nicole. You saw something else when you read her mind. Is my boy in trouble?"

He knew before Isaiah looked him in his one good eye. "I did. Sorry. I should've told you. She's letting what's-his-name—Vinnie, is it? She's letting Vinnie have full control over your son. At his garment factory. Deuce is in trouble, Tucker. He's been forced into child labor along with a couple hundred other kids Vinnie's got working for him."

Tucker dropped his food and jumped to his feet, madder than a son-of-a-bitch. "Where's this factory?"

Isaiah looked to the door, the color draining from his face. "Ten miles south of here on the west side of the Saigon River. He's not in pain though. Tucker, we can't save him. Not now. I just picked up a sharp image from Melissa. She's covered in blood."

Tucker punched the wall. "Move out!"

# **Chapter Nine**

"Son-of-a-gun," Melissa exclaimed to herself, softly of course. Simon was concentrating.

She knew there'd be blood and gallons of infection during an amputation this ugly, but so much? Her stomach began a slow climb up her throat at the river of greenish yellow goo slurping over the edge of the surgery table. The tendrils of bright red curlicues in the mess were not helping her breathe or think clearly.

The ugly smelling concoction splattered against her pant leg. It squished beneath the soles of her canvas sneakers, but what could she do? Only bathe later when the work was done and scrub her clothes and shoes.

She had names to go with the faces now, and Dang, the man whose leg they were amputating, needed the best help available. His poor wife, Tam, was still recovering from her narrow escape with the pit viper. For now, she rested with her children, Mimi and Peewee, in the same hut as Melissa. She suspected the children's names were Simon's nicknames, but they fit the little tykes, and it was endearing of him to have given them such sweet attention.

The abysmal humidity made the coppery scent of Dang's blood weigh heavy on her mind and in her nose. Melissa swallowed hard, fighting the creeping nausea.

For now, Dang breathed evenly, his poor body pumped with the stolen antibiotics and anesthetics from the supply trucks, his body draped in stolen sterile sheeting, and his diseased leg on the verge of becoming history. An IV line, probably stolen, too, kept him hydrated. Melissa no longer cared about the thefts. The supplies were being used for a good purpose. That was what mattered.

Simon had decided to perform the emergency surgery well after midnight while the rest of the camp slept. His men had curtained off a section of what would be the new clinic and set up spotlights for the amputation. Plastic sheeting covered the ground. The severely bloated leg was restrained within a wooden clamp Oreo had fashioned, itself surgically draped. If there was a more primitive operating room, Melissa couldn't imagine it.

"You doing okay?" Simon asked over his powder blue mask, his eyes sharp.

Melissa nodded, more determined than ever to assist and do it valiantly. There really was no one else. Ralph Jackman and Aaron Neumann were somewhere in the jungle on patrol. Tristan had gone with them while Oreo maintained armed vigil outside the clinic. So Melissa and Simon had both scrubbed and dressed in stolen surgical garb to keep the procedure as sterile as possible. She wished she'd doubled her surgical mask though.

Simon continued with his scalpel, slicing deftly through skin and tissue, inserting clamps to stop the hemorrhaging as he went. As skillful as he seemed, Melissa still looked away with every cut. Dutifully, she dabbed the sweat glistening on Simon's forehead with a sterile wipe and kept her gaze off the patient.

"Thank you, ma'am," Simon muttered, his brows furrowed and his eyes riveted on his work. "It's so damned humid tonight, I'm sweating bullets. Brows again, please."

She dabbed again and kept assisting, handing him the tools he needed. By the time the wretched sawing stopped, Dang's leg was separated just below the kneecap, and she was close to passing out. She drew in a deep breath and sent her mind across the Pacific Ocean to the East Coast of America, to Tucker. This was something he would do—save a man's life in the middle of nowhere with only his confidence in himself and the most basic tools. But he'd do it, and he'd be proud of the job when he was done. He'd brag about it.

That was Tucker, so much more than most, as if he'd been born to be a hero. A patriot. If anyone personified a military slogan, it was Tucker. The few. The proud. The army of one.

With Tucker there was only one way, and it was always up and over, forever forward. Not once that she could recall had he wasted time whining or complaining about the past. He just kept getting up each day and going to work, serving his country and putting himself in the line of danger while he did it. The man was a workaholic, born to fight the bad guys of the world. Born to win.

"Can you hand me the sutures?" Simon asked, nodding at the medical tray beside the surgery table. "I'm not sure what size. Give me the one with the biggest needle. That should work for now."

Melissa sized the sutures up and handed the already threaded larger needle to Simon. She'd met Tucker during an especially difficult time in her life. She'd just lost Brady and her reason to live, or so it had seemed. Every day was impossibly hard to get through then, and she'd fallen victim to the biggest scam on the planet—the one that offered a ray of hope where she'd thought she saw none. She shook her head thinking about how foolish she'd been. That hope had ended up being a siphon on her heart and a trap. A scam.

Alex ended up sending a team to retrieve her, but in the process they ran into an FBI agent already imbedded deep inside the cult. Things had gone bad. Tucker had been knifed. He'd ended up at Melissa's cabin, and from that moment on, she could barely stand not to look at him. He'd drawn her in with that sheer animal magnetism of his, that cocky male power of a man who knew why he'd been created. Darn him.

He hadn't known it then, but even with a knife wound in his shoulder, those deep blue eyes of his had swept her feminine receptors off their silly feet and her with them. How did a man get under your skin so fast? Or so deep into your heart? She honestly didn't know. The feelings she had for Tucker defied logic and biology, but not chemistry. There seemed plenty of that to go around, and all of it flammable with a *'Danger! Stand back!'* sign.

Ah, that man. He'd be in charge if he were there instead of Simon. No doubt about it.

"Ahem, could you snip this for me?"

"Oh. Oh, sure." She rallied out of her daydream and grabbed the scissors to snip the line Simon held at a right angle from the stump of Dang's leg. "Sorry. Guess I'm tired."

"No problem. Just stick with me a couple more minutes. I need to finish sewing this flap of skin, then we're done. Can you slide the leg out of the clamp and wrap it in plastic or something? It's attracting flies."

*Ewww*. Even with surgical gloves, lifting the separated leg out of the bloody clamp was a thoroughly disgusting job to have to do. Melissa ignored the queasy feeling in the pit of her stomach and carefully covered the limb in the small section of surgical sheeting she'd prepared before the surgery.

Thoughts of Tucker danced back to mind, if only because he'd be smirking at her if he'd been there, teasing her to be tough. To not be a pansy. He'd tell her not to chew on the leg bone or something equally gross, then he'd laugh because she had to be ten shades of green. Of course, then he'd wrap her up tight in his arms and press her against that heavily muscled chest of his. She'd breathe his masculine scent in and close her eyes. He'd kiss her neck. He'd call her babe, and she'd melt and wish life wasn't so complicated, that she could just throw herself at him, and that everything would work out.

Melissa set the limb on the farthest side of the makeshift counter where she didn't have to look at it. She knew better than to wish her life away. Marriage was a darned hard job and nothing in life was that easy. Happily-ever-after could change on a dime, and the hero you'd given your heart and soul to could come home without his legs or arms. Without the desire to live.

No matter how much you loved him, there would still be bleak days where it seemed the world was against the both of you. Where nothing went right. There would still be hospice. Tears in the middle of long, hopeless nights. The final vigil at the hospital you thought would never end, but when it ended, you wished it hadn't. The funeral parlor.

*The sad silvery notes of the bugle at Arlington...*

"You okay?" Simon asked. "You're not going to pass out on me, are you?"

"Yes, I'm good," Melissa answered quickly, nodding to prove it. Good and green and desperately homesick for Tucker. He'd come to her at the worst time in her life, a guardian angel with a potty mouth, an AR in his hands, and a heart as big as the sky. A risk taker.

Melissa stifled a sneaky sob that came out of nowhere. All along, she'd let Tucker believe he was the problem, that his willingness to sacrifice for his job was a deal breaker, but it wasn't. Not really. Deep down in her heart, she was so proud of him that it actually hurt to look at him sometimes. He knew who he was and what he stood for every day.

*She* was the problem. The coward. She'd already given her heart and soul to one man. One hero. But could she give the rest of her life to one so bold and as brash as Tucker Chase? Could she take the chance and live in the shadow of death again? She honestly didn't know.

"That ought to do it," Simon said softly, wiping his forehead with the back of his hand. "How's he doing?"

Melissa tugged the stethoscope off her neck and listened to poor Dang's heartbeat. He seemed to have come through surgery fine. "What do you think?" she asked the savvy jungle surgeon at her side. "What's a good heart rate after you cut a man's leg off?"

Simon peeled one of their patient's eyelids open. "Hell, I don't know. He looks good to me, though, and he's still breathing. That's a good sign." He transferred the packaged limb into a secure garbage can before he stripped off his gloves. "Come here. Lose your gloves and wash your hands. Wipe your face. You'll feel better once you get the smell of this place off your body."

She joined him at the plastic washbasin. While he pumped water from the ten-gallon reservoir, she washed her hands and arms thoroughly, then dried them with a long paper towel. Then vice versa—she pumped while he lathered up. Methodically. The man did have big, rugged hands. Calluses. But clean. Tanned. His cuticles were ragged, but his nails were trimmed short. A man's hands. *No wedding ring.*

A wave of heat flashed up her spine at that errant thought. Who cared if Simon Siegel was married? She didn't.

Very conscientiously, she dampened the paper towel and ran it over her neck, but there was no way to truly feel refreshed in this country. She needed a shower and to get out of her clothes and into something clean. Steamy humidity ran down her neck the moment she removed the refreshing towel.

Simon stretched, but the moment he did, his shirt pulled out of his pants and a fine athletic belly revealed the happy trail below his navel, not what she'd expected to notice after such a horrendous day. But there it was, a handsome tease. She averted her gaze and draped the paper towel over her neck if only to keep the sweat from running down her back and her flustered embarrassment in check.

"I could use a drink. How about you?" he asked, a husky drift in his voice.

She shook the invitation off, the intimate sight of his stomach along with it. "Not tonight. It's late, and I'm really tired."

"You did good, Melissa. You deserve a long night's sleep after all this, but I doubt you'll get it. Folks will be up and needing your nursing skill before you know it. Come on. If nothing else, it'll relax you so you can sleep better."

"I shouldn't," she insisted, rubbing the back of her arm over her brow again.

"Nurse Melissa," he scolded, a tease of steel in his tone. "Doctor's orders. One nightcap. Now. Then bed rest."

What harm could it do? She shrugged the tension off her shoulders. "One drink, then I'm history."

"Deal." He lifted the heavy canvas to their temporary surgical center and waved her outside. "Our patient isn't going anywhere. I'll come back and check on him, maybe stay the night. Oreo, are you out here?"

"On your left," came the quick reply from the shadows. Oreo stepped into view, his rifle over his arm. "How'd it go?"

"Just like I thought. The leg was a rotted mess," Simon acknowledged. "Glad it's over with. He'll feel better in a week or so."

"We hope," Melissa added, "but it's a good thing we did this tonight. I don't think Dang would've lasted another day."

"How'd it go with you?" Simon asked Oreo.

"No problems. Jackman's late getting in. Are you kids out of here?"

She blushed at the way he'd connected her to Simon. They weren't kids. They were very serious adults on their way to their own huts after one drink. That was all.

"For now," Simon said. "Keep an eye on Dang, will you? Tell me if Jackman shows. Would you mind burying that leg before it attracts rats? I stuck it in the garbage can outside the tent."

"You bet." Oreo peeked inside the tented clinic. "Man, this place stinks."

Simon clapped a wide-open palm to his back. "Thanks, buddy. Be back in a few."

His hut ended up being the one located away from all the others and closest to the parking lot. Most of the huts were large enough to house between four to six families, but his was small, more of a large shed than a hut. An open window framed each wall, but the door was locked.

Melissa waited, feeling out of place while Simon pulled a set of keys from his back pocket and unlocked his place. This simple drink after a gruesome surgery felt more like a date now that she was there. Wringing her fingers, she vowed she'd keep this short and sweet. Well, not too sweet. Maybe just short and—pleasant.

Simon bowed like a courtly gentleman and beckoned her inside. "Welcome to my humble hut in the middle of no-damned-where."

She hadn't noticed until then that he had a strong chin. A leader's chin, square and firm. There was a definite handsomeness to his looks. She hesitated. This seemed so wrong, her on the porch of another guy's hut, prepared to share a round of drinks while the man she'd meant to consider during these three months was thousands of miles away, and maybe deliberating exactly what she'd asked him to.

Oh, who was she kidding? Tucker wasn't deliberating anything. He probably hadn't even heard a word she'd said. She had no doubt he was involved in some high-speed chase or some other FBI adventure, and she was the last thing on his mind.

"Are you thinking too hard again?" Simon asked, his head tilted and his eyes sparkling against the moonless night. "I can bring your drink to the porch if that will set your mind at ease."

She swallowed hard at the velvet temptation in his voice. "Thank you, that would be nice. I'll sit here and wait."

Simon grinned, waggling those thick brows, but dragged a wooden chair out of his hut and onto the porch that was nothing more than ten or so boards nailed to a two-by-four framework. He dragged another chair out for him. "Take a load off. I don't have ice, but I do have authentic glass glasses."

For some reason, that made her giggle. "Glass glasses, huh?"

He winked and disappeared into the darkness of his hut while Melissa took a seat, thankful she was finally off her feet. God, it had been a long day. This just might be the perfect end to it—a drink to warm her tired soul, then a good night's sleep. For certain tomorrow would pose just as many problems as this day had, but she'd be rested and ready for it. She sighed. So. Tired.

"Here you go," Simon whispered as he brought a bottle of brandy and two small *crystal* glasses outside.

"However do you travel without breaking them?" she asked as he sloshed an ounce or two into one glass and offered it to her, while he poured the same into the other.

"I must confess," he whispered conspiratorially, "they've traveled in an old ammo box wrapped in a small Turkish towel. Don't tell anyone, but I like the idea of drinking good liquor from actual glass. It's more civilized and a good drink just tastes better. I had a set of Irish crystal once, but it broke when I... moved." He rested the bottle on his knee and lifted his drink to her, a thoughtful glimmer in his eye. "A toast to us, the luckiest medical team on the planet."

Melissa clinked her glass to his and offered a genuine smile. "I'm guessing we'll know how lucky we are in the morning, won't we?" She sipped the brown liquid and instantly closed her eyes as the fire in the drink scorched a path down her throat. "Blah. Eww. Yuck. That's what brandy tastes like?" She could barely draw in a breath.

He winked before he downed his glass in one swallow. His eyes didn't even water. "It'll warm you all the way to your toes once you get used to it."

She took another tiny sip, but shook her head at the nasty flavor on her tongue, needing to cough but afraid she'd choke if she started. "It's quite strong, isn't it?" she wheezed.

"That it is," he said quietly as he poured himself another round. "Like you, Melissa. I'm sorry you got caught up in this trouble we're in, but I'm glad, too. I couldn't have operated on Dang without you. You've dug in and made a difference in this pitiful camp since you've been here. You should be proud of yourself. Cheers."

She stayed her glass. She needed to know. "Why me?" *Was it for the ransom? Did they know she was Jed McCormack's daughter-in-law?*

Simon's lips pursed and his shoulders went up. He tossed his head back and emptied his glass before he said, "Luck of the draw I guess. I had intel that promised one of the clinic doctors would go after the supplies. My guys didn't know any different. Tristan said you looked smart, you could've been a doctor."

She took another sip, this one not as fiery as the others. The brandy did tend to go down smoother each time. "I need to go back to the city, Simon. I'm not trained for this. You need a real doctor."

"No, I don't," he said, his eye on the empty glass in his hand, steel in his tone. "I need another drink and so do you."

Melissa waited while he filled their glasses. She didn't need another drink, but at this late hour, she didn't need the confrontation that would ensue if she insisted on her rights as an American citizen. She didn't need to be stuffed back in that box, either.

She opted for a change in subject. The man had a quiet agony about him, a ghost. She recognized the far off stare that crept into his eyes. It was as if he was somewhere else seeing things that were neither present nor real. Tucker had that same look sometimes. So had Brady. "Whatever brought you to Vietnam, Simon Siegel?"

He winked. And that was the last thing she remembered...

# **Chapter Ten**

"Your choice. Which way do you want to go?"

Tucker stared at his fellow agent, his mind caught between two hellish firestorms and two impossible decisions. His eleven-year-old son on one side, the woman he loved on the other.

And there it was, the eternal dilemma of every hard man with an impossible job to do, whether as a SEAL, an FBI agent, a police officer, or a fireman. *Do I stay or do I go? Who do I save? The men who would die for me, or the family sitting safely back home waiting for me, counting on me?*

Which mission was more important—keeping the home fire burning or putting out the flames of war on the eastern front? Fighting side by side with his brothers and sisters at arms or fighting with his wife at home? Rescuing Melissa or rescuing his only child?

For the first time in his life, he honestly couldn't decide.

To lose one would cut as deep as the other. If he traveled ten miles south, he'd have to rely on Stewart to rescue Melissa. Alex could do it, but who knew what she'd suffer by the time Stewart got a team in country? If Tucker went after her, he'd have to sacrifice Deuce to the horrors of child labor for another long day, longer if the authorities caught Tucker in the country. He'd be back in jail. Knowing Nicole, Tucker might never see his son again, and God, the thought gutted him. He loved that boy so damned hard.

A heavy weight pressed in on Tucker's chest. The room spun. He looked westward to Melissa, the woman of his heart. Turning south, he faced Deuce, the child he couldn't live without. It all came down to this impossibly hard decision that only he could make, this pivotal moment when he stood to lose everything no matter who he chose to rescue.

He stilled, his heart pumping fire into his chest, and the most logical choice clear. Let Stewart do what he did best. He was right. His men would find Melissa. He was better equipped for jungle warfare with the creeps who'd abducted her. He'd have more men to get the job done. Besides, she'd made her position quite clear, and as hard as it was to let her go, Tucker knew to his soul that she would always love Brady first. There wasn't enough room in her heart for another man. For him.

He scrubbed a knuckle into his one good eye, tired beyond belief of fighting the world. *I'm just in the way, and I'm running out of time, and—*

Isaiah came unglued. "You stupid frog! Melissa loves you! How can you not know that?"

Tucker had to look twice at the angry guy he'd honestly tagged as nothing more than an intelligent nerd. Isaiah's fists were tight, his feet positioned to fight. Coiled muscles bunched at his shoulders, and damn, the kid had big shoulders. Big hands, too. That fist of his looked like it could do some damage.

Tucker strove for patience. "Look at us, kid. I'm in rough shape, and you're—"

"I'm not a kid!" Isaiah cocked his arm back, his right fist raised and all knuckles on target. "So what if you're in rough shape? Has that ever stopped you before? You're a SEAL, you moron. How many SEALs does it take to screw in a light bulb anyway, because you're sure making it look like an impossible job! So what if you're not on that jet out of Vietnam in a day? Stop having to be the biggest and baddest ass on the planet, Chase. Stop having to be Melissa's one and only. Her first. You missed that boat a long time ago, and God! Stop running on ego! So what if you end up in jail again? I'm here and I'm with you no matter what, so do what's right and let the universe sort everything else out! Go. Get. Your. Woman!"

*Well, now that you put it that way...*

Tucker stuck his chest out, daring Isaiah to do something with that big attitude of his. Maybe another knockdown, dragged-out brawl was exactly what they both needed.

Isaiah's fist came down on the wooden desk below the window. *"You're so stupid, Chase."* The mental message of disgust hit Tucker like a ton of bricks. Isaiah blew out a deliberate sigh through his nostrils just before he vocalized, *"I'm disappointed in you."*

Tucker came up fighting. He stabbed his thumb into his own chest to make sure the world knew. "Deuce is *my* son. *My* son! He's just like his old man—me! He's tough, and he's got what it takes. He wouldn't expect me to rescue him from a little hard work if it meant saving Melissa from kidnappers. He'd want me to rescue her first. Now load up. I'm getting Melissa back!"

"I knew you'd see it my way," Isaiah said calmly, every trace of his temper gone. "I've got a tarp to cover the pickup bed with. Step on it. It's starting to rain."

Tucker had to really look at the man beside him. Who *was this* guy?

They loaded the ammo and supplies in record time and secured the tarp with bungee cords, and damn, Isaiah had the makings of a top-notch agent. He'd thought of everything, even suppressors for those M4s, and those IED kits? Deadly miracles in the making as long as they were handled right. They were on the road within the hour and hustling through Vietnam's version of early-morning traffic.

"Can't you go any faster?" Tucker asked, his impatience rankling in his gut.

"Why? Wasn't one day in jail enough for you?" Isaiah wouldn't let Tucker drive. Made him ride shotgun. Not a good combination. "The last thing we need is a speeding ticket."

"My grandmother drives faster than you."

Isaiah paused for the space of a heartbeat. "Not true. Your grandmothers are both dead. You never even met them."

There went that mind-reading thing again. This kid was annoying.

"Annoying, yes, but you can't see out of both eyes right now, and I don't need to be in a traffic accident or back in jail. We do things my way or not at all."

Tucker chewed his lower lip to keep from telling his smart-assed sidekick to go to hell. He needed Isaiah more than the kid knew, but honestly, it seemed as if he were caught in a time warp with a brat who repeated everything just to irritate the hell out of him. And it was working.

Isaiah chuckled, but said, "I'm picking up Melissa again."

Why did Tucker have the feeling that his partner really meant to say he wasn't a brat? "Where?" he snapped, tired of the mind games. He was suffering from lack of sleep and a bruised ego. That tender spot under his left arm felt like a cracked or broken rib, neither scenario good, but he wasn't about to tell his partner he wasn't a hundred percent. Isaiah probably already knew.

"She's dizzy this morning. I'm not sure why. She's still with those men—at least one of them."

That didn't sound good. "I thought you level tens could get people to make different choices. Can't you influence her to get away from him, or whatever it is you do?"

"Sometimes..." Isaiah drew the word out while he steered around a team of oxen pulling a narrow wooden cart heaped high with green stalks of bamboo. "It all depends on the person. Melissa's thought patterns are quite... complicated."

"What's going on? Is she...?" Dare he say it? *Happy?* That was the last thing Tucker wanted Melissa to be, happy with another man. The notion boiled his blood.

Isaiah shook his head. "I wouldn't say happy, but she's... relaxed."

That didn't help either. "So you can't read Eden's mind, and now you can't get into Melissa's head, either?"

"Right. Eden's a level ten, same as me, but she's different. We can actually converse psychically, but only when she lets me in. Either Melissa is choosing not to let me in or she's not psychic at all."

"She's not psychic," Tucker growled. "She's normal. Like me."

"Ah, but you can pick up mental messages I push to you."

Tucker clenched his fist and looked out the side window. *Why me?*

"Because you're psychic, Tucker." Isaiah was smart enough to change the subject. "How's your eye? Feeling any better?"

Tucker nodded. He'd been worried whether that punch he'd taken had torn the lens loose, or worse, if it had permanently damaged his eye, if he'd be blind when the swelling went down.

"That's why I wanted you to see a doctor, Tucker. Eyesight's not negotiable. I'm not worried about the cochlear implant. Is it working?"

"No. It works off cell phone towers," he admitted begrudgingly. "It's useless right now. I'd have to request authorization for it to work over here."

"And I work off mind power. Do me a favor. See if you can pick up what I'm sending you."

Bourbon Street during Mardi Gras showed up loud and clear with all it's delightful aromas and sounds. The spicy drift of jambalaya piled high with crayfish, chunks of andouille sausage, and peeled shrimp. Sweat and swamp. The rowdy tones of sax and the *plinkety-plink* of honky-tonk piano mingled with trumpet, blues, and soul. "New Orleans," Tucker muttered. "Drive faster." *And stop playing games.*

Isaiah stepped on the gas. "I'm not playing games. I'm evaluating our ability to communicate with each other if we get separated. Your turn."

Tucker projected an image all right.

"Very funny, Tucker. The finger. Message received loud and clear. You're an ass. Got it." There it was again, a controlled sigh of annoyed disgust, exactly what Tucker had been going for.

They drove in silence while the pavement gave way to dirt and the dirt gave way to ruts and mud holes. The overnight drizzle stopped. Monsoon season would soon bring torrential rainfall, and Tucker wanted to be gone by then.

Suddenly, Isaiah steered off the road and into the nearby trees. "Hang on. We've got trouble."

Tucker stretched his neck to see, but nothing revealed itself. "What are you talking about?"

Isaiah kept going until he had enough room to turn the truck around to face the road. The man and boy with the oxen ambled by. "I hope they don't see us," Isaiah murmured.

"Who?" Tucker leaned forward, squinting and growing more impatient by the minute. "What am I looking for?'

"Wait for it..."

He waited. And waited. More cars. More bicycles. A few mopeds and scooters. The minutes ticked by, but at last, the ground vibrated. The air filled with the steady rumble of heavy equipment. Three camouflaged five-tons led the way. Truck after truck of soldiers in olive drab uniforms. Maybe a battalion. The Vietnamese Army was on the move.

Isaiah provided the news update. "One battalion, to be exact. They're going west like us. There's been a border skirmish with the Cambodian rebels."

Tucker craned his neck to see eastward past Isaiah. The line of troops and military equipment stretched as far as he could see, pushing civilian vehicles to the side of the road. There was no choice. "We need to get out of here. Leave the truck. Take what you can carry. Make most of it lethal. How far before we get to her?"

"We've got miles of jungle between us and Mrs. McCormack," Isaiah whispered, his eyes glued to the impressive display of military power, "but these guys will stick to the road, won't they?"

"Only until they reach their destination." Tucker rolled out of the truck, keeping low to avoid notice. "Scan one of the officers. See if you can get a reading on their bivouac through those brain buckets. Damn, that's got to be hot."

Isaiah scowled. "Brain buckets?"

Tucker tapped his head. "Helmets, genius. See if you can read one of those guys' minds through his helmet."

"Of course I can," Isaiah murmured. "This isn't *X-Men*. You ever heard of a city called Hà Tiên?"

"Yeah, it's on the south end of the Mekong Delta. Melissa's not being held there, is she?"

"No, but that's where these guys are headed." Isaiah slung his backpack over one shoulder while he carefully stripped the tarp from the pickup bed.

"She's directly west of our location. We'll cross the river at Tân Châu and swing north a couple miles to catch up with her."

Tucker armed himself with two M4s and as much ammo as he could pack. "You wouldn't happen to have a—"

Isaiah tossed one holstered SIG P226 Tacops, then another. "Sure thing. Extra magazines are to your right in the corner."

"How about a—"

"The knives are in that canvas bag by the ammo boxes. Gosh, how many weapons do you need?"

Tucker strapped one knife sheath to his thigh and another to his lower leg. One SIG went to his hip, the other under his arm. Carefully, he stacked all ten IED kits into a loose gear bag and rested it to the ground at his foot. He wanted more weapons. Tactical vests would've been nice. Bluetooth earpieces, too.

"No, I didn't think of tactical vests," Isaiah grumbled, "so don't go getting your ass shot. I've got water purification tabs, a couple lighters, plastic rain ponchos, and a few MREs."

"Tactical vests don't cover your ass, genius." This mind-reading stuff was starting to feel natural. Tucker only had to think of what he needed, and Isaiah made it come true.

"You wish," the kid huffed, a pistol on his hip and an M4 hanging off his shoulder, barrel down. "I'm not your damned fairy godmother."

*And he's starting to swear like a man, too.*

"You want to hear cursing?" Isaiah asked, a no-kidding edge in his voice. "Just keep it up."

Tucker put his index finger to his lips, a smirk tugging at the corner of his smart mouth. "Shhh. Don't ask, don't tell, remember?"

He got a stern eye roll for that. Isaiah jerked his head toward the jungle. "Lead on, funny guy."

Tucker grabbed a few more supplies until his pack was full and heavy. Clean socks would've been nice, but he intended this foray into west Vietnam to be quick, like any other SEAL infil/exfil. All he wanted was Melissa. He stashed as many MREs as he could in the small recesses of his IED pack until it could safely hold no more. Then a couple of aerosol cans of Deet. A smaller pistol fit in his belt. A bottle of water. The pack was filled to bursting.

"How long do you plan on staying in Vietnam, Tucker? Forever? Sheesh, let's move before we get caught."

Ah, the naïveté of the FNG. Any spec ops guy in his right mind knew the power behind packing the right supplies for a remote op. A guy could only rely on what he'd brought with him, and Tucker meant to be prepared. He tossed one bag to his shoulders and hefted the other. "Move out, Grandma."

He stayed close to Isaiah, trusting the guy's sense of direction as they honed in on Melissa. Tân Châu had to be close to two hundred kilometers southwest from Hồ Chí Minh City, around one hundred and twenty miles. He and Isaiah had already been traveling for hours. Highways were different in Vietnam, but they'd made good time until the army took over the road. Moving forward would prove more difficult now, but so what? Tucker had humped plenty before, and he'd done it better and faster and over steeper terrain. Ever heard of the Hindu Kush? Now those were mountains. He figured a good stiff pace would get them past Tân Châu by dark. Maybe farther. If all went well, Melissa might very well be back in his arms tonight. No later than morning.

"The Hindu Kush range is between Pakistan and Afghanistan, and you're limping," Isaiah murmured.

"No, I'm not," Tucker replied evenly as he picked up the pace and passed Isaiah, ignoring the burn under his ribs. "I'm marching, so get your ass in gear. Double-time it, soldier. Now!"

# Chapter Eleven

"Tucker," Melissa murmured sleepily, her back stiff and sore, her mind sluggish and dull. Stretching from side to side, her palm landed in the middle of a bare chest. Her nose twitched. She must have fallen to sleep on the couch, his body for a pillow. His chest hair tickled her nose, but he smelled different this morning. Less of mandarin and amber. More of sweat. But always gunpowder. But that strong heartbeat under her ear? That heavily muscled chest of her pillow? So familiar. His big hand on her—butt?

Not so familiar and not good. Not good at all.

*Here we go again.* He knew better than to take liberties with her while she slept. Touching her backside was off limits. Blinking awake, she shoved off—

*Simon?* Her heart stuttered up her throat. *Oh my. What have I done?*

Every muscle in her body cringed. She eased upright to find herself in his arms and on top of his bed. With him. She was still dressed, but a thin sheet draped them both—like something might have happened. The door was shut. They were alone. How had she gotten from the front porch to—here? They'd had one drink together. That was all. Just one.

*Make that two...*

Stealthily, she lifted to her feet, thankful she was still completely dressed. Well, except for her shoes. That was a good sign, wasn't it? It had to mean they hadn't done anything too crazy last night, didn't it? Her head buzzed—not a good sign. She couldn't remember what she'd done or what she'd said. *Oh my, indeed.*

"Don't leave yet," Simon muttered, his morning voice exceptionally deep and husky. He still had his eyes closed. "I'll fix coffee. 'Sides, I've got something I wanted you to see."

*I'll just bet you do.* "N-n-no, I... I have to go. Now."

"Melissa..." he taunted. "Come back to bed. We worked all night. We deserve to sleep in. Besides, it's too early."

*Or too late.* "No, no, no," she whispered, still not believing she'd sunk so low as to sleep with a man she didn't know. *Oh, my God, who does that? Hollywood divas and ladies of the night, maybe. Not me.*

"You dozed off. My bed's more comfortable than yours. I couldn't just leave you on the porch for the mosquitoes, could I? Hell, the rats around here would've carried you off."

"Did we...? Umm, did I...?" *Drat and double drat. Did I? Did you?*

Simon blew out a deep sigh before he opened both eyes and rolled to his side. "No, ma'am. You got a little silly before you dozed off, that's all. At least let me get dressed before you take off, will you?"

"Take what off?" She cringed, her foot in her mouth. *I didn't really just say that, did I? But if he needs to get dressed...* She spread one hand over her eyes.

"Will you relax?" he drawled mischievously.

She spared him a quick look through her fingers. Simon had one of those lazy, good-old-boy smiles, the heart-melting, panty-dropping kind. Darn, he looked like Tucker when he smiled like that. She could get herself into a world of trouble if she hung around this guy very long.

He flipped the sheet back to reveal two tanned, hairy legs and—*thank God*—camouflaged shorts. She had noticed he'd slept with the sheet tucked between them as well, not skin to skin. Well, not much skin to skin. His chest was bare, and it was a handsome, manly thing. Well-muscled. Athletic. Just the right smattering of dark hair over a deep tan, nicked by a few scars. Dusky man-sized nipples she shouldn't have noticed. Swoon-worthy, actually.

She rolled her eyes at her utterly foolish feminine responses to him and grabbed the wooden door latch for support. Sliding her toes into her canvas sneakers, she fingered the heels up nice and tight, and offered a quick, "I have to go. Really. Bye."

Simon grumbled, but she left him standing there.

"Morning," Oreo commented from his seated position at the end of the porch, his eyes bright and extra cheery. "Nice day for a walk, isn't it?" he asked as he wiped a rag over the long barrel of his rifle.

"Umm, yes," she said, brushing her tousled hair out of her eyes. "It is... early."

"Sleep well?"

She couldn't even begin to answer that leading question, her throat tight and dry. What did he mean by that? Sleep or—*oh, my gosh! Sleep with him?*

Melissa couldn't remember enough of last evening after the surgery to know anything for certain. She pivoted and nearly fell off the porch. Righting herself, she dusted her hands to her thighs and offered a quick, embarrassed, "I've got to run. Bye."

And off she went, straight to *her* mat in *her* hut before Oreo could ask anything else.

Wouldn't you know, sweet little Mimi was already snuggled there with her mama, Tam, both sound asleep? Well, alrighty then. Melissa tiptoed into the hut and leaned against the inside wall, her arms over her chest and her mind in disarray. How could she have done something like that? To Tucker? This was so out of character for her. Until this thing between her and Tucker was resolved, she meant to stay loyal and true to him. Faithful. If they broke up, he'd have to do the breaking up. Not her. He might have to get his priorities right, and she'd have to face her demons, but he was her man, and she was his woman and...

*What have I done?*

Another shiver skated up her spine. Darned if Oreo hadn't followed her. He peeked into the hut, cocked his head to the left and caught her hiding in the shadows. "Boss wants to see you."

She shook her head, her disheveled hair the perfect curtain to hide behind. "I need to use the bathroom first. I need a shower. I'll talk to Simon later." *A lot later.*

"I think that's why he wants to talk to you. He had us guys rig a special, umm, accommodation just for you. Come see. It's kind of cool. You'll like it."

She rolled her eyes to the thatched ceiling overhead where a glimmer of sunlight had broken through, not sure she could face Simon, not after last night when they didn't do anything. *Oh, drat.* She hoped not, but she didn't know for sure, and that not knowing made her nervous. Alcohol and her didn't mix well. After one drink of wine, she tended to think she was the sexiest woman on the planet, and there was a slim possibility that she'd said the most outrageous things. Until now, either Brady or Tucker had been there to keep her safe from her silly antics. Had she bragged how sexy she was with Simon? Had she made a fool of herself? Worse, had he taken her at her word?

She'd gotten a little carried away with Tucker more than once after a glass of champagne, but he'd never crossed that line. He might've stayed the night, but not in her bed. He might not have liked it, but he respected her. He loved her. It would sure be nice to hear it from his lips once in a while, but she knew he did. It showed, especially after that second glass of—

"You coming?" Oreo whispered.

*Ergh. Why'd he have to phrase it that way?* "I might as well. I can't very well use my mat. I'm on my way."

Oreo held out his hand to her at the doorway. She accepted his fingers and his gallantry and climbed down the three steps. "It's over here," he said, nodding back toward Simon's hut. Why not? If Simon meant the location of this special accommodation to keep her safe, why wouldn't it be near his hut? But if he intended something else...

A breathless shiver raced up her spine. She'd gotten too close too fast with a man she barely knew. No. More. Drinking.

"Ah, there you are." Simon's face lit up when he saw her from his open door. He nodded to the rear of his hut where another smaller hut had been constructed, a black-and-gray-striped curtain draped over the open wooden door. "Check this out."

She couldn't have been more surprised. Filtered sunlight from the thatched roof brightened the place up quite nicely. An actual porcelain toilet stood there on a framed-in bed of gravel, and next to it, a stack of white toilet paper rolls. A small table rested beneath an oval mirror nailed into the wall at her immediate right, with an assortment of combs, brushes, and toiletries tastefully arranged. Straight ahead stood an improvised shower with a shower curtain and towels, bottled bath gel and all.

"Oh, my," she breathed, not believing the reach of these men or their thoughtfulness. "You did this for me?"

"Yes, ma'am." Oreo beamed even as he flashed another one of those secret guy looks at Simon. "Me and some of the boys been working on it since you showed up. While you and the boss were engrossed in your surgery last night, we finished off the sewer line. It runs to a septic tank downhill a ways. Aaron sneaked into town and bought you a bunch of soaps and lotions. Some more Deet. We didn't put in any windows 'cause we figured you'd want your privacy, but once you're inside, there's a door you can lock. Aaron installed a hook behind the door for your clothes or your holster, whichever you're wearing. Hope you like it."

"I'll haul one of my chairs in later," Simon added, "in case you want to sit down while you brush your hair or paint your toes."

She could've laughed at the outrageous notion of painting her toes in the jungle, but swallowed hard instead. So this was what those guy looks had been about. They'd been planning a surprise. The genuine thoughtfulness behind this simple modern convenience took her breath. Until then, she'd gone into the jungle like everyone else to do her business. Her backside still bore the most outrageous mosquito bites on it, but she'd been more worried she might run into a snake each time. The last thing she needed was Simon taking a slice out of her and sucking pit viper venom out of her butt cheek. Wouldn't that be the sight?

"And the shower works." Simon's eyes twinkled like raindrops hitting some hidden jungle pool. "I broke it in last night after you fell asleep." The man had bedroom eyes. Deep, dark and the sexiest shade of green. Even though he'd just shot Oreo another guy look.

She took a step back, needing distance between them. "Yeah, about that..." Melissa ran a hand through her thick tangles and shoved them out of her eyes and off her face. "Did I honestly just fall asleep?"

Simon winked, the brat. He waggled those handsome brows like he'd done with Mimi. "Mostly. You did kind of brag how some guy you know is better than me before you passed out. Who the hell is Tucker Chase anyway?"

"I didn't?" she gasped. "Did I?" *Please tell me I didn't do that*, but then she thought twice. Naming Tucker was the perfect thing to have done.

"Your exact words were: '*worlds' better. Like out-of-this-universe better. Like he's stronger and cuter and braver.* Tucker's a lucky man," Simon said quietly, his brow lifted. "He must mean a lot to you."

Melissa swallowed hard at that absolute truth. What could she say? She lied just the tiniest white lie, but it felt smoother than that brandy had felt sliding over her tongue last night. "Tucker Chase is my fiancé." He was. Almost. He just needed to ask. "Thank you, Simon, and you too, Oreo. This is very thoughtful. I'm speechless."

Simon growled and rolled his eyes. "You sure weren't last night."

"Yeah, the boss said you drink like a sailor. I've got some whiskey in my hooch," Oreo teased, "if you wanna come over later."

"Oh, stop," she joked back. "I had one or two little drinks and I'll never do that again." *Ever!*

"Come on now, don't never say never." Oreo's black brows lifted. "Never has a way of coming around full circle. First thing you know, that never comes true, and there you are, doing exactly what you said you'd never do and eating crow while you do it. My place is always open. You might enjoy it."

His crass insistence bugged Melissa. So did Simon's lack of running interference. What exactly did they take her for?

Aaron ducked his head into the doorway. "You like it, ma'am?" he asked, his chocolate-colored skin accentuating the whites of his eyes. Of all the men, he was the youngest.

"You bought me all those toiletries?" she asked.

The cutest dimple showed up on his right cheek, and like a shy little boy, he toed the wooden flooring.

"Just got you a few things my mama would like. Hope they meet with your approval."

"Your mother must be proud of you. Thanks, Aaron."

"Yes, ma'am, she's a died-in-the-wool patriot, just like you."

Melissa cocked her head at him. *What an odd thing to say.* The tiny hairs on the back of her neck lifted in warning. She looked intently at Aaron, trying to understand why she felt ill at ease.

When Simon led the way outside where a group of excited children and adults had gathered, she waved them to join in. "Come see the house that Simon built."

"Great," he muttered. "Now everyone's going to want one." He and Oreo moved off to the side, their backs to Melissa's shower, their heads tilted together, obviously not wanting to be overheard.

The noisy static and squeal from someone's walkie-talkie broke the spell. The world stopped turning and, all at once, Melissa was standing in the chattering crowd, yet outside of it at the same time. Her heart thumped at the contradiction she found herself caught up in. She didn't belong there. *What have I done?*

Suddenly the magnanimous gesture of a fancy outhouse in the jungle seemed—contrived. Diversionary.

She felt used and very stupid.

Simon, Oreo, Aaron—all of these guys acted as if they were trying to accommodate her, but they weren't, not really. They'd simply honed in on her genuine empathy for the injured people and the children, and they'd capitalized on what they saw as weakness. Like a simpering idiot on a noble mission to save the world, she'd let them. She'd believed and trusted them—like she had with Lucien Kane in that twisted Palma Christi cult in Northern California.

Oh God. A shiver roared up her spine. She'd done it again. She'd missed the forest for the trees. Melissa rubbed her palms over her biceps, embarrassed at her naïveté. At her pride. This camp was a sham, the shower, the clinic, Simon's insistence that he needed her. Everything.

He didn't intend to let her leave.

That come-on from Oreo still made her skin crawl. Tucker never would've just stood there like Simon had without stepping in to Melissa's defense and doing it loudly. He might have made a spectacle of himself while he did it, but he would've knocked Oreo on his ass for the disgusting innuendo that she'd stoop so low as to warm his bed.

*Never say never, my ass.* These guys didn't respect her. Tucker did. He might not agree with her, but not once had he failed to defend her virtue and her right to be treated like a lady. Yet Simon hadn't said one word to set Oreo straight. He'd just stood there and watched.

*Like a spider with a fly...*

She swallowed hard at the very real sensation of being caught in a web. Melissa scanned the shower through different eyes. This *gift* was just another lure to keep her there, like Simon's insisting that he needed her when he knew she wasn't a trained nurse, not even close. Like that cozy drink last night after a surgery she had no business assisting with. Like this—*gift*.

These guys were—*liars*. All of them. The wounded men. Maybe the women.

Simon glanced sideways at her, then did a double take, honing in on her again. Studying her.

Melissa lowered her lashes, not wanting to look into his lying eyes. Not wanting him to see that she knew the truth.

# Chapter Twelve

Isaiah liked to hum. All the time. It was really annoying.

"Are we there yet?" Tucker whined just to piss him off.

"I'm not sure if it's the same for all psychics, but humming helps me keep my link with Melissa," Isaiah said instead of answering what they both knew was a childish question.

Tucker lifted his brows, wishing he'd known that earlier. "Oh yeah? What's she doing?"

"She's worried about some guy's leg, only he doesn't have a leg. Confusing. She seems—conflicted. I can't get a good read on her."

Conflicted? That wasn't like Melissa.

The jungle had given way to some kind of an animal trail, so for the time being, they zigzagged under the cover of tall brush and low trees with sparse branches. Birds fluttered overhead and in the greenery at their sides, but Tucker kept his one good eye on the alert for snakes, spiders, tigers, and other things that could hurt a guy. He'd heard some sort of high-pitched feline yowl a few miles back, but never saw the thing, probably because the rats in this country were bigger than the cats. One had probably chased it off.

"Seriously, are we getting close to her?"

"Yes. The river's up ahead. We'll turn north by northwest there. It'll be swampy in some spots, but it shouldn't take much longer."

"Stay undercover to this side of the river," Tucker warned. "We don't want anyone spotting us. Two Americans will stick out this deep in country." The closer they drew to Melissa's location, the more his hackles lifted. His SEAL instincts flashed into hypervigilance.

"Will do," Isaiah agreed, seemingly oblivious to the unseen threats around them.

Tucker took small comfort in Isaiah's lack of an internal alarm system. Most guys didn't come with one until they'd been in a firefight.

"Watch out for saltwater crocs," Tucker cautioned, stepping to Isaiah's right. "If you step on one, you might as well kiss your ass goodbye."

An obedient murmur drifted to Tucker, a good sign. The kid might consider himself trained, but Tucker was the one who'd actually served. He knew how fast things could go bad. Like now.

The ground turned to marsh and bog near the river. They had to backtrack to keep from sinking. It was then they came across cloven-toed tracks in the soft soil, possibly pig or deer. Lots of them. Nothing human, though. Those animals might just explain the heightened sense of unease and the twist in Tucker's gut. Maybe not...

"Ever hunt wild pig?" he asked quietly, his body on high alert for anything to indicate they had company. The snap of a twig. A rush of frightened birds thrown skyward. The sudden silence to the steady hum of insect life. Anything out of the ordinary in a habitat as teeming with life as the Mekong Delta.

"I've never shot a gun except for target practice," Isaiah admitted quietly, "and before you go all Rambo on me, no, I'm not a bleeding heart liberal. I believe in the right to bear arms, and I support the Second Amendment. I just don't think everyone needs to carry a concealed weapon. I believe in law and order. That's what makes our country work as well as it does."

Tucker grunted. Folks dumb enough to rely on all that law and order sometimes found it showed up too late to the party.

The jungle stilled. His heart rate kicked up a notch. He stepped closer to Isaiah, brushing the younger man's right elbow, hell-bent on keeping him safe. Something—*or someone*—was hunting them.

*"You're right,"* Isaiah's voice hissed inside his mind. *"We are being followed. One man in close*

*proximity, maybe fifty yards to your right. Heavily armed like you, and capable of killing. He's not alone. Maybe a dozen more with him. See anyone?"*

"Not yet. Take a sharp left, but keep your head down," Tucker ordered, his voice low and muted. "Let's circle back behind these jokers."

"Copy that." Crouched low, the two men moved stealthily through the tall grass until they came back to the mud, their bags, too. Only wild pig tracks showed, and Tucker didn't want to leave more. He offloaded his extra gear and hand-signaled Isaiah to sit, keep still, and stay. Making a circle with his index finger, he indicated his intention to get in behind their adversaries before he moved out and left his good buddy behind.

*"I wish you would communicate with your mind,"* Isaiah whispered mentally. *"I know you can do it. It'd be a whole lot easier than sign language. Quieter, too."*

*"Shut the fuck up,"* Tucker shot back at him, his M4 in his right grip. *"How's that for communicating?"*

*"See? I knew you could do it."*

Tucker dropped the psychobabble nonsense. Stealthy footsteps from up ahead took him to his belly, his rifle in his strong hand, his right hand. The predator within him sprang to life and flexed its sixth sense, energized despite the brutal shakedown of the day before and the long hours without sleep. He transformed into that big cat in the jungle, laying low and stalking the hunters stalking him, without making a sound while he did it. He let the beast within take over and take charge. Tucker became shadow and death, lurking, waiting for the right moment to kill his prey.

Adrenaline flooded his systems, his five senses hyper-tuned, transforming him into a human radar dish. This was who he was—a man who didn't take life if he could help it, but one who wouldn't back down from the dirty job, either. This was what he was created for—standing up for what mattered in a world gone bat-shit crazy. He'd fought and killed for his brothers- and sisters-at-arms in the service. Today he'd fight for his fellow agent, and, if God was willing, Melissa.

His sense of smell filtered the sweaty scent of man from the rich layers of the natural environment around him. His brain sorted the sweet stench of decay from human body odor. Cigarette smoke wafted on the air. One of these guys was an idiot to be smoking while hunting.

*"He just put his cigarette out,"* Isaiah reported, *"but you're right. He is an idiot. Cigarettes can kill."*

*"And I'm out here to stop guys like him from getting lung cancer, you moron."*

*"Stop name-calling, Agent Chase, and listen up. They haven't found our tracks yet. If you circle back to my position, we can get away without being seen or caught."*

Isaiah had it wrong. Tucker wasn't there to get away. Only to clear the way.

Elbowing forward on his belly with his M4 clear of the dirt, his hearing sharpened, straining for words among the quiet grunts and indiscriminate male grumbles coming to him through the brush and grass. Clothing brushed against leaves and branches. Voices. Some short and sharp in Cambodian. One whispered command with a southern drawl to, "Stop."

Interesting. *"What's an American doing here?"*

*"His name's Ralph Jackman. Ex-SEAL. Not like you, though. This guy's a straight-up killer. I can read him loud and clear. He's full of ugly sludge, Tucker. He means to torture us when he finds us. He wants to hear us scream. He's not thinking if—only when. Come on, let's get out of here while we can."*

The kid just didn't get it. Tucker blocked Isaiah's nervous energy. With him at his back and Jackman and his team ahead, the mission was clear. Tucker meant to end Jackman and his buddies. He lifted cautiously to his knees, his scope sweeping the enemy's flank. They'd fanned out, their backs to him, three to four feet apart. All were hunting.

Jackman wasn't hard to spot. He had to be the bearded guy walking point, the one in the center with the short-stock AR snugged under his chin and the foot-long knife on his hip. The one cammied-up with face paint and a dark green boonie hat low on his shaved head. The guy still wearing his trident. Damn him to hell for that.

Tucker despised traitors, but especially SEALs who turned on their country after swearing fealty to her and her alone. SEALs were supposed to stand tall and proud for all that was good in the world. They swore loyalty to country, team and teammate. They served with honor and integrity no matter where they were sent, and they earned their trident every son-of-a-bitchin' day. Not this guy.

*"You're right. Jackman's a traitor, but so are the three men to his right. They're Americans who served with him and they're nearly as bad as he is."*

*Good to know.* "They're all SEALs?" Tucker shot back at Isaiah, his inner sniper ready to take on his first targets, but damned disgusted. SEALs were the fighting elite. America's bravest and best. What happened to these guys?

*"One's Army."*

Small difference. Same brand of bastard.

Tucker brought his knee forward to balance his weight for maximum stability before he took a calming breath, and let loose a rapid-fire barrage. Jackman fell first, his arms spread wide, and his three buddies with him. When the remaining men returned fire through the long grass, Tucker dropped to his elbows for cover and swept the field to Jackman's left.

*"How many?"* he barked mentally at Isaiah since he no longer had a visual.

*"Eight dead, one mortally injured, four on the run headed west."*

*Shit.* Tucker lifted out of the grass and took careful aim at the guys on the run who'd thought they could hunt him and get away with it. He dropped two, but couldn't nail the last two cowards. Turned out he didn't have to. A weapon sounded to his right, startling him. He swung his rifle on—*Isaiah?*

Damned if the kid wasn't standing tall, an AR tight to his shoulder and his eye to his scope. Tucker watched the last two men drop just as they would've made it into the trees. He ambled back to his junior partner and gave his shoulder a solid knuckle bump. "You'll make a decent soldier yet."

"No, I won't," Isaiah said quietly. "I had to do that, but..." He swallowed hard, gulped, then dropped to his hands and knees and threw up.

Tucker let him have his moment of weakness. He'd tossed his cookies after his first kill, too, but right was right. Isaiah would figure it out. "Stay here. I'm going to chat with our survivor."

Isaiah didn't answer. He was busy... adapting.

Tucker kept his rifle ready as he advanced through the battlefield to the wounded man. Tucker kicked the guy's rifle out of his hands. He wouldn't last long, shot up like he was. "Who do you work for?"

The guy's face was a study in pain, pale and sweat dripping. Damn, he was just a kid. He had thin, stringy black hair in his face and a sad excuse of a beard sprouting up on his jaw, but damned if he didn't sneer. "Why would I tell you? Look at you. You beat to shit. I not tellin' you nothin'."

Tucker crouched beside the kid's twitching legs. "You should see the other guy," he murmured confidentially. "Listen kid, I've got a medic with me. I can help. Maybe get you something for that pain. Maybe get you back to your mother."

*"I'm not a medic, and I'm not helping him,"* Isaiah said weakly. *"He would've killed us, Tucker."*

*"Now you understand the law of the jungle,"* Tucker sent back to his good buddy, but to the dying kid at his feet, he said, "I can help if you tell me who you work for. How many more like you are out there? How many more will I have to kill?"

The poor kid spat a mouthful of blood, breathing hard and wheezing, not going to last long. "Go to hell."

Tucker shifted his gaze over the brush toward the Mekong, his voice deliberate, low, and thoughtful. "If you've been following me very long, then you know wild pigs thrive in this undercover. My guys and I passed enough tracks to worry us. I'm sure you saw them, too. You had to. They were everywhere." He paused to let the terror of his warning sink in. "The thing is, wild pigs are smart. They've got a helluva sense of smell, tusks as long as your arm, and ten to one, they've already picked up the scent of your blood. They're hungry and they're coming. They won't be choosy about who they chew on first when they get here. They're carnivores. They won't care if you're alive or dead. I hear they go for the belly first. How long do you think you'll last in a hungry, rutting herd?"

The boy's eyes widened, but he must've figured he needed to prove his manhood or something. "Eat shit and die," he muttered thickly, more blood staining his lips. "I no snitch."

"No, but you are a dead man if you stay here." The kid was already dying, and he had to know it, but Tucker hated to leave him behind. Kids were gullible and susceptible. They believed war stories and braggarts. He lifted to his feet and offered the boy one last chance. "Come with me. I might not be able to save you, but I can promise you death without pain."

"Go... to... hell..." The kid's last wheezing answer.

Tucker nodded once and stopped caring. *You can't fix stupid.* Every man was entitled to determine his own death. "Have it your way."

He turned his back on the dying boy and walked back to Isaiah, now sitting up, but pale and shaky in the tall grass. Isaiah swiped the back of his fist over his lips. "You're not going to leave him, are you?"

Tucker shrugged as he offered Isaiah a hand up. "He made his choice. How much farther?"

Isaiah gulped, but stood on his own, not wavering as he collected his gear. "Maybe a couple more miles."

Tucker glared back at Jackman's body. Two miles was nothing, and every last one of those guys had a two-way radio pinned to their collars. Nobody was answering the steady, "Jackman, are you there? Come in. Jackman?" Someone was bound to be on scene within minutes.

A SEAL could turn anything into an advantage, even this bloody battlefield, but Tucker would have to work fast. "You feel like playing with explosives?"

# **Chapter Thirteen**

Immersion. The act of being completely submerged in liquid, *completely* being the key word. In one instance, it happened when a person chose to be baptized. They went down under the water of repentance and willingly took on a higher set of values. From that day forth, they believed differently. They acted differently. They surrendered themselves to a higher power.

*Supposedly...*

Melissa rinsed her hair and let the trickle of clean water work its wonder of cleanliness. All of her worries should've washed down the drain, but they didn't.

Immersion also meant being submerged in another culture. Having to rely on the humanity of others while you caught your balance and learned their language and their ways in order to survive. In the process, you sorted through subtle hints and inflections for what was true and what was not. What you could trust. What you couldn't. You adapted because you had no choice. You relinquished your old world and you accepted the new one in order to survive.

*Supposedly...*

She stepped out of the shower and dried herself. Big surprise—Aaron hadn't exactly told the truth. None of the items he'd declared he'd gotten from his mother were new. Not even the towel. Not that it mattered, but everywhere Melisa looked she saw herself now immersed in Simon's world. Military-style vehicles. Military-style men. Military-style leadership. He barked orders. Everyone else obeyed. Even the children. Even her. He was the higher power in this ragtag outfit, and he cut an impressive figure as he made rounds with each of his wounded warriors. He cared.

*Supposedly...*

She ran the comb through her hair and wove a simple braid. But Stockholm Syndrome, where a person held against her will was gradually drawn into the culture and belief system of her abductors, also fell under the gentle guise of immersion, only it was done through force. Through the very ones who'd slapped her down and taken her choice. Who'd twisted her love of humanity to serve their own needs. Who'd forcibly changed her life and her future while they'd made themselves look like something they weren't.

She'd nearly succumbed to the desperate charm of this wretched place, the very real need of the women and children. And Simon? He'd read her like a book, like the simpering female she'd very nearly become. He'd banked on her sympathy for others to draw her in, and she'd stepped right up to his web and threw herself in with a snappy, 'May I please have another serving of bullshit, sir?'

Like a fool, she'd let her empathy rule her common sense. She'd taken everything at face value. Not anymore.

She dressed in her old clothes, as disgusting as they were, slid into her shoes, and ventured back to her hut. Shielding her eyes from the sun rising through the trees in the east, she watched Simon do what he did best—make rounds through the camp and chat with his men and their families. Schmooze like a politician.

His affection for them seemed authentic, but so did the quick glances she merited from the women and men he visited. One by one, they'd all looked her way and nodded, then jerked their attention back on him and whatever lie he was telling them. He never failed to shoot one of his charming smiles in her direction, but that was all it really was, wasn't it? Charm covering up the real reason he was there. Why *she* was there.

He'd been kind, yes. His men, too. But what was he really telling these people? She had no way to know, her immersion not complete.

Melissa waved, testing her theory and smiling like the proverbial queen of the welcome wagon. Tam dropped her gaze, not a hint of friendliness in sight. Melissa lowered her hand, not certain of the emotion shifting over Tam's pretty features.

As usual, Oreo stood too close by. "Hey, Miss Melissa. What's up? You need something?"

"What's Simon telling everyone?" she asked outright.

Her shadow grunted. "Ah, you know how he is. He likes people. He's probably telling them to stay out of your fancy shower." His tone carried a hint of teasing sarcasm.

*And I'm done playing your games.* "Have you seen Tristan?" Melissa smoothed the damp tendrils of her long hair off her face. Braid or not, for the first time in her life, she considered cutting her hair.

Oreo's brow spiked. "I haven't seen him today. What do you need him for?"

"I don't. Not really. I was just wondering. I haven't seen him since I got here. Is he out on patrol or something?" There was that immersion thing. It was happening. *Since I got here? Really?* She'd made her arrival sound as if she'd planned to be kidnapped and taken against her will. As if she was perfectly okay with being held prisoner and doing the work she'd foolishly volunteered for. It was no wonder Simon had manipulated her. She'd made it easy.

Her bodyguard went back to polishing his rifle, something he was never without. "Doubt it. His mother..." Oreo let his words trail off as he suddenly scrubbed at his weapon.

That was another thing. "Where is Tristan's mother? Why haven't I seen her yet?"

He shrugged, not making eye contact and still scrubbing that gun as if it wasn't already polished and gleaming.

The one thing a good Marine's wife learned from her husband was the embodiment and the spirit of the Corps. Brady might not have told her everything, but top-secret intel aside, she lived with him, and she'd absorbed some of the essence of the warrior he'd become. In one sense, she'd become that warrior with him, a part of his soul. Like his sixth sense. His gut feeling. His hypervigilance. It was immersion at its finest, and whether he knew it or not, Tucker had only enhanced her second skillset with his very rigid warrior ways. Melissa might not be able to shoot people, but she was decent at reading between the lines. At seeing the nuances and little details. The lies and deceit.

When she wasn't distracted by the misery of others.

"Let's visit Tristan. I'd like to meet his mother." She beamed innocently at Oreo.

He would've caught her act if he'd looked up. "She ain't here."

"How do you know? Come on. At least we can chat with everyone like Simon's doing. We'll start at the other end of the village and meet him in the middle. Maybe we'll run into Tristan."

Oreo refused, a first. "No, ma'am. Your job is to treat the sick and wounded. My job is to make sure nothing happens to you. You ain't here to chat. That's Simon's job."

"And you're here to make sure I don't escape." She leveled the accusation bluntly, without any feminine charm to make it an easier pill to swallow. "I'm your prisoner and that's all I am, isn't it? You're my guard, and you'll stuff me back in that box the minute I'm no longer useful. Right?"

"Why you got to make this so hard? You're the nurse. That's all. Got it?" Oreo's façade crumbled.

"Take me to Tristan," Melissa demanded. "Right now."

His lip twitched. "Simon ain't gonna like it, but fine. Follow me." He pivoted on the ball of his foot and ducked around her hut to the backside of the village.

Melissa ran to keep up. For a bodyguard, he had no problem leaving her in the dust, probably because he could kill her without batting an eye.

She saw it then, a hut hidden in the shadow of the trees. Then another. Four of them nearly concealed from view. When Oreo pulled to a stop, a slender woman peered out from the nearest doorway, a pipe dangling off her lip. Oreo called out to her in her language. She pointed to her left.

"Don't say I didn't warn you," he said, his tone flat and devoid of his previous charm.

Melissa followed, curious. She'd caught a glimpse of young girls staring back at her. Was this maybe where the single women stayed? "Why are you keeping these women and girls separate from everyone else?"

"We ain't. They're free to come and go as they please. You've seen most of them, you just don't remember."

But she hadn't. The deeper they went, the more the puzzle grew until Oreo climbed the three steps and rapped at the door to another hut.

Melissa couldn't have been more surprised when the woman answered the door.

"Kimmie?" Tristan's mother was—Kimmie? Her friend from Doctors for Charity? "You're here? But why?"

Kimmie glared over crossed arms at Oreo while he shrugged and explained, "What was I gonna do? Argue with the lady? Ain't no sense in it. She was gonna find out anyway. Might as well be today."

Melissa squashed the urge to hug the woman she thought was her friend, another automatic and really stupid female response. "What are you doing here?" It took a second before it sank in. The truth. The lies. The automatic rifle hanging off Kimmie's shoulder.

Wasn't this an awkward, horrible surprise? "You never planned to come back, did you? You're part of this."

"Stop the dumb blonde routine," Kimmie snapped. "You know why I'm here."

It hit Melissa like a pit viper on steroids. "You set me up."

Kimmie rolled her dark eyes, no hint of the friendly Vietnamese woman in sight. "I didn't set you up. We needed the doctor, not you. Hanks was supposed to come after me, not some bleeding heart American woman with no brain."

Gunfire sounded to the east, and Melissa ducked out of sheer instinct. Surprisingly, Oreo grabbed her wrist and dragged her away from the door. "We gotta go."

Melissa pulled out of his grip and demanded, "Where's Tristan?"

A sneer lifted over Kimmie's face. She chin-nodded toward the east. "By the sounds of it, he's hunting pigs. American pigs."

"He's what?" Melissa didn't understand.

Suddenly, Simon was there, breathing hard, his eyes fierce. "Jackman's in trouble." To Melissa he stated without one iota of emotion in his voice, "Good. You met Tristan's mother. Deal with it."

"Deal with it?" she shot at him. "That's all you've got to say, deal with it?"

There wasn't time to get more out of him, not with the tight clench to his jaw and the quick pace he set back into the village, the pace Oreo seemed determined to match. Another shock. Armed men were everywhere. Armed women, too.

"You're drug runners," Melissa accused. "You needed a doctor to treat your men, but they're not Cambodian soldiers afraid to go home, are they? They're nothing more than drug runners, and you're their leader."

He never argued, just kept marching, snapping out orders as he strode through camp.

"Simon," she called to him. "Stop it. Turn around and tell me what's really going on."

He turned on her, his face a deadly study in suppressed rage, his fingers spread wide. "We had a sweet thing going until those Cambodian rebels screwed everything up. And you! None of this would've happened if you'd stayed home in America where you belonged. I needed Hanks, at least one of his physician assistants, not some addle-brained woman who faints at the sight of blood."

"I do no such thing!" She could've slapped herself for letting that putdown get to her instead of everything else he'd said. Ah, pride. But he'd pissed her off. "So you and your little band of merry men run drugs through Vietnam, but the real refugees and the real war made it inconvenient for your business, is that it?"

She never saw it coming. One minute she was enflamed with self-righteous rage, the next she was on her knees, shaking the stars out of her head and blood in her mouth. He'd punched her. Hard. With his fist.

"Put her back in the box," he ordered. "The Vietnamese are sweeping north, and that bastard she's in love with is coming at us from the east. Let's give him a warm welcome."

Oreo half-dragged her to her knees. She could barely think straight. "Tucker? He's coming? Here?" It seemed unreal. "Oh, my God. Is that who Tristan's hunting?"

Oreo didn't speak. The way he twisted her arm behind her back was enough of an answer. Another burst of gunfire to the east sent Simon and the rest of the men scrambling to their trucks and cars.

*Not the box.* Melissa couldn't fight Oreo and win, so she feigned a silly female faint. She rolled her neck and bowed her head with a moan mixed in for good measure. Oreo's grip tightened on her bicep, but he'd drawn too close. Just close enough. She stiffened abruptly and rammed his nose with her head.

"Damn you!" he ground out as he lurched back a step, both hands clutching his bleeding nose.

She didn't wait to see if she'd broken it for him. Melissa ran into the jungle. There were worse things out there than snakes.

# Chapter Fourteen

"She's scared, and she's running," Isaiah offered out loud this time, a kick in the gut Tucker didn't need. He meant to be deliberate and methodical when he set these IEDs, not emotional. A warrior was always prepared. Always steady. They struck back and they struck hard, lightning fast before the enemy had a chance to regroup, but any mention of Melissa could turn him inside-out in a heartbeat.

"Where?" He slowed his breathing and dragged his mind off what might be happening to her and back to the task at hand. Isaiah couldn't do this job. He wasn't cut out for a warrior's life, not after he'd tossed his cookies a second time when that stubborn kid coughed and finally died. The poor guy had cried out for his mama just before he gave up the ghost. It got to Tucker, which was why he didn't want Isaiah near the mangled bodies where the ambush would occur.

It was sensitive work. The IEDs didn't need to be buried deep, just deep enough, but they were tricky. He'd wired three to one detonator, but spread the three at even intervals to get more bang for their buck. A claymore would've been better, but Tucker didn't have the time or raw materials to construct one. Sweat trickled down his forehead, stinging his eyes.

"West. She's on the other side of their camp. They're headed this way. She's going the opposite direction."

"Is she alone?" Tucker circled back around to Jackman. He buried a single IED a foot from the end of Jackman's pointed index finger beneath two inches of silt. Then he baited the trap with a single 5.56x45 NATO round, the round used in most M4s. Whoever came close enough to look at what Jackman was pointing at would end up in pieces.

But Tucker liked to underline his work with meaning that only another military guy would get. He made this booby-trap personal. With one punching blow of the side of his fist, he hammered Jackman's trident into his forehead. Jackman's buddies might as well know a SEAL was in the jungle and gunning for them

"So far she's safe, but I'm connecting her fear with a lot of anger. She's not sure where she's going. She's running scared. Men and women are chasing her. They're the angry ones, not her."

"Is she ahead of them?" Tucker kept his rage that Melissa needed, in even the slightest way, to be afraid of anything suppressed. He'd need every last flame of his darkest emotion and every spark for the battle ahead.

"She is." Isaiah sounded impressed. "Did your girl ever run track?"

"Only for UCLA." A big point of pride for Tucker. His girl was a California girl, born and raised near Pendleton. She'd moved east after she'd met Brady, and her parents had followed her when Melissa and Brady married.

Tucker finished his gruesome work but kept two IED kits back, knowing that whoever was running this slipshod army would be there soon. Wouldn't he be in for a surprise—if he survived? That was why the two leftover kits. Tucker never put all his bombs in one basket.

He gathered his gear and retreated to his forward position where Isaiah waited. They didn't need to be around when this went down. "Tell me when they're close."

*"Copy that."*

Tucker wanted to chew Isaiah out for using his mental talent instead of his voice, but mind-talking had worked incredibly well before. He could get used to it.

*"I forgot to buy ear protection."*

"You won't need it. We'll be far away by the time it blows." Tucker kept this voice low, slapping the dense shrubbery out of his way as he cut the distance between Melissa and him.

Isaiah was quiet for all of a minute. *"Will this make another mess?"*

"Hell yeah. Get your ass moving or you'll catch flack, maybe body parts."

Isaiah started humming while they set a steady pace west. Tucker counted to ten. It was either that or deck his musically inclined and very nervous fellow agent. He got to forty-nine when the whine of heavy engines and motorcycles growled through the jungle far to his left.

*"Keep low and keep moving,"* he commanded Isaiah, needing to get to beyond Siegel's camp to Melissa before those IEDs blew. Timing meant everything. He stopped short the moment he smelled campfire. "Which way?"

Isaiah pointed straight ahead. "She's still due west, but she's not running anymore."

"She okay?" The not knowing ate Tucker alive.

"Yes," Isaiah hissed, nodding ahead, "but you've got a kid with an AK walking perimeter around this camp. He's jumpy as hell. Watch your step."

"Got him." Tucker kept his eye peeled on the kid while he cut farther north, circumventing the camp.

He and Isaiah were ahead of schedule when the first IED blew and the ground shook. Two more explosions thundered in quick succession, a no-brainer when panic hits a densely packed grouping of soldiers or traitors. The moment they ran to get clear of the blast zone, they'd no doubt triggered the other two booby traps.

If this army worked like most, the cocky son-of-a-bitch in charge would've been the guy staring at the M4 round at the end of Jackman's finger, and wondering *what the hell?* If he was as good as he thought he was, he might have figured out the meaning of the bloody trident, but in the end it wouldn't have mattered. Tucker had rigged a simple detonator. All those guys had to do was get close enough to trigger the three sets of IEDs. By the time the trap was sprung, Jackman and anyone within a twenty-foot radius would've been dead.

Isaiah ducked behind a scrubby patch of pine. "Quick! Get out of sight!"

Tucker joined him as three men and two women ran eastward past them, all armed. He lifted his brows at his buddy.

"They're the guys who were chasing Melissa. She's on her own now. That way." Isaiah scurried around the pines, running.

"Is she okay? Anyone else coming at us?" Tucker asked, out of breath now and limping again. The pain in his side sharpened, but the twist in his gut hurt worse. He had to get to Melissa.

"She's five hundred yards ahead." Isaiah slowed, his fingers to his right temple, his face dark with shadow. "Damn. We need to hurry."

Tucker hadn't slowed down, his weapon up and his scope scanning for Melissa. "Just tell me where she is. What's going on?"

"The Vietnamese Army is in these woods, too." Isaiah put his index finger to his lips and crouched low. "She's directly up ahead, but so are they."

"How many?"

"All of them."

Tucker crouched into stealth mode, all but belly crawling like he used to do in training. He flattened his palm and motioned for Isaiah to do the same. "Stay to the undergrowth," he commanded. "Use the shadows below the brush and behind the trees. Where is she?"

*"We should see her any second now,"* came Isaiah's report.

Tucker tapped his right temple, wishing for that ocular lens tucked deep inside his swollen eyeball. He could spot Melissa sooner if both his eyeballs worked.

There she was, crouched alongside a downed log under an overgrown shrub with her hands over her head. *Good girl,* he sent to her. *I'm here, babe. Look for me. See me.*

Nothing. She stayed tucked into herself, no doubt shivering, and damn, he wanted that slender body of hers tucked up against him where he could keep her warm.

*"She can't hear you,"* Isaiah sent. *"She's not aware we're here yet. She's still panicked and hiding from Siegel's men."*

Tucker nodded his agreement with the astute observation. Seeing her was half the battle. She was alive and safe, scared but hidden for the moment. "Where's the army?" he asked Isaiah.

Isaiah nodded to his left. *"They'll be here soon."*

Tucker edged close enough to toss a small stone at the log where she was hiding, concerned if he stepped out into the open, he'd be seen. Melissa looked up at the soft thump, her face streaked with dirt. Their eyes connected. She bit her bottom lip, the sexiest thing he'd ever seen in his life. Tucker sent her the thumbs up immediately followed by the hand signal to hold her position. She nodded that she understood.

*"You've got fifty or so soldiers filtering through the trees at your left, Tucker. How do you want to do this?"* Isaiah asked mentally, his question laced with worry.

Tucker couldn't take his eyes off Melissa. Did she have any idea what just seeing her did to him? How much she meant to him? That he felt like he could finally breathe again just at the sight of her pretty face?

He held his index finger to his lips to signal her to keep quiet. "You tell me, Isaiah. Is anyone north of us?"

"Not as far as I can tell, but I've got to be honest. These guys are hard to read. Maybe it's because they're all wearing brain buckets."

Tucker stifled a smile. Isaiah was learning military-ese. "I'm going in," he breathed, not willing to wait. Shedding his gear bags, he blurted, "Cover me."

*"You're clear. Make it quick."*

Tucker did, a blur in the late afternoon shadows. He skidded into Melissa's boots first, sliding along her body, sandwiching her between the log and himself, his back to Isaiah. There were no words. All he could do was gather her into his chest, his nose in her hair and her face in his neck. "You're safe. I've got you now." *And I'm going to live.*

She hiccupped a funny, sad sound. "Tuck," she choked, clinging to him, her arms wrapped around his neck. "You're here. It's really you."

"Are you hurt? Can you walk?"

Melissa shook her head. "I'm fine. Just scared out of my wits. I heard shooting. What's going on?"

"This is dangerous country right now. There's a platoon of Vietnamese soldiers working their way north toward us. We've got to move. Can you keep up?"

She nodded. Her eyes brimmed with tears she hadn't let fall, but her chin was stiff. "I can. What do you want me to do?"

"See Isaiah?" He pointed over his shoulder back at his partner. "On my count, keep low and go to him. He's got you covered. Go fast. One. Two—now!"

She lifted to her feet, the warmth of her body the last thing his fingers wanted to release. But he let her go, and she flew. He made his return on her six, and carefully gathered his gear while the three of them angled northward and away from the nightmare.

Distant gunfire drifted through the trees.

"We've got another patrol at our east," Isaiah reported, his finger to his temple again. "It's a good thing we found you when we did, Mrs. McCormack. Those soldiers are engaged with your friends. Hear that?"

"They aren't my friends," Melissa said. "What are you doing here?"

"We saw your kidnapping at the airport." Tucker pulled her next to his hip, his arm around her, needing her inside his comfort zone, needing to be inside of hers. He shouldered his bags away from her, a dangerous, possessive heat taking over his soul. "Did they hurt you, baby? Tell me who did what." *And I'll go back and kill them.*

"We'd just landed, ma'am," Isaiah interrupted quietly, his weapon up and walking point like a good grunt. He truly had the makings of a decent soldier the way he scanned the way forward as well as keeping watch on their rear. "We saw the whole thing from the windows at Tân Sơn Nhất."

"They didn't hurt me, not after they took me to that camp back there. What a mess." Melissa ran a hand over her disheveled braid, but kept a straight path due north. "They acted like they were humanitarians, like Doctors for Charity, only they wanted me to think they were taking care of the Cambodian president's old guard. He said they couldn't go home, that they'd be killed by the rebels and shot for treason, but they were really running drugs. And I'm so stupid, I fell for that lie."

Tucker caught the anguish in her tone, but he needed a name. "Who's he?"

"Simon Siegel. He's their leader and he's a Navy SEAL, too. Did you know him?"

Contrary to popular belief, all SEALs did not know each other. "Never heard of him," Tucker admitted, matching his gait to Melissa's, his palm flat to the small of her back, and his heart full. "We ran into Jackman and a few of his guys. That's what drew Siegel out of camp."

"That was you? All that gunfire and noise was you?"

"Isaiah did it," Tucker teased, feeling lightheaded and at peace for a moment.

"Hardly. Your man's the real deal, ma'am. He's got nerves of steel." Isaiah stepped lightly but doggedly through the jungle fauna, clearing the way when the brush was too thick and holding back branches so he didn't accidently whip Melissa. The kid was quite the gentleman.

*"You did good,"* Isaiah offered, out of breath but still going strong.

*"I always do good."*

*"No, I mean psychically. You connected with me in your head, like you're doing right now. You're a psychic. I told you so."*

Tucker could only growl at that annoying revelation, but the kid was right. They had stayed in contact without speaking. Mental communication had become second nature without Tucker consciously intending it to. *Damn it to hell.* "Don't you need to hum or something?"

Isaiah just grinned. *"No, but tell her you love her. Stop being the conquering hero. She needs to hear it. She's waiting and you're hurting her feelings by not saying it."*

*"I am?"* The thought had never occurred to Tucker. She was there in his arms—wasn't that enough? Women were so complicated. *"She's smart. We might have had our problems, but she already knows how I feel."*

*Does she?"* Isaiah rolled his eyes skyward, his brows arched. *"She's a woman, Tucker. She's sensitive and she needs to hear you say it. Tell her. Give her what she needs, not what you think she needs, you moron."*

Ha. That was humorous, Isaiah calling him a moron, but if the kid was right? Tucker stopped walking. This wouldn't take long.

"Melissa," he said, his heart on the line and suddenly climbing up his dry throat. He licked his lips and tried hard to swallow. Not happening. His throat clamped shut. Somehow, this felt entirely different than when he'd said those three little words to Nicole. This time it felt like he was betting his soul in the biggest gambling den on the Vegas Strip. Like he stood to lose his ability to breathe because no air would be left on the planet. This might take longer than he'd planned.

He tugged Melissa into his arms, scared out of his wits now and wondering, *what the hell?* "There's something you need to know."

"Yes, Tuck?" She came easily. Expectantly. Her blue eyes glowed, setting his blood on fire. How did she do that, get under his skin just by looking at him?

He framed her gentle face in his big callused palms, his thumbs rough and ragged on her petal soft cheeks, so thankful he'd caught up with her, and really afraid for the first time in his life that he could've lost her. She meant everything to him. The sun. The moon. Every last star in the sky. Nothing else existed, but her. *And Deuce.*

Melissa lifted her fingers to his swollen face, worry etching the laugh lines at the corners of her eyes while she feathered the touch of an angel over his bruised cheek. "You look like you've been in a war. What on earth happened to you?"

"This isn't about me, babe. This is about you." And there, in front of God, Isaiah, and that tiny slice of Vietnam, Tucker closed the distance between him and the woman he loved. He kissed her lips softly. At first. But fire was a dangerous thing to play with, and Melissa was the perfect accelerant to the overly dry tinder in his tough-guy heart. He'd waited so long for her.

Heat burst through every cell in his all-male body at first contact of his mouth on hers. Her breath fanned his lust into a bonfire. He wanted her more than he'd ever wanted any other woman before. His body hardened. God, she had to feel what she was doing to him. He couldn't exactly conceal what had to be the father of all hard-ons. The flash fire of what had started as a tender kiss morphed into an inferno of blistering need to protect and love her. To shelter her. It threatened his military control on the situation.

He eased a fraction from the honey of her mouth and whispered his secret into her moist, wet lips. "I love you, Melissa," he ground out, his fingers sliding down her arms and waist to purchase the curve of her hips. "I love you so much I can hardly breathe when you're out of my sight."

She whimpered, her fingers on his collarbones, holding him tight. "Say it again."

He growled playfully. "I love you, damn it, woman. I have for months. Hell, since I first saw you in California. You're my every second of my every day. Marry me, damn it."

He glimpsed another eye roll from his smart-assed junior partner over Melissa's shoulder. *"What?"* he sent to Isaiah mentally.

*"Wow. How romantic. Did you ever consider that maybe, just maybe, Melissa doesn't like your foul mouth? She's a lady, Tucker. Treat her like one. You might be surprised what a difference it makes."*

That was it. Isaiah had to go, but hell. The kid might be onto something. Tucker stammered, his question still unanswered. "Umm, I mean, what I meant to say was..." he thought fast, "... would you do me the honor of accepting my name as yours? Of taking my hand in yours? Of... of..." He grasped for something just as flowery and twice as romantic.

*"Of letting me love you forever, you dumbass,"* Isaiah prompted, his brow spiked, *"only don't say 'dumbass.'"*

"Of letting me love you forever?" Tucker finished.

Melissa's pretty pink lips parted. Her mouth dropped open. "Who *are* you? Where's the Tucker Chase I used to know?"

He almost swore, but caught himself just in time. She turned him into a needy little boy who wanted to please her more than he wanted a new rifle for his collection. "I'm not taking chances. Not anymore. Not with you. I love you, Melissa McCormack. God knows I do. Hell, I'll quit the Bureau if it makes you happy. Marry me." *Please say yes.*

Isaiah crossed his arms over his chest and turned away, his head shaking, but Tucker purposefully forgot he existed. His lovely lady had yet to reply, but she'd placed her fingers on his chest, her eyes glistening. Her lashes came down, and...

She wasn't going to turn him down, was she?

"Oh, Tuck." The tears spilled over. She chewed at her bottom lip, and his heart sank. She didn't want to look at him. Why not? Because of Brady? *Here it comes.* Melissa was too smart to marry another military guy. She'd been through enough hell with the first. What made Tucker think she'd want to go through that again?

He gulped what was left of his pride and prepared for the letdown. Damn. It would be a long, lonely walk back to Hồ Chí Minh City to catch that red-eye flight if this woman scorned him. He swallowed the lump in his throat. Felt like a Bradley tank.

"Yes," she said softly and sweetly, sniffling as she lifted her chin and met his gaze. "I love you, Tucker Chase. From the very first moment I saw you, I've loved you." Up on her tiptoes, she leaned those pillowy breasts to his chest and...

*Oh, what the hell.* He scooped her off her feet and into his arms. He dipped her backward, one hand under her head to hold her steady while he kissed her good and proper.

The aching fire of lust roared up his spine, an electric shot mingling with the rock-solid surety of his love. This woman was breaking his heart. There was no way he'd let her get away now. They were meant to be together, and this time, there would be no stupid mistakes to foul things up. He would listen better. He'd work harder. Hell, he'd quit the Bureau if it meant making her happy.

For two cents he would've laid her down right there in the grass, but Isaiah was close by. Hopefully keeping an eye out for trouble and not gawking. And the Vietnamese Army was too close for comfort.

He tucked her back under his chin, his heart pounding with that flood of endorphins and his head in the clouds. He needed a cigar.

"Ahem," Isaiah murmured. "We really ought to keep moving."

Suddenly aware that he'd taken far longer than he'd planned with his declaration of love and the impromptu marriage proposal, Tucker took his eyes off Melissa. It had all spilled out of him once he'd started, but he knew he'd been meaning to say it for awhile now. "Oh, yeah. This is my junior agent, Isaiah Zaroyin."

"*Your junior agent?*" Isaiah offered an incredulous eye roll before he shifted his weapon and offered a hand to Melissa. "It's an honor to meet you, ma'am."

She beamed and returned the handshake. "Hi, Isaiah. It's very nice to meet you."

Damned if a distant gunshot didn't spoil the magic.

# **Chapter Fifteen**

Tucker tugged his rifle off his shoulder into a steady grip. "Let's move."

Melissa meant to follow him anywhere. She'd never been so happy to see anyone in her life. How incredibly lucky could one woman get? Downright miraculous, was what this was.

Another spat of gunfire erupted at their rear, the very real need to run and hide adding speed to her feet. Tucker pulled her into an easy lope at his side, but something was wrong. He ran with a limp, and he'd winced when he'd hugged her. One eye was black and swollen shut. Dark bruises marked his cheekbones and brow. The skirmish with Jackman must've been rough. He looked as if he'd been in a brawl instead of a gunfight.

She doubted he'd tell her what happened, so she hadn't asked. She knew how closed-mouthed special operators were. Brady never shared, either.

Tucker kept his fingers intertwined with hers as they ran. They were good this way, running side by side, her long legs keeping up with his ground-eating stride. She could imagine them on the beach, him in his swimming trunks, her in her one-piece bathing suit. Running. Laughing. The sea breeze in their noses and sunlight on his handsome face. He'd be tanned and morning scruffy, his chin unshaven and his black hair mussed. Sexy. He'd wink that sinfully wicked wink of his, the one that melted her core every time. The one that made her knees weak. The world would stand still.

She licked her bottom lip at the thought. Isaiah, the man to her right, was every bit the athlete. Tall, dark, and handsome, with bedroom eyes, but Tucker? Eye-candy, pure and simple. Heart-throbbing, panty-melting soul food. There was no other man in the world for her.

After they'd put a couple of miles between them and the sporadic gunfire far at their rear, Tucker slowed to a stop beside a grove of tall, spindly bamboo. "Take a load off."

She crouched to the ground, her palms to her knees, thankful for the breather. He handed out two water bottles, one to her, one to Isaiah. Melissa took a quick gulp and offered the rest to him. Tucker upended it and swallowed, and...

*Man, oh man.* She could've knelt there all day watching the way the strong muscles on his neck worked as he gulped the liquid down. How his Adam's apple bobbed with every swallow. He hadn't shaved in days, the shadowy scruff on his chin and neck tempting her libido. She curled her fingers into her palms, wanting to trace that strong chin and neck just to hear him purr.

When he crunched the plastic in his fist, he looked down at her. She couldn't look away. The man glowed. Even as battered as he was, he absolutely glowed, and she knew it then. This was Tucker in his true element, a jungle cat on the loose and against all odds, untamable, lethal, and one hundred percent deadly.

She got it then. The world she'd signed onto with that impromptu marriage proposal wouldn't be easy. The road would be long and hard, and there'd be more lonely days and nights wondering and worrying. But Tucker Chase was not Brady. This man standing proud and ready to take on the world didn't need her to fight his bureaucratic battles for him. He didn't need her to run interference with doctors, nurses, and lawyers. This was a warrior to the bone. Healthy. More than able. More than willing. Strong to the point of brash, maybe even daring to the point of foolhardy.

He cupped his chin like he was sizing her up, his gaze narrowed, flicking his thumb over his whiskers as if he ran through the jungle for his life every day. "You're sure a sight for sore eyes."

"You mean eye," Isaiah teased. "I'm gonna call you Cyclops."

Tucker leveled a spiked brow at his partner and grunted. That broke the magic spell.

"What happened to you?" She had to ask. Isaiah sported a few bruises, but nothing like Tucker's.

Predictably, he winked. "Nothing for you to worry about."

She swallowed hard and lowered her chin, all of her feminine receptors tingling, her fingers itching to get him alone and out of his clothes. To run her hands over every plane and edge and furrow of his rugged body. To nibble and lick and...

A lightning bolt of craving for this outrageously brave man shot through her. The hairs on her arms lifted as searing heat unfurled in her blood. Living on the edge had opened her eyes and she saw him. Finally. She got it.

Tucker Chase wouldn't change. He couldn't. This bigger-than-life warrior standing before her, the handsome guy bristling with weaponry and shouldering an over-sized pack that looked plenty heavy, needed that brash, cocky part of his soul to do the impossible jobs others shirked. To face the evil in the world and run it to the ground. To fight the odds and save people like—her.

Simon had a veritable army at his disposal, but Tucker had one man, yet there he was. Winking and telling *her* not to worry. Denying his pain. Putting her first when he obviously needed someone to put him first for a change.

Tucker Chase was fighting the world alone. Something in her gut told Melissa he always had been. It was no wonder he'd continually pressed her for intimacy since they'd met. The man was lost. He had to crave stolen moments of peace like this one amidst the battles he fought daily. How else could one stay sane while fighting the good fight if not for the recharging lift from a soul mate, if not for someone standing at his side, loving him, trusting him? Willing to fight for him.

Her heart swelled. Love for Tucker lifted its head and roared. Melissa wanted to seduce him in every way she knew how.

"Are you coming, babe?" he asked, his hand reaching for hers, his voice uncommonly husky.

"Yes," she answered, her tone definite and sure. Wasn't he in for a surprise?

She let her gaze drift down his belly to his zipper, hoping he caught her brazen signal and that Isaiah hadn't. It was no wonder Tucker could barely speak with that bulge in his pants. Every last nerve ending responded to the sight. Her muscles clenched with an insane need to grab hold of him, to feel him moving inside of her. To be the one who saved him for a change.

She lost her voice when she placed her fingers in his palm and that manly hand closed around hers, pulling her up from the ground and against that tremendous hard-on. It was a simple, ordinary action between a man and a woman, but it seemed so much, umm, larger. Maybe even life-changing. He wanted her the same way she wanted him, and he'd meant for her to know it.

"You're breathing hard," he murmured into her cheek as he rubbed his nose into her hair and inhaled. "God, you scared the shit—I mean, the life out of me."

A smile tugged at her lips. If they'd been alone, she would've surprised him by smoothing a palm over that bulge in his jeans. The idea was tempting, but they weren't alone. She opted for casual conversation instead. "Are you trying not to cuss?"

His mouth roamed over the curl of her ear and ended with a moist nip at her earlobe. "Maybe. Isaiah seems to think it's a good idea. Is that what you want, me to clean up my mouth?"

And there he was, that tender man hidden beneath the rough, macho exterior, trying to please his woman. Her eyes brimmed. She blinked to keep the tears from falling. "I don't care if you cuss like a sailor," she managed to breathe out. "Kiss me, Tucker, just kiss me."

A groan lifted up from his gut as Tucker framed her head with his palms. His mouth closed over hers, devouring her lips and the last of her self-control with it. He hooked one hand under her knee and drew her leg up to his thigh, and she let him, needing him, wanting him with every fiber of her being.

Liquid fire pooled at her core as his scorching male brand rubbed against her, whetting her appetite for that more he'd always wanted, that intimate part of herself she'd not yet relinquished to any man besides her husband.

"Ahem," some guy mumbled.

"Go away," Tucker growled, his lips still fast at work, his tongue still dancing over hers, trailing a warm, moist line of desire that arced straight to her core.

Melissa giggled. She honestly felt like a treat in Tucker's arms. A treasure brought out of the dark into the light. She felt—alive.

"They're getting closer." *Isaiah. That's his name.*

Melissa caught her breath and whispered, "He's right, Tuck. We have to go."

He growled, barely easing back from her. "I want a rain check to do this right."

She had to smile. "I don't think you'll need a rain check with your wife," she said softly and suggestively, her tongue sliding slowly over his bottom lip.

"Woman, you're killing me." He bumped her nose with his. "Have I told you yet today how much I love you?"

"Guys, enough already," Isaiah hissed, his rifle sweeping their backstop. The noise of men and machinery had gotten closer. "Stop making out. It's time to go."

Enough said. Tucker geared up, and after one more kiss, he disengaged, and they headed north into more jungle. The afternoon faded into evening. They stopped for another break before Tucker turned away from the sun and headed east.

"How much farther?" Melissa asked. These two men seemed ready to walk all night, but she was tired. They needed a safe place to stop for the night.

Tucker shot a questioning glance at Isaiah. "How far are we from the city?"

"How would I know?"

"Because you're psychic."

"I'm psychic, not omniscient."

"But you found Melissa."

"Of course I did. I was there when they took her. I knew who I was looking for."

Tucker grumbled, his hands on his hips. "Well, I thought you knew where we were going."

Isaiah's chin stuck out. "You're the SEAL. How would I know?"

"Because you're psychic!"

Melissa chuckled at the banter. For as capable as he was, Tucker could be so obtuse. "Guys. I'm pretty sure we keep going east, but not during the night; it's too dangerous. Let's stop here. I don't hear gunfire anymore. I don't suppose either of you has any blankets in those bags?"

Isaiah tugged out three plastic packets. "I've got rain ponchos."

She turned to Tucker, her brows raised expectantly. "What do you have?" She shouldn't have asked the question, much less allowed her gaze to flutter down to his zipper again. It was very obvious what Tucker had.

He shifted his stance when she noticed. One stern eyebrow spiked in her direction. "I'll find us something to eat," he muttered and stomped off, grumbling, "How the hell would I know where we are? I'm not a mind reader."

She suppressed another giggle. Yes, they were all hungry and grumpy. Once they ate—if they ate—things would settle down, and they could plan sensibly for tomorrow.

Isaiah shook one of the ponchos out of its plastic wrapper and offered it to her. "This will keep you warm and dry."

"You wouldn't happen to have any Deet in that bag, would you?"

"You bet." He rummaged in his backpack until he found it. "Here you go."

"Ah." She sprayed a layer up her arms and around her neck. "Thank you. The mosquitoes have been eating me alive. They don't seem to bother you guys."

"We sprayed up when we ditched our truck." Isaiah wandered into a stand of nearby bamboo. "Did you see that stream we crossed back a ways? One of these might make a good fishing pole if I had some line and a hook."

"I'm going to find a bush." She looked around for suitable cover wanting privacy within a reasonable distance. "I'll be right over there."

"Scream if you need me."

"She doesn't need you," Tucker muttered, startling Melissa.

"That was fast," Isaiah commented drily. "Forget something?"

"No, I found something," Tucker said as he slapped a big ugly fish with black whiskers at Isaiah's feet. "Clean this. Skin it while you're at it, while I make a fire."

Isaiah frowned at the still gasping fish, his nose wrinkled in dismay. "Where'd you get that? You've only been gone a couple minutes."

"In the creek." Tucker jerked his head to some vague place behind him. "It's shallow. You've just got to know what you're looking for. Why? Isn't it big enough for you?"

Isaiah sputtered at Tucker's snarky tone. "It's not that, but I... I don't know how to clean fish."

"Stop whining. It's easy." Tucker dropped to his knees, pulled a knife out of the sheath at his hip, and promptly cut the fish's head off with one clean slice. He held it up at the end of his knife, a glint of despicable mischief in his eyes while the rest of the fish kept wriggling and slapping its tail. "See? Nothing to it."

When he dropped the head to the dirt and poked the point of the blade into the fish's yellow belly,

Melissa turned on her heels and headed for cover. "I'll be right back," she said, giggling, not wanting to watch what happened next.

"I'll make a fire," Isaiah volunteered.

Dinner that night was a little charred, but tasty.

# Chapter Sixteen

"That fish was good, even if I do say so myself." And the company wasn't so bad either. Tucker settled with his back against a fallen tree and Melissa curled on his lap, her head on his chest and her slender hand tangled in his. He loosened the thin piece of rag she'd used to tie off her braid, and tugged the different strands out of their tightly woven pattern. Crimped ribbons of honey gold slipped through his fingers like silk.

The jungle nearly felt like paradise, full of bugs and unknown animals skittering up the trees, but peaceful. A man couldn't ask for more after a tough day than to rest with his woman safe in his arms. Melissa filled an empty hole in his heart, the one he'd tried for months after his divorce to fill with hard liquor, living on the edge, and flat-out denial that he had feelings.

Isaiah ended up roasting the fish on a bamboo spit he'd rigged. The kid knew how to cook, and the meal was surprisingly good, but it was Melissa's butt planted on Tucker's lap that made the night perfect. Her slender frame fit inside the shelter of his larger body like she belonged there. He didn't mind that she used him like a sweater, snuggling under one arm for warmth, and wrapping his other arm around her.

But something was missing. Something very essential to the end of a good day—a little guy named Deuce.

Tucker had no doubt he could get his kid free from Nguyễn Vin Li, aka Vinnie. He just wasn't sure the guy would live to talk about it, and that could pose a problem. Killing Vinnie meant trouble if Tucker got caught. He needed to know more about his adversary, how well connected he was, who he knew, and exactly which authorities he had in his pocket before he faced off with the jerk. A powerful man in a foreign country would twist the truth to suit his agenda. Tucker couldn't risk going back to jail and losing Deuce and Melissa forever. He had to do this right. What a dilemma.

Isaiah leveled two more broken chunks of some rotted tree into the fire, sending a rush of orange-red sparks skyward like falling stars. Tucker watched them drift back to earth. They weren't stars. Not really. They were like him. Falling back to—nothing.

He worried. Melissa might have said yes to his marriage proposal, but he had his doubts. Adrenaline tended to skew people's thinking when they were running for their lives. Of course she'd said yes. She would've agreed to anything in that intense moment. The problem was the timing. Would she have agreed if he'd asked her when they were safely back home? Something deep in his gut told him no. She was too good to be true.

It might be better if she backed out and left his sorry ass. She could live her quiet, sedate little life and forget about him. He had too many ghosts hanging over his head and sitting on his shoulder. His old buddy, the Grim Reaper, kept showing up like the ghoul he was, demanding blood. Sometimes Tucker worried only his blood could pay the price for what he'd done in the name of the gods of war. It felt like an honest trade somehow, that whole eye-for-an-eye thing, but Melissa didn't need to be a part of it. She'd had enough crap. One dead husband was enough.

Tucker had struggled with the dilemma for years. He'd never let himself get carried away or go too far in all the firefights he'd been in. Not once had he let the blood lust win. As pumped up as a man got in hand-to-hand combat, he'd always kept the rage controlled. He'd stayed sane and followed the rules of engagement religiously, but this next battle would be different. No father followed ROEs when it came to his son.

Once he had Melissa and Isaiah on a plane to America, he'd go after Deuce. Then they'd need a way out of this country. Tucker wasn't about to double-back through Cambodia. There had to be a smarter way.

*"Alex will help if you ask,"* Isaiah whispered in the farthest recesses of Tucker's mind. That was odd, a psychic whisper. It almost felt like his own thought, but he knew it wasn't. He looked at the kid sitting cross-legged on the other side of the campfire from him, his hands on his knees like he was meditating.

Isaiah shrugged, like it was no big deal to read minds. *"Some thoughts are quiet. That's the best way to get through to people."*

"You did good today." Tucker meant it. *"So don't spoil it. Get out of my head."*

Isaiah sighed the warning off. "Sorry. It's a habit," he said out loud, his dark eyes drifting over Melissa. "Is she asleep?"

"No." She snuggled under Tucker's chin, her voice thick with slumber. "I'm just thinking about all those children in Simon's camp. What will happen to them?"

Tucker tightened his grip. "Weren't their parents with them?"

She nodded. "That's the problem. Their parents put them in danger to begin with."

*Like me... I'm the reason Deuce is in the fix he's in today. None of this would've happened if I'd been a better father. If I'd been a better husband.*

"And there were so many girls. I think they were orphans."

He kissed the crown of her head. "This is a different culture, Melissa, and these people are poor. They do what they think they have to do to survive. We'll never understand what motivates them."

"I really thought I was helping refugees," she murmured, squeezing Tucker's fingers up to her lips and ending with a kiss along the pad of his thumb. "That's the whole reason I came here."

"Yes, but you didn't plan to be kidnapped. You did good," he told her with certainty. "Your heart was in the right place. Simon's the problem, not you."

"Still..." Her voice trailed off.

"Mimi and Peewee will be okay," Isaiah assured her. "That's who you're worried about right now, isn't it?"

She straightened on Tucker's lap. "I've been meaning to ask, are you really psychic? Can you see them?"

"No, I can't actually see Mimi and Peewee in my mind, but I can get a sense of them. We're close enough to the camp, but I'm not detecting the negative energy an injured child would project into the universe." He smoothed the dirt in front of him with a wide sweep of his palm. "I'm what's known in psychic circles as a precognitor, Melissa. I can read some people's thoughts, but only if I'm in close proximity or if there's a link already established. I find it curious that I can't read your mind. All I get from you are impressions. It's as if you're blocking me somehow. Have you ever been tested for psychic talent?"

"She's not psychic," Tucker declared firmly. "She's normal, like me."

Isaiah rolled his eyes emphatically. "Tucker, in the entire world of normal people, you're the furthest—"

"Shut it, Zaroyin. I can make you disappear."

Again with the eye roll. "So now you're a magician?"

"I wasn't planning on using a wand, smart guy."

"But you're sure Mimi and Peewee are okay?" Melissa pressed, ignoring their jabs.

"Yes. Children's energy is different from adults. It's more..." Isaiah paused for a heartbeat, "... pure. It's clearer."

That seemed to do the trick, at least for Melissa. She relaxed into Tucker's arms again. "As long as they're okay."

Isaiah shot Tucker a darker thought. *"But there are other children in that camp, Tucker. Girls. All under twelve, and they're not releasing good energy. They're scared to death, and they've been hurt. They want to go home to their mothers."*

*"What do you mean other girls? Sex trade, maybe?"* Tucker asked, but out loud, "What about my boy?"

"I can't hear Devlin at this distance."

"Damn it, Zaroyin. For the last time, his name is Deuce!" Tucker snapped, shielding his angst for the children caught in Siegel-Rat-Bastard's trap. If it were anyone else, he would've gone ahead with his plan to save Melissa and Deuce, but a guy just doesn't leave defenseless kids behind. Maybe this part of the mission wasn't over yet. Maybe there was a way to go back.

"You're right," Isaiah conceded, "and I'm sorry I used the wrong name. I know better."

"You think? I've told you often enough." Tucker growled for effect, not so mad at Isaiah as Siegel. *But those little girls...*

*"You're all right, you know that, Tucker?"* Isaiah murmured on their private channel.

"What does Deuce have to do with anything?" Melissa asked, weariness in her tone and oblivious of the covert conversation going on in her midst.

She already knew Tucker had lost custody, that it ate him alive. She'd even met his ex and said she understood his dilemma after that one hostile encounter with Nicole, but honestly? No one knew what a sucking hole in their heart felt like until they'd lost their only kid. She might have lost her husband, but losing a kid was different. It just was. Brady McCormack went down fighting, but Deuce never stood a chance, not against his shrew of a mother. "That's why I came to Vietnam, babe. Deuce is here. I was after joint custody, but knowing what I know now, I'm taking him home."

Melissa tilted her chin up to Tucker's face. "What aren't you tell me, Tuck?"

*God, can she read my mind, too?*

"Deuce—" Isaiah directed that at Tucker, saving the day with his timely interruption, "—is being forced to work in Vinnie's garment factory. Vinnie is Nicole's new husband, and he's using Tucker's son to keep the other children in his factory in line. He's been pretty rough on Deuce. We need to get him out of there and soon."

Anger hissed out of Tucker. "You never told me Vinnie's hurting my kid."

That woke Melissa up. She moved out of his arms to face him. With a toss of her head, the rest of her braid unraveled, spilling coiled tangles of firelight over her shoulders. "How dare he? What are we doing here, Tuck? Let's go get Deuce."

*So that's what a real mother looks like.* Melissa was breathtaking. Tucker could've kissed her for her righteous indignation over a boy she'd never met. The sight stirred him to his soul. It was one thing to date a woman within the confines of refined society where gentlemen held doors for ladies, and ladies responded with flirtation and gentle conversation, but to see her in the wild jungle with fire in her eyes, her dander up, and her face smudged and flushed. To hear her proclaim her intentions for his boy...

Something dark and feral and primitive within him lifted its head and took notice. His nostrils flared. Like an apex predator to its mate, his hunger for her dialed into the generous curves of her warm body. The glimmer of flames washing over her blonde hair like a fiery halo. The mother bear called Melissa.

Red-hot embers sprang to life in his gut. And lower. Every nerve lit with need and hunger. The male in him was all at once hyper-aware and ready to capitalize on the insatiable chemistry between them. To claim her, mark her, and make her his.

"Tomorrow," he promised, his voice filled with pure intent.

"The problem will be to get Deuce out of the country once we've got him," Isaiah added. "We're not sure how powerful Vinnie is yet or who he knows. He could have some influential connections. We might ignite an international incident if we're not careful."

"Humph," she declared staunchly, her jaw set in that stubborn mode Tucker knew so well. "I know a couple of influential people, too. Alex will help, just ask him."

"No, he won't," Tucker explained. "He already told me he wouldn't handle a non-custodial parent kidnapping. We're on our own."

"Bet me. I know Alex. He's a hellcat when it comes to children. He'll help," she declared vehemently, tossing those tangled curls. "Does he know Deuce is being used for child labor? That he's a slave? Have you told him?"

"I haven't had time." Tucker flicked a red-striped beetle off his thigh. "I've been kind of busy rescuing a damsel in distress."

That should've carried more weight than it did. All it did was make Melissa angry. "Are you serious? Are you telling me…?" She pinned him with her meanest gaze. "Tell me you didn't. Tucker. Did you trade saving your son for chasing after me?"

"I made a choice." Tucker felt that familiar angst creep up his spine, the one that told him everything was slipping through his fingers. "I chose to rescue you because—"

"Because I couldn't get a good read on you, ma'am," Isaiah interrupted. "If anyone's to blame for saving you before Deuce, it's me. I sensed that you were in a box, Mrs. McCormack, and that you were covered with blood. You seemed dazed, and then you were focused on a bloody leg. How could we not come after you when we thought your situation was more critical? Deuce was just unhappy, but you were in more desperate straits."

She swallowed hard, her throat muscles working. "Oh. I see. Umm, yeah. I wasn't bleeding, though. It wasn't me. They put me in a wooden box at first, but then they let me out and started to build me a real clinic. I thought I was helping refugees, not drug runners. Not that I wouldn't have helped just because they were drug runners. Those poor people—"

"Were probably in a drug war with either the Vietnamese or the Cambodian Army, which is how they were injured in the first place. Hell, they might have been fighting amongst themselves, for all we know." Tucker tugged her wrist gently, and she mellowed and let him hold her. "What's with the bloody leg Isaiah saw, though? You're not hurt."

She gulped like she was swallowing a frog. "It wasn't my leg. Dang. His leg, it had to be amputated and I..." Big noisy gulp. "It was awful. I helped with the amputation." She wiggled as a shiver shook her entire body. "I almost threw up in the middle of it."

Tucker smoothed his palms down her back, ending at her waist instead of gripping her ass like he would've if he'd thought he could get away with it. "You didn't say you had a doctor with you. Who did the surgery?"

"Simon," she said so softly Tucker had to strain to hear. "None of that matters. We have to save your son, Tucker. We have to save Deuce. Tomorrow. First thing. Before the sun comes up."

There was that crusader again, the Joan of Arc within Melissa, wanting to right the world when they weren't even back in the city yet. She felt it too, the compulsion to save others. His fingers wandered lower. "Come with me," he whispered.

She knew what he wanted, but he didn't dare say it out loud. Her eyes widened and her breath hitched high in her throat, reading his signals like he was reading hers. He needed to finally be inside of her, locked together once and for all. He needed a home for once in his sorry life, and damn it, it was that light in her eyes and the banked heat in her body.

"Keep the fire going," Tucker ordered as he pushed off the ground and dusted his rear pockets. "We'll be right back."

Isaiah didn't look up, just nodded, his gaze fastened to the flames. "Take your time."

"And stay the hell out of my head," Tucker warned, his index finger in Isaiah's face.

The kid shrugged. "I'm not stupid."

Tucker snagged two of the plastic ponchos and all but dragged Melissa through the vines and brush, back toward the creek where he'd found dozens of those carp-like fish lounging in the shallows. That was the only reason he'd caught one so easily. He'd been lucky. He needed to be that lucky again and actually reel this woman in.

He settled the ponchos to the ground, keeping to the shadows along the eastern creek bank, the moon in the west at his back. The jungle was alive tonight with croaking frogs and insects. With life.

"Sit," he ordered brusquely, his blood on fire and his heart climbing up his throat. He needed to know. Did she mean yes? Was any of this real?

"No," she replied evenly, and there it was, defiance and femininity all rolled into one. "Not unless you sit with me."

*Damn it, do as you're told.* He shot her a nervous look, his fingers curled in his hair again and his heart on the line. "We need to talk."

She unbuttoned her top button, the one he'd been staring at half the night. "You're right. We do need to talk, but first..." She unbuttoned the second and the third until moonlight glimmered over the creamy flesh of her upper breasts.

*What did I want to ask?*

The shirt slipped off her shoulders to the ground, her breathing as heavy as his. The sight of her full breasts and flat stomach curled his toes. The flair of her full hips, too. She unsnapped her jeans, each snap a sizzle on a hot plate, and, sensually and slowly, she revealed high-cut bikini panties. He couldn't make his eyeballs move off of her when all his dreams came true—when she stepped out of her sneakers and jeans and toed the bunched clothing to the edge of the plastic poncho turned *tablecloth*. He'd intended it as a blanket, but now...

He licked his lips at the long-legged feast bathed in moonlight, her hands sweetly clasped together as if in prayer, her dark eyes sparkling in the night. He needed a queen-sized bed.

"Tucker," she said, her lips offering an air kiss he meant to catch. "Come here. Now. Please."

She reeled him in. This woman had him by the balls, and he knew it. His breath hitched up his throat. He moved as fast as that moonbeam to her side, his hand instantly cupping second base, thumbing one peaked nipple through the silky fabric of her bra, his other hand curled possessively at the nape of her neck.

"Melissa," he breathed, his body one giant, throbbing hunger for her. All of her. "Why?" he asked, his brain searching for the other half of that important question he could no longer remember.

"Because I love you, Tucker Chase, and I want you. Tonight and always." Her voice quavered with need. "Especially now, Tuck. Right now."

"And I want you," he admitted. "But why now? Why me? God, are you sure about any of this?" *Because you're scaring the hell out of me with this quick change in direction. What's really going on? How can you possibly love me?*

"No," she admitted huskily. "I'm not sure of anything. I thought I was. I thought if I controlled everything around me, I'd never have to lose anyone again, but..."

That cooled his jets. Enlightenment struck him like a line drive to second base. That was why he'd gotten the continual push and shove from this woman, the come-hither come-on always followed by the quick reverse gears and the leave-me-the-hell-alone routine. Tucker stilled, his throat gone dry but his eyes most assuredly opened. He should've known.

Life had dealt Melissa one helluva knockout punch when it took her husband the way it did. All this time, she'd been fighting to catch her balance. That was why she hadn't let Tucker get too close. It wasn't that she didn't want him. It was her need to make sure he was safe and accounted for before she gave her heart away again. Poor Melissa had been trying to control everyone and everything in her life so what happened to Brady wouldn't happen again.

*It's called hypervigilance, you dumbass,* he scolded himself. Most soldiers, Marines, airmen, and sailors came home with it in one form or another if they'd been in combat. Why couldn't their wives catch it? They sure as hell suffered along with their men.

Tucker didn't want to hear a single word about What's-His-Name, not now. He didn't want another man in this sacred place, but the damned ghost had to go. The words had to be said.

"Brady's not coming back, baby," he told her gently, like she didn't already know.

A sad whimper lifted up her throat. "I... I know but..."

*Smart move, Chase. You killed the mood.*

Those luscious breasts heaved. She swallowed hard, chewing her lip. "Brady's dead. I really do know that. He's... he's really gone, but I tried, Tuck. I tried so-o-o hard to make him live, but he left me anyway, and you... and you..." She burrowed into him, her ear to his chest and his nose in her hair. "You deserve someone better than a crazy woman like me."

He fell for her all over again. There was no way in hell he deserved better than her because there was no one better—or kinder—or more gracious. He was the sinner, not this woman who'd come halfway around the world to help refugees. He wrapped her up in his arms and laid her down on their skimpy bed by the creek.

She collapsed into him, quaking with grief. "He died, Tuck. And I'm glad he's not suffering anymore, but..." A hiccup wrenched out of her. "I'm sorry. I know you don't want to hear about Brady, but I miss him every single day."

He couldn't speak, could only enfold Melissa against his heart while she shattered in his arms and wept for her dead husband—the first boy she'd fallen in love with. It wasn't the wailing of so many other women worldwide, though. It was more the sobbing acceptance of a woman who'd been strong for too long, who was finally letting her guard down. Finally coming to grips and letting love seep back in to her valiant heart.

Awareness trickled into his hard head. Maybe that was all she'd needed this past year, him to help shoulder the load, to act like a wingman and carry her when things got too hard for her, instead of always trying to impress her to get her attention. Instead of acting like an insecure ass. He'd wasted a lot of time feeling threatened by a dead man.

Tucker gulped at his flaming arrogance. Yeah, he'd gotten sick and tired of *Brady this* and *Brady that*, but all this woman had wanted was someone in her corner who understood the fire she'd walked through. Someone just as strong and brave and...

*I am such a moron.*

So what if Brady's ghost hung around? He was entitled to watch over the woman he'd loved when he was alive. Correction. Whom he still loved. Brady McCormack was one of the good guys. He had to have been, if Melissa loved him. Two hard-assed warriors watching over her for the rest of her life couldn't be so bad.

"Don't be sorry," Tucker murmured softly against her ear, striving to be that better man she needed and not just an arrogant tough guy who thought he knew it all. "Never be sorry for honoring your husband, Melissa. Of course you miss him. You should. Who wouldn't miss their first love? Brady McCormack was a hero through and through. You tell the world about him. Tell me. I'll listen. We'll never forget him together." He blinked away the moisture blurring the vision in his one good eye. Damn it, he was starting to like Brady McCormack. Who would've thought?

"I've been so foolish. So scared to live."

"You've got a funny way of being scared to live, baby. Look at you. You came to a foreign country to help others. That doesn't say scared to me."

She blinked hard, struggling for composure.

He tried again. "It's life, Melissa. Just life. You can't control it. None of us can. Bad things are still going to happen. Life's a risk and a rush and a downer, all in the same day—hell, sometimes in the same five minutes. It's a ten-second ride on some bull named Daisy, and it's a sweet baby boy named Deuce. It's a flag flying half-mast at Arlington and the same one waving high and proud at Quantico. You've got to grab life by the horns and not miss a single second of it. Keep moving forward, even when it knocks you down and stomps on you. Get up again. Don't be afraid to live because of what happened in the past.

Trust me to love you for the rest of your life. Come live it with me."

She wept until her voice turned ragged and soft, and he kissed every tear off her cheeks and every whimper off her lips, so grateful for the tremendous heart of his woman.

A glitter of fireflies had lifted up from the reeds and hovered over the shallow end of the creek, the reflections in the water creating a magical space and time where dreams might really come true.

"You rode a bull named Daisy?" she asked, her voice small and tired.

*Aw, shit. Of everything he'd said, she had to catch that.*

He sighed, mostly at his big mouth for revealing yet another moment of supreme stupidity. "Yeah. Two-day leave. A couple of us guys took in the sights at the Dallas stockyards. One of us thought we were tougher than Daisy."

"While you were in the Navy?"

"We were SEALs by then." *Cocky, know-it-all, tougher-than-shit SEALs.* "One of the guys handling the stock bragged no one could ride Daisy, not even us."

"Why name a bull Daisy?"

"Good question, but that bugger sure didn't like it. He was the meanest SOB behind the rails."

"And you were the meanest on the other side of the rails. Let me guess. You took the dare?" Melissa leaned back enough to look Tucker in the eye. "Seriously?"

He couldn't lie. "I never said I was smart, babe. Younger then, but yeah, it was the longest ten seconds of my life."

"Did you get hurt?" Of course she would ask that. Empathy ran through Melissa like the lost vein of gold in the Sierras.

"Just my pride. Old Daisy put me on my ass before he kicked up his heels, then he spun around a couple times like he was part tornado, and came at me with his horns. I swear they were ten feet long and sharp as sin."

"Are you done taking dares, Tucker Chase?" She took his breath and all of his heart away with that quiet question. Why did it feel as if he were on the edge of a monumental precipice, staring death—and life—in the eye again? Maybe taking the biggest dare of all?

He gave her what she needed to hear. "Yes, ma'am, I am. With you I am."

Tucker shoved out of his boots and pants. He pulled his shirt over his head and tucked it into a pillow for Melissa's head. With infinite tenderness, he gathered her into his arms and undressed her with the reverence of a monk. This was the right woman. Finally. He meant to make her his slowly. Tenderly.

All the way...

# Chapter Seventeen

She loved his mouth. The smoldering taste of him lifted goosebumps up from her skin like a magician with a wand lifted playing cards from his deck. He commanded her soul with a brush of his whiskered lips, or the slick heat of his tongue over the seam of her mouth, so insistent and gentle and demanding.

Nearly ruthless. He'd framed her head, his forearm at one side, his palm cupping the other while he took control, his body a wall of sheer muscle. So warm. So Tucker.

He was her exact opposite and her one true complement. The male. The dominant. The alpha protector. She would always be the female half of the equation, the nurturer and the bearer of his children, the willing accomplice to all his craziness. His anchor. And she loved him. She didn't want him any other way.

He held her immobile while he nibbled at her lips and explored her mouth. The farther his tongue ventured, the harder her stomach and that deeper, other part of her anatomy clenched. Her womb. Need for him flickered into a voracious appetite, then hunger. She meant to take it easy on him. The poor guy *was* black and blue and bruised all over. He still couldn't open one of his eyes, and she was fairly sure he might have a broken rib, but this man... she'd wanted him this way for far too long, and honestly, he didn't seem to mind her hands wandering over him.

Skin to skin wrought waves of sensual sensations over her naked body. Shivers raced up the inside of her thighs, up her spine, and over her shoulders. She arched as his palm covered her breast, his thumb strumming her nipple while he made love to her mouth. Her fingers tunneled into his thick, black hair, holding his head.

She'd expected a wild and crazy rush of hot, heavy sex, not gentle lovemaking so deliberate and slow that she ached for more. Desire dripped from her core, needing him to extinguish the flames he'd lighted, but he took his time. Was he doing this to torture her on purpose? Did he know he held her in the palms of his hands—that she was on the verge of combusting?

He drove her insane with his delicious mouth, her lips bruised with pleasure before he trailed a liquid line of molten lava straight down her centerline to her full breasts. The sound of his groans of satisfaction when he covered one nipple with his wickedly warm mouth sparked a surprisingly wanton side of her. She wanted him to taste all of her. Her knees parted, not waiting for encouragement.

His whiskered face crinkled into a smile against the tender skin of her breast. "Tell me what you want, baby," he growled, his breath moist and hot and melting her to her core. More sizzle.

She could barely whisper, "You. Inside of me. Now."

Another smile grazed her nipple, but the man was taking his time and making a feast out of her while he dallied. He made love languidly, deceiving her yet again while his fingers wandered lower. Lower.

Melissa arched her back, needing him—there. Trembling with a desperate appetite to be loved. "Please," she begged, her voice tight and needy, her body on fire. "You're torturing me."

"Not yet I'm not," he whispered, his mouth at her ear again and his fingers working magic. "I'm not going to rush this. I've waited too long." He strummed her most feminine desires until she was taut with need, lifting her butt off the ground with lust while he took possession of her mouth again. "Is this what you want, baby? Is this what you need?"

"More," she breathed into his lips, aching for him.

"Soon," he whispered, thrusting his tongue deeper, pushing her closer to the edge.

*Enough!* She bucked him off and rolled him to his back, straddling his hips, and thrilled at the surprise written on his rugged face. She'd put it there. He might have expected a nun because she'd certainly portrayed herself as such over the past year. Not anymore.

"You want to play?" she taunted, the curtain of her hair creating a secret world of just him and her.

Black eyebrows lifted, then dipped to a salacious, smoldering *V*. "Woman, I'm not playing," he growled, a tremor of danger in his tone as his palms gripped her, his fingers splayed over her butt and his thumbs digging into her hips. "Keep teasing me like that and I'm going to spank this bare ass of yours. Trust me. I play for keeps."

Ah! Her entire body clenched with arousal. Her sweet patient lover had just turned into a tiger. She groaned at the notion of being turned over his knee. How dare he? But, *ahhhhh. How dare he...*

She let the pleasure of the spicy threat shift up her spine while every muscle southward clenched in anticipation, and she could wait no more. With a quick whimper, she plunged her body onto his, impaling herself, filling her tight female core with the rough friction of him. A needy moan lifted up from her gut. He fit tight, deep, and right where she'd wanted him.

With her hands pressed to his chest for balance, she lifted up on her knees to view the advantage she had while she still had it. Wide and muscular, she could barely straddle him. Dark, coarse hairs sprinkled his chest before they narrowed into a line down his belly and below. Eternally cocky, he seemed coiled and ready to pounce. His neck was thick, and the fingers kneading her backside were rough and callused.

Tucker Chase was danger in its most primal degree. Deep. Dark. Damaged with all she still didn't know. Sensually, sinfully wicked. Less gentleman. More bad boy. And all hers.

His fingertips fluttered on her bare bottom. "Don't stop now," he urged, his eyes narrowed and black with lust.

She had to say it before her heart burst. "I love you, Tuck. I love you so much."

He growled out a delicious, "You have no idea how much that pleases me," and set the rhythm, his hands on her hips holding her in place while she rode.

She knew it then. Brady might've been her first, but Tucker would be her last.

He couldn't take his eyes off of her, not even if he tried. From the sway of her curvaceous hips to the swing and bounce of her plump breasts, she was everything he needed and more than he deserved. A goddess of silken honey with a hint of tease. Ambrosia and manna to a dying man lost too long in the desert. She was rain on parched lips, life-giving, life-saving rain, and sunshine pouring down on him.

And she loved him. He'd known it before she'd ever said it, before she'd stepped one foot out of her clothes. It was written in the moon glow in her eyes. The tender lilt in her sexy voice. The blatant come-hither dare in the tilt of her chin. He let her play, knowing full well he'd never be able to live if he let her go.

Just before her legs stiffened, just before she climaxed without him, he tucked her into his chest and rolled her over. He seated himself deep inside her sweet body, home at last, and not going to forget this perfect moment in a million years.

She moaned and writhed beneath him as he began their ascent again slowly, then built up to the sweetest... highest... pinnacle of sexual glory. He gave her his all when her muscles contracted around him, a glove so tight he felt every last vibration thrumming through her fierce, feminine body. The rumble of every delightful moan she uttered, every last aftershock clutching him.

He suffered the roar in his heart as stars burst over, around, and through him. Lightning and thunder filled the air and he felt like a god at the power of his coming. Never had he soared so high and been so humbled at the same time. He owed it all to Melissa.

She hadn't screamed like other women, but groaned, her heels dug into the backs of his thighs, grinding against him for every scintillating touch. When he was certain she'd finished round one, that she was safely back to earth and her ten-second ride complete, he bowed his forehead to hers, his unruly bangs flopping over her face and into her eyes. He kissed the tip of her pert nose, breathing hard, but not quite ready to break into two halves yet. One was so much better. He would live inside of her forever if there were a way. God knew he wanted to. This was what he'd been missing. This woman right there.

"Mine. All mine," he vowed. "You're all mine, and I'm never letting you go."

The sassy woman had the nerve to giggle in his face. "Who says I'd leave if you were dumb enough to let me?"

He'd lowered his body to her side before he saw the teardrops clinging to her lashes. "I love you, woman," he ground out, his heart suddenly stuck in his throat at the gift she'd freely given him. Men were such base creatures, inclined to rut like animals and content to live like pigs. But Melissa sparked a need deep in his core to be a better man. To protect her with every beat of his heart and every breath of his worthless life. To love this woman in the way she needed to be loved. "Don't cry."

She ran the back of her finger under one eye, wiping a tear. "I can't help it. I'm..." She gulped. "...happy. I never thought it could be like this."

He fought the urge to ask her if he was better than Brady, but tugged her under his chin and against his heart where she belonged instead. He didn't need to know which of her lovers were better. It didn't matter. He had her now.

Tucker drew Melissa into his arms, her back to his front, and they talked for hours by the side of the creek. No subject was taboo. He answered her questions about Nicole, and he didn't mind hearing about Brady and their short, tragic marriage. How they'd honeymooned in Cancun. How much he'd loved his mom and dad. How he'd doted on Melissa, and how hard it had been for him to come home a lesser man.

"The thing is, he was still my Brady even though he could barely move," she said quietly. "He told me to file for divorce when he first came back, that I needed to find someone better and let him go, but I couldn't. I wouldn't. I loved him, Tucker. I'm sorry if I'm rambling on about this, but I loved my husband. I truly did."

He kissed her bare shoulder, trailing a path up her neck to her ear, somehow the second luckiest guy in the world because of Melissa. "Brady was a good troop," he murmured at her earlobe. "Trust me. I never met the guy, but I'll bet he's still on duty. He's still looking down on you, baby. He's got your six. Why wouldn't he be? That's what I'd be doing."

She shivered. "I think you're right. There have been times I was sure I felt him near me."

"See? What'd I tell you? Jarheads don't know how to quit, even when they're dead. They're dumb like that. He's still hanging close, making sure you're in good hands." Tucker clenched his fingers around her breasts to make sure she knew he had a good hold on her.

Melissa pulled his arms tighter around her. A deep sigh escaped her body. "This is crazy, huh? Me talking about my husband after we just made love."

He lowered his nose to the sensual crook of her neck, that tender spot where he was lost in blonde tangles and soft skin, and he planted a kiss. The warmth of her lush body against his was working its magic. She had to know he was ready for round two. "I don't know about that. Most people go through life and never find the right person. You've found two of us. I'm proud he took good care of you for me."

"Me too," she said on a long sigh.

The fireflies had drifted away, but the moon smiled down behind them, its reflection glimmering in the ripples in the creek. Tucker tossed a bug he'd caught walking over the poncho into the water. Immediately, a foot-long silvery devil breached the surface and gulped the insect down before it could drown. A life for a life. The circle of life. Just plain life...

Melissa giggled. There was that little-girl quality again coming to the surface. He nestled back into her neck. "How big of a wedding do you want? Are we talking the National Cathedral or the White House for a venue?"

She rubbed her cheek against his forehead. "Small. Just you and me and our closest friends."

"Huh. That won't be very small. I'm a Navy guy, remember? I belonged to a fleet, and I'll bet your parents are dying to show you off. You'll be a beautiful bride. They'll want to put you in all the papers. McCormacks will, too."

"But it will be our wedding," she emphasized. "What do you want?"

Good question. Good timing. Tucker turned her to face him and covered those pretty lips with his mouth, needing her to know that it all started there and then. He meant to live for her. Every day. "You tell me," he said as he eased away from her wet lips. "I'm just a guy. What do I know about weddings?"

She rubbed the tip of her nose to his. "You know you love me."

"I do," he agreed wholeheartedly.

Her brows raised. "And you promise to love me forever."

"I do," he agreed again, his heart climbing back up his throat.

"You may now kiss the bride." She lowered her lashes and pinched her lips together, ready for that kiss.

"Did we just get married?" he teased just before he covered her mouth again.

She mumbled, "Uh-huh."

Enough said. He rolled her onto her back and thrust himself back into her slick, secret place. When she groaned at the first thrust, he asked, "Do you promise to love, honor, and obey me?"

Melissa looked up at him with moonlight in her eyes. She clamped onto him with her core muscles, surprising him with her womanly strength. "I do love you, but I've never been good at that obedience thing. I can't promise that, but love and honor? Oh, yes."

"Listen up." He thrust again. Harder. Needing to brand her, deeper and deeper. She needed to be sore and marked and his. All his. "Exception noted. Do you promise to bear all my future children and light my fire?"

She squirmed, her fingers gripping his chest muscles and her temperature rising. "Like I'm lighting your fire now?"

He poked her yet deeper. "Stick to the vows, woman," he ordered playfully, his heart back on the line. "Just say 'I do' or 'I don't.'"

Another wiggle and a moan and an, "Umm, yes, I do-o-o." She drove him crazy the way she fit him like a glove, clenching so tight, he nearly lost track of what he meant to say. "I'll bear all your children, and I'll love the son you have now, and I will most definitely strive to light your fire every day, sir."

*Sir?* He liked the sound of that, but he knew better. This woman was no simpering weakling without a mind of her own. She was tough. From this moment forth, Melissa would be the first and most important boss in his life. She'd forever rule, and he'd be thankful to serve her. To tickle and please her. To prove himself worthy of her in every way.

He got lost in kissing and nuzzling her ticklish neck for a moment before he said, huskily, "I now pronounce you mine, Melissa McCormack Chase. All mine. Forever and ever—"

"Amen," she breathed.

# Chapter Eighteen

Despite the raucous birds in the trees that should have awakened her, Melissa still slept. Tucker kept his arms protectively around her at daybreak. She'd turned into him during the night, her breath on his collarbone and her soft bare breasts mashed against his chest. Sweetest thing for a guy like him to wake up to, the pliant body of the sleeping woman he loved more than life itself lying soft and warm in his arms.

They hadn't gone back to the fireside, just lingered out of sight. Isaiah was already up and about. Tucker could hear him breaking camp, but Tucker wanted one more stolen moment. He pressed his lips to Melissa's forehead, loving the salty taste of her mingled with the scent of him on her claimed body.

It would've been heaven in paradise if the hairs on the back of his neck hadn't lifted on end. If acid hadn't poured into his gut. He covered the back of her head with his man-sized palm, his nerves on full alert and his eyes on the jungle. *"Isaiah,"* he called to his right-hand man.

*"Already on 'em,"* came the quiet affirmative. *"Four big guys with face paint closing in on our position. Not Vietnamese Army regulars though. These guys are quiet as shadows. Might be Americans—they're big enough. Stay down."*

Not going to happen. Tucker shifted to one knee at Melissa's side, his left hand holding her flat to the ground, his right swinging his rifle into his arm. He dressed hurriedly. Frightened deep, dark eyes riveted to his. "We've got company," he whispered in her ear. "Get dressed. I need you up on your knees, baby. Get ready to run."

"Not if you want to live," a gruff male American voice rumbled at his six.

Tucker rolled to his butt shielding Melissa, his rifle dead in the center of a face smeared with black and green paint. This guy had gotten too close too fast. Who the hell did that? "Back off, Siegel!"

"Who the hell's Siegel?"

Tucker blinked, not believing his eyes. It was Maverick Carson standing just feet away, his eyes black and his breathing heavy, his rifle aimed at Tucker's head. "Damn you, Chase, you're supposed to be long gone by now. Lower your weapon."

Relieved, Tucker did just that while three more of Stewart's finest, Taylor Armstrong, Gabe Cartwright, and Ky Winchester, emerged from the greenery. All junior agents and all suited up with body armor and enough weaponry that they looked like they were going to war and prepared to win. When Tucker lowered his weapon, they did the same.

"Hi guys," Melissa said brightly.

"Morning, ma'am," Maverick returned calmly.

"You guys mind?" Tucker asked, nodding slightly to the future Mrs. Chase still wrapped up in that flimsy poncho. At least the ponchos weren't see-thru, but these guys needed to turn their backs so she could get dressed. No one but no one got to see her lovely naked body.

Ky and the Fearsome Threesome chuckled, coughed politely, and complied like the gentlemen they were. Melissa scurried into her clothes. Cutest sight ever.

The presence of Stewart's men instantly brought a measure of calm. Carson, Armstrong, and Cartwright were somewhat revered in ex-military circles and reverently referred to as the Fearsome Threesome. All three had served on a failed purple operation in Kandahar, Afghanistan. Camp Leatherneck. Helmand Province. Lashkar Gah. Tucker knew well the cost of confronting their target, a psychotic Taliban cleric and his army. Gabe had left the better part of a leg behind. Maverick had lost his baby brother.

All were heroes, but it was Taylor Armstrong who'd singlehandedly carried Cartwright on his back and dragged Carson out of harm's way. Taylor, as quiet as he was, led his band of Marine Corps brothers back to the cleric's hideaway in the mountains days later. They smoked the Taliban's ass that day. Burned the cruel cleric back into the hell he'd crawled out from. Taylor should've gotten the Medal of Honor for all he'd done that day. *Shit. Shouldn't they all?*

Tucker had been on that hillside with them. He knew exactly what had happened. He'd survived the same ambush. He'd seen the bravery of all troops in action. But he had his own share of survivor's guilt. His best buddy died on that same hillside. All he'd brought back was the body in a bag.

"Hey, Tucker." Ky Winchester grinned when Melissa was at last presentable, another welcome sight. He'd survived his own brand of hell in Afghanistan at the hands of a madman known to torture American soldiers for the sport of it. But there Ky was, bright-eyed, married, and happily in the employment of Stewart. The guy had a definite knack for pulling only the bravest and the best into his TEAM. It was too bad they were mostly Marines.

"Ky. Maverick." Tucker held out a hand in heartfelt greeting. "Good to see you, Gabe. You too, Taylor." SEALs would've been better, but these ex-Marines were a welcome sight.

A round of quiet back slapping ensued. "Morning, Mrs. McCormack." Maverick nodded with a quick two-finger salute to Melissa. "Sorry if we scared you, ma'am, but we're your ticket home. Hoverboat's waiting on the Mekong. We don't have much time. Get ready to move."

"She stays with me," Tucker growled, his hand shackling her upper arm.

"She stays with me, too," Isaiah announced as he stepped out from the jungle. "You do know you were followed by Vietnamese regulars, don't you?"

"'S okay," another familiar American voice rumbled from the direction of the creek. Damned if Mark Houston didn't clear the thicket, decked out in body armor and carrying an arsenal the same as the rest of his team. He stood there like a wall, his boots spread, his hands on his hips, and a bemused grin on his face. "I popped yellow smoke to their rear. They're following it at the moment, not us. That gives us maybe thirty minutes to clear out. Melissa. Alex sent us to get you out of Vietnam. Now."

Tucker tugged Melissa into his side. "I can't leave yet," he said firmly. "Neither can you. Siegel's running a child sex-slave business. I'm almost sure of it. We've got to get back into his camp and rescue the girls he's keeping there."

"He's what?" Melissa asked, her voice edged with disbelief. Her eyes widened. "How do you know? Is that what those...? Oh, God. Tucker. That's why all those little girls are there, isn't it? That's why the separate camp. Those poor babies."

He pulled her back under his arm. Melissa hadn't seen the world like he had. It was no wonder she hadn't recognized Siegel's operation for what it really was. "I'm going back," he declared evenly. Mark Houston could like it or lump it.

"Are you certain of this?" Mark asked, the lines of his face taut with worry.

"I am," Isaiah piped up. "Hey, Mark. I've made contact with one of the women guarding the girls. She's not talking to me, but I've been in her mind. Siegel's running girls by truck from Cambodia through the Mekong. He links up with his contact near the south end of the delta. Contact Alex. If you're quick enough, he can run an intercept before these girls get sold and are gone for good."

Mark shot an appraising stare at the FBI agent on loan. His brows narrowed. Tucker knew Mark had been with Ky Winchester the day they'd rescued Isaiah from certain death. He'd seen the two psychics in action, Eden and Isaiah, He'd witnessed their direct link, their uncanny ability first hand. He, more than anyone else on The TEAM, believed in Isaiah's power to do the impossible. Still, he hesitated. "Are you positive? Alex will be pissed if we deviate from our main objective."

"Your main objective will always be children." Melissa stepped forward. "Alex will understand."

Tucker held his breath. Stewart did tend to stick his neck out when it came to kids. He and his team had single-handedly gone after the Black Dragon Syndicate years earlier and saved hundreds of orphans in the process, all without receiving one dollar of compensation. How he'd managed to keep his head above fiscal waters amazed Tucker.

"And then what?" Mark asked, his voice ominously low. "You need to understand that these girls probably weren't kidnapped by Siegel. Their parents and families most likely sold them into this ugly business. Once we rescue them, what do we do, take them home where their parents will surely sell them again? Siegel's not the source of the problem. Simple economics is. These people are dirt poor. They're doing what they can to survive."

The same old question. *Do I stay or do I go? Do I follow my heart or do I turn a blind eye and pretend I saw nothing when I know damned well what I saw? And what about Deuce?*

"Then go," Tucker spat, his mind made up. "Siegel might not be the problem, but he's sure as hell willing to capitalize on human suffering, isn't he? Shit, Houston, I can't save the world, but I can save these..." He glared at Isaiah. *"How many?"*

The answer came quickly back quickly. *"Twenty-one girls, Tucker."*

"I can save these twenty-one little girls. What if those were your girls were in Siegel's camp, huh? How can you be so sure those girls' parents sold them? Who even cares how they got there?"

"Damn, you really care, don't you?" Maverick asked, one brow lifted as if he was considering the option. "I'm starting to like you, Chase."

Mark blew out a soft sigh through pursed lips. "We give a shit, which is why we're here, and you don't have to tell me how bad little girls in these countries have it. I'm just trying to save them from more of the same. Let me check with a friend of mine in Phnom Penh. He runs a safe house there for girls caught up in the sex trade. He might be able to help."

That floored Tucker. "You have a friend in Cambodia? You speak Khmer?"

Houston's dark brown eyes twinkled. "Why would you think that? He's an American. Ex-Marine. He still thinks he has to save the world, too. Ring a bell?"

Tucker had no answer to that smart-assed question. Some men were hard-wired to protect the innocent. He was one of them. Go figure.

Mark turned ninety degrees, his finger at the earpiece in his right ear and speaking in terse, short clips. All Tucker caught was, "You heard me. Twenty-one."

*"Melissa's proud of you,"* Isaiah whispered. *"Look at her."*

Tucker glanced down at the genteel lady under his arm, the one with the soft glow in her blue eyes and the smile on her face. "Don't worry. We'll get this figured out. We won't leave 'em," he told her gruffly.

She lifted to her tiptoes and graced his lips with one feathery angel kiss. "I know you won't, Tucker."

*Wow.* A guy would do somersaults for that kind of a smile. And then some...

"I just talked with Rory and Zack," Mark muttered, one hand raking through his dark head of hair. "They're manning our exfil out of here. It'll be a tight squeeze with one hovercraft, but Zack knows a guy. I called my buddy. He's got an underground railroad set up between Vietnam, all the way to Thailand. He's standing by to take the girls. He'll make sure they don't go back into the business."

"Your buddy got a name?"

Mark nodded. "You know him. David Tao."

"No shit?" Tucker hadn't seen that one coming. "He quit working for Stewart?"

"Not exactly," Gabe muttered, a hint of mischief in his eyes. "This was David's idea, but Alex is backing him. It's a two-year assignment for now. David and his family live in Phnom Penh. His kids are having a ball with the whole cultural exchange thing."

"Didn't he adopt one of those little orphan girls from the Black Dragon Syndicate?"

Gabe nodded. "Get ready. Alex is thinking of going international. You want in at the ground level? I'm sure he could use someone like you."

"Guys," Mark hissed, "stow the chatter. We're on the clock, remember? Our biggest problem will be getting those girls out of Siegel's camp and all the way to the border of Svay Reing. It's not far, but it will be tough going with a bunch of frightened girls."

"You do know there are Cambodian rebel forces between here and there," Tucker added.

"Understood, but most of them are farther south in the delta. David's got friends who'll be looking out for us along the river closer to the border."

"Then why are there Vietnamese Army patrols in the area if the rebels aren't this far north?" Isaiah questioned.

"My guess is they're after your buddy, Siegel." Mark turned to his men. "Guys? Your thoughts on throwing a wrench in the sex trade while we're here?"

Maverick leveled a truly malevolent eye at Tucker. "I've pissed Alex off before. I'm good with whatever you decide, Mark."

Gabe pointed a finger at Maverick. "Yeah. What he said."

Taylor, looking the part of the stoic American Indian with his long, black braid, his arms folded over his chest, nodded. "It's what we do, isn't it?"

"Then it's settled. What's the plan, Chase?" Mark asked, one hand on his hip. Interestingly, the rest of his guys assumed the same pose, the jokers.

Tucker studied his options. The plan had been simple when it was just him, Isaiah, and Melissa. Rescue the girls and run like hell. Okay, so it wasn't a great plan, but it would've worked. At the least, it would've given the girls a fighting chance.

But Mark had proposed a no-kidding, viable solution to the real problem. The girls could still go home to their families if they wanted to, but they'd be safe if they chose to stay with David Tao. Mark had solid connections, and he'd brought enough manpower with him to get the job done right. Better yet, David Tao could get help for the girls after they were rescued. Mark's plan came with a little more vision.

"May I propose a solution?" Isaiah raised his hand like a kid in school.

"Yeah, what?" Tucker twisted to look at his partner. Isaiah had changed the last few days, his eyes a little darker, the laugh lines etched a little deeper. But he still wasn't a covert operator, and he, along with Melissa, had no business being caught up in the middle of what might be a tough battle.

"Let Mark and his team rescue the girls while you and I get Deuce." Tucker could've hugged the kid. Finally. He got Deuce's name right. "We can be back before the hovercraft leaves. Then we'll all go visit David at the same time." *"Unless you go Rambo on me and kill your kid's stepfather."*

*"Vinnie isn't Deuce's stepfather, damn it. I'm not dead yet!"*

Tucker caught the disparaging glimmer in Isaiah's eye, the whispered, *"See what I mean? Vinnie is Deuce's stepfather whether you like it or not. That doesn't mean he's adopted him, Tucker, only that he married Nicole. Think about it. If you can't control your temper, you might lose your son for good."*

Sobering.

"What's up with you guys?" Mark asked, his tone suspicious. "What's going on? Are you...? Damn,

Chase. Are you psychic, too? Are you talking behind our backs?"

Tucker glared at Mark, daring him to say it again. "Isaiah's plan is plausible, but still risky," he muttered through gritted teeth, not willing to admit to any such thing as psychic ability, although it was fairly obvious. "There's a problem, though."

Mark headed him off at the pass. "Don't even go there, Chase. There is no way Melissa doesn't leave with us. Understand that right here and now. She goes with me while Taylor, Gabe, and Maverick proceed to rescue the girls. Sound good?"

All four TEAM agents nodded affirmative like trained marionettes, but Tucker hit the roof. "No way in hell. She stays with me."

Mark shifted his entire wall of a body toward Tucker and Isaiah, an outright threat. "This isn't open for discussion, Chase. I'm not running a democracy. I'm taking her out while I still can. We'll wait at the hovercraft to rendezvous with the rest of you guys, but if things get hot before you make it back, she'll be safely out of the frag zone. Isn't that what you really want?"

It made sense. Tucker just hadn't planned on telling her goodbye. Not this way. Not this soon. "Yes," he admitted, tightening his hold on her just the same.

"Besides, Tuck." Isaiah just kept opening his big mouth. "Those little girls will feel safer with a woman once the guys get them away from Siegel's camp and link up with Mark. Let Mark take Melissa, so she can help those twenty-one girls while we go get your son. It's the best solution."

*Shit. Just shit.* A glimmer lifted at the corner of Tucker's still swollen eye. He wanted Melissa and Deuce safe, not just those girls. "Fine. Good plan. I... I wasn't thinking. I—" His gaze dropped into two pools of the purest blue love.

"It's okay, Tuck." Melissa winked, her palms flat to his chest, but not pushing him away like before. Her fingers were knotted in his shirt this time, tugging to stay with him, and God, he wanted her to. He wanted this ugly business behind them so he could start living again. So he could breathe. He just couldn't take the chance that she'd get hurt. He stowed his overly possessive streak, set his need to be the dominant alpha aside, and he let Mark step up to do what was smart.

"You're hurting," Melissa said tenderly. "Your eye's still swollen, and I know something's wrong with your side that you're not telling me about. Your rib's cracked or broken. I can hear the hiss when I listen to your heart. And you're limping."

Tucker chuckled, his hand trapping hers over his heart. Wasn't that just like her to be worried about him? He kissed the center of her forehead. "This is nothing. I'll be fine, babe."

"Don't worry. I'll take care of him, ma'am," Isaiah promised.

She looked to Mark, her fingers interlocked with Tucker's like vines that wanted more time to grow together. "You promise you'll wait for Tucker and Isaiah and Deuce? I won't leave without them."

"You know we will," Mark's head bobbed as he answered. "We never leave a man behind."

Tucker knew where Melissa needed to be, so he headed her off at the pass. As much as it galled him to let her go with another man, this particular guy was the one for the job. "Go with Mark, Melissa. He's right. This is about saving twenty-one little girls, not me. They'll need your help, and Mark's a good man. You can trust him."

She melted into his side, her arm around his waist. "I know that, Tuck. Just don't take too long."

He framed her face between his ragged hands, the hands that had taken life in the name of freedom and self-defense, the hands that didn't deserve to hold a creature so pure and noble.

She lifted up on her toes, wrapped her arms around his neck, and there, in front of God and a goodly portion of Stewart's almighty TEAM, she planted the wettest, sweetest kiss on his lips, murmuring as she did. "I love you, Tuck. Be careful."

He lifted her off her feet, needing more than just one stolen night in paradise. The world needed to take a break from avarice and greed and mayhem, damn it. Wars needed to stop. The power mongers, the pillagers, and every other brutal jerk out there needed to drop dead and let the planet heal for once.

Just so Tucker could stop worrying. So he could stay with her.

"I love you, babe," he whispered, easing her out of his arms and back to her feet. "Wait for me. I'll be coming home to you."

"I know you will," she said, tears glistening on her lashes. "I love you, Tuck. I'll be waiting."

And damned if he didn't let her go again.

# Chapter Nineteen

Two days later, Tucker and Isaiah made their way out of the jungle and through the rice paddies to Hồ Chí Minh City. Mark had hooked them up with earpieces, but there wasn't much in the way of chatter between the teams. Tucker wanted to talk with Melissa, not Mark. Besides, he had Isaiah. If anything went wrong with the planned extraction of the girls, or if Mark got waylaid for whatever reason, Tucker assumed his psychic buddy would tell him.

They hitched a ride the last thirty miles on the back of a wagon filled with assorted vegetables. By then, the night was the same as all the others: dark, humid, and sweltering. Isaiah took point, secured a room on the outskirts of the city, and reported in. Wouldn't you know? Stewart was still pissed.

"Twenty-one girls..." he hissed over the speakerphone.

Tucker ignored the blatant hostility aimed at him. The odd trick was that as ornery as Stewart could be, he commanded agents so loyal to him they'd die for the guy. He was the kind of leader who could literally lead his men into hell and they'd follow. Of course, he brought them home alive, too.

"You would've done the same, Boss," Isaiah piped up.

"Don't tell me what I would've done, Junior Agent." But Stewart took a breath, and Isaiah winked at Tucker. The conversation settled into a normal status report of precise details, who went where, and which guys were doing what.

"You haven't heard from Mark yet?" Tucker asked, his gut churning. "Not even after he left with Melissa?"

"Time out," Isaiah interrupted. "He and Melissa are already near Zach and Rory's location on the delta. They're both safe. I've been keeping track of everyone."

Tucker glared at his partner. *"That would've been good to know before now."*

"You can do that?" It was hard not to miss the incredulity in Stewart's voice.

"Sure, Alex. I've been tuned into Melissa since she was abducted. The link with her isn't as clear as I'd like, but I've always had a link with Ky Winchester."

That admission surprised Tucker. Isaiah, the mind reader, winked at him. "Ky doesn't believe he has psychic talent, Boss, but he does." *"Just like you,*

*Tucker.*" "He and the guys have already infiltrated Siegel's camp while Siegel's preoccupied fighting off the Vietnamese Army with what's left of his men."

"Wait." Tucker scowled. "Siegel's still alive?"

"Yes—at least that's what Ky believes. There's enough confusion in camp that Ky and the guys think they can sneak in and remove the girls before they're noticed. I'll continue to monitor the situation as it evolves."

An audible sigh of relief came over the line. "Keep me informed."

"Sure thing, Boss." There it was again, sublime obedience to Stewart from a guy who was supposed to be working for the FBI. How the hell did Stewart do it?

"Anything else?"

"We've got a bead on Deuce," Tucker offered, not sure Stewart cared about his kid any more.

"About that..." Stewart paused long enough to make Tucker nervous. "There's been a recent push by the authorities in Hồ Chí Minh City to locate and eliminate child slavery in the garment factories. The deplorable state of some of those places has gotten worldwide attention, and the UN is threatening sanctions if Vietnam doesn't clean up its act. Be careful. You may run into a police presence."

That was good to know. "Thanks for the heads-up," Tucker said sincerely.

"I assume you'll take Deuce out of the country with Mark's team?"

"That's the plan," Tucker replied, "unless you've got a better idea."

"I do if things go bad and you miss the connection."

"I don't miss connections unless all hell breaks loose, but go ahead. Whatcha got?"

The sound of fluttering drifted over the line. Possibly an old-fashioned *Rolodex*? Interesting. "Call this number. Ask for Smoke. He'll shelter you until you can get clear." Stewart rattled off a phone number.

"You're shittin' me. Smoke Montoya?" Tucker had to ask. It had been years since the guy had been last seen, so how the hell did Stewart know his phone number when the rest of the world wondered whether he was alive or dead? And to top it off, Stewart was nothing but a dumb jarhead. Why was he cozied up to a Navy SEAL hero?

"He owes me. Leave it at that," Stewart groused.

Could things get more bizarre? A Navy legend owed a Marine? Tucker scrubbed a rough hand over his face. The world was a pretty messed-up place when a Marine knew where a hero SEAL lived while no one else did.

"Are we done here?" Stewart asked, his tone edgy and impatient as usual.

"I asked her to marry me," Tucker announced. He might as well get that out in the open.

"Good. It took you long enough."

Oddly, that grumpy retort set Tucker's mind at ease. "I'll be in touch."

"Copy that." The line went dead.

"You should've kept me better informed," Tucker growled at his cocky partner.

"You never asked."

"I'm agent-in-charge. I don't have to ask."

"True, but until tonight there wasn't much to tell. Ky and the guys just got to Siegel's camp. Mark and Melissa just arrived at the hovercraft."

"And?" Tucker glowered, not buying this line of bullshit. The timing was off. Mark's guys should've gotten into Siegel's camp long ago and been gone by now.

"You're right, the timing is off," Isaiah readily agreed, "but the Vietnamese Army has Siegel's camp surrounded. Ky and the guys had to go through enemy lines. It took time."

"And now?"

"And now..." Isaiah paused, one finger to his temple. *"Melissa is safely aboard. Mark, too. Ky and the guys are advancing on the huts. The village is deserted except for a few of Siegel's people. Ky's afraid the girls are either dead or restrained, or they wouldn't have been left behind."*

"Out loud, Zaroyin. Is he sure the girls are there?"

Isaiah nodded. *"Yes. He and the guys have been watching the huts. They saw several women leave, but no girls. Why do you refuse to admit your talent? Don't you realize that your psychic ability might explain why you're good at everything you put your hand to?"*

Tucker gave Isaiah the evil eye. "Out. Loud."

The kid had the nerve to lift his chin in defiance. It was mild defiance, but a challenge nonetheless. *"Where we're going tomorrow morning, there will be no chance for verbal communication. Garment factories in these countries are noisy, dirty, and dangerous. Trust me. You'll need to use your talent if you expect to save Deuce. Say it with me. I am psychic."*

Tucker sneered. "Say it with me, Zaroyin. You're a dead man if you don't start following orders."

"You're a dead man if you don't start listening. Why are you so stubborn? This ability is a rare gift from the universe. Don't throw it away. Use it. Make the world a better place." His eyes glazed over. *"Tucker! They're under attack."*

It took more time getting through the Vietnamese Army patrols than expected. By afternoon of the second day, Melissa was exhausted, but glad to see Zack Lennox and Rory Dennison, two of Alex's best agents. She knew their wives and had been to their homes. They were a sight for her sad, tired eyes. The camouflaged hovercraft, too. Sitting low in the water and reeds along the riverbank, it sported two large upright fans at the rear of a long sleek cabin, and hopefully a hot water heater for a nice, warm shower.

"Melissa," Zack all but purred as he hoisted her out of the raft and aboard the hovercraft. Tall, muscular, and his head shaved close, his biceps barely rippled when he lifted her off her feet. "It's good to see you again. You're as pretty as ever."

She doubted that, but the man was a kind liar. "Thanks, Zack, but I know better." She tucked her dirty hair behind her ears, anxious for information. "Any word yet?"

"Nothing from Agent Chase, but our guys are entering the first hut now," Rory called out from what looked like the communication center in the open cabin, a set of earphones strapped over his head, his dark blue eyes somber and attentive. He'd married Ember, one of Alex's genius technical assistants, and they'd been happy ever since.

Melissa hurried to his side, along with Zack and Mark.

"Gunfire to the south of their location," Rory reported. "They've found five girls in the first hut, all chained by their ankles to the center post. All scared to death."

She took a seat alongside Rory, her heart climbing up her throat. "Can they break the chains?"

"They can pick those locks," Mark said matter-of-factly. He'd settled one knee to the floor at her side, listening to Rory. "Don't worry. They're prepared for all scenarios. They'll bring them out safely."

*Or die trying,* she thought. These men didn't know the meaning of quit. They thrived on the adrenaline rush of saving others. They were just like Tucker.

"Taylor's taking the first group out. He'll wait at a predetermined location. Second hut. Six girls. Same sorry condition as the last." Rory blew out a low hiss. "Ky's pissed. He's pretty certain one of them's been abused. She's going to need you, Melissa. Gabe's taking this group out."

"Are they resisting?" Mark asked.

"It doesn't sound like it. Ky's getting through to them," Rory breathed. "You know how he is with kids."

Ky had an uncanny knack with teenagers. On his off time, he worked with Kelsey Stewart at her home for wayward street kids in D.C. He was one of those rare guys who wasn't afraid to mix it up with some of the most misunderstood people in America—teenagers.

"Tell him there's food in the only hut with a wooden door," she told Rory. "It's to the west if they can get to them. They'll need to feed the girls if they can't make it back tonight."

Rory passed the word, then nodded at Melissa. "Ky says good to know. Is there water, too?"

"And bug spray."

Huts three and four revealed the same—frightened little girls, none older than twelve, Ky guessed.

"Stop frowning so hard," Zack teased. He'd taken the bench seat behind Rory, his big hands on his knees. "Agent Chase won't recognize you the next time he sees you. You're giving yourself wrinkles."

"This is so intense," she murmured, her fingers knitted tightly on her lap.

"But it's going smooth. These guys are good at what they do. Take a deep breath, Melissa. They'll be back here before you know it."

She tried to smile, but it was difficult with her heart stuck up high in her chest like it was. It felt as if she'd swallowed a rock.

"Maverick just hooked up with Gabe and Taylor. They've got all the girls," Rory said calmly. "One altercation. Some woman caught Ky in the act. He says to tell you he feels bad he had to smack her, but he doesn't feel too bad."

Melissa clamped her hand to her mouth. That might have been Kimmie. Things had happened so quickly, she hadn't thought to ask her about Tristan. He'd seemed a genuinely nice young man. Where was he now? With Simon? Or with that Jackman fellow?

Mark's warm hand settled on her shoulder. "Take it easy, Melissa. They're almost clear of the camp. We'll see them in a day or two if the girls cooperate with this exfil."

"Ky's still at the edge of the huts," Rory reported. "Rapid gunfire to the south. He's spotted two more kids. He can't leave them." Rory stilled, listening, no expression on his face while Melissa's heart pounded. Could it be Mimi and Peewee?

Rory cocked his head. "Maverick's taking the rest of the girls to safety, but Ky's going back in, Mark. He's got to."

"Understood," Mark replied evenly.

The cabin stilled. All of these men were fathers. They didn't have it in them to leave a child behind, but the tension turned palpable. Melissa ran her tongue over her dry top lip. Four men. Twenty-one traumatized girls. Now two more tiny children. How could a rescue of this proportion go smoothly?

"I should've stayed there," she murmured.

"Maverick just rejoined Ky," Rory said. "It's hard to hear Ky's transmission. All hell's breaking loose."

Melissa couldn't hold still. "No, no, no," she prayed, her hands to her temples. "Hurry, Ky. Save the kids. Get out of there."

"Rocket fire, Mark," Rory reported. "They've got incoming."

"Do they have the kids yet?" Melissa barked, her angst uncontrollable.

"Not yet," he replied evenly, not a hint of panic in his tone. "The two little ones ran for cover. They're scared. They're hiding from our guys."

"They'll be killed."

Mark's hand squeezed her shoulder. "Ky will get them, you'll see."

"Maverick just caught the little girl," Rory reported. "She's screaming but he's got her."

"Mimi," Melissa declared. "Tell him to call her Mimi. If it's her, using her name might settle her down."

Rory passed on the scant intel, his hand cupping his headset. Melissa clutched her forehead, willing Peewee to come to Ky. *Oh please, go to Ky, little guy. He'll keep you safe.*

"Maverick's retreating with the girl. She's quieted down, but Ky's going in after the boy."

Melissa leaned over Rory's shoulder. "Peewee. His name is Peewee. Where is he? In the main camp?"

Rory nodded, but he didn't speak.

"The farther he goes into camp, the more adults he'll run into. There are injured men there and they're all armed." Rory nodded again, still silent until Melissa couldn't take it anymore. "What's he doing? Does he have Peewee yet? Say something."

Rory turned to Melissa, a sheen of tears in his eyes, his gaze transfixed. Melissa's heart stopped at the tender compassion she read on his face. As calm and collected as this man had appeared, he was worried now. Panic rained down around her. *No. Not Peewee. Not Ky.*

At last Rory hissed and shook his head. "No, but that was damned close. Sorry. The little guy's crying. He's got a bloody bump on his head, but Ky's got him. Don't worry. He's bringing him in."

"Oh, thank God!" She collapsed on the bench opposite Zack, her heart wrung out and her forehead in her hands. Rory looked a little worse for wear, too.

He had a son he adored, Tyler. He had to have related personally with that frightened little Peewee. She could only imagine what those children were going through. "How do you guys do this? They all could've been killed."

"But they weren't," Mark said calmly. "Take it easy, Melissa. We've done this before."

"But... but..." She had no words. This was the kind of thing Tucker did every day. Save someone's life. Put himself in danger. Protect the innocent. Take ungodly chances that could get him killed, and she'd barely touched the tip of the iceberg. "Are you all crazy?" she had to ask, embarrassed with at the way she'd taken over and ordered Rory around. She'd turned into a maniac while these guys had handled themselves like pros during the extraction. "Why do you do this?"

Zack lifted his shoulders and grunted. "Someone has to."

# Chapter Twenty

Tucker couldn't sit still. "Who's attacking them?"

Isaiah held a palm up for silence, his gaze vacant. "Shhhhh. I'm reading Ky Winchester. There's... turmoil in the camp."

"For God's sake—!"

Isaiah blinked, shook his head, and fixed a stern stare at Tucker. "You need to be quiet. I'm working here. I can do a lot of things, but I can't be in two places at once."

Tucker stifled a comeback. He'd thought Isaiah meant Mark and Melissa were under attack, but this was about those little girls. He swallowed hard and kept his mouth shut, every nerve stretched to the breaking point. His fists clenched ready to fight. God help Siegel if he'd hurt those kids.

Isaiah closed his eyes, his face etched with worry. "I'm having trouble reading Ky. He's under serious stress, but..."

*But what?* Every nerve in Tucker's body reached out to Melissa, needing her to be strong no matter which way this rescue attempt went. He couldn't be with her, but she needed to understand. Sometimes, even the best men failed. They came back with empty arms or worse—body bags.

The longer Isaiah didn't speak, the harder it was for Tucker to think positive. He should've stayed to assist Stewart's men. He never should have listened to Mark Houston and left Melissa. *Damn it, Zaroyin. Talk to me.*

At last, Isaiah swayed, then dropped to the edge of the bed, his head in his hands, and his chest heaving. "Ky and the guys have the girls, them and a few others. They're on their way to the delta."

The air whooshed out of Tucker's lungs. He dropped to a knee at Isaiah's side. "You're right. I need to read minds like you do. Teach me. Now."

Isaiah shook his head before he flopped back onto the mattress, his arms spread wide. "Later," he whispered. "I'm beat. It takes energy to maintain a psychic link, and this one was tough."

It must've been tough. The kid's shirt was drenched with sweat and he looked pale. Tucker leaned over him, peering closer. "Are you okay? Can I get you anything?"

Isaiah had his eyes closed. "Sleep. I just need sleep."

The day was well gone by the time Ky and the Fearsome Threesome returned to the hovercraft. They'd not only rescued Mimi, Peewee, and the girls, but they'd also brought Dang and Tam with them. Melissa wept for joy at the sight of all those sweet, sad faces, as well as the sacrifice of those brave professionals. By then, the army patrols seemed to have moved on. Zack was able to run into the nearest village to purchase additional food and what clothing he could find for the girls.

Once his men and their charges were safely aboard, Mark and his men turned into medics and cooks, taking care of the needs of the many. Zack had crazy skills in the kitchen. He dug in and whipped up a meal of sticky rice, spring rolls, and a platter of Thit Bo Xao Dau, a beef and green bean dish.

The sweet girl who'd been assaulted clung to the others, avoiding eye contact and attempts to comfort her. Melissa wanted to mother them all, but they needed each other more than a strange American woman, so she backed off and accepted them on their terms.

In America, this would've been a crucial time to collect evidence. There'd be specific emergency room protocol, a rape kit, and a detailed medical examination, but in third-world countries rife with child sex trafficking, the chance of prosecuting the child's attacker was next to nil. Children weren't protected from such crimes.

The TEAM's beleaguered passengers had so many needs, but that was exactly why Melissa had come to Vietnam. To help and to serve. In all the commotion, Tucker had contacted Mark to let him know they'd made it into the city. Missing his phone call hurt, but she had plenty of work to keep her busy.

By nightfall, everyone was fed. Dang and his family were together in a berth below deck, the girls in several others. Mark and his men had sprawled topside with sleeping bags, hammocks, and a few cans of American beer.

Melissa was dog-tired, but worried for that sick little one. The little girl showed definite signs of trauma to her face and neck, bruising as if she'd been held down. Melissa had tried over and over to get the injured child to let her examine her, but her overtures were rejected, so Melissa erred on the side of patience. It just hadn't worked yet.

Patience was not her strong suit.

She stood at the rail, her hair loose and catching the cooling breeze off the water. The river was dark with gentle waves rippling the surface. A big fish—or something—splashed nearby. It could've been an alligator or a crocodile. She didn't know the difference but she'd seen one off the bow of the hovercraft.

The jungle was alive with night noises. Frogs. Insects. Birds called as they settled in the high branches overhanging the bank. Monkey's chattered. It would've been perfect if Tucker had been there.

"This boat is bigger than what I expected," she said to no one in particular, her heart in her throat and missing Tucker.

"That it is," Mark replied quietly. Now that his guests were in bed, he'd taken the bench seat near the rear of the craft, his hands on his knees, a weapon in his holster. "It's a refurbished Navy rig. In its day, it hauled a payload of thirty tons, but not anymore. Alex keeps another just like it available for David's needs."

"He comes across enough children that he needs a boat this big?" The notion appalled her.

Mark stared off into the jungle, wiping the sweat off his brow. "Kids don't have a chance in some parts of the world, Melissa. You know that. David's been busy."

She had to change the subject. Her heart couldn't bear the thought of all those desperate children beyond David's reach. "I didn't expect you to bring Dang back with you, but I'm thankful you did. That had to be hard, transporting him through the jungle as sick as he is."

Maverick offered a grunt from the hammock he'd strung at the corner of the deck, between railings. "It wasn't once we got him and his missus settled down. Knowing we already had Mimi and Peewee turned the tables. They were happy to go with us then. Gabe rigged a litter and away we went. It was the girls we were worried about. They didn't trust any of us."

If ever there was a cowboy, it was Maverick. Tall. Broad-shouldered. Prone to brooding silence. When he spoke, people listened.

"Yeah, but Ky always carries five pounds of caramels with him." Gabe chuckled. He stood at the opposite rail, alert, continually scanning the shore. "Bribery works on kids. The girls came around."

"The U. N. ought to try candy instead of sanctions. Might sweeten the whole world," Ky added somberly. Melissa didn't know his story, just that he'd come home injured from the Mideast war. She never would have guessed it to look at him, not the way his eyes lit up when he teased Maverick every chance he got.

"Those girls were awfully hungry when they got here," Zack commented. "Food always calms the savage beasts at my house."

"Those little girls of yours aren't beasts," Melissa said. "But I know being safe helps, too.

"I cleaned Tam's snake bite," Taylor said. "It was ugly. She's got a good case of necrosis going on. It'll need to be flushed twice every day."

"I can do that," Melissa offered. "I was there right after she got bit. I think she trusts me."

"That Peewee's a cute little rascal," Maverick added. The toddler had refused to be set down once aboard, so Maverick ended up carrying him throughout dinner, and then some. It didn't look like either of them minded.

"I noticed he latched onto you," Gabe tossed out. "I think it's your drawl."

"Damn straight," Ky agreed. "It's that cowboy thing you've got going on. Kids love it."

"I don't drawl, and I'm not a cowboy."

"Keep telling yourself that," Gabe teased. "Any guy who owns a herd of horses is a cowboy in my book."

"Just twenty-eight," Maverick murmured. "China wants a grand champion. We're breeding again."

Gabe choked on his beer, not bothering to wipe the grin off his face. "Come again?"

An empty beer can sailed through the air and bounced once off Gabe's hard head. "I meant the horses, smart-ass."

Melissa eased into the cushioned bench near Mark, glad to be sitting with this company of elite snipers. Alex knew how to pick honorable men. These guys were Tucker's kind of people.

"The only problem is Dang," Mark murmured. "If he's in this with Siegel, I'll have to turn him over to the authorities. Maybe his wife, too."

Melissa's heart sank.

"I'd let David make that call if I were you," Zack said quietly. He'd stretched out on one of the two pilot seats at the front of the cabin. "All we really know is Dang and his family were in trouble, and they needed our help. We assisted their escape from a bad situation. I wouldn't jump to conclusions, not in this part of the world."

"He's running a temp," Taylor added. "I gave him a double dose of the strongest antibiotic we've got aboard and some pain killer. I hope David knows a good doctor. Dang will need one."

"You guys might be right," Mark admitted. "I don't want to take sides, not between a father and his kids. Why the hell didn't you take Alex up on his offer, Zack? You'd make a helluva senior agent."

Zack crossed his heavily muscled arms behind his head, his shirt stretched tight across his chest, and his teeth extra white against his mocha-latte skin in the twilight. "I like field work, not being stuck behind a desk running interference for the boss."

"But I'm here," Mark growled, "not behind a desk. I'm still on active ops."

Zack grinned. "Feels good being useful, doesn't it?"

"You have no idea." Mark blew out a long deep sigh. "Libby's not happy that I'm halfway around the world again, though. It puts her in a tight spot between taking care of the kids at home and her job at the hospital, but she knows how it works. Sometimes I travel. It's part of the job."

"Tucker loves the travel and adventure," Melissa murmured, her mind on that missing man and wondering what he was doing. "I don't think I've understood how much he's still needed in the world until now."

The men stilled.

She could almost see the devil-may-care smirk on Tucker's handsome face. "You're all like Brady. Brave. Courageous and—"

"Dumber than dirt," Maverick interrupted, his fingers stretched to the floor as he pushed the hammock to and fro, his dark eyes drilling Melissa's. "Please don't go calling us heroes, Mrs. McCormack, because we're not. The heroes are the ones who didn't come back. We're just the guys who did. It isn't anything to be proud of."

"We're just the lucky ones, ma'am," Gabe agreed. "That's all."

"It's who we are." Rory had been silent until then. He'd stayed up front with Zack near the radio. "Not everyone's made for this kind of life, but some of us are. I know I am. I guess it's a gift, though I doubt you'd see it that way. Sure, we'd rather be home safe with our kids and wives, but when trouble comes calling, we owe it to our families to do what's right. I couldn't live with myself if I didn't at least try to make this world safer for them."

"But there will always be someone who needs saving." Didn't these guys get that?

"And there'll always be horseshit," Maverick muttered, pulling his TEAM cap down over his eyes. "It's like taking care of the barn. It's got to be done, or the shit stacks up and the horses get sick. I'm not about to sit on my butt while China cleans stalls. I'd rather she ride to her heart's content with the wind in her hair and let me do the grunt work any day."

Taylor arched his back from his post at the rear of the hovercraft. As calm as these guys appeared, all were still armed, a couple, like Taylor, on guard. "At the risk of sounding trite, Mrs. McCormack—"

"Melissa. Please, all of you, just Melissa."

He nodded. "It's as simple as this. You'll never know if you're born to fly until you lift your wings and face the wind. The only problem is that once you do, there's no going back. You either fly or you fall. I guess we've chosen to face the wind and try."

"Turkeys don't fly," Maverick grumbled. "They fall out of the sky like boulders."

"But eagles do," Mark said softly. "Like it or not, Maverick, you're a frickin' eagle."

That elicited chicken clucks and coos from Gabe and Ky. Maverick turned his back on his buddies, with a surly, "Goodnight," but Taylor's dark eyes didn't stray from Melissa's. "You wouldn't be happy being less than what you are, would you?"

She swallowed hard. Answering in the affirmative made her feel as if she were running full bore over the edge of a mighty steep cliff into the unknown. "I hate being the one left behind all the time," she admitted. "I know it's selfish, but I hate never knowing if I'll see him again."

"Believe me, he hates that, too."

"There isn't a one of us who wouldn't rather stay home with our wives and kids." Mark stood abruptly, stretching his back and his joints cracking. "I'm going to bed. Will you need another blanket, Melissa?"

"No." Her eyes turned northward to Tucker's last known position. She didn't need a blanket. She needed Tucker.

# Chapter Twenty-One

Melissa couldn't sleep. She'd lain wide-awake for hours listening to the quiet sounds from the next room until she could take no more. Frightened or not, that abused little girl needed a woman's help.

The birds in the jungle had just started their early morning chatter when Melissa knocked on the door next to hers and peeked inside. The four girls were huddled around their friend, all in the center of one of the two bunks.

"Sweethearts," Melissa whispered softly. "May I come in? Please let me help."

All five shook their heads, but she was not to be dissuaded. Closing the door quietly behind her, she crossed to the bathroom and ran a tub of warm water. If nothing else, a bath would soothe the girl's discomfort. "Come with me," Melissa said to the battered little one, her hand outstretched, and her own eyes brimming at the fear in these children's eyes. "Come on. I can help you feel better," she promised. "At least cleaner."

It took a few minutes, but with much sisterly chatter from her friends, at last the tiny thing gulped and lifted up from the bed. As one, the girls closed ranks around her and walked slowly to Melissa. It tore her heart out to watch the girl clutching her stomach and walking like an old woman. Finally, Melissa reached for her, and the tiny thing collapsed into her arms. She went to the floor with her, cupping the child's head. "There, there," she crooned.

The rest of them sank alongside their sad friend, stroking her hair and offering gentle words in their language. All were thin and dark-haired. They could've passed for sisters.

Melissa tapped her fingertips to her chest, hoping to get them to talk with her. "Melissa. My name is Melissa."

Shyly, the girls began. The one with the brightest eyes spoke first. "Dara."

Melissa nodded and smiled encouragingly. "Hello Dara. You have very pretty eyes."

The poor thing in her arms looked up. "Pich," she said, her fingers searching for Melissa's, pulling them to her tear-stained cheek.

Melissa pressed her forehead to hers. "I must help you most of all. Will you let me be your big sister?"

She might not have understood a word Melissa said, but Pich sighed, and that was good enough. The ice was broken. The other's followed suit. Sotheara. Maly. The only one not willing to share, the sweet little girl with a ragged scar on her cheek, looked away, her chin lifted in defiance.

Sotheara opened her mouth as if to tell the secret, but Melissa raised her index finger to her lips, shook her head, and said, "It's okay. I can wait. It must be a very good name if it needs more time to be spoken." She knew the girls didn't understand, but this tiny, gentle step made the difference. "I think the tub is full enough. Shall we all take a bath?" she asked her flock of lost girls, her voice subdued and low. Carefully, she eased to her knees, lifting Pich with her.

Bath-time was a community affair with all the girls eager to help undress each other until all were naked in the tub or sitting on the edge of it. Melissa could've cried at the tender scene of these future mothers nurturing their hurting sister with tender care, all smothering poor Pich with attention and love. Not one of them owned a thing. All were destitute and themselves rescued from the worst circumstances, but even the grumpy one who refused to look at Melissa helped bathe and comfort her friend. It was enough to humble anyone.

At last, the community bath was done. Melissa coaxed all of the girls into the bedroom, but left the bathroom door open while she discreetly examined Pich, now sitting on the counter. The poor thing was torn and bleeding where no child her age should be torn. That her stomach hurt concerned Melissa the most. Mark and Zack had daughters. They might know what to do.

When the girls were towel-dried and dressed in the cotton shifts Zack had bought at the market, the bedroom door cracked open. "Mind if we join your pajama party?" Zack palmed the door wide to allow the rest of the girls to enter. "These young ladies have been out in the hall."

"I'm so glad you're still awake." Melissa waved him in.

He leaned his hip to the doorjamb instead of entering. "You look like a mama duck with her flock of ducklings."

Tears brimmed her eyes at his gentle compliment. "This little one needs a doctor, Zack. Her name is Pich, and her tummy is tender. She needs stitches, too." Melissa pressed her lips tight, not going to fall apart if she could help it. "Can we get word to David to bring a doctor with him when he meets up with us?"

"So Ky was right? She was…?" Zack left the ugly word unsaid.

Melissa nodded. "I'm sure of it. I don't want to leave Tucker and Isaiah behind, but she can't wait."

Mark cocked his head around the corner, his dark hair mussed, but no sign of sleep in his eyes. "I heard. Don't worry, Melissa. I'll advise David and Agent Chase of the change in plans. How can we help in the meantime?"

"Are you sure?" Melissa had to know Tucker and Isaiah would be safe, that they'd make it home in one piece.

Mark nodded. "Tucker's savvy. I'll check with Alex to make sure he gets the help he needs to get out of the country. He might even make it home before you."

"We've got several antibiotics onboard if she needs them," Zack offered.

"I'm sure she does after what she's been through, but do you have any morning after pills?" Melissa asked. She'd volunteered at Kelsey's home for homeless kids in D.C. enough to know what happened on the streets. There might be time to stop the next tragedy for sweet little Pich.

He shook his head. "No, damn it."

"Those meds work up to seventy-two hours after the act," Mark said quietly. "If we leave now, we might make it to David in time. I'll tell him to come prepared."

Melissa gathered Pich into her arms, needing to comfort this tiny one, needing Pich to feel safe despite the way she'd been used. "I hate cruel men," she declared even as she rocked the child in her arms. "They should all be drowned at the bottom of the ocean."

Zach's chocolate brown eyes connected with hers. "Now you know why we do what we do."

Tucker had barely fallen asleep when his internal alarm went off. The night was pitch black, but there was Isaiah, coming through their hotel door with bags in his hands. Tucker bolted upright and snapped the bedside lamp on, his feet to the floor. "Where have you been? I thought you were sleeping. What time is it?"

"It's around midnight. This city never sleeps, you know," he whispered.

The bright light shocked Tucker's bleary, good eye, the other still swollen and sore. It worried him. He'd never had a black eye that felt this bad for so long. It had to be because of the implanted lens. He used to think it was a godsend, now he wasn't so sure. "What's that supposed to mean?"

"Infiltration. That's all. Go back to sleep. You need your rest more than I do."

Tucker wiped the back of his finger over the puffy seam of his eyelid. It hadn't stopped tearing up since he'd left Melissa. Kind of like his heart. "You've been inside the factory?" Unbelievable.

Isaiah shrugged. "No, but I've been to the Internet café down the street. Want to know how close we are to your ex-wife's place?"

Tucker tugged his pants on. Sneaking out alone at night was unacceptable. It wouldn't happen again. "Where?"

Isaiah flipped the desk lamp on and spread a map of the city for Tucker to study. "See this dot right here? That's us." He traced his index finger along one of the many yellow lines. "Did you know there are more than eight million people living in this city?"

"I don't care. Where's she live? Where's the factory?"

Isaiah traced the yellow line across two rivers. "Right there."

Tucker peered closer at the map, squinting and his head throbbing. "She's got a home east of the Saigon River?"

Isaiah leaned over and tugged a laptop out of another one of his bags. "I wouldn't call it a home. It's more like an estate, a big estate. She had a French architect design it. I checked."

"You've been shopping again?"

"I've been taking care of business," Isaiah purred while he flipped the computer lid up and turned it on. An image of a lavish estate sprang to the screen. "Welcome to your ex's new home, Tucker. Nice, huh? It's a *poteaux-en-terre* design."

"Stop trying to impress me. The what?" Tucker ran a tight hand over the pain climbing up the back of his neck. The mansion was Nicole all right, and it was more than nice. The lavish home had been set back in a palm grove with a wide expanse of manicured emerald turf at the front. More palms and ferns. A pond the size of a small lake with a waterfall. Peacocks. Swans. Geese. All those pretentious things Nicole needed.

"The vertical columns of the wraparound porch. See? They run from roof to ground. No concrete footings."

"And I care about this why?"

"I'm just providing detailed intel in case you decide to breach the place."

Tucker gritted his teeth and peered closer. Flowering shrubs ensconced a wide stone walkway to the two-story *home*, the face of it bright yellow stucco that stood out against all the green. Wrought-iron balusters lined the wraparound porches on both levels. There were two points of egress from this view, one at the front door, the other on the second level balcony. A brick chimney stood at the right. Eight windows faced the front, the largest to the left and filled with plants and trees, maybe a two-story arboretum. *Fancy.*

"She's got staff. Maids. Chauffeurs. A music teacher."

Tucker grunted. "Of course she does." Nicole always wanted to be richer than everyone else. Now she was. "What's the music teacher do, teach violin while Deuce is sewing shirts for Vinnie?"

"I don't think he's there for Deuce. That's what's interesting. Look at the latest family portrait." Isaiah scrolled to another page. "Do you see your son?"

Tucker peered closer. Two chubby boys of the same approximate age stood between Nicole and Vinnie, both smiling with violins in their hands. No

Deuce. Alarm lifted the hackles up the back of Tucker's neck. "Where's my kid? What's going on?"

Isaiah leveled a piercing eye at Tucker while he brought up a series of photos taken at the home, one of Nicole in an elegant, lace bridal gown. Other family sittings. Still no Deuce.

"Where the hell's my kid and how long has Deuce been working in that son-of-a-bitchin' factory?"

Isaiah narrowed his eyes. "There's a ball at the American Embassy in two days. Your ex will be at Madame Antoinette's at noon today for her dress fitting. I think it's time to do a little shopping. Ask me how I know."

"Where's the damned factory?" Isaiah didn't need his psychic ego stroked.

The kid was smart enough to bring up another screen. Bright red lettering on the front of Vinnie's factory declared *Ham Thủ Thiêm Sewing Distributor*. Housed in what looked like a refurbished airplane hangar from the Vietnam-war era, an eight-foot-high metal fence surrounded the place. The limousine parked in front might have been intended to make it look classy. It failed.

"Vinnie's factory's on the opposite side of the Saigon River from his mansion. See where the river bends west at Ham Thủ Thiêm?" Isaiah tapped his index finger to the screen. "The bridge there links District 2 with downtown District 1. It's very congested. Very industrial."

Tucker forgot how bad his body felt as he absorbed every last detail. According to the online photos, the inside of the old hangar had been modernized. Plenty of smiling employees at clean workstations operated gleaming, industrial sewing machines, forklifts, and fabric tables. All of them looked happy, and all were adults or older teenagers. It appeared there were no children Deuce's age working at the factory. In one group shot, the cheerful liars all waved. Everything looked legal. *Like hell.* He didn't buy the propaganda spin. "Gear up."

Isaiah faced him. "Thought you'd say that. Where first? Nicole's home or Vinnie's factory?"

"The factory. You haven't showed me one thing to convince me he's at that... home." Tucker seethed. "Nicole's nothing but a hard-hearted, greedy bitch who lives for herself. She made her bed. Let her sleep in it."

"But she does have legal custody. You can't just barge in and take your son without proof. You will need to speak with her."

*That might be a problem.* "Not if I can prove Deuce has been mistreated. You know he's in a bad way, right?"

"No judge will allow my testimony, Tucker. You know that. I'm an unknown quantity. A psychic. I'm the guy everyone in the judicial system thinks is a scammer, a con artist. We need solid evidence, so..." Isaiah drew several mini-cameras up from that magic shopping bag of his. "Let's see if we can get the proof you need. Don't you want to know how I know where your wife will be today? Come on, ask me."

"Do not tell me she's psychic," Tucker warned. That was all he needed.

Isaiah winked. "She's not, but your son is."

Tucker about dropped his teeth. "Deuce? He's... like me?" He hadn't meant for that to sound like a good thing. "Can I reach out to him? How's that work anyway?"

"With a little bit of effort, yes, you can do it." Isaiah grinned. "Guess who's taking him out for lunch right after her dress fitting today?"

"Nicole?" *Son-of-a-bitch.*

Isaiah had all the makings of a good covert operator. His eyes glittered. "What say we get into Ham Thủ Thiêm Sewing Distributor and steal Deuce out from under her nose?"

"You're all right, kid," Tucker admitted. "So show me. How do I call Deuce? I want to talk to him. Do I just, I don't know— ring him up or something?"

Morning stretched across the Mekong, waking the world with golden light from the east. The sight couldn't have been lovelier.

Melissa stayed with the girls at the back of the boat, getting to know them better while the hovercraft floated its way up the delta. Instead of meeting David at the border of the Svay Reing province, he'd suggested they rendezvous farther south to bring the medical care to Pich and Dang instead of the other way around. It was still risky with the Vietnamese Army on the hunt for the Cambodian rebels, but doable.

Zack had been in Vietnam and Cambodia before, quite a few times by the sounds of it. He stayed close to wait on Melissa and the girls, entertaining her with trivia and stories, one about an odd fellow called the Coconut Monk, so named because he only ate coconuts for several years. Zack knew plenty of other Vietnamese trivia, but he wasn't fooling anyone. Melissa hadn't married a spec ops guy without some of his training rubbing off on her. Zack was armed. He was keeping her distracted.

"Tucker ought to bring you back to Vietnam someday. It really is a beautiful country. You could visit the Thien Mu Pagoda in Hue. The Citadel there, too."

The melodic Vietnamese words seemed to roll of Zack's tongue. "You've been here before." She made it a statement.

"Once or twice," he hedged.

She didn't press the issue, her mind and heart on the man she had yet to hear from. Mark had talked briefly with Alex and Tucker. He and Isaiah had reached Hồ Chí Minh City, but something was wrong. She could feel it in her bones.

"We're coming up on our stop," Mark came by to report, "but we've got Vietnamese Army patrols watching the shoreline. We'll need to do this transfer quick. Stay sharp. How is she?"

Melissa glanced at Pich, sound asleep in her arms. "She's feverish, Mark. I'm worried."

He nodded, the light in his eyes grim. "I am, too. Have you given her any antibiotics?"

"Just a child's dose," Zack answered, "and something for pain."

"That's probably for the best, but darn…" The tenderness in Mark's tone caught at Melissa's heart. All of these men had hovered over the girls, waiting on them the few times the girls had ventured forth from their rooms. For the most part, they preferred to cling to Melissa, and she didn't mind. This was her calling in life, to do for others, and she truly loved it.

"Did David bring a doctor?" she asked.

Mark nodded. "Nancy's with him. Don't worry. These girls will be in good hands. This is the best solution."

Melissa had expected David's wife would be there, but Pich needed a doctor. She ran her fingertips over the girl's brow, smoothing a strand of hair out of her open mouth. The poor thing had fallen asleep after a light breakfast of rice porridge that Zack had made especially for her.

"When we're done here," Mark said quietly, "you'll fly out of Tân Sơn Nhất International Airport with the rest of us."

"We're not going back for Tucker?" she asked, surprised. "But I thought—I hoped—"

"Sorry, but plans changed. There's a battle between the rebels and the army in Tien Giang province right now—"

"That's smack dab between us and Tucker," Zack interpreted.

"Right," Mark agreed. "He won't be able to get to us like we'd originally planned, but don't worry. I talked with Alex. He gave Tucker a solid contact in case things didn't work out. He'll be okay."

"But Mark..." Melissa paused, her worst fears tapping at her shoulder. "You guys are supposed to work miracles."

He winked at her. "So can Tucker. Just wait. You'll see."

# Chapter Twenty-Two

Reaching out psychically to Deuce ended up a big fat zero. Isaiah explained over and over how to project an image or thought, but Tucker couldn't make the mental connection. With every attempt his head pounded a little more. The night turned to morning. His swollen eye oozed tears. He'd focused until his back teeth hurt from concentrating, but not once did he get a hint of his son's voice in his head. Not a whisper.

Isaiah's laughing at him didn't help. "Enough already. Stop with the faces."

Tucker scrubbed a palm up over his forehead and through his hair, frustrated he couldn't do what Isaiah could. "Then how?"

"Keep it simple. Picture him. Talk to him just like you would if he was sitting here with us. It's easy. Block the world and focus on—"

"*That's* what's wrong. I can't stop thinking about everything else."

"Deep breath..." Isaiah inhaled, his demeanor calm and steady, his chest barely lifting.

Tucker'd had enough. He stopped trying to be something he wasn't. "I can't do this bullshit. I'm not psychic anyway. Give me a truck to fix. A sink or a toilet." *Something that makes sense.*

Isaiah shot him a raised brow. *"Then what are you doing right now? Are we not communicating psychically?"*

Tucker's fists clenched. "I'm better with my hands." *"You smart-ass."*

*"You're new at this. Trust me. It will come."*

Tucker rolled one shoulder, his dander up, tired of looking like a one-eyed fool. "Let's roll."

Isaiah had the good sense not to argue. Once on the street outside their hotel, he hailed a cab, and phase two of this operation began in earnest. He carried the padded canvas guitar case he'd bought to conceal the bulk of their M4 assault rifles. The kid must've watched too many gangster movies.

The early morning traffic was lighter, but it still took forty minutes to get across town. Tucker kept his mouth shut and let Isaiah do the talking. His sore eye throbbed with an increasing drumbeat that matched his pulse. It didn't matter. He'd soldiered through worse injuries, but God. He needed one day of downtime. Just one.

After a slow crawl through the densely populated industrial neighborhood, the cabbie deposited them at the Ham Thủ Thiêm Sewing Distributor. Vinnie's factory looked the same up-close as it had on Isaiah's laptop, only dingier. Grimier. Locked up tighter than a Nevada brothel, the building hummed with a peculiar electrical vibration. Cast off plastic bottles, papers, and other debris tumbled on the breeze down the alley alongside the factory.

"Look there," Tucker cautioned his sidekick, pointing at the roofline. Security cameras adorned each corner, but they hadn't been properly synced. The timing of their rotation was off. When one camera panned to the left, the other hadn't yet completed a full rotation. There was no overlap. No continuous coverage. Tucker meant to capitalize on Vinnie's poor excuse of a security system. "Stick close. Keep your head down. We're going in."

Isaiah sucked in a deep breath. "Don't we need a plan first?"

"I do. You do your mind thing while I grab Deuce. Once I've got him, we'll split."

Again with the eye roll.

"Listen, smart guy. Do you have a better idea?" Tucker hissed.

"I just thought we'd have a definite strategy with a foolproof fallback plan before we risked our lives."

"Is that what Stewart taught you? Sit around and waste time planning? Strategizing? Talking?"

Now it was Isaiah's turn to growl. "You know things could go wrong if we're not on the same page once we're inside."

"There's only two of us. How many pages could we be on?" Tucker rolled his shoulder to suppress the growing pain in his neck. Isaiah did look worried. This was probably the kid's first time breaking and entering. He really wasn't a covert operator. *Time out.*

"Okay, how about this?" Tucker drew in a steadying breath for his sake as much as his junior agent's. He'd almost forgotten Isaiah was the FNG. He needed everything explained in triplicate. "We'll enter through the rear exit. That's most likely their staging area. There ought to be storage there, a loading dock, maybe deliveries incoming or outgoing, hopefully some place to hide while you do your mental stuff. Once we're inside, we'll lose that clever guitar case of yours and get real. We'll split up. You'll plant those bugs you brought with you, while I find Deuce. How's that for strategy?"

"Do you intend to grab Deuce if you see him?"

All the leadership courses ever written tell you there are no dumb questions, but that one took the cake. "Of course I'm grabbing my son. Why the hell do you think I'm here?"

Isaiah chin-nodded him forward, gritting his teeth and clearly frustrated. "Never mind. Let's just go. I'll follow your lead and do my—" He rolled his eyes. "—*mind thing.*"

"You roll those eyes one more time, and I swear I'll slap the crap out of you," Tucker warned, his angst climbing up his spine. "Let's do this quick and clean. In and out. Once we're inside, keep your rifle tucked in tight to your chest and out of sight."

"Copy that," Isaiah replied.

Tucker led the way, sticking close to the building and out of sight of the security cameras. Getting inside was easier than he'd expected. The rear of the factory was precisely what he'd said—shipping and receiving. Poorly lighted. Dirty. Plenty of twelve-foot-high shelves stacked with bolts and bundles of cloth. All colors. A train of rolling bins full of scraps and remnants lined the narrow way forward.

"Stick to the shadows," Tucker whispered over the din of what sounded like hundreds of sewing machines. It was no wonder the place hummed.

*"Now would be a good time to use your covert operator voice, Agent Chase."*

Tucker hated when Isaiah was right. *"Copy that. Lose that guitar case. I want my rifle."*

Isaiah complied quickly. Dropping to one knee, he looked nervously over his shoulder before he unzipped the case and revealed the weaponry. With hands shaking, he lifted the first rifle for Tucker.

*"Take it easy, kid,"* Tucker said. *"I haven't lost a junior agent yet."*

Their eyes locked. *"I haven't lost a senior agent either. I'd like to keep it that way, but if—"*

Tucker put a palm in Isaiah's face to stop the *'but if'*. *"Stow it, Zaroyin. We've got work to do, now get off your knees and plant those cameras in plain sight. Get it done."*

Isaiah nodded, chastised and obedient. *"Copy that, Boss."*

At last. What sounded like submission. There'd be time for chitchat later. Tucker waved Isaiah forward, wishing he'd taught the kid spec-op hand signals. A firm palm at his shoulder and a quick, *"Stop worrying, I've got this,"* eased his mind.

Tucker scanned the enemy camp with a meticulous eye. Vinnie didn't believe in modern conveniences or employee safety. The factory was not only stuffy, but rank with the combined odors of unwashed bodies, mildew, and the smell of leftover oil, no doubt absorbed into the concrete floor from aircraft of a long ago era. There was no air-conditioning. No fire extinguishers and no marked exits.

The long rows of low hanging fluorescent shop-lights that didn't come near to providing the bright light needed for close, tedious work, comprised the overhead lighting. Glass walls divided the second level, itself a good twenty feet above the working level. Tucker guessed Vinnie's office was up there, where he could survey his kingdom and his slaves.

Stern men and women with long bamboo rods in their hands patrolled. Guards or enforcers, Tucker counted ten on the catwalk directly over the work area, others on the floor.

A latticework of wooden framework supported electrical lines to each workstation. To the far rear of the building, young men manned long tables, feeding fabric into machines to cut pieces of patterns, Tucker guessed.

Row after row, child after child, all had their heads bent over their work. The front doors were for show, judging by the heavy equipment stacked against them.

Tucker wiped the sweat running down the back of his neck. He had yet to spot Deuce. This place was stifling and a father's worst nightmare. All it needed was a match and everyone would be trapped. They'd die or be trampled to death during the stampede to safety. Glancing sideways, he kept track of his partner crouched behind one of those rolling remnant bins.

Isaiah nodded toward the work area. *"Grab a bin, Boss. It's a good place to stash your rifle. Hurry. I need to do more of my* mind thing."

*"Smart-ass."*

*"Just watch out for the rats."*

Tucker raised his eyebrows. *"Seriously?"* He'd almost forgotten the vermin of the underbelly of Vietnam.

Isaiah nodded. *"They're everywhere. And they're big."*

Tucker saw them then. Terrier-sized rodents slinking in the shadows beneath the tables and chairs.

Cockroaches the size of dollar bills skittered away from the rats.

He latched onto the nearest cart and kept his head low, his ball cap pulled down, his eyes wide open, scanning for that sweet boy of his in the multitude of unclean bodies. Machines hummed. Pieces of fabric flew through the assembly lines while older kids made the rounds and collected the piles of sewed pieces. Surely Henry Ford didn't have this nightmare in mind when he'd invented the assembly line, not slave labor for little kids who should've been in school learning how to be good citizens and future leaders. *Or playing baseball.*

Where the hell was Deuce?

*"I haven't spotted him yet."* Isaiah answered Tucker's unspoken thought. *"There are eight main vertical supports along the walls in this warehouse. Solid eight-by-eights. I've already placed a camera on four of them."*

*Good thinking,"* Tucker sent to his fellow agent.

*"Believe it or not, I do have some skills."*

*"Then cover the other four uprights."* Despite his terse comeback, Tucker nearly smiled. He hadn't expected Isaiah to man up like he had on this mission, especially when it had turned into a rescue op instead of a simple re-establishment of parental rights. A definite bond had grown between him and Clark Kent. Isaiah had initiative and Tucker trusted him, a definite plus amongst covert operators.

Dropping his rifle into the nearest bin, he rolled toward the opposite end of the building. Rounding the first aisle, he jerked to attention when a woman shrieked. Looking over his shoulder, he caught sight of a young kid punching another in the face, knocking him down. The bully screamed up to the woman, pointing to the kid he'd just pummeled into submission. The witch yelled again, pointing her rod at the fallen kid. Several older boys zeroed in on the poor boy on the floor, screaming while they kicked and punched.

This garden party had to end. Tucker rolled his bin up the aisle. He hadn't spotted Deuce yet, and he didn't want to intervene unless he had to, but that puny little guy on the floor had better get up and offer one lick of resistance if he meant to live. *Fight back, for hell's sake. Punch someone. Anyone.*

And then another voice lifted above the din of machines and bullies. A familiar, commanding voice. "Leave him alone!"

Tucker's heart stopped. *Deuce.*

At any other time, Tucker would've been proud, but the bullies heard Deuce, too. They turned as one. Words were exchanged. Deuce answered, but Tucker couldn't see him until he shoved his bin between two sewing tables. There Deuce stood down the aisle, facing three older boys, his face sweaty and his fists clenched at his side. The kid blinked like he was going to cry, but not for a second did he stand down. He meant to fight those boys, and, damn it. Tucker couldn't get to him fast enough. This could go so bad.

He powered off the ball of his foot, but upset a stack of pattern pieces with his boot in the process. The old woman shrieked from her lofty perch. Tucker shot her a quick glance. She wasn't looking at him. Only Deuce. Damned if her face didn't twist into a snarl, her pudgy legs carrying her straight into the fray, and that damned rod twitching in her hand.

Tucker matched her pace, his fist clenched and ready to knock the glint out of her beady eyes. "Don't you dare touch my boy."

*"Don't do it. You can't break cover,"* Isaiah cautioned. *"Remember why we're here. You need proof to support your case, Agent Chase."*

*"Bullshit!"* Tucker put a wealth of authority in his tone to back Isaiah off. "I've seen enough." He left his rifle concealed in the cart, but eased his pistol up from his thigh holster.

Things happened fast. A cry went up, and the bullyboys charged Deuce. When he went down swinging, Tucker jumped the workbench blocking his path, but someone grabbed his ankle on the way over. He pitched to his hands and knees, dragging a shelf filled with fabric down on him. Scrambling to his feet, he shoved the shelf aside, but slipped on the fabric on the floor. Barely on his feet again, he caught sight of the old woman, her arm cocked and—

*STING!* The bitch struck Deuce.

A smoldering red haze filled Tucker's head. Logic flew out the window.

*"Wait,"* Isaiah called to him.

*"Nobody hits my kid."*

She cocked her arm for another strike, and Tucker turned into a bull in a china shop, but before he could engage... *BLAM!* A single shot rang out.

He whirled on the shooter, shocked. *Isaiah?*

The kid was scared, hyperventilating, and shaking, but what a sight. Isaiah aimed his pistol at the woman, his eyes wide. *"O day co ai biet noi tieng anh knong?"* came screaming out of his mouth— whatever that meant.

*"You speak Vietnamese?"*

*"No, but this phrase was phonetically diagramed in my travel guide."*

*"You've got a travel guide?"* Tucker closed in on his son, daring that old hag to stop him. *"Keep going. You're doing good."*

*"That's all I got."* The gun in Isaiah's hand shook. "Deuce Chase!" he said with tense authority, his nervousness barely under control. "Get off the floor and get over here. Bring your friend."

The machines ceased clattering. Everyone within reach watched as Deuce lifted shakily to his feet, wiping his bloody nose against his shoulder. He tugged his friend off the floor, glaring at the bullies before he ran to Isaiah. Catching sight of Tucker, he changed directions. "Dad?" he cried. "Dad! You're here! You came!"

He hit Tucker hard enough to hurt him, but Tucker gladly took the hit. Broken ribs or not, he smothered his son under his arm. Nothing felt sweeter than that boy back where he belonged. "Deuce," he ground out, assessing both boys' physical condition with a glance.

Shadows dogged Deuce's eyes. His nose was bleeding and his cheeks had lost their boyish plumpness, but that smile? One in a million.

His friend was another story. The poor boy ducked behind Deuce, not meeting Tucker's eye. He was of a slighter build and a good foot shorter than Deuce. One bloodied eye was swollen shut, and Tucker had to roll both shoulders that time, loosening every single vertebrae for the slap-down headed Vinnie's way.

"I couldn't let them hurt Luke, Father. I mean Dad," Deuce blurted, his eyes shimmering and his fingers clinging to Tucker's wrist. "Luke's small than me, and we were just talking, and... and... it was my fault. I was just trying to do what's right."

"You did good. Your friend's going home with us."

"I happen to speak perfect English," a haughty male voice declared from the catwalk. Had to be Nguyễn Vin Li. The bastard.

"So the hell do I, and I've come for my son." Tucker stared him down, not sure why Nicole's new husband led with that info byte. Who cared how many languages he spoke?

*"Because that's what I asked before,"* Isaiah admitted. *"Sorry. It's the only Vietnamese I knew. I had to say something."*

"You have no custodial rights in your country, Mr. Chase," Vinnie stated clearly as he looked over the railing instead of confronting Tucker at ground level. "Certainly not in mine." He looked the part of an aristocrat in his linen trousers, his white shirt unbuttoned, the cuffs rolled to his elbows.

"Why don't you climb off your perch and fight like a man?" Tucker snarled, his son tucked behind him.

Step by step, Vinnie complied. Deliberately, he closed the distance, the metal stairs creaking under his weight, his palm sliding down the smooth metal banister. The crowd parted, and there he was. The worst kind of bully. An adult who preyed on children and used them for profit. A pimp by any other name.

"Your witch had no right hitting my son," Tucker growled, his Irish up. He slanted a deadly glare at the old woman, daring her to fight an adult who could knock her on her bony ass. "Deuce and his friend are coming with me," he told her in no uncertain terms. "Get the hell out of my way."

"I think not, Mr. Chase." A look passed between Vinnie and his nearest guard, a thick-necked guy with long, greasy black hair. "The laws concerning child labor in my country are different than yours. Children here are often required to work long hours to serve their families, their elders, and their betters. It's a sign of respect and the least they can do." He lifted his palms, playing to the crowd gathered around him, now infiltrated with thugs with clubs and knives who seemed to be translating what Tucker had said. "Isn't that right?"

Murmurs and shifting glances answered timid affirmatives.

*"I don't think those guards are translating, Tucker,"* Isaiah mentally whispered. *"I think they told Vinnie's workers you're here to put them out of a job. At least, that's the vibe I'm getting."*

Tucker let a low hiss between gritted teeth. *This is going to get ugly.* "I don't give a shit about your country or your laws, Vinnie. Only my boy. He comes with me. His friend, too."

A half-smile slithered over Vinnie's lips. His thugs were already weaving into the crowd, tightening the noose. Tucker tried again. "Sorry, folks. I'm just here for my son. You got a problem with Ham Thủ Thiêm Sewing, you take it up with management, not me. Now move aside. Let me pass."

He didn't see the knife as much as he felt the vibration in the air when it sliced toward his kidneys. Without thinking, Tucker whirled on his attacker before the blade struck, keeping hold of Deuce's wrist, shielding his son and Luke.

The tip of the knife caught the edge of his elbow, but not before he landed a boot dead center of the thick-necked guy's chest. The knife skittered to the floor when Thick Neck flew backward. He didn't fall, but settled one hand to the dusty concrete, his fingers splayed and ready to charge.

Tucker's pistol was instantly in his palm and ready, a round chambered and hell on its way.

"You'd better think long and hard before you try that again," he ground out at the man in his sights. "I can make two of you at this range, and it won't be pretty. Go ahead. Try me."

Deuce tucked his fingers into his dad's belt. "I wanna go home, Dad. You're bleeding."

"I'm fine, son. Get ready to run. If anything happens to me, stick with Isaiah."

Thick Neck never took his eyes off Tucker, just chin-nodded, a sure signal to the other guards.

Tucker put every deadly intonation into his voice, daring the moron to start this war. "You heard the boy. We're going home. Now move your ass."

The noose had tightened. Vinnie's thugs were closing in. Vinnie, too. Tucker had no doubt the man was armed. This was no standoff. It would be a massacre.

*"Get my boy out of here,"* he mentally commanded Isaiah.

*"Like hell. I intend to appeal to their despicable natures. Watch and learn, Agent Chase."*

Again with the watch-and-learn bullshit. The fluorescent lights flickered once before the place went completely dark. The steady hum of noise died, making the silence nearly as loud. Tucker plastered Deuce against his hip where no one could get at him.

"Whatever happens next, you and your friend stay with me."

"I will, Dad. I've got a good hold of Luke."

*God, a man loves it when his kid was one hundred percent on his six.*

"Come out with your hands up!" a loud voice bellowed from the rear entry.

*"Are you doing that, Isaiah?"* Tucker had to know. He didn't relish running into any real cops.

*"What do you think?"*

*"I think it's time to get the hell out of here."*

*"I can do that."*

"This is the police!"

*BLAM!* Isaiah upped the ante with a single shot, and chaos took over. But Thick Neck still had a hard-on for Tucker. He charged with his head down, plowing the few workers out of his way to get Tucker.

Tucker barely had time to hand Deuce off to Isaiah before he intercepted the guy with a come-on-over embrace that put Tucker on his back and sent Thick Neck flying over his head. *Crash.* The big guy went down hard.

Back on his feet, Tucker thumbed his nose and danced to the adrenaline racing up his spine. He'd been in bar fights and brawls galore since his dad did what he'd done. He could take more than one of these guys. The rifle slung over his shoulder proved that, but first—he just wanted to play.

Another man came up behind him, but Tucker was on his game now. He bobbed to his left and pulled the idiot in close enough to crunch his nose onto his thigh, then pushed him into yet another thug who'd gotten in too close and too fast. Too bad the third guy never got a chance to lower that fancy knife of his. He'd inadvertently knifed his buddy. The second idiot went down screaming and swearing in a puddle of his own blood.

Isaiah must've mentally flickered the lights on just enough to give Tucker a visual, and to let him know the crowd wasn't in the game as much as the guards were. He found himself in a ring of a dozen fighters while the workers shifted away. Isaiah, Deuce, and Luke were nowhere to be seen. Just the way Tucker preferred it. His kid didn't need to see his old man in action. But Vinnie was missing, too. Not good.

Thick Neck was back on his feet. He and another guy, both with knives, charged Tucker.

*Not today, boys.* The basic science behind hand-to-hand fighting was how to use an enemy's energy against himself. How to throw him off-balance and keep him guessing while you killed him.

Tucker kicked out at Thick Neck the same time as he punched the new guy in the throat with a hard right. He earned a knife slice up his left bicep with that move. It cut his shirt and bloodied his arm, but New Guy went to his knees gurgling, his larynx crushed. Thick Neck tucked his gut in to avoid the kick, but couldn't recover in time to dodge Tucker's one-two punch to his ears. Fatal mistake. Thick Neck went down with a pathetic squeal, both eardrums shattered if the tactic worked like Tucker meant it to.

"Who's next?" he growled, still dancing and still buying time for Isaiah to get Deuce and his friend to safety.

*"We're clear of the building,"* came Isaiah's voice loud and clear in Tucker's head. *"You've only got one good eye, or did you forget? Get your dumb ass out of there."*

*"One eye is enough. 'Sides, I'm just getting started."*

The lights flashed again, and, God bless him, Isaiah was a good man to give Tucker a final warning. Tucker thumbed his nose again, surprised it was bleeding as much as it was, and not exactly sure how he could get from point A to point B in the dark. He dropped to one knee, no longer sure which way was out.

*"Turn one-hundred-and-eighty degrees and go straight. I'll tell you when you're at the exit."*

Tucker complied, jostling through the congested, groping crowd as he weaved between sweaty hips and thighs in the dark.

*"Keep moving."* Isaiah's voice sounded tight and stressed. *"You're running out of time."*

*"I see it now."* Tucker feinted to his right, truly wondering about all that psychic crap. His five senses seemed to be on some kind of souped-up hyper-alert. He felt the guys coming for him before they passed by, four hulking guards with clubs and rods. Thick

Neck was now packing a sawed off shotgun. The guy had to be dizzy with those busted eardrums, but there he was.

*"Keep my son safe. This might take a while,"* Tucker commanded Isaiah.

*"But—"*

*"But nothing!"* He couldn't take the chance. Tucker launched himself at Thick Neck, needing to end this confrontation. *"Do it. Do it now!"*

# **Chapter Twenty-Three**

David Tao's warm brown eyes glittered with approval. He stood with his hands on his hips at the wooden dock as the hovercraft sidled alongside it. Dressed in khaki pants and a yellow printed button-up shirt with his wife, Nancy, at his side, he looked the picture of contentment.

When Rory turned the engines off, he beamed. "Melissa! What an unexpected surprise."

David Tao was a true friend and one of the first agents Alex Stewart had hired way back when he'd first founded his covert surveillance business. He and his wife, Nancy, had always been in the background, solid supporters during the bad times and quiet cheerleaders during the good times. He had to be pushing forty by now, but Melissa had never seen him happier.

This next part was going to be hard, but she offered him a genuine smile despite the goodbyes in her imminent future. "It looks like Cambodia agrees with you."

"That's because he's incorrigible," Nancy declared, her dark eyes scrolling over the sweet girl in Melissa's arms. "He's always coming up with another way to help. Is that Pich you're holding?"

Melissa looked past Nancy to David. "Yes. Where's the doctor?"

David nodded at his wife with a serious smile. "She's never a heartbeat away from me. You're looking at her."

"You? You're a physician?" Melissa hadn't known.

"General practitioner, mid-wife, and nutritionist," Nancy replied as she climbed onboard and took her place alongside Melissa, her hands already smoothing over the sleeping girl and diagnosing as they went. "Tell me all you know about this child's situation. Fever? Contusions? Abdominal swelling?"

Melissa breathed a sigh of relief as she filled Nancy in. Her angst fled. Nancy was the answer to her prayers. "Yes. I'm sure she's been raped, but we didn't have any morning-after pills in our first-aid kit."

"Don't worry. I've got something for that, plus I've got something to calm her nerves. She'll be okay."

"Do you have any idea when this happened?" Melissa had to ask. "I mean, can you tell by the color of her bruises like they do on all those forensic murder shows on TV?"

Nancy allowed a small smile. "The people in Hollywood make everything look easy, don't they? But yes, we can make a calculated guess." She peered closer at Pich's wrists. "There's no yellowing. If this was her first assault, I'd say we're still inside the seventy-two-hour window as far as preventing conception goes. I'm more worried about internal injuries. Let's take care of first things first. David? Can you come get this little one for me?"

"Please don't let anything happen to these girls," Melissa pleaded when David eased Pich out of her arms. "Please take good care of them."

Nancy took hold of Melissa's forearm and pulled her in close. "All of these girls will live with us at our private compound, Melissa. I will personally watch over them as if they were my daughters. Don't worry. The minute you get back home, check your email. I'll send a progress report and pictures so you can see for yourself."

Melissa could've cried with relief.

"I need to run," Nancy murmured as she pulled Melissa in for a tight sisterly hug. "Pich will be feeling better within forty-eight hours. You'll see. I'll make sure of it."

"Thank you," Melissa said, her eyes squeezed tight against the pain climbing up her throat. "They're just babies. They deserve to be happy."

"And they will be," Nancy promised as she let go. "Remember, check your email. If you can't wait to talk to me until you get home, have Mark get in contact with David or Alex. We're never more than a phone call away, and I'll always make time for you. Bye now."

"Goodbye," Melissa said sadly. "Thanks again."

Mark and Zack transferred the Dangs and the rest of the girls into the waiting vans, all except for the five she'd fallen in love with. These five were hers, every last one of them. It broke her heart, but one by one, she said goodbye to stern but kindly Sotheara, then shy little Maly. There were no words as she pressed a tender kiss to bright-eyed Dara's forehead. And then there was the tense and taciturn child with fire in her deep brown eyes and a healthy dose of attitude.

"Goodbye, sweetheart," Melissa said calmly, not sure if she should risk kissing this little one, if that would only push her further away. "I'll never forget you."

The girl toed the deck mat. Her gaze shifted to the waiting van and back to Melissa. And God, this was the hardest thing in the world. At last, she shrugged like it was no big deal and turned and walked away. And that was okay. It wasn't fair to expect adult behavior from children who'd been traumatized the way these girls had.

She swallowed hard, the knot in her throat pumping tears up into her eyes. She'd grown fond of these lost little ducklings, Zack's name for the troop that had followed her around on this one-day trip up the Mekong. She tried to be brave, even stood there and watched David lift the last little girl into the van.

Melissa waved, determined to put on a brave face in front of these five gentle warriors who had her back. David swung the van door shut and waved goodbye. Melissa bit her bottom lip and returned the wave. Rory revved the hovercraft engine. The giant propellers aft commenced spinning, and carefully, Mark tugged her to her feet.

Melissa stood leaning against him until she couldn't see the vans anymore. Until she lost sight of the dock at the bend in the river. Until she'd left Tucker and every one of her ducklings...

*Behind.*

There was no way out. No light at the end of the tunnel, and even if there had been, Tucker couldn't have seen it. He'd been too busy taking Thick Neck down in a chokehold, squeezing the breath out of the big guy while he watched his back. The man's knees had buckled, but not before the three guys with him piled on Tucker with kidney punches and hammer-sized fists to his head, neck, and face.

He was losing, but Tucker held on. He'd always known it would come to this, that he'd die in some far off country fighting for freedom. A man couldn't ask for a better death than to give his life for his child. Still, he refused to let go, bound and determined to take as many of these child-slavers with him as he could. When Thick Neck went limp, Tucker came up swinging. He elbowed the guy on his right, but the man at Tucker's left whipped one of those damned stinging rods across his face, blinding him.

Tucker hit the deck, out of breath and nearly out of strength. Sucking in enough air for one last attack, he crouched low, his head down, his fingertips splayed to the floor. Tucker feigned defeat, his one eye watering. The third guy leaned over him screaming. The dumbass. Tucker just needed a moment to power up for what he expected would be the end of him. His heart flew to Melissa, hopefully on her way home by now. To Deuce, the baby boy Tucker never thought he'd see again. God, he loved them both. His heart ached for one more chance.

But it was not to be. He was done resting. His thigh muscles bunched. He clenched his fists. He endured one last rant from the big mouth spitting on him. Tucker growled, his fingers now tightened into fists and his knuckles to the floor, his heart the heart of a SEAL to the end. This—*this!*—was how real men died. For others. For the ones they loved. For home and family, for God and country.

With a mighty roar, he propelled his battle-hardened body off the ground, coming up fast, and surprising the two still pounding on him. One flew backward, righteous rage the only weapon Tucker had left. His son *would* live, damn it. Deuce would grow old and hopefully marry better than his old man had. He'd raise a family, and he'd play that violin as long as he wanted if Tucker had anything to say about it.

Enraged, he let the nasty predator within him come out to play. These bullies were accustomed to slapping children around. They didn't know what it meant to fight a real man. They did now. He rammed his hard head into the only guy still on his feet, then took a running leap at the wall, bounced off it, and clothes lined the next guy, chopping his neck as he swung by.

The first guy fell with a hard thump, but climbed unsteadily to his feet. The second tilted sideways, his arm extended to the wall. Dropping to his haunches, Tucker kicked low and swung wide, sending both adversaries to the concrete.

On his feet and moving fast, Tucker ducked behind the racks of shelves on his way out of Ham Thủ Thiêm Sewing Distributor. He hadn't expected to get this far. He cleared the metal fence in an easy, adrenaline-induced leap with several more guards nipping on his heels.

Isaiah was nowhere in sight.

*"Yes, I am. See the dirty brown garbage bin across the street?"*

*"You're hiding in the trash?"*

*"No, you moron. Vinnie's hiding in the bin. I thought you ought to know. Deuce and I are in the car I just stole. To your left. The rust bucket."*

*"You've got Luke?"*

*"Give me some credit, Chase. Of course I've got Luke. Now move it!"*

It didn't get better than that. Tucker blew out a deep breath as he ran to the stolen vehicle and climbed in. Deuce burrowed into him once his butt hit the backseat. Tucker tipped his head back, relief flooding him at the miracle of holding his kid in his arms. Nothing felt better.

"You're hurt," Deuce cried.

"I'm fine," Tucker insisted raggedly. "Let's get out of here."

"Are you sure?" Isaiah's dark eyes met his blurry gaze in the crooked rearview mirror. *"You've got Vinnie right where you want him. Now would be a good time to call the authorities."*

Tucker peered at the garbage bin out of the slit that, until this morning, had been his good eye. Vinnie, with his shiny shoes and white shirt was in there? Had he really thought with all Isaiah's light flickering that the police showed up? *What a chicken shit.*

"Another day," Tucker said. "Move it before everyone runs out of that building."

"You're hurt, Dad." Deuce's eyes were wide. His battered little friend barely nodded from beside him. Poor Luke's mouth was bloodied—his nose, too.

"Yeah, well…" Tucker watched the factory fence slide open, at least two-dozen more workers after him now, all armed with rods and brooms, and a couple with pistols. All headed his way. "Step on it," he urged his buddy.

The Chevy shuddered. Isaiah ground the gears, shifting when he should've been clutching.

"Depress the clutch, damn it! The middle pedal. Don't you know anything?"

"Right. Standard transmission. Not automatic. I-I-I've…" Isaiah slammed the vehicle into drive, "… got it!" And they were off, racing down the street, around traffic, tires squealing and gears grinding at every shift of the poor clutch popping.

"Turn right," Tucker ordered at the first intersection. "Go across the river."

Why?" Isaiah argued. "The sooner we get away from the city, the better."

"That's what they'll expect. Go right."

"But that will take you east." Isaiah shot Tucker a quick look. *"Are you going back to talk to Nicole? Is that why we're going east when we should be headed west?"*

Tucker couldn't answer. He honestly didn't know why he needed to go east.

Isaiah rounded the corner on two wheels while Tucker glanced over his shoulder, keeping an eye out the rear window. "Tell me again. What's your friend's name, son?"

"Luke," Deuce replied. "He helped me figure out how to work the steam presses so I didn't burn my fingers. I had to help him. He's my friend."

"I'm prouder than hell of you for stepping up to those bullies back there."

Deuce's big blue eyes shimmered, his lips pinched tight, but not crying. "I missed you, Dad."

And God, Tucker wanted to go back and punch that witch who'd hit his son, right in the middle of her ugly face. He thumped his son's knee instead, not going to break down. He reached out to Deuce's too-quiet friend. "It's good to meet you, Luke."

Luke nodded shyly, a tear tracking over his bruised cheek. He wasn't much taller than four feet and couldn't have weighed as much as Deuce.

"Does your friend speak English?"

Deuce grinned. "And French and Vietnamese, too."

A lump closed Tucker's throat. Of course Luke spoke Vietnamese, but it was so cute the way Deuce declared it, like he was proud of his friend. "Where's your mother? Weren't you supposed to have lunch with her today?"

Deuce blinked. "She says stuff like that all the time, but she doesn't mean it, Dad. Mom's not nice like she used to be."

Tucker couldn't begin to explain how Nicole never really was nice. He palmed his son's knee to distract him when Deuce's eyes brimmed. Vinnie wasn't the only one who still had a smack down coming. "I'll bet you and Luke are hungry. How about a cheeseburger and a bucket of greasy fries?"

"Yeah!" Deuce's eyes lit up, but Luke had yet to speak. Tucker planned to check the boy for injuries if he could keep his eyes open. His head pounded like a mother. "Isaiah, my boy's hungry," he hinted, his voice weaker than he'd expected.

Isaiah gunned the Chevy into the dense traffic crossing the Saigon River. It would've made Tucker feel good if he hadn't spotted a police cruiser behind them with its lights flashing. A shiver galloped over his shoulders. He'd come too far to lose Deuce now.

*"Sheriff's on your tail,"* he warned Isaiah. *"Step on it."*

"I see that," Isaiah murmured as he slowed to the speed limit. "Let me handle this."

Tucker bit back the urge to order his junior agent around. Isaiah had yet to do him wrong. The kid couldn't drive a stick for shit, but Tucker was willing to trust. He blinked hard at the pain in his chest. Man, a guy needed a day off once in a while.

The cruiser dodged traffic on its way east behind them, then moved in close and tailed them. Isaiah kept watch in the rear-view while Tucker strived not to turn around. Isaiah pressed his index finger to his temple. When he slowed down, Tucker's heart rate kicked up. The police car cranked up its siren and—

Shit. Tucker was sick of fighting the world. He gripped the door handle, intending to make a run for it the second Isaiah stopped, to draw the police away from the boys if push came to shove. Deuce deserved a better life, and Tucker meant for him to have it.

But the police car swerved around the Chevy and roared into traffic. Away. *Thank God.* Tucker exhaled heavily.

*"I'd appreciate it if you didn't call me God,"* Isaiah whispered into his mind. *"A name like that could stick to a guy. Now sit back and rest. You look like hell."*

*"I feel like hell. You did that? You tricked the cops?"* Tucker slouched back into his seat, utterly spent.

*"I made an astute observation, that's all. I told them the donuts were fresh out of the fryer east of the river, but they'd better hurry."*

Tucker would've laughed at the outrageous stereotype if his gut didn't hurt like it did. *"You did not."*

*"Actually..."* Isaiah glanced at him slyly. *"I simply planted a suggestion. I told the driver we were not who they were looking for. I told him they needed to stop bothering us and to hurry, the bad guys were getting away."*

Tucker closed his eyes, fighting the urge to hug the daylights out of his boy. Maybe even poor Luke. Maybe Isaiah, too.

# Chapter Twenty-Four

By the time they got close to Vinnie's, Tucker knew he was in trouble. He couldn't draw in a deep enough breath, and dark blotches compromised his vision in what was left of his one good eye. Ha. What a misnomer for an eyeball that dripped what he hoped were just tears. He didn't dare look at his kid in case it was blood trickling down his cheek. He kept his head down to wipe the leaking fluid without being seen. Crap. A man shouldn't feel so bad on such a good day. He had his kid back. He was on his way to the altar with a damned good woman. He should be buying a round for the whole world down at the local pub.

Instead...

He lost track of exactly when and precisely where Isaiah turned off the highway. He didn't want to move when the car stopped vibrating. He wanted to be left the hell alone.

"Is he okay?" Deuce asked somewhere off in the distance, and honestly, Tucker tried to come up with some pithy SEAL-type answer, but shit. The room he'd stumbled into spun, and he didn't have a clue where he was or how he'd gotten there. Not a good scenario for the lead dog to find himself in—accepting assistance when he was used to being the one who dashed in and rescued others.

Instead...

He collapsed onto the first bed he came to, his arm slung over his eyes because the light hurt his eyeball. Someone took his boots off, and he couldn't remember securing his gear or his weapons. Little by little, the cool breeze from the air conditioner wafted over his sweaty body, and he knew he was sick, a rare event in his life.

"Melissa," he growled, his lips dry and his throat sore. He reached for her, his arm flung wide even though he was pretty sure he was dreaming. Some guy pressed a bottle of water to his lips and he gulped a few swallows down. Ah. Finally. Some relief.

"It's me," Isaiah answered. "Melissa's with Mark and the guys, remember? We saved your son. He's in the shower and Luke's watching TV. Are you hungry? I've got noodles and—"

"Deuce?"

"Yes, Tucker. Deuce is safe. He and Luke have been playing video games and watching TV while you slept."

"Did we... get 'em?"

"Get who?" Isaiah wiped a cool rag over Tucker's forehead. Just once. Tucker snagged it out of his hands before he tried that crap again. "Did we get...?" He shut his mouth. He couldn't remember who he was supposed to get.

Isaiah kept talking, but Tucker's mind soared through dizzying spirals where eagles dared to fly and Navy SEALs were never wrong. A few words filtered through to him. *Airport. Mark. She's gone... home.*

Tucker swallowed the pills Isaiah shoved between his lips with one long gulp of lukewarm water, and he tried. He really tried to keep his mind alert and his eyes open, but...

A man's just a... man's just a... damned sick man.

He dozed off.

Tân Sơn Nhất Airport to Reagan International. Twenty-six hours of international flying discomfort as straight as the crow flew—if that crow stopped for a two-hour layover in Seoul, Korea. And if that crazy bird flew over the Arctic Circle, then hovered in a hold pattern over JFK International Airport until a passenger was ready to scream. The long flight home wore on Melissa's last nerve.

Not for Mark and the guys, though. Like her, all were sprawled out in first-class where they usually traveled. They'd dropped off to sleep the moment the jumbo jet's landing gear lifted up from Vietnamese soil. Maverick had nursed a whiskey sour until he gave up the ghost. Not Melissa. She couldn't sleep. Her heart was still in the country she'd left behind with Tucker and all those little girls.

Taz was one happy puppy when she retrieved him from her parent's place. They were happy to see her, especially after hearing her harrowing story, but he wriggled in her arms all the way home.

*Home.*

Somehow, her tidy bungalow-for-one didn't feel like home when she unlocked the door. It felt—bereft. Lonely. Empty. It didn't make her happy like it once had.

She'd always taken care of herself. Exercised. Ate a nutritionally balanced diet. Worked for charitable causes mostly because she didn't need the money. Yes, everyone thought she'd given her wealth away to that crackpot cult in California, that madman Lucien Cain, but she wasn't that dumb. She'd done the same thing Cassidy Dancer's husband, Jude, did before he'd gone looking for his missing daughter, Judith. She'd created a shell company and buried her assets, every last one of them, so deep that no self-professed prophet could reach one dollar of her wealth.

Yes, she'd stumbled into depression, and she hadn't made the smartest decisions for a short time in her life, but give every last day of her future away? Strip herself of Brady's hard-earned investments? Never. She'd been inconsolable and heartbroken after she'd lost Brady, but she hadn't been *that* dumb or *that* lost. She'd been confused. Not anymore.

Melissa wandered through her apartment with faithful Taz dancing at her heels. The reality of what she'd become stared bleakly back at her from her immaculately cleaned rooms. From her tidy refrigerator with not a single bottle of Sam Adams beer –Tucker's drink of choice—in it. From her well-organized closet without a single man's crisply ironed shirt or rumpled jacket or sweatshirt hanging alongside hers. Tucker preferred his ratty sweatshirt with bright yellow NAVY stenciled across it when he watched football at her place. She wished he'd left it behind. It'd be comforting to snuggle inside something that smelled like him.

But no. For too long now she'd resisted the male chaos Tucker brought into her life. She'd forced him to clean up after himself. To keep his hands to himself. To be some stupid idea of the perfect man. She'd tried to change him to fit her standards. What a ridiculous notion, to tame a man as big and wild and free as Tucker Chase. *What was I thinking?*

She lifted the sleeve of her favorite blazer to her nose. Not a hint of amber spice. No whiff of gunpowder. No sizzle. No Tucker. Just—her.

It might as well have been sterile. That was how she'd lived. Careful. Cautious. Steeped in other people's causes. Always running at someone else's noble beck and call and always doing it alone. At the end of every cause, she'd always ended up there. In her bedroom. Without one piece of Tucker to call her own.

Her gaze drifted to the floor. Most women had a pair of men's boots under their beds. Socks on the floor. Dinner to cook and men's clothes to wash. She had—nothing.

It was time to change.

Tucker wasn't perfect, but he loved her, and she wanted inside that man's arms. She wanted her life back. Her real life.

"I never should've left him," she told Taz as a plan began to percolate. There was a way to turn this around. She'd have to be discreet when she called Alex, careful of what she said and how she phrased her questions. She couldn't give her intentions away. Alex was sharp, and Tucker might already be on his way home, but if he wasn't...

The sweet dog in her lap narrowed his eyes at her the way contented dogs do. She stroked him from the crest of his silky head to the tip of his fuzzy tail. "I'm going back to Vietnam, Taz."

Tucker wavered at the edge of feeling like crap and wanting to die. Some old guy leaned out of the dark and hovered over him for a moment there, but didn't pull him back. Tucker wasn't sure if he was real or not.

"Stewart?" he croaked, seeing things for sure. Couldn't be him. This guy had rheumy brown eyes, not startling blue lasers that pinpoint welded a guy's backbone to the wall like a deer hide stretched out to dry.

Stewart was like that though, charging into the fray to rescue his guys. Working outrageous miracles when missions fell apart. Like that op in California. The one in Morocco. The one in the heart of Alexandria, Virginia, in Stewart's own Sit Room. But the blue-eyed devil wouldn't be charging to the rescue this time, would he? Tucker wasn't one of his guys.

Somehow that—hurt.

The brown-eyed ghoul came and went, a smart decision. It wasn't the first to hover over him. A guy with a raging fever sees a lot of old buddies and dead enemies when he's half out of his head. Some flowing black shadow with bony fingers and a long silver scythe kept passing over his bed. He was sure of it.

Tucker tossed and turned and dreamed of Melissa. Needed her. Ached for her. Burned for her petal-soft skin. The warmth of her lush breasts rubbing against his chest. The taste of her slightly salty skin on his tongue. Her midnight beauty and her exquisite scent—apples and cinnamon and—virtue. Until he'd met her, he hadn't known virtue had an odor, but it did. Crisp and clean with a bite—a lot like bleach. Too clean. Too straight and too narrow. His

Melissa. The woman needed to learn how to play. How to relax.

He floated between reality and shadow, sure that Melissa was perfect just the way she was. *Too perfect.* As thrilled as he was that she'd kept herself pure and clean after she'd lost Brady, Tucker wanted to mess her up again. To brand her and make her his. To bite her, bruise her, and kiss her lips until she was swollen and wanting.

But she wasn't there, was she? No. She'd gone off with that handsome bastard Mark Houston and left Tucker behind when he was damned sick. Not good. Covert operators died when they got this sick, and... and... that pesky old guy loomed over him again. Why Tucker had ever thought he looked like Stewart made no sense. It had to be the way he kept slapping Tucker's hand away and growling, "Do as you're told."

"Go 'way. I'm good." Tucker came back at him with as much SEAL positivity as he could muster. He struggled to his elbows, a tough job that shouldn't have made the dark little room spin like it did. But damn. The ceiling dipped and bucked like he was back aboard ship in choppy seas. The walls closed in.

He sank back to his pillow to control the nausea lifting up his throat. A shiver raced over his body. That was another thing. *Why's it so cold in this dive? Who left the air conditioner on high? Where's Isaiah and Deuce?*

*"Take it easy, Tucker,"* came the instant answer. *"The air conditioner isn't blowing on you, but you do*

*have a one-oh-five fever. Your son knew a good doctor, so be nice to Doctor Trang. Stop fighting him. Let him do his job."*

Tucker's head lolled to the side. He squinted through the fog in his head, pushing the sight in his one good eye to cut through the bullshit. *"Where the hell are you?"*

Isaiah stepped out of the shadows to Tucker's bedside. Deuce was right there with him, worry etched on his face, but a welcome sight for Tucker's one good eye.

"Son," was all he could say as he reached for his kid. His arms had turned to lead. He settled for fluttering his fingers.

Deuce grabbed hold of his old man's hand like a good boy. "Dad, you're sick so relax. Dr. Trang's got some medicine for you. Please don't argue with him."

"I'm... not... arguin'," Tucker asserted as clearly as he could with a thick tongue and thicker lips. It was easier talking with Isaiah. *"Am I?"*

*"You never quit. You're a very belligerent patient. Deuce and I tried to take care of you. We didn't think you'd want a doctor involved, but it's been three days, and you weren't getting better. Take your medicine and be good for a change—can you do that? Dr. Trang is going to give you a strong antibiotic."*

*"Bullshit."* Tucker tried to put enough determination into that one word to make Isaiah

understand. *"SEALs don't get sick, you moron. We're invincible.*

Isaiah had the good sense not to argue.

*"Where are we?"* A good operator needed to know where he was at all times.

*"We're on the east side of the Saigon River, like you wanted. We're at the Happy Dragon hotel, less than ten miles from your ex's place. Once you get feeling better, we'll swing by for a visit if you still think that's a good idea."*

Thinking took more mental dexterity than Tucker had at the moment. *"Why the hell do we need to visit her?"*

Isaiah snickered. *"My thoughts exactly. Roll over, Tucker."*

Tucker closed his eyes and rolled over, not sure why he needed to be on his side to talk with Isaiah. *"There. I'm over. You happy?"*

He heard another quiet snicker as he closed his eyes and—

Damn it! Dr. Trang stuck a needle in the left cheek of his ass.

# Chapter Twenty-Five

Melissa cleared customs easily on her return trip. It was simple with only one carry-on to declare. Borrowing Tucker's over-confidence, she'd caught the first flight back to Tân Sơn Nhất, but didn't dare tell Alex or Mark, not even to have them contact Tucker and let him know she was on her way. They'd be angry, and there was no reason to tell either of them her business in the first place. She and Tucker would be back home before Alex or Mark were any the wiser.

At least, that was the plan.

She hadn't an idea where to find Tucker, but she knew where to find his ex. That was Melissa's first stop after she dropped her bag off at her hotel, the pricey five-star Hotel Majestic Saigon. The stunning hotel of French colonial design boasted a splendid view of the Saigon River, a view she had no intention of relishing once she got Tucker back. Not if she had her way. She meant to wine and dine and molest him to her heart's content on that plush king-sized bed in her room. They deserved one night of pure unadulterated bliss together before they ended this— mission. She liked that word. That was exactly what she was on, a mission to get her man back.

By now, he had to have located his son, Deuce. He and Isaiah worked well together. Surely they'd accomplished their one and only goal, hadn't they? They had to be having that final confrontation with Tucker's ex. She nearly giggled in anticipation, a very un-Melissa-like response, but wouldn't Tucker be surprised to see her? Wouldn't he be thrilled she'd tracked him down?

Melissa fully realized this impulsive trip might not turn out the way she expected, but she meant to give it all she could, just in case. She didn't plan to confront the ex-Mrs. Chase, but she did intend to follow her. A woman who's just lost track of her son and her only bargaining chip would surely be on the hunt for him. Melissa intended to tail Nicole. If anyone could lead her to Tucker, it would be his borderline psycho ex. This mission shouldn't take long.

Leaving Tucker behind two days ago had drained her, but returning had the opposite effect. She was energized, even after two long back-to-back international flights. Taz was back at her parents. Finally, the stars had lined up.

Melissa dropped her bag at the hotel. She caught a cab and proceeded with her plan. The cabbie headed east on the Vo Van Keit Highway and into the Thu Thiem Tunnel under the Saigon River. Everything seemed so much easier in the bright light of day. The cabbie was polite and spoke proper English. She had enough VND, Vietnamese Dong, in her tidy backpack for her mission. She'd purposefully chosen denim jeans, a light sweatshirt, and a sturdy pair of walking shoes for the day. She could do this.

At least, that was the plan.

*I'm alive. Finally.*

Tucker opened one bleary eye, his good one. The sunlight cracking through the window blinds didn't ping like shards of broken glass in his skull. He drew in a slow breath, relishing the comparative lack of pain. He swallowed, his throat parched, but no longer raw.

"You're awake."

He turned to the weary tone in that familiar voice. Isaiah sat in a worn overstuffed chair opposite the bed, his long fingers stretched over his brow and tunneled into his black, curly hair.

"Hey," Tucker rasped, surprised at the weakness in his own voice. "You got some water around here?"

"I'll get it," Deuce jumped up from the floor and offered cheerfully. Damn, he was a sight for Tucker's sore, tired eye.

Tucker straightened his back against the headboard, hating that his son was waiting on him, but thrilled at the honest familial tone to it. Deuce made him smile. The kid was nothing like his mother.

He brought two bottles of dripping wet, ice-cold water. Tucker popped the cap off the first and drained it. *So good.* By the time he'd crumpled the plastic, Deuce had the second bottle open and ready. "I knew you'd be thirsty," he said, his dark eyes bright when he traded for the empty bottle. "You look a whole lot better, Dad."

Tucker grunted and downed the second bottle. "What have you two guys been doing while I've been sick?"

Isaiah shot him a quelling look. *"Watching your sorry ass sleep and listening to you complain. What do you think?"*

"Me and Luke been watching TV and playing video games, but that's okay." Deuce shrugged one shoulder. "He doesn't have a television at his house, so I'm making sure he has fun."

Luke? Oh yeah. That skinny little kid from the factory. Tucker looked across the mussed bed for the boy. Luke faced the TV, a game controller in his grip, totally absorbed with the brightly colored antics on the screen. "Doesn't Luke have a family to go home to?" Tucker asked his son while he pushed a question to Isaiah. *"Is Luke well? Did you have that troll of a doctor look at him?"*

Deuce wrinkled his nose and shook his head. "No, Dad. He doesn't. His grandpa died last year, and he's been alone since, and I kinda thought maybe…"

Tucker closed his eyes, thrilled at the wheedling pitch to his son's voice. God, he'd missed being a dad. Deuce sounded—normal. Not the prissy boy Nicole had tried to carve him into. It was possible he had more of his old man's genetics in him than Tucker had suspected. "Let me guess. You want to know if we can keep Luke?"

Isaiah answered, *"Dr. Trang checked him. He's as well as a kid on the streets in this city can be, Tucker. You should've seen him eat the first time I brought food. He needs a family or he won't last long."*

Deuce shrugged. "Well, now that you mention it, yeah. He needs someone, and he could live with us, and he could be my brother, and—"

Tucker closed his eye and chuckled at Deuce's simple outlook on life. He hadn't seen his kid in well over a year and the first thing Deuce wanted was to bring home a brother. Life didn't get any more normal than that. Bizarre maybe, but normal to an eleven-year-old's way of thinking. What was odd was that Deuce had yet to ask about his mother.

Running a hand over his head, Tucker came up with fingers full of bedhead hair. His mouth felt like something had crawled in there and died. He needed a shave. "Son, I'm going to shower first, then we can sit down and eat breakfast or whatever meal of the day it is. Then we'll discuss what we can do with Luke if his story checks out. We can't go kidnapping a Vietnamese national just because we like him, can we?"

Damned if Deuce didn't fall into his father's arms instead of arguing. "Dad," he ground out, his voice packed with emotion. "I missed you so much."

Tucker buried his nose in his kid's hair, his heart about as full as it could get. There was nothing better in the world than the love of your son, the warmth of his gangly body in your arms, and your future suddenly brighter. Tucker closed his eye and let the tears track out of it and down his scruffy cheek. This was precisely what he'd come to Vietnam for. "I missed you too, Deuce."

"I love you, Dad. I'm sorry I left you, and I'm sorry I—"

"Let me up." That bullshit had to stop. Tucker tousled his son's curly black hair.

Deuce pulled away, but didn't let go of his old man's hand. Tucker cupped his very intelligent child's chin and looked him in the eye. Man to man. Deuce was a helluva lot smarter than his old man. He'd understand. "Don't you ever be sorry for anything. You had no say in what happened between your mother and me. It's my fault. All mine. Not yours. I screwed up. I should've been a better father, and I should've been a better man. If I had, none of this would've happened."

"Do you still love Mother?" the innocent, hopeful boy asked.

"No," Tucker said bluntly. That needed to be out in the open. There was no going back to Nicole. "But I don't hate her either. We had our chance together, and we both blew it. I've got a new woman in my life, and I want you to meet her as soon as we get back to the States. You'll like her."

It was hard not to miss the disappointment shifting through Deuce's eyes, but Tucker kept going. "Her name's Melissa McCormack. She's a good woman. You ever heard of McCormack Industries?"

*"You're rambling, Tucker. Deuce doesn't care about prestige and power. He just wants his mom and dad back like they used to be, and that's not going to happen. Don't lie to him."*

Tucker shot a quick glance at Isaiah. He sounded like he knew what Deuce had gone through. He might be right. Tucker gripped his son's arm. "The thing is, people change. I'm not the guy I used to be. I want to be part of your life, and I'm going to do anything I can to prove it to you and your mother."

Deuce sank against his father, his arms wrapped around Tucker's neck. "You don't have to prove anything to me. Don't change. You're my dad, and I love you. I want to stay with you. I'm almost old enough I can decide for myself. I choose you, Dad."

Not likely. Deuce wanted to believe he had a choice in the matter, but the truth was divorce laws varied from state to state. No matter what Tucker or

Deuce thought or wanted, some impartial judge would make the final determination as to which parent was the best for this bright young man. Unfortunately, the way Tucker had gone about getting his kid back would weigh heavily in the final outcome.

Tucker's heart swelled. He blinked hard and failed miserably at pretending he was tough. "Listen, Deuce. You keep thinking positive, and we'll take this up with a judge the minute we get home. Now let's go eat."

A sharp knock at the door startled everyone. "Are you expecting company?" Tucker asked his partner. That would've been nice to know.

Isaiah shook his head, his shoulders off the chair back he'd been lounging into. "Not room service, either." Damned if the kid didn't have his pistol already in his hand like a good operator should. Like Tucker wished he had. "You seen my gear bag?"

By then Isaiah was at the door, his index finger to his lips and his eyeball to the peephole. "It's your ex," he whispered. "She doesn't look happy. What do you want me to do?"

"Mother? She's here? How...?" Deuce asked, a tremble in his tone. "Don't answer it, Isaiah. Please don't open that door."

Tucker ran a hand over his head, not sure how Nicole had tracked him. He wasn't ready for a showdown, but there she was, probably tapping her high-heeled toes and pissed that no one had answered yet. He looked to his son for the best way forward. "Do you want to talk to your mom?"

"No." Deuce shook his head slowly. Deliberately. "She told me I had to learn how to work like a man. She told me that guy's boys are better men than me, but Dad, there's two of them. She said I was soft, but they're both fatter than me, and I'm not soft. Feel." He bunched his bicep for his dad.

Tucker's temper flared. "She told you that? After all the crap she gave me about you not playing baseball and not going to the gym with me? After making you play violin?"

"But I love my violin." Poor Deuce glanced at the door, his eyes wide. "But I don't like it when she lets him hit me. She says it will make me a man. Don't make me go, Dad. I don't want to. Please—"

"Never," Tucker growled, sorry he'd caused his son to think for one second he'd have to go back with his mother. "Deuce, go over there with Isaiah. Take Luke with you while I talk to your mom, and don't worry. You're staying with me."

*"This isn't a good idea,"* Isaiah cautioned. *"You're not well and she looks mean enough to hurt you. Look at you."*

*Yeah, well...* Tucker shoved his hair off his forehead, determined to end this family feud once and for all. He stretched his hands over his head to get the kinks out of his spine, then ambled to the door and jerked it open to the surprised bitch who'd made his life, and now Deuce's life, hell. "What do you want?" he asked bluntly, "and how did you find out where I'm staying? And what's this bullshit that you let your asshole husband hit my boy?"

"Tucker. Sweetie," she breathed, not answering. Her fingers fluttered at her throat, drawing attention to her scooped neckline and her over-abundant cleavage. "Oh my God, it's so nice to see you again."

He grunted, not buying that line of BS. How she got those fake big boobs into that tiny tee amazed him. There was a day he'd wanted her stacked. Not anymore. Her platinum hair looked over-sprayed and stiff. Her nails were too long and too red. Too twisted. Like her. Even her heels made her bubble butt jut out more than was physically attractive.

"My doctor called and said Devlin was staying here with you. He told me how sick you were. Naturally, I had to come by to see if my son was okay or if you needed anything." She minced a step forward, leading with those knockers he used to love playing with, like she thought she could use them to get inside. Like she thought he'd still let her.

Not happening. Tucker stepped outside and pulled the door shut behind him. Isaiah had set him up in a ground-floor room with an outside exit. Smart kid. He'd learned. But the sun was up and hot, even through the leafy fronds arched over the walk on this side of the hotel. Tucker leaned his bicep to the doorjamb, squinting at his ex. "Cut the crap, Nicole. What do you really want?"

"To help," she insisted, batting those incredibly long eyelashes. "I mean, look at you. You're beat up like you always used to be when you came home. Do you need some ice for that eye? It looks really bad." She drew out her last words. Like she cared.

Damned if she didn't get up close and personal, though, her ample cleavage nearly touching his chest. He stared her down, not backing off and not once falling for those silicone knockers or that slick tone to her voice. "Back off. I'm good."

"Why, Tuck," she demurred as if she had a shy bone in her black widow body. "I've missed you, you know. It's been so lonely over here."

"Is that why you never called? Never wrote? Never answered my emails, voicemails, or text messages asking about Deuce?" He pressed his butt to the door, wondering what he'd seen in this conniving woman all those years ago. "Is that why you took off without letting me know you were taking my son out of the country? Is that why you ran off and got married? You *missed* me? Give me a break. I've been out of my mind for months, but not once did you do what was decent, and let me know where you'd gone. No, I had to track you and Deuce down myself, and then I find you've let your jerk of a husband beat on my kid. What the hell do you want?" He ran a hand up the back his neck, pissed and suppressing the urge to knock her on her ass, once and for all.

She had the nerve to tap her manicured fingernail to his lower lip. The woman never could answer a straight question. "Remember how good we used to be together?"

He brushed her hand away like the annoying fly it was. "Cut the crap. Don't act like you don't know what I've been doing. Surely Vinnie's climbed out of the stinking garbage bin by now and told you his version of what went down."

She blinked big, wide eyes, her fake lashes fluttering and those red-tinted lips pursed like she hadn't a clue what he was talking about. "Vinnie was in a garbage bin? Really? My Vinnie?" Something about the way she lifted her chin when she asked *'My Vinnie?'* raised Tucker's sniper sense to full alert. Nicole wasn't there for Deuce.

Right on cue, her dark eyes shuttered. Her lashes lowered. She shifted her heels into proper model stance, the heel of one butted into the arch of the other. It made her wobble, as high and as big as her centers of gravity were. She tilted forward, whether deliberately or out of sheer stupidity, but she landed in Tucker's arms, plastered against him with her chin raised, her mouth too close for comfort.

He peered down into her heavily shadowed, outlined eyes, wondering what the hell he'd ever seen in there. This woman wore so much makeup, she'd probably used a trowel to slather it on and a putty knife to scrape it off.

"Vinnie's not the man I thought he was," she said breathily. "I've changed my mind. I want you, Tucker, and I'll do anything to get you back. Please don't make me leave." She wrapped her arms around his neck, her breasts pressed to his chest, and that was the last straw.

Tucker arched away from her. She made his flesh crawl. "I didn't make you leave last time, now get your grubby hands off me," he growled, not taking no for an answer. Deuce was going home with him.

# Chapter Twenty-Six

Things were going splendidly! Melissa couldn't have been happier. After she'd located Nicole's address, she'd paid her cabbie extra to keep up with the silver Mercedes that pulled out of Nicole's estate.

"Follow that car," she urged her cabbie on, a zing of excitement zipping up her spine at the movie line that sprang so naturally to her lips.

"Yes, ma'am," he said cheerfully. He ought to be cheerful. He was getting paid enough for this joyride. "I follow you anywhere."

"Not me. Just that car." Melissa couldn't help but smile. She'd employed the perfect driver for this adventure. This was her lucky day.

Surprisingly, Tucker's ex was driving, not what Melissa expected after seeing the lavish estate. The cabbie got hung up at a train crossing that took forever.

"Oh no. We're losing her," Melissa cried.

"No worry. We find. I good driver. I sharp eyes. We find," he replied in his broken English.

She tugged at the long blonde curl draped over her shoulder, loving his enthusiasm and willingness to help, but how would they ever find that Mercedes now? This wasn't one of those sleek bullet trains. Her magnificent plan to surprise Tucker had been brought to its knees by a diesel workhorse of an engine with a hundred or so dirty cars lumbering behind it. Doing five miles an hour.

"Darn," she whined, straining to catch a glimpse of that Mercedes beyond the clattering rail cars. "We lost her."

"No worry," her cabbie repeated, even as he tuned his car radio to a local station of soft and soothing sounds that only irked her more. Maybe this wasn't her day after all. Okay then. There was always tomorrow. If her cabbie was willing, they could—what was the word? Stake out Nicole's place until she came back? Tail her again tomorrow? The day seemed hopelessly lost until the last rail car rumbled by. Thank goodness.

"Hurry," she urged the cabbie onward before another train came by.

"Look! I find your silver car," he exclaimed when they were no more than over the tracks.

Melissa rolled down her window and peered closer at the vehicle in the parking lot. It looked like the same Mercedes, but why would Nicole park there?

The hotel wasn't much to look at. More of a motel, it boasted ground-level rooms within the noisy screech of the railroad at its doorstep. Broken-down vehicles and more than a few mopeds filled the lot, but Nicole's silver Mercedes was parked in the fifth stall from the front door. Melissa could tell by the license plate.

The cabbie slowed down, then parked at the curb. What a piece of good luck. What a piece of...

*Oh. My. God.*

Melissa's gaze landed on the plump backside of a platinum blonde who could only be Tucker's ex. She had some guy cornered at one of the ground floor rooms.

Melissa's heart climbed up her throat, along with her stomach. She would've recognized those tanned and incredibly sculpted biceps anywhere. That shock of black hair, too long to be military, too short to be shaggy. That lock that never failed to flip into his eyes when he kissed her.

Nicole took a step into him, and...

*Oh hell.* She kissed him. *Him.*

Tucker.

Tucker unwound his ex-wife's sticky tentacles from his neck and set her a full step away from him. "You're not taking Deuce," he stated clearly, the sun too bright and hurting his eye. At this rate, it wouldn't be good for long. "That's not why you're here anyway. Spill. What do you really want?"

She grunted, an airy snort whistling from her nose, the loving wife act stowed and her claws out. "I've been wondering when you'd show up and demand custody. It took you long enough."

He could've slapped her for disrespecting Deuce if her words hadn't made him deep down, intrinsically happy. But he needed to make certain she knew what she was up against if this was just another one of her games. This time, he'd fight tooth and nail for his son. Nicole wasn't getting anything but the end of his steel-toed boot. "I've got video proof Vinnie's beating the children in his garment factory, Deuce included. Know right here and now, I'll do everything I can to bring him down and you with him."

Nicole shook her head. "You've got nothing on me, Tucker, just Vinnie. I've never set foot inside his factory, and I don't intend to. It's a disgusting, dirty place. I'm too good for him, and you know it. Why do you think I'm so happy to see you? You're the answer to all my problems."

She reached one long finger to his bicep, but he dodged her touch, never wanting her hands on him again. "I'm not staying. Deuce and I are on the first flight out of here."

Her chin lifted in a dare. "I don't think so. Not after I tell the police where you are."

He narrowed his gaze at the she-serpent in her tiny tee. She knew something.

"Yes, Tuck, my wonderful ex-husband." She cocked a fist to her hip. "I confess. I did hear from Vinnie. After he told me what you'd done to him at his factory, I knew I had all the leverage I needed to get away from him."

Tucker waited. *Here it comes...*

Nicole's manicured brows pinched to a *V*. "He's abusive, Tuck. To everyone, not just his workers. He honestly thinks he can use people to get what he wants. I had no idea he had two sons when he married me. Stupid me—I should've insisted on a pre-nup, but no—I actually trusted him. Do you believe that? I believed the lying son-of-a-bitch. I thought Devlin would inherit Ham Thủ Thiêm Sewing and all Vinnie's other factories. I thought... I thought..." She sputtered, her nostrils flared. "Never mind. The point is I'm not even in line to inherit that Mercedes I drove here. Devlin isn't either. Everything goes to Vinnie's sons. The factories. The mills. Even the stupid delivery trucks. Heaven forbid if something should happen to those two whiny brats, but if it does, and don't think I haven't thought about it—Vinnie's old nag of a mother's next in line. I'm not even in his will! His ex-wife is, but not me. Do you believe that?"

That explained her swift departure from the States. Nicole, the gold-digger, had grabbed an opportunity that hadn't panned out as she'd expected. He didn't miss the subtle death threat against Vinnie's two boys, nor the utter shock in her tone that anyone could be as devious or as manipulative as she was. Tucker grunted. *There really is a god.*

But worse, he'd caught the undertone to her drama, the real reason she'd wanted that pre-nup. This wasn't about Deuce inheriting anything, not as quickly as she'd offloaded him to Vinnie's sweatshop. This was purely about Nicole.

*"Yes, Tucker, you're right,"* Isaiah whispered on their secret channel. *"She's capable of killing you and your son. She only sent him to work in the factory after she discovered Vinnie's will. Be careful. She might be armed."*

"We're done here," Tucker declared evenly. If Isaiah thought she had a weapon on her, she most likely did. His head had set to throbbing with rage, and his back hurt. He needed to lie down before he hit something—or someone. "Do your worst. You can't touch me, and you're sure as hell not taking Deuce."

"Devlin," she spat.

"Deuce!" Tucker roared, his sore fingers clenched to do the deed, his heart ready. "He's my son and his name is Deuce."

"Don't you have a twenty-four-hour charge against you to get out of the country?" she hissed, her eyes flashing. "Aren't the police looking for you even as we speak? Don't you stand to lose that sniveling eleven-year-old snot hiding in the hotel room behind you? What's going to happen to him then? Did you ever think about that?"

*"How does she know about my twenty-four-hour deadline?"*

*"This is Nicole, remember? She knows people in low places. Cops. Scumbags..."*

That obvious revelation made Tucker rethink how he'd lost Devlin in the first place. What exactly had Nicole done to influence the judge in that case? It didn't matter now, but what exactly was she capable of? How low would she stoop to get what she wanted?

Damned if the door didn't open behind Tucker, nearly dropping him to his butt.

"Sorry, Dad," Deuce said as he steadied his old man, one surprisingly strong palm to the middle of Tucker's back. "Hello, Mother. What? No dashing Vinnie at your side? No chauffeur? No servants?"

Tucker's lips twitched into a no kidding smile at the nerve of his kid. Deuce had changed—a lot. He was no little boy any more.

She rolled her eyes. "Shut up, Devlin. Your father was dashing. Vinnie's just... convenient."

Deuce cocked his head at his mother, his hand on his father's bicep in an outright show of solidarity. "Leave us alone. Stop hurting everyone who loves you."

Nicole tossed her head. "Why'd you have to turn out like your father, Devlin? And don't go telling me about love. You know nothing about it. Get it through your thick skulls, both of you. Love's in the eye of the beholder, and from my point of view, it's all about the diamonds and gold I'm going to be holding. Love is for losers, but money talks. I'm after Vinnie's real investments. His mutual bonds and marketable securities. I want his land. Get a clue, Tucker. He owns more than that two-bit factory. I'm talking about assets. Real assets."

"You never loved me, did you?" Tucker asked quietly, his past life with this shallow dame now crystal clear. Everything about Nicole was false. True, he'd bullied her into the 38Ds, but his immature desires had certainly struck pay dirt. She'd used her wiles and her looks, her brilliant mind, and her over-sexed body, but for what? To destroy others? To make herself rich?

"Yeah, once. Maybe." She scrunched her nose like the feline she was. "That night on the bridge was kind of hot."

Heat flamed up his neck at that foolish fifteen minutes and the dare to take her from behind while she faced the brightly lighted Jefferson Memorial. Young kids did stupid things for the thrill of sex in public places. For the adrenaline rush of being caught. Hell, he'd been home on a two-week leave, sex-starved, and still thinking she loved him. It was late and dark and—suddenly, it seemed like a long time ago. "You'll never be happy, will you?"

"Yes, I will." She stuck a finger in his face. "As soon as you waste that prick Vinnie, his two brats, and that decrepit mother-in-law I'm stuck with."

*"Ah, so that's what she wants—a hitman to clean up her mistakes so she can move onto bigger, richer*

*prey,"* Isaiah murmured in Tucker's head. *"Was she always like this?"*

"Mostly," Tucker admitted, *"but she's gotten meaner. Uglier. Bitchier."*

Nicole kept going. "Do this for me, Tuck, and I promise I won't tell anyone you're still in town. It'll be our secret. I won't sell you out. Hell, I'll fly you out of the country on Vinnie's private jet. Just do this one teensy little thing, for old time's sake." Nicole launched herself into his arms, her lips puckered and her eyes lethal. "You owe me that, Tucker."

He pushed her out of his space one last time. "I don't owe you shit."

Melissa had seen enough despite the tears in her eyes. "Take me back," she whispered to her faithful cabbie, her eyes on the floor along with her shattered heart. She couldn't stop shaking. Bile pressed up her throat. "Please. Just take me back to my hotel."

He lifted his bony arm over the seat, his gaze skating over her. "Why you so sad? We are here where you wanted to be."

Her heart thudded with all of her foolish, lost dreams. Yes, she was there, right where she wanted to be. Enlightened. Shattered. So disappointed. She had all the proof she needed. Tucker wouldn't change. He would always have a woman in every port. Every hotel. And she, Melissa McCormack, was a very stupid woman to have believed otherwise.

The gentle cabbie waited on her answer. He wasn't an old man, but he was older. Maybe fifty. Age amongst Asian people was difficult for her to determine. She huffed through her nostrils, holding herself together, her arms tight against her stomach to keep it from heaving. "Please. I just want to go back to my hotel. Don't worry. I'll pay you what we agreed on."

"That not problem." He huffed and murmured something more she didn't understand, but turned to the steering wheel and said, "If you think."

Most likely he'd meant, 'if you think so,' but his words struck a familiar chord. *Think.* Alex Stewart's favorite and often-used word, sometimes expressed with a shot of venom to get his point across. *Think, damn it.*

*Well okay, Alex,* she thought to herself. Breathing hard, she lifted her lashes and let her gaze scroll back to the scene at the hotel. *Tuck,* her heart cried out. He'd seemed so ardently in love with her back in the jungle. He'd been so romantic. So different. Hadn't he?

She cringed at how wanton she'd been. How willing to throw her values away just to be with him in every sense of the word. How foolish. God, she'd thrown herself at him. Swiping the back of her finger through the tears on her lashes, she fought for a grip on her emotions. To not let anyone hurt her again.

The cabbie shifted the car into drive while Melissa blinked her blurry vision away. A young man had joined Tucker at the open door. That was a good sign. Maybe this wasn't a hook-up. Tucker wouldn't be with a hooker if he had a kid with him. Melissa knew that much for certain. He might reek of raw sex and testosterone. He might be tempted, but he reeked of honor, too.

She looked closer. *Is that Deuce?* That young man looked to be the right age. He did look a lot like Tucker. She straightened her spine. "Umm, I'm sorry, but can we wait here a moment longer?"

Her cabbie shoved the stick into park. "For you, anything. You take all the time to think and wait. I wait with you."

She wiped the condensation from her breath off the passenger window, wishing that blonde, who was very probably Nicole, would move to the left so she could see the look on Tucker's face better. Of course, the woman didn't, but the few seconds more of watching gave Melissa time to think. If Tucker had Deuce, Isaiah was nearby, maybe in the same hotel room. "Do you have a cell phone I could borrow? I need to make a call."

Her cabbie turned around. "My name Jacob Giang. What is your name?"

She gulped at her rudeness. "I am Melissa McCormack," she said contritely. "Please excuse my ignorance."

He handed an older-style flip-phone over the back of the seat. "Do you know how to make a call in my country?"

"No, I... don't." She glanced at the hotel. "But do you see that man standing there? I need to call that room. I'm looking for a man named Isaiah Zaroyin. Can you place the call for me?"

Jacob smiled. "Yes, I can. For you."

She clung to the back of the front seat while he placed the call and chatted with the front desk in his language. He paused and waited, then asked in English, "Excuse me, sir, but are you Mr. Isaiah Zaroyin?" With a smile, he handed the phone over.

Melissa pressed it to her ear. "Isaiah?"

"Who's this? Melissa? Oh my God, what are you doing here?"

"Never mind." She smiled at the surprise in his tone. "I'm outside the hotel. Is that Nicole talking with Tucker? Can you hear what they're saying? Do you know?"

He blew out a slow hiss. "Umm, yeah. She showed up a few minutes ago. She's trying to blackmail him into killing her current husband in exchange for Deuce's safe passage out of the country."

"She's what?" Melissa's righteous rage boiled over. "That bitch."

"You've got that right. I can't for the life of me figure what Tucker ever saw in her, but he's getting a tough lesson in paybacks right now."

"He's not considering her offer, is he?" The question blurted out of Melissa's big mouth. "Never mind. I know that answer. Sorry, Isaiah. I was just a little stressed when I thought they were kissing."

"Tucker, kiss *that*?" The shock in Isaiah's tone made Melissa smile. "He might not be the brightest guy in the world, but he's a helluva lot smarter than to kiss a skank like Nicole. Sorry for the language, ma'am."

Melissa squeezed her eyes before she burst into tears of relief, so thankful for Alex and that darned smart word of his. "I'm coming in, Isaiah. Please put a pot of coffee on. We've got a lot to talk about."

"Yes, ma'am." It was hard not to miss the respect in Isaiah's quick response.

With a deep breath, she handed the phone back to the honorable Jacob Giang. "Thank you so much for helping me. May I enlist your services for the rest of the day?"

# Chapter Twenty-Seven

*Holy shit. I'm dead.* Tucker's heart lurched up his throat. His lungs failed, as in flat stopped sucking in air molecules. He wanted to die. Straight ahead at his twelve o-clock walked the woman of his dreams. Make that strutted. No, make that marched. And there he stood, chatting with the other woman—his ex.

Miss Melissa McCormack had her swagger on, a funny lift to her chin and a cocky tilt to her head, but he couldn't miss the hellfire sparking in her eyes. She didn't look happy. Dressed in boots and jeans, not her usual classy get-up, she took long, determined strides, her sumptuous hips swaying like a sexy predator on the hunt. A lioness. With her head tossed high and her long blonde hair streaming behind her, she licked her lips like she needed to kill something. Like him.

He couldn't force a swallow down his dry-as-hell throat. No woman would ever believe he hadn't just kissed Nicole, not the way she'd been all over him. His heart fluttered to a dead stop, but he met Melissa's steely-eyed glare. She didn't bat an eye. *I am so dead.*

Death was coming for him in the sweet, sexy—and very deadly gaze of his all-American girl. His nostrils flared to draw in the sultry scent of apples and cinnamon on the breeze. He ran the tip of his tongue over his bottom lip remembering the taste of her silkiest skin. The night of unbridled passion when she'd given herself to him. All the things he'd never have again. His one good eye watered at all he stood to lose.

*Damn it. Why now? Why here?*

*"Relax big guy."* Isaiah quietly chuckled. *"Melissa knows what's going on. She's not here to kill you, but your ex ought to run for her life. I keep getting impressions of 'He's mine, bitch' from Melissa—or something like that."*

Tucker ran a quick hand over his weary eyes, wishing this face-off could happen when he felt better. "Isn't she supposed to be with Mark? What's she doing here?"

*"She's here because she's loaded for bear, and she loves you, dumb-ass."*

*Oh yeah. That.* "Hi babe," Tucker muttered, his eyes set on the real woman in his life. The one who could hurt him.

"Tuck!" Melissa stepped between him and Nicole, brushing his nasty ex out of her way while she tangled her fingers in his hair and pulled him in tight and close, so damned... hot. She planted her wet lips on his mouth, and *wow*. He wrapped both arms around her, staggering back to catch his balance. That kiss would've fogged up his digital lens if it still worked.

He plastered his ass solidly to the doorframe, his fingers tunneled in her beautiful, sweet-smelling hair, his heart on fire for whatever she had in mind next. The fresh taste of her minty mouth brought him back to life. She trusted him. She loved him. He was going to live. His energy level spiked. A couple other tired body parts spiked, too.

He took over the kiss, groaning into her deliciously hot mouth, tangling his tongue with hers and not having to beg for it. She opened and gave back as good as he gave her. His heart swelled in his chest at the incredibly strong-willed woman in his arms. The right woman. The only woman.

Some witch whined and huffed and tapped her pointed shoes in the background, but honestly? Who gave a rat's ass what Nicole thought? Not Tucker, and by the sounds of his boy's 'oohs' and 'ahhs,' Deuce didn't mind meeting his soon-to-be stepmother, either.

After a few more nibbles and downright tonguing each other—if that was even a word—Tucker eased back enough to really look at the courageous woman in his arms. The deep blue eyes. The pride. The swollen wet lips. Yeah, her. Jealousy looked good on Melissa.

"Hi there," he purred. Somehow, when she was in his arms like this, with her breasts flattened against his chest and her arms wrapped possessively around his neck, all was right with the world.

"Hi there, yourself," she breathed, her fingers combing around his ear to his neck before they came to rest on his shoulder. "I missed you, Tuck. I'm sorry if I surprised you by showing up unannounced like this, but I knew you were still in town, so I had to run right over."

*The fibber.* He could read it in her eyes. She meant for Nicole to know right where she stood, and it was six feet behind her, those big boobs of hers smashed under her crossed arms and her snazzy toes tapping. Like anybody cared.

Melissa tossed her head at the witch in question, her gaze dropping to those expensively clad toes. "Who's this? The maid?"

Tucker couldn't suppress a smile at Melissa's cute catty side. The woman had her claws unsheathed and her tail twitching. "She's no one important." God, he'd wanted to say that to Nicole's face for years.

Melissa's brows arched, more mischief glittering in her pretty blues than Tucker imagined was possible. "Was she fun times?" she egged him on, and damn. After that remark, she deserved what she had coming.

He didn't think twice, just lowered his palm to her ass and gave it a solid slap. "You know better than that, babe. You're my only fun times, good times, all-day-long times."

He loved that her breath caught with that single spank, and that something playfully naughty came to life in her eyes, something he seriously wanted to explore if they ever had one moment of privacy. And thick soundproof walls. Maybe a bottle of wine. A tub of honey. Slick, sweet chocolate. And a paddle for that sweet ass cupped in his hands. It seemed good little Melissa had an impishly rowdy side that might need a little hands-on attention after her self-imposed abstinence.

*"Easy boy."* Isaiah snickered. *"You're killing me with all this erotica."*

*"Get out of my head,"* Tucker bellowed—as much as a guy could bellow a thought.

"Oooo, Tuck." Melissa rubbed her nose against his scruffy cheek, her eyes closed. "Do that again."

*"Ahem,"* Isaiah just kept interfering. *"Will you two stop acting like horny teenagers in front of your son? You're embarrassing him. He's only twelve."*

*"He's eleven."* Tucker tossed a wink at Deuce, his hand still on Melissa's ass. The kid might as well get used to it, because his old man wasn't going to change. "Son, this is Melissa. She's going to be my wife. My real wife. Melissa. Deuce. My kid and my best man."

God—those words. *My wife. My kid.* They made a man proud was what they did.

"Excuse me, Tucker," Nicole grated out, like fingernails on a dry chalkboard. "Aren't you listening to me?"

Tucker tugged Melissa under his arm and faced the troll who'd made his son's life a mess. All at once, he didn't feel so crapped on. He had everything he'd ever wanted, and she had Vinnie and his boys and his mother.

He stared his ex down. "I already said all I've got to say on the subject. I'm not a gun for hire. I don't kill people to make you happy, and I won't run from you one more day. Neither will my son, you hear that, *Nicki*?" he threw a depth of sarcasm into his once-upon-a-time nickname for her. "Deuce is *my* son. *My* boy. I've got enough evidence to put you away for life. Now beat it."

Tucker shot a quick question to Isaiah. *"I do, don't I?"*

*"Yes, sir, you do. Not only do you have the video downloaded from the mini-cams at the factory, but I've been recording everything she's said since she showed up. You've got her cold."*

Tucker blew out a deep breath of relief. Once again, Isaiah had him covered. "Hit the road, Nicole. Take your Mercedes and get your uppity ass off my doorstep. I've got a life to live, and you're not in it."

"And just so we're clear on this, *Mrs. Nguyễn*," Melissa patted Tucker's chest, her fingers splayed over his heart, but a definite hiss to her tone. "This man is *mine*. You'd be smart to keep your hands off of him from now on."

"But Tuck..." Nicole glowered, shooting daggers at him while she ignored Melissa, her lips pinched into a stern pout as if she could will him to do what she wanted. That would've worked back when he was young and dumb, running on testosterone instead of brains. Not today.

He meant to wave her off, but Deuce beat him to it. "Mom," Deuce said, his hands on his hips. "Grow up, why don't you?"

Nicole stamped her foot. "Shut up, Devlin. I'm talking to your father."

"My name is Deuce," Tucker's boy declared loudly and proudly, pointing at his chin like he needed to make sure his mother knew who he was. "Why don't you go tell your lies to that Vinnie creep you let slap me around, huh?"

Tucker lowered one hand from Melissa's soft body to shackle his son's wrist before the kid got carried away and hit his mother. A smile breached his lips. There he was, holding back the two people he loved more than anything in his world, keeping them from charging to his rescue. Somehow, it didn't get any better than those two declarations of loyalty. Nicole's reign was finally ending.

She must've sensed it too. Her upper lip curled. Something deadly sparked deep and dark beneath those thick, fake eyelashes. "You'll both be sorry."

Melissa took Tucker to bed—as in, she collapsed with him on the turned-down bed, the one nearest the door. The man wasn't well, his skin damp with the humidity of the day, and his body burning with fever. "You're sick."

"Nah, I've never felt better." He eased her on top of him, one hand at the back of her head. "Turn up the AC. I'll be fine. You're quite the jealous cat, aren't you?"

She couldn't help but growl. "That ex of yours has a lot of nerve. If she'd come one step closer, I would've decked her. I mean it."

"Come here, babe."

She didn't resist until he'd satisfied himself with another long, wet kiss. Then she pushed away from his prehensile lips. "You are too sick, and your son's watching. Let me up."

He grumbled but released her. "He's a big boy. He can handle it, but yeah. I guess. Been out of it the last couple days."

She pushed up on one elbow, still hovering over him as she traced a finger along his brow, pushing his unruly hair out of his eyes and smoothing it back to where it belonged. "What happened? You've been fighting again, and you're sicker than the last time I saw you."

He groaned under her caress, then grabbed her fingers and trapped them against his ear, kissing her wrist. "I'm better now that you're here. Just need a nap. Lay down with me?"

She wanted nothing more than to rest beside him, but the thought alone conjured intimate positions that required a bigger bed and no audience. Pressing a kiss to his chin, she could've cried. He wasn't the cheat she'd thought she'd seen, and for that she felt both ashamed, and just as relieved he'd proven her wrong. "I need to pay Jacob, my cabbie. Come with me, Deuce?"

"Yes, ma'am." Deuce scrambled to her side as he offered a hand and assisted her to her feet.

"Stay here, Tucker. I'll be right back."

"That's my boy," Tucker mumbled, his poor good eye closed and the other still as puffy and discolored as ever. "We'll have to move soon. We can't stay here any longer now that she knows where we are. Can't trust her. Can't... trust anyone... any..."

The poor guy drifted off to sleep in the middle of talking. Melissa nodded Isaiah out of the room with her and Deuce. "Okay. Spill. What's really going on? And who is that poor little boy sleeping on the other bed? Who's been beating on him? My God, what have you guys been up to?"

"That boy is Luke," Isaiah answered quietly, his ear cocked toward their room. "Deuce rescued him back at Vinnie's house of horrors, then Tucker and I rescued them. I checked. Luke's got no family, so he's staying with us. Anyway, Tucker took the brunt of it coming out of the factory. They roughed him up pretty bad, and Dr. Trang says he's got a mild case of pneumonia."

Melissa peered toward the street and waved for Jacob to come join her. "Pneumonia?" she questioned. "I think he's got more than pneumonia—maybe a broken rib and a punctured lung. He wasn't breathing properly when we were in the jungle, but he sounds worse now. We need a real doctor. Where did you dig up Trang? He should've taken care of that injury."

Deuce arched his brows. "Dr. Trang treated me once when I had the flu and got dehydrated."

Melissa tapped her toes. That explained everything. Trang was as trustworthy as Nicole. "Didn't you think twice about using Nicole's doctor?" she grilled Isaiah.

"I needed somebody fast," he replied, "and I thought I could influence him once he got here."

"You thought wrong," Melissa pointed out as Jacob brought the cab around. She walked to the passenger side and pulled the door open. "Jacob, can you please help me find a good doctor for a very sick man?"

His brows narrowed, nearly touching in the middle. "Oh, yes, ma'am. My uncle good doctor. He know many ways of healing. Why? What you got?"

She took a seat, one foot on the pavement. "It's my friend. I think he has a broken rib, maybe a punctured lung. Can your uncle treat that? Does he use antibiotics?"

"Oh, yes. Hurry. We go now." Jacob waved Isaiah and Deuce into the cab. "Come now. Hurry. I call him on the way."

She paused, not willing to drag her kindly cabbie into foreign intrigue. "It's not these two guys, Jacob. My friend is inside and he might have a broken rib, but there's also a young boy who's been beaten. He needs our protection so I'm bringing him, too."

"Yes, yes. Bring everyone." Jacob waved again. "Hurry fast. My uncle busy man."

Enough said. Isaiah and Deuce got Tucker on his feet and into the back of the cab while she brought Deuce's poor little friend. The boy weighed next to nothing, but the way he moaned when she lifted him tore at Melissa. Holding Luke was like holding Pich. They were both too young and too tiny to face the world alone. Maybe David Tao could find room for one more lost child?

"Did Trang look at Luke?" she asked.

"Mostly just Dad," Deuce answered. "Luke was scared of Dr. Trang."

"Listen, guys, we've got to move. I'll follow with Deuce and our supplies," Isaiah muttered, gesturing toward a rusted out Chevy near his hotel door.

"Don't tell me you stole that," she said, nodding at the car.

He brushed a hand over his head. "I had to get everyone out of Vinnie's place fast. It was... available."

She shook her head. "You're just as bad as Tucker."

"Thanks!" he said with real energy, not the reaction she was going for.

# Chapter Twenty-Eight

The room kept swaying. He was sure of it. Tucker just wasn't sure where the hell he was until he heard the first gunshot. Until he heard Melissa scream. He shoved up off the back seat of some car, disoriented and searching for his gear bag and his pistol. His knife. Anything.

"Stay down," Melissa ordered as the cab they were in took a sharp right, tilting him to the left.

"What going on?" he snapped. "Where are we?"

"Near the river," she shot back. "Now lie down and shut up. We've got a shooter on our tail."

Them were fighting words. Tucker Chase never laid down and shut up. Clutching the edge of the front seat by his fingernails, he shot a quick look over his shoulder at the silver Mercedes coming up fast on his bumper. *Nicole?* "Is she crazy?"

"Don't ask me. You married her."

"Yeah, but... Nicole?" That was a sight he'd never expected to see, but it was her, by hell, big round Hollywood sunglasses and all. What she do, fall off the deep end? She punched the gas, ramming the back of the cab with her pricey ride and pushing them into a spin. He hung on tight while the cabbie struggled for control. The cab swung too far left, then over-corrected the other way before it righted itself and landed firmly on all four wheels.

"Will you get down, Tucker?" Melissa barked. "You're not well enough for this. Do what you're told for once."

"Bullshit," he snarled at his dearly beloved, the woman whose ass he was definitely going to paddle if she didn't stop telling him what to do. "You got a weapon?"

"You can't kill your son's mother," she shot back at him.

"No, but I can blow her tires." *"Speaking of which, where the hell is Deuce?"*

*"He's with me,"* Isaiah replied promptly. *"I'm trying to get between you and your crazy, umm, relative."*

*"You got a gun? I've got nothing."*

*"Yes, you do. I stashed a pistol under Melissa's seat just in case things went bad like they usually do."*

*"Thank you, sir,"* Tucker replied humbly as he bent over and fingered the weapon out of its hiding place, racked it, and took aim out the back window.

"Where'd you get that?" Melissa barked, her eyes wide with fright and her arms full of Deuce's frightened friend. "Stop, Tucker. Don't shoot her. You can't."

"I'm not going to, but…" Tucker shot her a baleful glare, "… you and I are going to have a serious talk about who's in charge the next time we're in the same room together, young lady. Keep it up and I'm going to tune your backside good when we get home. Now get down and keep Luke safe."

Her eyes were wide at his blatant threat and she ducked to the floor, but damn it. She had to understand that he, and only he, ruled the Tucker Chase roost. Only him. *When guns were involved.*

Another round hit the cab, striking the rear window frame before it ricocheted to the left. The poor cabbie hunched into the steering wheel, grumbling but still going. Melissa screamed. Safety glass flew everywhere, and still that damned Mercedes plowed into the back of the cab again. What drugs was Nicole on?

Tucker aimed low even as his psycho ex pointed her shiny silver pistol out the window and took a shot at him, screaming her guts out by the looks of it, her blonde hair rife with the wind.

"You bitch," he hissed as he put one round in her front tire. "Shoot me, will you."

She screamed something at him, her mouth wide open and her lips working, but honestly? He'd heard it all before. Sirens shrilled in the distance. The police were coming. Things were about to get damned ugly.

She slammed on the brakes when her tire blew, and the cabbie left the ex-Mrs. Chase behind with the police on *her* tail for a change. From there, the cab took a sharp left down a narrow alley lined with blackened dirty bricks, then another left and a quick right while Tucker tried to hang onto the seat and stay on his knees. Where'd this guy learn to drive? Running moonshine in the back hills of Tennessee?

At last, the flustered driver pulled into a garage so narrow, it seemed they'd never be able to open the cab doors. Tucker tapped Melissa's shoulder, his heart still pounding like a mother. "Are you okay?"

She lifted her tear-stained face. "It's Luke. She... she shot him."

Tucker scrambled over the seat to Melissa. "No," he growled, pissed at the getaway that should've ended better. Not like this.

The cabbie had already hightailed it through an inner garage door, and in seconds, he returned with another man in spectacles. The older guy sidled alongside the cab and gently pulled Tucker out of the way. "You go now," he said. "I fix."

Tucker stood back while this guy took over, but Melissa was covered in blood, and he couldn't do anything but stand there and watch.

"He my uncle," the cabbie offered somberly. "He good doctor."

"I'm sorry, who are you?" Tucker asked, his memory spotty at best.

"I Jacob Giang. Your girlfriend driver," he replied, his dark eyes glued to what was taking place in the front seat of his cab. Tucker listened to Melissa's soft, sad murmurs as she crooned over Luke.

"I owe you," Tucker said humbly. "I owe you a car and for helping us and..." *God, not this.*

*"Tucker, what's wrong? Did you guys get away safely?"* Isaiah asked from wherever he and Deuce were.

*"No,"* he reported sadly. *"One casualty. How about you? Is my son safe? Please say yes, damn it."*

*"Yes, but... who? Not Melissa."*

Tucker didn't want to say until he was sure. He held his breath, hoping against the odds that ricochet hadn't wasted a young boy's life. That Nicole hadn't gotten the revenge she'd promised with her final threat.

Jacob's uncle lifted his head, sadness in his eyes. He blinked and took his glasses off. He never said a word, but Tucker knew the second Melissa let out a slow, sad whimper. He gulped hard and projected the heartbreaking news to Isaiah and Deuce. *"Shit. Man down. Luke is... dead."*

He heard it then, the high-pitched mental anguish of his son for his only friend. *"No, Dad. No! He can't be dead. He... he can't!"*

"You hold still for me." Jacob's uncle was a patient man. Somber. Old. He smelled like fish and the river, probably because his home was a solid wood Vietnamese junk. Tied up alongside a city of shanties on stilts along the polluted Saigon River, the two-level pagoda-style craft was no small boat like the bevy of sampans beside it. This elegant watercraft bobbed in the gentle waves and wakes of other boats. It looked fairly modern from what Melissa had seen of it. Clean, wooden plank floors led to a hall and several small examination rooms. It seemed Jacob's uncle was a traveling doctor, tending to patients and families up and down the Saigon.

But Melissa couldn't hold still. Sorrow kept sneaking up and choking her. Poor Luke, most likely Luc, Jacob had explained, a simple mistake for a naïve American boy to have made.

Jacob brought her another cup of tea while his uncle stitched the crease on her left bicep, the wound Nicole's bullet had left on its way to murder an innocent child.

Jacob had taken Tucker below. She'd checked on him before she let herself be treated, but he was mercifully sound asleep. Melissa suspected Jacob's uncle had given him something to knock him out or he never would've succumbed as quickly as he had. Not after this.

Another tear trickled down her cheek.

"There, there," Jacob murmured, patting her back, still her faithful companion.

His uncle wrapped a sterile length of gauze around her arm.

"May I know your name, please?" she asked, fighting her emotions.

"My family name is Giang, but you may call me Dr. Noah," he said kindly.

"You have unusual names for Vietnamese."

He nodded, his eyes on the tape he'd pressed to her bandage. "We have taken Christian names."

"You're Christian?" Another surprise.

"And Buddhist and Taoist." Jacob shrugged, winking at her. "All are good."

She got that, but this day hadn't been good. Because Isaiah and Deuce had witnessed the shot that killed Luke, they were both held at the scene for questioning. Isaiah had actually used that beat-up Chevy to box Nicole in until the police got through the traffic to her. It was a brave move with a psychotic woman with a gun, especially for a man with a record, which now she understood both Tucker and Isaiah had. What a mess this goodwill mission to Vietnam had turned into.

Isaiah had provided a first-hand account of Nicole's other underhanded activities up to the point of the shooting. Poor Deuce was held for questioning, too, but when Isaiah handed over a copy of the audio clip of Nicole's brash proposition for Tucker to murder her husband and his two sons, the cards were stacked against her. Karma proved she couldn't get away with everything. Just most things. Just all the wicked things she and Vinnie had heaped on Deuce before his father had shown up. Just killing Luke.

That close encounter with the police had raised another problem: Tucker's failure to adhere to the imposed deadline to get out of the country. The police officers on the scene hadn't seemed too interested once they understood all that Deuce had gone through at his stepfather's hands. They all knew of the wealthy garment manufacturer. Nguyễn Vin Li was on their list of child slavery suspects. They just hadn't caught up with him yet. After they released Isaiah and Deuce without further questioning, they took Nicole off to jail.

Jacob returned to her side with a steaming pot of tea. "I fix," he said simply as he arranged the pot alongside a row of porcelain cups.

"Do you live here with your uncle, Jacob?" It seemed strange there were no women or children on their boat.

He lifted his shoulders, his answer for many of her questions. Handing a steamy cup to her, he motioned for her to take a drink. "You feel better soon."

"What's in it?" she asked, not sure if she really cared as long as it helped her sleep. She'd trusted this simple cab driver and his uncle more than she trusted most people.

"It is an herbal blend. Try it. You will like."

Melissa took a long sip of the scalding-hot brew. Lemon. Rosehips maybe. Something else she couldn't quite decipher. "Thank you, gentlemen, for helping me and my friends. You don't even know me."

Dr. Noah nodded, his dark eyes unsmiling. "The body requires rest to heal. The mind, too. You must go below. Sleep."

He made it sound easy. Melissa nodded, then headed downstairs to the room where Tucker lay on his side on the double bed, softly snoring and out cold. Deuce had lain down with his dad, his back against his father's chest. He'd pulled the light blanket over his legs, his hands folded under his chin, his face blotched from crying, and his eyes closed tight. It was the sweetest, saddest picture of a father and son Melissa had ever seen.

She leaned against the doorframe, content to soak in the sight of this passionate father who obviously loved his son more than life. Most men she knew didn't hug their children, much less sleep with them. It looked as if Tucker would never let Deuce go. She was thankful for the strong men in her life, especially the one with his nose buried in his son's curly black hair. Deuce could've passed for Tucker twenty years ago. At least Nicole had done one thing right. She'd given birth to the little boy that obviously held his father's heart.

Isaiah would be back soon from the Cho Ray Hospital where the police had taken Luke's body. Due to Isaiah's evidence, no official investigation would be conducted. There was no need. Sweet little Luke had no family to insist on one, and the medical examiner who'd come to Noah's home had already confirmed cause of death, a simple conclusion when a bullet was involved. In seven days there would be a funeral. Until then...

Melissa shuddered at what Tucker might do. He was a man of action. Many things were black and white, clear-cut, to be done quickly without over-thinking. He had a father's hatred for Vinnie. He wouldn't just sit around and talk about it. He would act.

"You want mat?" Jacob asked, ever the watchful friend, gesturing down the narrow hall, "or better room? More private for woman. You take?"

Melissa released a heartfelt sigh. "Thank you, Jacob, but I'd rather sleep with my guys. A mat on the floor will be fine."

Tucker woke slowly. Carefully. Feeling no pain, an odd sensation after spending so many miserable days with something hurting, he stretched.

It was midnight-dark in the room. Deuce wasn't beside him, and that was okay. Tucker no longer had the rising panic to hunt his boy down to make sure he was safe. He could hear him somewhere on this small boat, chatting with Isaiah about astral projections and other crazy, psychic stuff.

Tucker didn't want to believe he was psychic. It messed with his tough-guy image, yet he *had* heard

Deuce cry out when Luke was killed. Somehow Tucker *had* heard him. That mournful scream of pain inside his head was his boy's. Tucker had no choice. He had to admit. Blessed or cursed, he was a teensy bit psychic.

The sounds of gentle waves lapping against the hull of the junk comforted him. Tucker had barely eased one foot to the floor when he spotted Melissa curled on a simple mat a few feet from his bed with her back to him. Her massive tangles of honey blonde curls were tossed behind her in a lovely pile of gold on the mat. Nothing but a light woven blanket covered her. Her shoulders barely rose with each breath. The crazy woman had come all the way back to Vietnam for him. It didn't get any better than that. *Beautiful. Just plain beautiful.*

Lifting off the bed, he knelt beside her, then rolled to his hip and cradled her delicate feminine form within his bigger frame. She fit like a lamb inside its shepherd's arms. He nestled closer, one arm beneath his head, the other draped along her side, his fingers tucked in behind her knee. "I love you, babe," he whispered.

She pushed her backside into him and sighed the husky, breathy murmur of a sleeping woman. Warm. Quiet. Trusting.

He nuzzled his nose to her ear. "You make me complete," he said simply. Honestly. From the bottom of his hard man's heart. "I've been looking for you all my life, Melissa McCormack. Don't ever leave me."

She groaned a luscious, grumbly, "Never."

# Chapter Twenty-Nine

Mornings on the Saigon River were noisy and busy. Tucker stood with his arms crossed over the heavy wooden rail at the bow of Noah Giang's junk, taking in the view. The doctor's boat was a spectacle of a thing, right out of a tourist destination poster. Its diesel engine was stowed aft behind a modern and well-equipped pilothouse. It boasted eight cabins in all, four on the main deck and four down on the second deck, all with en suite heads. Tiled showers. Hot and cold running water. Real toilets instead of bombsights.

Both decks boasted full-size, shuttered windows instead of the customary portholes. Two orange sails lifted loftily overhead, their canvases rippling in a stiff south-by-southwest five-knot wind that made Tucker long for his days in the Navy. He suspected the rig had once been a commercial tourist enterprise, as squared away as the galley, mess, and cabins were. The teak bulkhead still gleamed with a good, thick coat of marine varnish, as did the rails and deck. You wouldn't know it to look at the old guy, but Dr. Giang must turn a goodly profit to be able to afford a junk this grand.

It was early. Tucker hadn't seen Isaiah or Deuce yet, but they were around somewhere. They couldn't have gone anywhere, not with the junk set loose from the dock, its sails billowed and full of morning sun and wind. He'd seen plenty of kids and guys scramble from one sampan or barge to the next, but that was what folks on the river did. They got around.

When Melissa joined Tucker at the rail, she planted her hip firmly against his as the sounds and smells of the busy river drifted their way. Tucker smiled at the simple contact. It might seem like nothing to most people, but with it came a sense of oneness he'd never experienced before. He felt as if he were half of a matching pair of salt-and-pepper shakers, she being the better half.

He could finally see out of both eyes, probably because of the herbs and seeds in that poultice he'd found plastered on his eyeball when he'd woken up. Whatever was in Dr. Noah's homemade concoction, it worked. The swelling was gone, and his eye didn't feel like raw hamburger any more. It didn't even sting when he'd peeled back the eyelid to see if the FBI's mechanized lens still functioned. Thank God for small favors. His pupil dilated and closed properly, and the lens zoomed in and zoomed out like it should have.

His bandaged ribs felt better, too. He felt stronger. Healthier. Too bad his heart still hurt like a mother. Too bad Deuce still felt like shit. A father never stopped wanting to shield his child from life's hard knocks. What had happened to Luke hurt most of all.

River life was busy with entire families hauling their wares of fish, vegetables, and fruits to market. Colorful rafts piled high with oranges and melons floated by. Parents called to children. Men shouted at their neighbors. Others fished what looked and smelled like polluted waters. Life and business abounded.

He wished it would stop. Take a break. Call time out. Game cancelled. It never seemed right how Time marched on after Death called, like it had with Luke. There ought to have been, at least, a moment of silence out of respect for the passing of a motherless child from this life. The sun should hold still in the sky for one minute. It should! People should stop their senseless squabbling and fighting and listen up for a change to what really mattered. They really should.

Because a kid *had* died, and that singular life *did* matter. A child's death was enough reason to stop all the wars in the world if Tucker had his way. Melancholy shifted over him like a cold, wet blanket. Maybe a shroud. He wrapped an arm around Melissa's waist, settling his palm to her hip, his fingers splayed on her backside. At least the barriers between them were down.

He needed her in ways he'd not realized until then. She wasn't just his better half, she was the light to his darkness, the glimmer of hope that kept his head above water when he was drowning. She was the goddess who made him want to strive to be a better man.

He'd always thought of himself as the toughest dog in the fight, but now, he wasn't so sure. Melissa had always radiated a calm peace that called his bluff and bluster from the first time they'd met. If anything, she was the quiet eye of the hurricane and he the storm whirling around her, needing her to center him. To give him something real to hold onto. Something permanent.

The good doctor's houseboat offered many amenities, including phone service. Of course, Melissa had already called Nancy Tao to ask how Pich and the girls were doing, Mimi, Peewee, and the Dangs, too. Nancy had sent a picture over Jacob's cell phone of Pich in a pretty turquoise silk dress, her hair in two pigtails off the sides of her head, and a shy chocolate-fudge ice cream smile on her face. It did Melissa good to see those girls safe and happy, after the hardships they'd endured.

That phone call gave Melissa what she needed, but it didn't help Tucker. Now that those kids were safe, his thoughts turned to Vinnie, the scumbag of Hồ Chí Minh City. To Mr. Big Stuff and that one night of hell in jail. To Simon Siegel and his flesh-peddling cohorts.

The world was still plenty wicked. Something needed to be done.

He stuck his fingers deep in his jeans pocket and retrieved the keys he'd stolen from that smart-assed jail boss. He had no doubt he could get back inside without being caught. Wouldn't that bastard be surprised to see him again?

Tucker snapped the keys into his palm before they jingled. Too late.

"What do you have there?" Melissa asked. "Keys? For Isaiah's rusty Chevy?"

He glanced at the innocence in her eyes, the ready lie on his lips suddenly unspeakable. He didn't usually have a problem inventing stories that sounded good if they got him his way or out of trouble, but with Melissa, they'd gotten harder to tell.

He confessed rather than disappoint her. "They're keys to the jail I was in. I stole them from the guard who threatened to kill me if he ever saw me again."

"No," she breathed fire with one word. "He said that? When was this?"

That was the difference between Melissa and the rest of the world. He didn't have to fight her to be heard or accepted or understood. She was instantly in his corner and on his side. He had to tell her the whole story then, didn't he? How he'd raced after her abductors only to end up caught for stealing the mayor's car and stuck in a jail cell when he'd gotten stopped by a train. How Alex sprang Isaiah out of jail first, but couldn't get Tucker out because he'd stolen the mayor's car. How he'd been roughed up, then saved by Alex at the last moment.

She melted against him, her teacup on the flat railing, her fingers on his face, and her soft breasts cushioned to his pecs. So gentle. So sweet. So much everything he didn't deserve. "That's what happened to your eye, isn't it? That's how your ribs were broken. Those jerks. They beat you while you were their prisoner, didn't they? We should do something about them."

He wrapped her in his arms and tunneled his fingers through her silken locks, surprised at the vehemence in her tone. He knew it to his core then. She would always fight for him and with him. She'd always be there for him at the end of every hard day. Melissa was not the betraying type.

It was odd how, when you got what you thought you wanted, the world shifted, and all at once you wanted something different. Something better. Like her safety more than Mr. Big Stuff's comeuppance. Like her peace of mind more than his revenge.

"Nah," Tucker mumbled as he pressed a kiss of utter fealty on the forehead of his all-American girl. His queen. He paused there, drawing in the scent of her, now mingled with a hint of lemon soap instead of apples and cinnamon. Still Melissa. "It's done, babe. I'm not going back to jail for any reason, especially not for guys like them."

"Not even to report them?" she asked, her nose in his neck and her breath soft and moist on his skin, teasing him with her love. "There ought to be something we can do. They deserve to be taught a lesson. Are you sure?"

Tucker pulled her flat against him, her ear to his heart, relishing the pleasure of her lush body, and the sea in his nose. She had a way of smoothing his rough edges, of filling in the pits and scars that life had left in its wake. Of making him whole again.

"I'm sure," he said calmly. It was unlike him not to feel the compulsion to fight back. He took a deep breath and proved it. He dropped the keys into the river. "There. Now it's done. It's over."

"What about the guy who hurt Deuce? You're going to have a talk with Vinnie, aren't you?"

His body stiffened at the image of that slick weasel in his fine linen trousers while sweaty children groveled at his imperious feet. Vinnie definitely had a thing or two coming. The only part of that payback that Tucker struggled with was the guy's two children. He had sons. If not for them, Tucker would be in Vinnie's face right then, pounding a definite message home. But the boys in the picture that Isaiah had found on the internet were close to Deuce's age. They needed their father. Hell, they might even be the reason Vinnie did what he did in his cruel, mixed-up mind.

Tucker understood a father's devotion to his sons. Love drove a man crazy. It might even drive him to take the law into his own hands. Vinnie might think he'd gotten away with what he'd done to Deuce, but from this day forward, he owed his life to those two kids of his. Who knew? Maybe with Nicole out of the picture, Vinnie would straighten up, at least until the evidence that Isaiah gave the police caught up with him. It could happen.

Tucker looked down into his world, the one in those trusting blues with the cutest laugh lines at the corners. He cocked his head to place a kiss on her lush, plump lips. "Don't worry. One day, the police will raid his factory, and he'll get what's coming to him. We might even read about it in the papers back home."

"You're awfully mellow today," she murmured against his mouth, her breath minty fresh on his tongue. "This week has taken a lot out of you."

He grunted and tugged her back under his chin, his nose in her hair. "It has," he sighed. "Guess it's been hard on everyone."

"Did Dr. Noah bandage your ribs?"

"Yes, and he gave me some oils to rub on my bruises, too. I actually feel good for a change. I can breathe. It's too bad we can't take him home with us. I could use a decent family doctor."

Melissa relaxed, her body heat seeping into that cold spot in his soul, the one that cried for Luke and all the lost children like him. A SEAL saw a lot in his travels across the globe. South America. India. The

Mideast. It didn't matter where Tucker had gone, the motherless were there. Even in America.

Tucker cocked his head. He sensed him before he heard him. Isaiah. Out of breath. His gut churning with acid and panic. Tucker's heart kicked into high gear. With Melissa in his arms, he turned to the open bridge just as Isaiah pounded up the ladder from below. "What's wrong?"

Isaiah's face said it all. "Is Deuce with you?"

"The last I heard him you were telling him about some psychic babble."

"He said he needed to talk to you. He said he'd only be a minute, only he didn't come back and now…"

Tucker's heart leapt out of his chest. Somehow he knew. "Shit. He's going after Vinnie."

"Where? The factory or his house?" Melissa asked, her fingernails digging into Tucker's forearm.

He turned on Isaiah. "Do you know?"

Isaiah closed his eyes and lowered his head. He dropped his palms to his knees, shaking and sucking in great draughts of air, his chest heaving. "Give me a sec."

"I'm going with you," Melissa declared.

"No, you're not," Tucker shot back at her, his focus still on his fellow agent. She might have his six, but she needed to stay here with the Giangs where it was safe. "You'll stay here and—"

"I'll do no such thing. I didn't fly all the way back to Vietnam to—"

He whirled her into his arms, his thumbs stuck below her collarbones, his stare lethal. "You'll stay and that's the end of it."

Damned if she didn't narrow those pretty blues, and glare right back at him. "He's going to be my son too, Tucker Chase. Get over yourself and—"

"You don't understand. It's not that simple. I can't—"

"You can't what? Make room in your life for me? Let me love your son as much as you do?" She spiked a malicious brow at him, her lips pinched thin and tight. "I thought a big, tough Navy SEAL could do everything."

"I can't..." He growled, his tenderized heart on his sleeve. "I can't chance losing you, damn it. Things might go bad. Don't you get it? I finally found you. I finally have something good and decent and pure and I... I just can't."

"But Tucker." She moved in fast, her hands gentle on his neck instead of wringing it like he half expected. She'd shoved one foot between his boots, her body aligned perfectly with his. "You're the one who told me I can't control life. It's a rush and a downer all in the same day, remember? It's a bull named Daisy and a sweet baby boy named Deuce, and I'm here, Tucker. For you. Do you think it's any easier for me to sit home and worry while you're in danger? I'm sorry I yelled at you, but I'm in this with you all the way. To the end and beyond. Let's go get that boy of yours back once and for all."

God, he loved this woman so hard. Tucker mashed his mouth to hers, his heart on fire and his mind made up. She could come with him, and he'd be proud to have her on his six. He wouldn't want it any other way.

He licked her luscious lips to seal his promise to her. "Now that we've got that settled..." He glanced over Melissa's shoulder to Isaiah. "Where are we going, kid?"

Isaiah looked damned bleak. "He's at Vinnie's house."

# **Chapter Thirty**

Melissa rode shotgun. It hadn't taken long for Tucker to drive Isaiah's rust bucket to Vinnie's estate. Tucker pulled into the brush just off the end of Vinnie's wide circular driveway. He'd already let Isaiah out down the road, and now they waited for Isaiah to get in position at the rear of the estate. Two snipers with a psychic link were better than one.

Climbing out of the battered vehicle, she hefted the AR that Tucker had allowed her to carry, intent on matching him step-for-step. He seemed to think he was the boss of her, allowing her to do anything. Silly man. For now, she let him think that. His son's life was at stake. They didn't have time to squabble. If Deuce was in this place, she meant to do whatever it took to get him back. Tucker needed to understand that. She could handle herself.

The estate was quiet though. Too quiet. The last time she'd been there, noisy peacocks strolled the front lawn. There'd been quaking ducks in the pond, and long-legged, white cranes in the reeds by the waterfall. But today there was nothing—until she and Tucker drew deeper onto the estate.

Someone had raked the lawn over with rapid fire. She saw the peacocks then. All dead, their lovely sapphire-blue bodies torn and shredded. A poor turtle floated belly-up on the pond. The stucco walls of the house carried plenty of pockmarks. Melissa swallowed hard, her throat dry at what had taken place there. At what Deuce might not have lived through. Summoning Tucker's salty vernacular, she muttered a guarded, "Shit."

"Deuce didn't do this," Tucker cautioned, his voice rife with tension. "Isaiah, can you get a read on my son? Is he still here? Where's Vinnie? What the hell happened?"

She stilled along with Tucker, waiting on his command to move forward.

"Isaiah?" he asked again, his head cocked. "Can you read me?"

Her pulse quickened at the worry in his voice. He turned to the house, his fingertip to his ear as if that could help the psychic connection. "Damn it, where are you? Talk to me."

"What's wrong?" Mental links were always supposed to work, weren't they?

He nodded for her to follow him around the pond, behind the palm trees to the side of the house. "Not sure. I've never *not* had him in my head on this trip until now. Let's find out what's going on. Keep your weapon up and ready."

She got that. Brady had always said there was no foolproof plan, that Murphy's Law could and would ruin any and every way forward. A sudden chill passed over the back of Melissa's neck despite her thick mantle of hair now tied into a ponytail. She'd practiced shooting alongside Brady at gun ranges before he'd been injured, but this was different. Her fingers trembled alongside her rifle's trigger guard. She licked the sweat off her upper lip. This was real.

Step by step, she and Tucker advanced. He led, his broad shoulders blocking her view, the point of his weapon sweeping back and forth, his massive body like one rippling jungle cat ready to pounce. How a big man like him could move so quickly and be so light on his feet intrigued and amazed Melissa. She honed her pace and her movements to match his. To keep as quiet as sin—until they cleared the rear corner of the estate and saw the pergola.

He snapped his rifle on the lone man standing there. She followed suit. It was a trap. An evil, wretched trap of death and dare, and Deuce was caught in the middle of it, along with Vinnie, his son, and Isaiah.

The pergola, constructed of eight-by-eight red-stained wooden uprights, stretched the width of the backyard. Ropes laced over the top beams in the center of the wooden structure. Vinnie sat in one of two chairs beneath the beams, his neck in a noose, a gag in his mouth, and his hands tied behind his back. He'd been beaten, his cheek bloodied. Tears ran down his face. He sobbed, his head cocked to the side, but his gaze fastened to the chair at his side.

Isaiah sat in that chair to his left, unconscious, his head on his shoulder, and his neck also in a noose. Blood trickled from a gash over his brow.

But worse were the marionettes dangling by their necks at the other end of those ropes. Deuce and one of Vinnie's boys. They stood on the back of the men's chairs, their hands tied behind their backs, their feet slipping, striving for balance. If either boy fell, they hanged the man at the other end of their rope while they strangled themselves.

Deuce danced nervously over Vinnie's chair back, Vinnie's son over Isaiah's. Deuce would die getting the revenge he'd wanted. If Isaiah didn't come to, he'd never know what killed him. It wouldn't take much. Just one slip. One frightened boy.

The man at the opposite side of the pergola held an equally impressive AR trained on his hapless victims. Simon Siegel. He looked as if he'd been in a war since she'd last seen him, the left side of his face raw and blistered. Patches of hair were missing from his bare head. One ear was a melted piece of raw flesh.

Melissa's heart sank. How could anyone be so evil? So cruel? She leveled the barrel of her weapon on his head, mentally judging distance, praying she could get a shot off before he did. That's all it would take to end this despicable farce. Just one lucky shot.

"Dad," Deuce cried hoarsely, his eyes wide with terror. "Dad, I'm sorry."

Tucker sucked in a sharp breath. "You're doing fine, son," he encouraged the impossible, his rifle also aimed at Siegel. "Stay calm. I'll get you out of there."

"But I—"

Melissa licked her bottom lip, wanting Simon to look away. To blink. To give up so she wouldn't have to kill him.

"But nothing," Tucker said evenly. "Take a deep breath, Deuce, and keep your eyes on me. You can do it. Hang on. This'll be over soon."

Melissa didn't argue. Deuce needed to trust his dad. He nodded slightly at Tucker that he understood, his neck already rubbed red and raw from the nylon rope stretched taut between him and Vinnie. It had no slack to it, but at least Deuce's tennis shoes had some grip. Between them and the tension of the rope, he seemed able to maintain a shaky balance.

Vinnie's son was another problem. The poor boy looked as if he'd been on his way to a dance or to church in his white shirt and slacks. Sweating profusely, he tipped forward and backward in slippery dress shoes on the back of Isaiah's chair.

Blubbering for his father, he wouldn't last. He'd be the first to fall. Vinnie would react, hanging Deuce, and Isaiah would most certainly strangle to death.

Melissa's heart kicked up as she planned for that worst-case scenario. Tucker would most likely end Siegel the second this game changed. Isaiah's chair was closest. She would run to him, cut the rope from his neck with the knife in her back jeans pocket on her way to catch Deuce before he fell. It could work.

Simon nodded his burned chin at Melissa, a salacious twitch at the corners of his mouth, jolting her back to square one. "I'd say it's good to see you again, Mrs. McCormack, but hey..." He waved a bandaged hand at the beleaguered performers on his stage. "I'd be lying. You're certainly a clever bitch, though. Not once did I connect you with McCormack Industries, and I should have. I could've used you a whole lot better if I'd known you came from real money. I wouldn't be here now, would I?"

He winked at Tucker. "So you're the almighty Senior Chief I've heard so much about. It's time we met face-to-face, Chase. Did your lady-friend there tell you how quick she gave it up to me once I let her out of her box? She tell you how fast she cozied up to me and some of my boys, how happy she was to put out so we wouldn't kill her worthless, rich ass?"

Melissa's indignation nearly got the best of her. He sounded as if he knew someone that Tucker knew. Just who had he been talking to?

"Liar," Tucker hissed as if he'd read her mind. "What do you want? Money? Is that what this is about?"

Siegel's peeling nose twisted, along with the rest of his burned face when he shook his head. "Them little girls are what this is about. They were the real money, Chase, but you're too late to the party. I'm past that now. Look at me. Do I look like I need cash? Do I look like I care about screwing rich chicks like that whore behind you just to get my hands on a few billion dollars?"

*Well, yeah.* Melissa almost nodded. Wasn't everything about money to guys like Simon?

Tucker's rifle hadn't wavered an inch off his target. Shaking with adrenaline, Melissa tried to keep the barrel of her weapon as steady, but her emotions were all over the place. Anger for what Simon had done to Pich surged through her veins like molten magma. Her soul burned to shoot him in the face for what he was doing to Deuce and Isaiah. For what he'd done to those little girls. To Tristan.

Fear for Tucker and Deuce, for Vinnie and his son, roared up her spine, shaking what little composure she had left. Outright panic pulsed through her mind, making it difficult to think clearly. How could Tucker stay so cool and calm in the face of such evil? That was his son's life on the line, riding on Vinnie's chair back. All Vinnie had to do was panic and try to save his son, and Tucker would lose Deuce and Isaiah. Was there ice in his veins?

Vinnie's kid's foot slipped, jerking Isaiah's head nearly off, stretching his neck, and lifting the chair legs up from the concrete. The poor kid flailed and spun. He grunted and pitched, his eyes bugging out until he regained a semi-solid foothold, his slippery shoes braced at the finials at each side of the chair crest. The rude awakening startled Isaiah, his wild-eyed gaze shifting back and forth as he quickly assessed his predicament. He ended with his dark eyes riveted on Tucker.

Tucker never made a sound, just grunted at Simon. "So you're here to end me—is that right, Siegel? Is that what this is about? Revenge? And just how did I offend you?"

Melissa couldn't believe the insolence packed into his tone. He cocked his head like a prizefighter before a brawl, and suddenly, she felt it. The power. The danger. It roiled off Tucker like heat waves on an asphalt road in July. His spine stiffened and yet his shoulders had relaxed. The tight cords of a powerful predator flexed beneath his sweat-stained shirt. She didn't know how, but she knew with certainty. *Deuce and Isaiah were going to live.*

A quiet snort expelled from Tucker's flared nostrils as he shifted his weight from one foot to the other. He'd transformed into a living culmination of his years worth of training and experience, a veritable I'm-going-to-kick-your-ass father.

Beads of sweat trickled down the valley between her breasts, inciting an uncommonly feminine response to her man at the worst possible time. She fought off the fierce desire to caress the back of his proud, suntanned neck. To bump her hip to his just to be sure he knew she was there *for him,* and that she'd fight to the end *with him.*

Simon Siegel didn't stand a chance.

"Ending you won't get me those girls back, Chase. It took me awhile to track you down, but now, I know how to hurt you." He took three steps to Vinnie and stuck the tip of his boot to the chair leg. "Let's play."

Even as Siegel curved the sole of his boot to Vinnie's chair leg, taunting Tucker to take the kill shot, Tucker recognized the signs. The man was a clone of bullies the world over. He needed the drama. The dare. The puffed-up sense of power when cowards held the lives of weaker prey in their grip. When they thought they were invincible.

Tucker'd seen the same evil glint in his old man's eyes before one of the many thrashings he'd endured as a kid. Siegel wasn't going to tip that chair over. He needed Tucker to take that first shot, to make that fatal decision for him. That way the outcome would be Tucker's fault, not his. Siegel had a death wish and Tucker intended to fulfill it, but first...

He had to know. "You know my ex-wife." Tucker made it a statement. It was the only thing that made sense and explained how Siegel knew where to find

Vinnie. Nicole finally had what she wanted. A hit man. Deuce's being there at the same time was just bad dumb luck.

The Navy was a tight knit family, but family was still family, full of as many friends who'd give you the shirt off their backs as enemies who'd stab you in the back. Tucker might not know all Navy SEALs, but he wouldn't put it past Nicole to have used that family connection to serve her grasping need for power. God, how long had she known Siegel? How far did her web of lies and deceit stretch? All the way to Cambodia? Was she Siegel's partner in the sex trade? Was that her real motive for moving to Vietnam? Worse...

Who worked for who? Was Nicole Siegel's partner or his boss? That actually made sense. She must've had him on speed dial. The clawing reach of his ex shocked even Tucker, a hardened warrior. He'd let Nicole into his life. He'd given her all of himself, his heart, his paycheck, and his kid. There was a time he'd told her everything the way husbands and wives did, and she'd used that intimacy against him.

Siegel answered with a grunt, as if his knowing Nicole was a foregone conclusion, and suddenly it was. Tucker's heart skipped a beat. God, he was the dumbest shit in the world. This entire hangman's game was simply Nicole at work again, moving on. She was clearing her game board, ending the men she could no longer bleed before she moved on to another. She'd said it herself. Love was in the eye of the beholder.

The truly scary thing was she'd orchestrated this hit from inside a Vietnamese jail cell. Even that made sense. Tucker almost felt sorry for the jail guards. Almost.

"You won't like what you've got once you've got it," he warned Siegel, knowing the man was too far gone to understand that Nicole was no prize, but reaching out to him just the same. Nicole was that insidious black widow spider. Attractive and slick, she'd suck Siegel dry and then kick his hollowed-out shell of a corpse aside the second she found someone better—like that jail boss.

But like attracts like—birds of a feather and—all that bullshit. Siegel had obviously worked hard at his crimes. He deserved Nicole. "Don't matter to me one way or the other. I'll be long gone and living the life. You'll be ashes."

Tucker swallowed hard at the disgust creeping up his throat, disgust at Nicole for using Deuce to get to him. Disgust at himself for thinking she was ever worth one second of his life.

*"What the hell are you waiting for? You can take him, Tuck,"* Isaiah all but spat into his mind. *"Kill the son-of-a-bitch. Don't worry about me. I'm expendable, not your son. Save Deuce!"*

*"Shut up, kid. There's no way you can mentally convince him to blow his own brains out and let us go?"*

Isaiah's nostrils flared. *"I'm psychic, not a magician. Save Deuce!"*

"Just thought I'd ask. Guess I'll have to do this the old-fashioned way then."

"It's been good working with—"

*"Shut the fuck up, Zaroyin."* Tucker shot his buddy a barely perceptible brow-lift of scorn. He'd already used his meched-up bionic eye to survey the backstop for another sniper, some guy on his belly out there in the leafy jungle beyond Vinnie's elegant estate. Someone desperate enough to forget to smudge his sweaty brow and the damp patch of skin above his lip. Someone in too big of a hurry to remember that a good sniper always covers the sharp and shiny lens of his scope. Someone stupid enough to follow the likes of Siegel.

Tucker needed more time to make a more accurate judgment call, time he didn't have. *"Hey, kid. Can you get a sense if there's another guy laying for us? I need to be sure."*

Isaiah's expression went blank, but he came back quickly with, *"Just Siegel. He's pissed you killed his friends, Jackman and some guy named Oreo. Most of all, he's pissed you killed a kid named Tristan. You left him lying in the jungle."*

*"Oh. Him."* Tucker remembered the scrawny kid in cammies, the one with the wispy excuse for a beard. The kid he'd lied to when he'd said he could save him. *"Tristan, huh? Shit. Now I feel bad."*

*"Don't. Kill this bastard, damn it. Kill the son-of-a-bitch before he ends Deuce!"*

Tucker cocked his neck. *"I must be rubbing off on you. You sound like me."*

*"Just tell me when."*

*"Copy that, kid."* Tucker kept his cool. This was your basic no-win situation. Either way, one of these kids would not land on his feet. Necks would get stretched. Someone would die.

Worse, Tucker had brought Melissa straight into Nicole's hellish game with him. He could hear her short, sharp intakes of breath behind him. He could hear her heart jackhammering in her chest. Despite the barrel of her rifle aimed at Siegel, he knew Melissa had never killed a man before. He felt her rising panic for the thing that was to come. This was go time, but he was damned if he'd let her suffer the after-effects from taking a life. Not his woman. She needed to stay as pure and as sweet as she was.

If there was one thing Tucker understood besides ballistics and the sea, it was baseball. A good pitcher controlled the game. He knew his batters. Their stats. Their strengths. Their weaknesses. He knew the base runners, the prima donnas, the guys most prone to hit a sacrifice fly or to swing at everything within the strike zone when they'd lost their cool. He knew which player's batting average hovered at three hundred. Or four hundred. Whose on-base percentage was worth worrying about. Worth ruining.

He knew who was on first. Itching for second. Diving for third.

And a SEAL knew a bastard when he saw one. They all looked like Simon Siegel. Shifty. Sneaky. Over-confident losers. Every single one of them.

Tucker rolled his shoulder without moving his sights off ground zero. The bases were loaded. He set up his first shot. His second. His third and his fourth. It could work provided everything went according to plan, which would be a miracle.

Time to batter-up.

*"When,"* he sent covertly to Isaiah.

The kid blinked hard, signaling message received. He stiffened his shoulders and straightened his spine to take a hit that could very possibly break his neck if things went bad. *"I'm ready. Do it."*

"You're a SEAL," Tucker said evenly to Siegel, for once in his life not a ripple of anger or vengeance up his sleeve. Not a spike of adrenaline. The boys didn't have much strength or fortitude left. Things had to happen soon.

"Was." Siegel snorted in derision. "Not now. It's just plain old me standing here gonna kick your ass, Chase. What you see is what you get. I'm the last man you'll ever lay eyes on."

"I see a traitor. A liar. A dead man."

"I don't give a fuck what you see," Siegel shot a snarl back at him instead of a ballistic round that would've carried more weight. *The fool.*

Tucker wasn't there to chat, only to play games. "Batter up," he said so softly that Siegel cocked his arrogant head just a smidge to the left, like he hadn't quite heard.

*BLAM!* Tucker let him have it. Head shot. Pink mist. Then again. Another round. Just to prove he'd meant what he said. Why settle for a single tap when a double-tap sealed a better deal? Why do a half-assed job?

Tucker moved with lightning speed. Shifting his weapon on his predetermined targets, he fired two more rapid rounds, one at the rope stretched above Deuce, the other at the rope above Vinnie's kid's head. Vinnie made the mistake of ducking at the thunderous report at the same instant that Deuce landed on his feet. The reflex action meant Vinnie's neck got stretched before the rope disintegrated under the energy of Tucker's red-hot round.

Vinnie's kid fell backward when Tucker nipped his noose. In anticipation, Isaiah had pushed up to his feet and out of his chair as far as his ties would let him reach. It was barely enough, but his neck didn't get stretched like it had before. That was a good decision since Vinnie's kid landed on his ass, rolled to his side, crying and blubbering because he was scared to death. *Poor little guy.*

Just like Tucker planned: One neck stretched, albeit not enough to kill Vinnie. One kid on his butt, but still alive. And one bastard dead, precisely what Siegel deserved.

Score: Tucker, four for four. He'd taken four shots without getting any of his designated targets killed, but Siegel wasssss... out!

Isaiah collapsed back in his seat, a little worse for wear but breathing. *"Thanks, Tuck,"* he projected. *"I really love you, man. I mean it."*

*"My pleasure,"* Tucker sent back to the FBI's newest covert operator.

This was why Tucker loved who he was and what he did. He knew this game of real men who laid down their lives for their brothers. Of warriors who pushed back against the atrocities of the devil and sometimes won. He'd played it enough. He'd ended skirmishes and firefights. He'd taken down assholes and saved the people who'd mattered, and he'd sent the bastards to hell. And he'd do it again.

Vinnie's kid crawled over to his dad while Deuce scrambled to loosen Isaiah's feet and wrists. Melissa was having some kind of an emotional breakdown at his six, so Tucker grabbed her under his arm where she belonged and let her burrow her face into his shirt.

"I wasn't much help, was I?" she asked tearfully, still shaking, but her weapon safely secured, its barrel pointed toward the sky. "Everything happened so fast, and I... I meant to shoot Simon, but I just stood there and watched."

*Just the way I planned it.* He pressed a chaste kiss to her forehead, saving the heat for later when they were finally alone. "You did great, babe."

"Dad!" Deuce plowed into him, his head to the other side of his old man's chest, crying like a baby. And it was okay. Even hard men cried once in a while.

# Chapter Thirty-One

"Mr. Chase." Vinnie stuck his hand out, his scuffed cheek bloody and repentance shining in his eyes, his other arm fastened around his kid's shoulder. "I can't ever repay you for what you did here today."

Tucker grasped the unexpected handshake and jerked the guy up close and personal. Nose to nose. Father to father. "If you ever hit my son again, I'll rip your fucking head off, you understand?"

Vinnie nodded, his head bobbing fast and hard. "Yes, sir. I was wrong. I know that now. I'm sorry for what I did to Devlin. He didn't deserve how I treated him." He swallowed hard, his Adam's apple ratcheting up and down in his throat like it was stuck on the apology. "I've made some bad mistakes. I'm going to fix them. All of them."

"His name is Deuce, damn it! You do know your wife's in jail, don't you?" Tucker released the man's sweaty hand, still playing hardball, his voice filled with acid. "She killed that kid you had beat the other day. His name was Luke, you bastard. He's lying on a slab at the city morgue, and it's your fault. You put him there as much as she did! You should be in jail with Nicole for what you did to him. Shit. He was just a kid."

"You're right," Vinnie said with a whole lot more humility than Tucker expected, his eyes on the ground, not daring to meet Tucker's wrath.

Tucker expected some pushback after his verbal attack, but Vinnie only waved one of the police officers who'd responded to the emergency call over to him. "I promise. I have means. I can't help Luke anymore, but I will change. I will be a better boss to my people."

Tucker growled, not buying one word of this crap. Talk was cheap. "They're not *your people*, you moron. They're moms and pops and, God, most of them are kids. Why'd you do it?" His temper spiked. "How does an adult male torment children just to make a fast buck?"

Vinnie closed his eyes, his shoulders heaving with a deep breath while the officer waited on him. At last he met Tucker's glaring gaze. "I didn't used to be like this," he said weakly.

Like that meant anything. Tucker turned away before he punched the guy in the face. Vinnie had connections. He deserved a helluva lot more than what he'd get out of this ugly fiasco. Changing business practices did not atone for endangering children's lives the way he had. The man was full of shit.

"Officer," Vinnie said as Tucker walked away. "I have a confession to make."

It would have been nice if it were true. Tucker didn't hang around to find out.

Police officers and detectives were everywhere, as well as the local medical examiner. Tucker had been separated from Deuce, Melissa, and Isaiah long enough during the questioning phase. He was weary and the adrenaline rush had worn off, leaving him cranky and tired. He wanted out of there, his son back safely on the boat, and Melissa in his bed, preferably beneath him. "Are we free to go yet?" he asked the nearest officer.

The officer turned to Tucker. His gaze narrowed. One brow lifted. His ugly face twisted into a sour lemon expression. "You," he hissed.

Damned if it wasn't that prick from jail. The guard who'd threatened Tucker with a slow death the next time he saw him. Tucker raked a hand over his hair. If he didn't have bad luck, he'd have no luck at all.

"Yeah. Me." Tucker stuck out a hand, wishing he hadn't tossed those keys into the river.

The guy had the nerve to fumble a metal whistle up from his shirt. He puckered his cheeks and blew it in Tucker's face. What could Tucker do? He growled at his own stupidity, looked for his son and his wife-to-be, and prepared to be cuffed. *Shit. Just shit.*

"Officer," Vinnie called across the yard. "Excuse me, Officer!"

Tucker's worst nightmare snarled something at Vinnie before sharp words in their language and rapid hand signals commenced, flying back and forth. Tucker held his breath while Melissa joined him, her hand shackling his forearm, the other splayed between his shoulder blades. "Oh, my gosh, what a racket. What's up?"

He had to tell her. "It looks like I'm going back to jail."

The officer didn't look too happy, but he also turned away. Vinnie shook his head. "No, Mr. Chase. You're not going to jail, not after what you did here today. You're free to stay in my country as long as you want. Don't worry. I'll take care of this misunderstanding. Thank you again for all you have done for me and my sons."

*Speaking of which...*

"I thought you had two kids?" Tucker asked. "Where's your other boy?"

Vinnie's face blossomed into a tired smile. "He's with my mother today. There's a ball at the American Embassy later this week. He loves to shop, so Grandmama took him with her."

Tucker winked at the boy standing beside Vinnie. "Make your old man proud, kid."

The young man nodded shyly.

"Mr. Chase..." Vinnie paused while the unhappy police officer stood at his side waiting, cooling his jets. Vinnie extended his hand to Tucker again. "I would very much like to repay you for your kindness. Please. Let me prove I can be half as good a father as you are."

That hit Tucker hard. He'd never been called a good father. The courts in Virginia certainly hadn't thought of him in that light. "Just take good care of your kid."

He shook Vinnie's hand again. This time, he meant it.

It was their last night in Vietnam, and Melissa was beyond tired. Tucker had persuaded Jacob's uncle to take the junk out into the South China Sea. Tucker was her quintessential guide for all things sailing. She now knew the lovely orange sail billowed tight with wind overhead was called a lugsail. Of Chinese origin, the rigid horizontal ribs spanning the full width of the canvas that made it look like bat wings were called battens. All sails depended on the spar of the ship, the mast. She stood at the bow. The diesel engine was aft. And she knew a bunch of other nautical jargon she'd never known until then that she wanted to learn.

He'd rambled on about other kinds of sails and how different the concept of sailing was from country to country. She now knew about the Dhow, an Arabic version of a sailing ship, still very much a part of daily business on the Persian Gulf. The Spritsail of Greco-

Roman invention. The Lateen. The Bermuda Rig. Something called a Square Rig. Honestly, the man could talk ships and boats nearly more than she could listen.

But listen she did, because Tucker came to life when he talked ships and boats, and she loved the light in his eyes. She'd seen yet another side to him today. He adored his son and that adoration had put him in harm's way, yet not once had Tucker hesitated to step into the line of fire for his child. And that was another thing. The man had turned into a bigger-than-life predator. One minute she had truly doubted him. The situation with Simon Siegel seemed hopeless. All looked lost from her point of view and her limited outlook. She didn't know how Tucker could ever live without his son—especially to see the poor boy hanged in front of his eyes. To see him choke and kick—ahh! Just thinking about it broke her heart. She wiped the backs of her fingers through her lashes.

But Tucker must not have seen what she'd seen. He'd just acted. Now Deuce and Isaiah were below deck playing a card game called Tiến lên over bottles of soda, and even a little bit of laughter. Deuce was still heartbroken at the death of his friend. It would take time to heal, but it would happen. She of all people knew that.

Her heart swelled with peace. Tucker had gone below to get her a wrap. It gave her time to think and time to be thankful for the men in her life.

She never thought she'd fall in love again, but fall she had. The FBI agent she'd once found more attractive than civilized, she now saw in a different light. Yes, she still lusted after his body, but she loved him. Tucker wasn't perfect, but he was perfect for her. They'd walked on different paths, and yet they'd walked the same path, too. A path of hardship and struggle, loneliness, and sometimes despair, yet there they were. Both had come full circle to find what they were looking for in each other's eyes.

A woven wrap fell softly over her as Tucker leaned into her neck with a hot, moist kiss, his hands clamped onto her shoulders. "Melissa," he breathed, his voice hoarse and raspy, a tremor of something she couldn't name in his tone. "I need to know. Did you mean it? Would you really...?" He turned her into his muscular arms, his big broad chest taking up her view.

"What's wrong?" she asked, her fingers to his roughened cheek, her heart aching at the thought he might still be unhappy. She smoothed the pad of her thumb over his cheek, filled with the desire to kiss his poor eyelid that had barely just opened. To kiss the still healing scrapes and bruises from all the beatings he'd taken. To make love to this incredible man until he forgot all of his troubles.

He dipped his nose to hers. "Nothing's wrong, babe. I just want to marry you. Would you ever—"

"Yes," she bit out quickly and certainly, not a shadow of doubt in her mind. "Yes, Tucker. I'll marry you." She eased her palm to the nape of his neck and tugged his forehead to hers just so she could look into those sexy blue eyes that right then reflected the sea and the sky and all of her heart. "I love you, Tucker Chase. Right here. Right now. And every single day after this one."

A choke caught in his throat, a funny little sound, and she knew she was witnessing a rare thing. Tucker Chase wiped his eyes before his tears spilled, but she'd seen them glimmering at the edge of his eyelids. She knew. This man had the tender heart of a lion. Pure gold.

He growled and turned her around to face the cabin and living quarters, and there stood Jacob and Noah in traditional Vietnamese costumes. Isaiah and Deuce too, both grinning like cats that had eaten the proverbial canary. They almost looked like priests, decked out in simple black brocade tunics with the stiff mandarin collars. Obviously borrowed clothes. Obviously up to no good. Obviously not playing cards like she'd thought.

"You mean right now?" She had to ask.

"Yes, babe. Right here and right now. Noah's the captain of his boat. He can do it." Tucker engulfed her under his arm. His hand snaked under her long wrap and settled like a catcher's mitt over one cheek of her ass. He gripped her hard enough that he started a chain reaction that launched from her suddenly pebbled nipples to her clenching tummy, and all those other body parts reserved exclusively for Tucker.

Her heart exploded with the implications of this wonderful, rash decision. She'd be Mrs. Tucker Chase by nightfall. By bedtime. By hell—

"Yes," she breathed, never so sure about anything before in her life.

"You must dress," Noah said sternly, his arm extended and his finger pointing for her to go below.

"You have a... a wedding dress... for me?" She couldn't believe these devious men in her life.

"And pretty shoes," Jacob answered while Noah nodded solemnly, both indicating she should go.

"Hurry," Tucker muttered as he shooed her along with a sharp smack on her ass. "Don't take all day."

She couldn't help it. She giggled like a little girl as she rushed to do his bidding. Darn that arrogant, smug man of hers. He did things to her. And that spank to her backside? It stung, but it also elicited a wash of feminine tears between her thighs. It made her want to be compliant, to please him. To put that smoky, sexy light in his eyes while she drooled all over him. To do anything that would get her hands on him and him inside of her body where he belonged.

She hurried back to his side after she'd dressed in the simple long, red silk gown laid out on her bunk. Just for grins and future giggles, she left her underwear in her room. He'd promised something with that hard sting on her ass, hadn't he? This would be a short ceremony, right?

Anticipation swept through her veins like molten lava. By the time she'd maneuvered the stairs up to the deck in the pretty stiletto heels, her body was in sexual overdrive, half predator and completely famished.

Tucker's mouth dropped when she came straight to him. He pulled her easily into his chest, that misty shimmer in his eyes again. "God, I love you," he ground out, "so damned hard, babe. Look at you. You're—"

She made sure Deuce was out of range before she tipped up to her toes to nuzzle Tucker's ear and whispered, "Wet."

The stifled groan that came from his gut was all Melissa needed. "You're killing me," he grumbled back at her, his voice pitched low and feral. Hot as hell.

She loved the power she held over this wickedly dominant male who thought he ruled the world, and that every woman wanted to be with him. Ha. That day was past. Tucker Chase was effectively off the market and unavailable for future engagements. He was spoken for and about to get what he had coming to him.

The sun was low on the western horizon. The whole world turned pinkish orange as if it were on fire along with them. Even the river reflected a golden heat, and this—this was where her life began again. This was her bright and glowing future and her renewal, a definite baptism of fire if those male fingers smoothing over her ass, probably searching for a panty line, meant what she hoped they meant. Tucker needed to burn with her, to leave his past with all its heartache behind him, and to jump into this new life with her.

He turned her to face him, his dark eyes smoldering with some unspoken question. What could she say? She wanted this man in her heart for the rest of her life. And longer. "Are you ready for me?" she breathed, licking her bottom lip with one slow, sensual sweep of the tip of her tongue.

His eyes followed the movement. He swallowed hard, lifting her hand to his mouth to bite her knuckles, never breaking eye contact as he pressed a warm, moist kiss to the bite. "I've been ready for months, woman."

Animal heat shuddered off of him, melting her into a puddle at his feet. The man was sinfully dangerous and gloriously handsome. And now he was hers.

Melissa could barely swallow past the hard knot in her throat. How could she last through the ceremony and a reception? Breathing hard, she turned with Tucker to face the honorable Noah Giang as one, their fingers intertwined, Tucker's other hand possessively cupping her hip. Yes, she was going up in flames.

Noah offered a delightful prayer in Vietnamese, then repeated it in English before he pronounced the impulsive, happy couple man and wife. Jacob presented them with a stunning porcelain vase covered in blue vines and flowers, along with the symbols for double happiness. He took careful time to explain the lovely story behind the Vietnamese tradition, but Melissa could barely contain herself, her body weeping with desire for the stalwart warrior at her side, the man etching circles of lust with his fingernails over her hip bone.

Isaiah offered a gentlemanly bow, then offered a toast to the happy couple.

Deuce lifted his goblet and belted out an unexpected, "Oo-rah!"

Tucker grumbled, "I have got to teach that boy not to say jarhead shit like that."

And Melissa McCormack became Mrs. Tucker Chase. Forever.

# Chapter Thirty-Two

After a quick snack of grilled tiger prawns, sticky rice, and enough rice wine toasts to make a man see stars, Tucker politely excused himself and his new bride. They had an appointment to keep, and he would make certain they kept it.

He aimed a stern finger at Deuce as he snagged Melissa by her elbow. "You. No more wine, and you—" The next pointed warning went to Isaiah. "Make sure that's his only glass. He needs more than wine in his stomach. Make him eat more shrimp and rice. Vegetables. They're good for him."

Isaiah grinned. "Will do, boss," even as Deuce whined, "Aw, Dad."

Tucker didn't think twice. He had a woman to make love with and the hard-on from hell. That red silk kimono thing Melissa had slithered into had to go. It hugged her sumptuous ass and her tantalizing hips like a fine-fitting glove, teasing him with the promise of a warm, wet welcome home, but damn it. Her nipples had been on high beam since she'd put the thing on.

Did she mean for that slinky piece of silk to slither over her thighs and hug her toned tummy and hips like it did? Did she have any idea what she was doing to him and most likely every other horny male topside? Maybe even Deuce? He had to get her out of sight and naked and bent over something, his body speared inside of hers before he lost his mind.

She giggled as he escorted her, maybe a little too quickly, away. "I'm coming as fast as I can."

"No, babe, you're not," he growled down low in her ear. "Trust me. There's no such thing as a woman coming fast enough for a guy. Now get your ass downstairs."

She leaned her hip to the banister, sliding down it, a little tipsy from one too many toasts for all that double happy marriage business. Those Giangs could certainly hold their liquor. Tucker wasn't feeling it, but Melissa sure was.

Never in a million years had he expected her to be so impulsive—or so naughty. The woman had sex on her brain. It showed in the way she rubbed up against him, the way she let her fingers stray down his gut to his belt. He meant to give it to her, any and every way she wanted it.

"This way, babe." He steered her down the hall and into the one and only double-bed cabin onboard.

"Get rid of that dress," he ordered even as he jerked out of his pants and unbuttoned that annoying high collar on his ridiculous black tunic. It made him look like a priest, the last thing he was. He made quick work of dragging the bed covers and pillows to the floor. He wouldn't need blankets for a while, but he did need a nice flat surface for this next mission.

*She's mine,* he thought. *Finally. She said yes, and she meant it, we're married, and she's all mine. How'd I ever get so lucky?*

"But Tuck... er..." She slurred his name, her high-heeled feet spread and her bright blue eyes full of enough stars to make a man's heart swell with pride. And that damned dress still on. "You could be a little more... ro... man... tic. After all, it is our wedding night."

"Romance comes later," he quipped. With one quick step into her space, he bent to catch the hem of her silk and stripped the dress up and off her lush, tempting body. Yep. She was stark-ass naked beneath that dress, just as he'd suspected. The tease.

This was a different side to Melissa McCormack. Her eyes widened in surprise. The silly woman actually covered her overflowing breasts with both hands, her fingers splayed. She might have been able to hide those mouthwatering mauve nipples, but she couldn't conceal much of the billowing, creamy pillows he intended to bury his face between the minute she was on her back. Not the uniquely feminine scent lifting into his nostrils, either, nor the triangular garden of delight at the juncture of her legs.

But those heels? *God, help me now.* His blood boiled at the sight of her long legs, and what he could do to her with them wrapped around him. He'd been hard for days, but seeing her stripped naked, watching her dare-me chin lift, and the soft tipsy glow of love in her eyes... knowing she loved him...

He tugged her into his arms and angled her over his knee. With one sharp but playful smack to that wiggling ass, he growled, "No bra? No panties? On a boat full of men? You're a tease, little girl. You've got this one coming."

She arched backward, her head up while she brought one hand around, trying to cover her derrière, but still giggling like a naughty little girl. "You're spanking me?"

He leveled her head toward the floor just to tilt her ass higher, but then...

His red palm print on her tender flesh stopped him cold. He couldn't do it. He couldn't hurt her. Not Melissa. A tremble started in his heart. Memories of the abuse he'd suffered at his father's hands and fists rolled back on Tucker. No. He couldn't let himself morph into that monster. The blustering, pig-headed, obnoxious level he'd sunk to wasn't him. It had to stop. Here. Now.

He placed his palm over the heated mark on her backside and bowed his head even as she squirmed and giggled. "Tucker! You're making me laugh."

*Yeah, well...*

"I'm sorry," he whispered, more contrite than he'd ever been in his life. More ashamed. Not once had he ever raised a hand to Deuce. Why the urge to unleash his angst on Melissa now? On her wedding night? For fun? The compulsion blew Tucker away. This was not who he wanted to be. Not at all.

His heart deflated along with the rest of him. He swallowed hard, bringing Melissa upright on his knees, her face still aglow with rice wine and love, her body flushed. That humbled him more. He'd taken advantage of her when she was compromised, when he should've been the one taking especially good care of her, instead of rutting like some egotistical—SEAL.

He could barley meet the question in her eyes. God, he'd been such an ass. Everyone was right. Melissa deserved someone better than him.

She hooked one elbow around his neck, her other hand at his chest and her breath in his face. "Are you okay?" she asked, still dizzy enough she tilted backward.

"I am now," he growled, steadying her with a palm to the middle of her back, "and I promise I'll never hurt you again."

She cocked her head, looking at him through a mess of silky blonde tangles. "You didn't hurt me, Tuck. Honest." She blew at her strands of hair, but they went nowhere. "I knew you were playing. You'd never hurt me."

"Yeah, but I was playing rough. Too rough." Besides Deuce, Melissa was that one pure thing in his life. Tucker quelled his emotions. He dipped one hand to her cheek and smoothed her hair out of her eyes, tugging the loose strand behind her ear. Leaning in to kiss the end of her nose, he manned-up and took control of his and Melissa's future. "I'd like to get it right this time, babe. For once, I'd like to be the man you think you see in me. I'd like to be—" he gulped "—worthy of you."

Her lips curled in a sexy, drunken half-smile. "Then give me a kiss, big guy, because I'm on fi-i-i-r-r-r-r-e and I'm tired of waiting."

Tucker very nearly grinned at the salacious pout to her delectable lips. Melissa did tend to think she was a sex kitten when she'd had a glass of wine. Until this moment, he'd always maintained that line of propriety between them. He'd put her to bed when she'd gotten like this, and he'd done nothing more than snuggle with her. Not once had he taken advantage of her inebriated state. He'd been honorable.

"Are you sure you're up to this?" he asked, giving her a way out.

She nodded, saucy curls bouncing at her shoulders, dripping over her bare breasts in a luxurious cascade. "I love you, Tucker. I need you. Please make love to me again. Don't make me wait. Give it to me. I want all of you. Every day. Maybe twice." She ended lifting her shoulders with a shrug.

Enough said. He couldn't refuse his woman on her wedding night, could he?

Tenderly, Tucker eased Melissa onto the bed, laying her head on the pillow. She stared up at him, breathless, her pulse throbbing at the satiny hollow of her neck. The time for talk was over.

Melissa gave him no time for second thoughts. With a cute growl, she latched onto the nape of his neck and drew him into the heavenly warmth of her wet mouth. That was all it took to get him back in the game. One taste. One promise of forever.

He eased one knee between her thighs while he smoothed a hand over her ribcage to her breast. The sweet tango of tongues began in earnest. Tugging at her nipple, he scraped the pad of his thumb over the tip, pebbling it. Tucker made soft, gentle love to her mouth, urging her to climb that celestial staircase with him, needing her to fly with him. That was what made her different than others. She aspired to be with him in everything he did. She wanted him like no one else ever had.

She writhed beneath him, setting his body on fire. Tucker fit inside the cradle of her hips as if he'd been made for her, as if he'd finally found where he belonged. He was lost in a sensual world of silky hair, satin skin, and the luscious scent of his all American girl.

When Melissa scraped her fingernails over his scalp, digging into his back , the moment came when they could no longer refuse the impulse to mate. To growl at each other in soaring passion. To bear witness with muffled cries that declared they'd climbed to the highest stars, that they'd exploded into each other in blinding bursts of what could only be two souls joining together. The fireworks ended too fast. Too soon. They fell back to Earth in each other's arms.

Tucker let out a shuddering sigh as Melissa quivered beneath him. He loved the word *coming*. It held so much promise with her. So much—everything.

Stiffening his spine, he gave her the depth she needed, every last inch, going in deep and inducing aftershocks that rippled through her core. The sublime comfort of the act took his breath. He'd never felt so much for any woman in his life. So much tenderness. Devotion.

The moment robbed him of his arrogance, of the desperate loneliness haunting him. It was very much as if he'd died in her arms and risen anew. As if joining with her sweet spirit had finally chased every last ghost away, the grim reaper, too. He couldn't speak, the love welling up in his heart too reverent. So damned sacred.

Melissa snuggled into his neck, rubbing her cheek against him like a cat. "I really needed that," she purred, her body stretched languidly beneath his, her fingernails tracing lines up the back of his head, then down his neck to land on his ass. "Tucker? Are you okay?"

He nodded, fighting for composure. Damn it, real men didn't cry. She'd proven herself ready, willing, and certainly able to take him on, so why the intense emotion sweeping up from the lowest levels of his heart? Why couldn't he get a grip already?

Because this time wasn't just about good sex. It was that elusive *more* he'd been searching for, finally found. It was Melissa and the light she'd filled his life with just by showing up. It was Deuce. Isaiah. America. God, it was—everything.

Soft kisses landed on his ear as her fingers raked over his head, gentling him. Settling the broken, ragged pieces of his heart back into place. Healing every rough edge. Vanquishing his demons. The anger of years lifted out of him like an ugly wraith that had attached itself to his soul for too long. It hurt losing the tentacles that had dug themselves in deep around the cords of his solitary heart—in a really good way.

He, Tucker Chase, was no loser. He wasn't his old man and he wasn't a killing machine. Better than that, he wasn't just a good SEAL. He was a good man and a good father again. Deuce was safe and would live a long and prosperous life, if Tucker had anything to say about it. Melissa would get fat and pregnant with however many kids she wanted, and they'd all know they had the best mom and a good dad. He'd never spank her ass again, but if he did, it would only be in play. In bed. *Maybe...*

He swallowed hard. God, he'd been fighting the world all of his adult life and most of his childhood. To finally be free of that desperate need to control the spread of evil in the world, vanquished the last of his ego. How pretentious had he been? Eliminating evil was never his job or his mission. There wasn't a man on Earth who could do it. But living for Melissa and Deuce?

Yeah. He could do that.

Shuddering, he breathed in a deep cleansing breath, and it was her sweet scent he inhaled. It filled his entire being. He drew in another breath as a man reborn and ready to try again.

Her delicate fingers cupped the back of his head, holding him to her. She pressed her lips to his ear. "I want a tattoo."

He couldn't help it. The notion of this prim, bossy woman with an anchor tattooed on her bicep made him laugh. Melissa was one outrageous surprise after another. "A tattoo?" he asked, finally lifting up from the warm recess of her neck, but still joined together as man and wife. As soul mates. "What kind of tattoo, babe? And where would you like it? On your ass?"

Melissa giggled, still buzzed. "Believe it or not, not everything has to do with my backside."

He nuzzled in deep, scraping his whiskered chin over her jaw while he landed a moist kiss in her ear, loving it when she wiggled against him. "Bet me."

"I get that. You're a man, but..." She tilted her head, granting him more access, sparking another flame in his groin. "But I want a heart with our initials right here. Over my heart."

He lifted his torso up from her, thrusting his hips forward, needing to see. "Where?"

"Here," she whispered, her blue eyes gone dark with lust at the hardening of his body, her womanly curves molding to his thighs. She traced a circle between her breasts, but her breath hitched. Her body clenched, pulling him in for more.

"You can have whatever you want, babe, but if you do, I'm getting the same one. Same place as yours." He ended that dare with another thrust of good intentions.

She nodded, clenching him, an obedient little wench with a gleam in her sexy blue eyes. Her lashes fluttered. "Hmmm. Maybe I will put it on my ass then."

Tucker couldn't help it. He laughed out loud. She might not remember this crazy conversation when she sobered up, and she might change her mind, but one thing was sure. He'd met his match and he knew it.

# Chapter Thirty-Three

Vietnamese funerals were different. Strange to American ways. Still sad.

Tucker refused the painkillers Dr. Giang offered for his still healing lungs. He wouldn't take them, not when his son was hurting so badly he could barely speak, just cry, unashamed of his tender feelings for his lost friend. Melissa hadn't left Deuce's side since this hard day began, her hand firmly in his as if she were his real mother. As if she had always been there.

Tucker had stood proud at Deuce's right when Luke's body was brought to the Giangs' junk for final preparation, his arm tight around the boy whose mental anguish he could now hear loud and clear. The utter grief. The immeasurable pain in an innocent young man's broken heart. It was almost more than a father could bear.

Nicole couldn't make it. The bitch was finally where she belonged, in the bowels of the same jail where Tucker had been harshly detained. Tucker only hoped she'd get the same treatment he had, but knowing her conniving ways like he did, he doubted it. Hell, she'd probably rule the roost before nightfall. Mr. Big Stuff might even be suffering along with all the other guards with the drama from their latest inmate. Who cared?

When a person passed away in Vietnam, the surviving family held a five-day vigil, a wake of sorts filled up with friends' and neighbors' visits, condolences, lights, and prayers. Often, a funeral took every last bit of the family's hard-earned money. Since Luke had no one to claim his body, Tucker had stepped in to assume the costs and responsibility of a father.

With Jacob and Noah's assistance, he'd performed the preparation ritual the night before. He'd washed Luke's fragile body, the one Vinnie's thugs had pummeled into bruises before Nicole shot him. The poor kid never stood a chance in this world. With every gentle swipe, the message struck home again and again. *This could have been Deuce.*

Tucker had gritted his teeth, bit back his tears, and carried on. After Luke had been carefully clothed in the new suit Melissa had bought for him, Tucker had laid a clean white chopstick between Luke's teeth per Uncle Noah's instructions. In Vietnamese tradition, it ensured Luke's mouth remained open for the grains of rice and coins his friends or visitors might insert before his burial. After all, the motherless child might get hungry on his way to eternity.

Jacob's uncle said a quiet prayer then, which Jacob translated, but he addressed Deuce when he said the gentle words, "Being born from the earth, one must return to the earth. It is the way of all things."

Deuce had nodded as if he'd understood, but Tucker knew his boy didn't have a clue. Death was beyond understanding for most kids. It was one of those harsh, bigger-than-life realities a guy never really comprehended, no matter how old he was. Maybe women were better at handling grief. Maybe not. Tucker only knew he was carrying a boatload of sorrow for his lost buddies and friends in his own heart. The pain never went away. It just got shifted around to make room for another.

Now Deuce would be carrying his own pain, maybe two if losing his birth mother counted. Tucker honestly didn't know. He hadn't talked with Deuce about what had happened with Nicole yet. He'd let his son pick the time and place for that discussion. *If ever...*

At the end of the ceremony, Jacob and his uncle had helped Tucker swaddle Luke's body into a clean white funeral cloth, careful to keep the chopstick in place. Then came the hard part, putting Luke down inside the four walls of that wooden box. Of letting this homeless and unloved child go.

Tucker could barely let Luke go. He'd held onto his body a little longer, his heart shredded while he'd fought for composure in the face of such awful tragedy. That poor little guy. This lost soul. Tucker had curled Luke into his chest and cradled him, his head bowed to Luke's forehead, wishing to hell that God's plan hadn't been so harsh.

There were no words to bring Luke back from the grave. No words to bridge the gap between life and death. No words to reason away man's inhumanity to man, to explain it so a boy could understand what Tucker still couldn't grasp.

He'd offered what he could. "Sleep tight, son," he'd whispered gruffly into Luke's ear. "You are hereby relieved from duty. May you forever know fair winds and following seas."

At last, he'd laid Luke down and let him go, and the casket, the best money could buy, was closed.

But today was harder.

Tucker walked with Deuce at one side, Melissa at the other. They followed the somber procession to the place of burial, a cemetery farther along the Saigon River to the south. Noah had chosen the site for Luke's final resting place.

In the tradition of the land, geomancy, the location and position of the grave, determined a person's fortune in the afterlife. Luke's gravesite rested beneath the long tendrils of a weeping willow facing the river. Jacob had previously lined the trail with lighted votive candles. So many lights along the way. How appropriate. How sad.

Much of this culture's tradition had to do with ancestors, the spirits who were supposedly able to reach back through time and space to help their living descendants. Tucker grunted at that stupid belief. No ancestors had shown up to help Luke when he'd needed them most. No one had come to his rescue except another lost kid who'd gotten his butt kicked for trying.

After a lot of chanting and more praying, Luke was finally laid to rest. Jacob explained how it was tradition to leave rice at the grave for the deceased. How after forty-nine days, the family would stop bringing rice. How after one hundred days, Luke's family and friends would gather back at his grave to celebrate something called *tot khoc*—the end of tears.

Tucker knew better. Tears never ended. They just went underground and turned into hidden wellsprings in a guy's heart that might pop a geyser of remorse and sorrow up to the surface at the most inopportune time. Look at Deuce, brave but fighting for composure every step of the way. Look at Melissa, her pretty blue eyes puffy and red-rimmed, as they'd been most days since Luke had died in her arms. Not fair.

Even Isaiah had grown more somber. He'd taken a long walk by himself last night, and Tucker knew he needed to chat with the kid. Isaiah had voluntarily assumed responsibility for dealing with the authorities, but something had been bothering him since that showdown at Vinnie's. Isaiah's gloom seemed to have faded during Tucker's wedding, but today, it had returned with far-off stares and brooding stretches of silence. Tucker couldn't even reach Isaiah mentally.

Tucker cussed himself. He should've shot Nicole sooner. Faster. In the head. Before she'd taken this little guy's life. But he hadn't, and he couldn't understand why not. He wouldn't have hesitated if it had been anyone else gunning them down, so why had he with Nicole? He didn't love her. That wasn't the reason. She'd killed those feelings long ago. The only thing that made sense was what Melisa had said. A father shouldn't kill his son's mother.

He shouldn't have had to.

At last, Deuce dropped to one knee at his friend's graveside. He'd been carrying a bulky duffle bag the entire walk. Tucker couldn't help but smile when he saw what was in it. The poor kid removed a small bag full of rice from his bag and tucked it inside the coffin alongside Luke. He transferred a black nylon wallet full of Vietnamese paper dollars into Luke's hand.

"I know he's not really gonna need this stuff, Dad, but I wanna make sure he's got enough," Deuce ground out, his voice cracking, "just in case. Is that okay? Do you think I'm being stupid?"

Tucker blinked hard. "No, son. I think you're the bravest man I've ever met."

The son Tucker loved to the depths of his battered warrior's soul broke his father's heart all over again. Deuce pulled his violin case out of that duffle bag and something else—his Little League baseball cap and the ball Tucker had given him the fateful day he'd lost him. Vinnie had the grace to let the boy take whatever he'd wanted when Tucker had driven him to the estate for the last time.

With tears dripping down his face, Deuce laid his violin across Luke's chest. He choked as he secured the cap to Luke's head, nice and tight, the brim backward like Tucker had taught him. Very carefully, Deuce lifted his friend's hand from the shroud and wrapped that baseball inside his stiff fingers, his shoulders heaving when he said, "I can't go with you this time, buddy, so you need to practice real good so we can play together when we meet again, okay? 'Cause I'm gonna find you in heaven, Luke. I mean it. I promise. You'll never be alone again." Deuce scrubbed a hand over his face and climbed to his feet, and in the way of all little boys falling apart, he turned into Melissa's arms instead of Tucker's, sobbing. "I m-m-miss him. He shared noodles with me when I was hungry. He was my friend."

Melissa's teary gaze met Tucker's over the top of Deuce's head. *'I love you,'* she mouthed, but Tucker turned away, his heart raw at the injustice of life. It wasn't that Deuce had chosen the comfort of her arms over his, it was the whole jacked-up mess of it all.

What was God thinking to make life so damned hard for little kids and animals and old people, huh? Why did Luke have to die? Him? A little boy who'd never had a break in his short, pitiful life? What was so important in Heaven that God couldn't let the kid live a little longer? *Shit!* Tucker's angst boiled over. Why didn't people understand how little it took to be kind to each other?

He pressed a fist to his forehead, as angry as he'd ever been. He might blame God for a lot of things, but this time it was his fault, every last bit of it. Not God's.

*"No, it's not,"* his faithful conscience whispered. Isaiah. The kid should've been named Jiminy Cricket the way he kept chirping up at all the wrong moments. Like now.

*"What do you know?"* Tucker shot back at him as he ran a quick hand over his face, shoving his grief back down in his gut where it belonged, ashamed he'd let it get away from him. The guy might not be within sight, but Isaiah was always there. Always at the back of Tucker's mind. And now inside his breaking heart.

Isaiah sent back a drawn-out mental sigh that spoke volumes. *"I know, believe me. I was the guy the Bicks forced to do a lot of crap while I was under their, umm, care, remember? I hurt you and Eden and my dad—a lot of other people, too. You have to let this go, Tuck. Bad things happen, and sometimes we're just there when they do. Sometimes we can help. Sometimes we can't. Sometimes we're God's avenging angels, but most of the time, we're helpless bystanders, and all we can do is stand and watch and bear testimony against the evil in the world. We can't carry the blame for everything that goes wrong. We just can't. It will eat us up."*

Tucker exhaled a deep breath, wishing it were that simple.

*"You saved your wife and your son, Tuck. Some helpless little girls, too. You would've saved Tristan if he'd let you. You're one of the good guys. Stop beating yourself up."*

*"Yeah, well..."* The good advice was easier said than done. Tucker stared out at the busy river life with all those junks and sampans and little rickety motorboats. All those houses on stilts along the riverbank. There it was, happening again. *Life.* It never stopped or slowed down, and maybe that was a good thing after all.

He let his gaze scroll over the cemetery, searching for Isaiah but not seeing him. *"So what's wrong, kid? You're quiet lately. Do you need to talk something out?"*

Isaiah's breath caught. *"I'll tell you about it someday."*

Tucker knew instantly. Go figure. Maybe he was a mind reader. *"Your mother?"*

*"Yes,"* Isaiah came back wistfully. *"I miss her on days like this."*

Tucker never had a mother he could remember, only his mean old man. He clenched his jaw so hard that his back teeth creaked at the pressure.

*"Deuce is crying, and he's not ashamed to do it,"* Isaiah whispered on the breeze. *"You should be proud, Tucker. Your son's a better man than either of us will ever be."*

*"You've got that right."* Tucker bowed his head, so damned tired of fighting the world. Just when he thought he'd found safe haven, it reared its ugly head again. He needed back in Melissa's arms where things made sense. Where comfort lived. *"You're a good man, Isaiah. I hope you know that. If there's anything I can do—"*

"Dad?"

Tucker froze. *Shit. Just shit.*

Deuce stood behind him. Needing him. Expecting him to turn around and be tough and all that heroic crap that heroes never really were. Didn't anyone get it? They were just the guys who showed up and tried not to get killed while they did their job. That was all.

"Yeah, son?" he ground out, still facing away, his fists clenched. Any second now the dam would break, and he'd cry like a baby, make a fool of himself, and—

Deuce wrapped his arms around Tucker's waist and laid his head on his back. "I love you, Dad," were the only words he had to utter to break Tucker. Grief shuddered from his kid's true blue heart through Tucker's body, resonating to his tough guy core. He clutched Deuce's clasped hands fiercely over his gut in a grip he swore he'd never take for granted again.

When Melissa sobbed behind him—

*Oh, what the hell. If Deuce was man enough...*

Tucker turned into his son, his eyes squeezed tight as he pressed his kid to his chest and cried with him. "I love you, son. You're a good boy," he muttered, swallowing hard before he fell completely apart. He was that close.

Melissa snaked a hand under Tucker's suit jacket and around his waist, her fingers sliding below his belt. "And I love the two of you."

He pulled her into the Chase family circle where she belonged. Deuce sealed the deal when he snuggled in tight against his old man's bigger, wider body and whispered, "I'm gonna be just like you, Dad."

Tucker squeezed his eyes tight to squelch more tears, but it was Melissa who surprised him when she said, "You already are, son."

God, he loved this woman.

# Chapter Thirty-Four

Damned if some guy in pitch-black sunglasses, a dirty ball cap, and a worn leather jacket didn't show up at Tân Sơn Nhất International Airport to see Tucker and his new family off. Black-haired and deeply tanned with a thick, dark scruff on his chin and cheeks, he stopped where Tucker sat with Melissa, Deuce, and Isaiah. He stood there with his feet spread like he meant to start a fight. "You," he said gruffly.

Tucker couldn't believe his eyes. He scrambled out of the seat, one arm outstretched to shake this legend's hand. "Smoke Montoya? Melissa, come meet this guy. Isaiah. Deuce. This here's a real no-kidding hero. It's Smoke Montoya."

Smoke grasped Tucker's forearm in a warrior's grip. "I had to see it with my own eyes, you son-of-a-bitch. You're still around."

Tucker hadn't a clue what that meant. He slapped his brother SEAL's back. Hard. "Course I'm still around. Why wouldn't I be? Man, I never thought I'd see the day we were in the same place at the same time. Where you going?"

Smoke jerked his head to the side. "Nowhere. Just came here to meet the guy who faced off with those thirty-plus piece-of-shit insurgents in that battle with the Kurds in Iraq. That was some mean work and a brave thing you did saving those eleven missionaries. I heard you took a round, but you held off that horde all by yourself 'til help showed up. I'm damned proud to know you."

"You're kidding? You came to see me?" That made no sense. Smoke was the hero. Not Tucker. Everyone who was anyone knew that. "It was no big deal—honest. I was just doing my job. How do you know Stewart?"

"He's been around."

Man, this guy was hard as a rock and about as forthcoming as Alex.

Smoke planted his feet, crossed his arms over his chest after that one handshake, but didn't crack another hint of expression, much less a smile. He didn't lower his dark glasses when he nodded at Isaiah and Deuce, nor when he acknowledged Melissa with a gruff, "ma'am."

"Hello, Mr. Montoya. Any friend of Tucker's is a friend of mine." She lit the world with her dazzling smile, but Smoke seemed impervious to a woman's charms. He didn't budge an inch. Didn't offer to shake her hand. Isaiah's or Deuce's either. Just stood there like a brick wall.

"Do you have time for a drink?" Tucker asked, star struck with his superhero standing this close. "I'm buying. Beer? Whiskey? You name it."

The guy wasn't very old, but to finally meet the Navy SEAL sniper who held the current record for confirmed kills against an enemy that had no problem beheading women and children? Priceless. Tucker was pretty certain that was how Smoke got his handle—his uncanny ability to get in close enough to take out five or six bastards at a time without being seen by anyone but his spotter. The man was exactly like smoke—there one minute, gone the next. Tucker couldn't recall Montoya's real first name any more.

Smoke stuck his hands in his pockets and looked away. "No, thanks. I've got places to be."

What did you say to a guy who acted as if he'd rather be anywhere else than there with you?

Smoke solved the awkward moment with an abrupt, "See ya around."

"Hey, wait up a second. You got a number?" Tucker pressed, not wanting this once-in-a-lifetime moment to end. He pulled out his brand new cell phone to take Smoke's contact information. "I'll hook up with you when you get back to the States. We'll grab a beer. Tell a few lies. Tell me where and when, and I'll be there."

Smoke shook his head. "No," he said without hesitation. "I'm not going back to the States any time soon."

Well, alrighty then. Tucker backed his enthusiasm off. As far as he knew, the guy had never married and he hadn't gone home once he'd left the Navy, just disappeared and migrated from one foreign country after another. Tucker didn't know why, but he understood. Some scars ran deeper than others, that was all. Some ghosts never let go.

"I'll never forget this day," he admitted honestly. "I mean it. It's been a privilege just to shake your hand. I hope you'll come home someday. I hope I'll get to buy that drink for you. God knows you deserve it."

Smoke grunted and Tucker couldn't miss the hostile vibes rolling off the guy. It might've been disgust. Maybe anger. He wasn't going to double it by adding, *'Thank you for your service.'* Sincere or not, most veterans hated the attention they got for doing their job when so many others had died.

Isaiah and Deuce stood there quietly, when, with a curt nod, Smoke took a step back and pivoted, his hands still in his pockets.

"It was nice meeting you, Mr. Montoya," Melissa said sincerely to his broad back. "Maybe next time we can talk longer."

Tucker saw it then, the coiled rattlesnake embroidered under the shoulder blades of Smoke's leather jacket, and the gold *Don't Tread On Me* stenciled beneath it. Enough said. This man wanted his space and he wanted it now.

Tucker had said all he could anyway. He snaked an arm around Melissa's waist and watched the hero walk away, an odd lump in his throat. A man shouldn't be so lonely. He shouldn't have to live out his days in foreign countries. He should've gone home. Why hadn't he?

"He's not very talkative, is he?" Melissa asked, her palm on Tucker's chest, but her gaze on the solitary man intent on getting lost in the crowds of people coming and going.

"I guess not," Tucker answered, wondering what the hell had just happened, and what Smoke's story was. It must've taken a helluva lot for the reclusive guy to come all the way into this busy airport just to shake hands with the wrong hero.

Tucker didn't have time to worry about it. His flight to America was just called.

He and his family were going—home.

# Epilogue

"You're bullshittin' me. You want me to do what?"

Tucker should've known they were up to something when he received a personal request to meet with FBI Director Zachary Strong and his nemesis, Alex Stewart. There they sat opposite Tucker at the conference table in Strong's office, in their matching gray business suits and both wearing blazing red power ties. What'd they do? Call coordinate their apparel for the day? Who were they, the Bobbsey Twins from Hell? Request nothing. This was an ambush.

"You heard me," Director Strong said evenly. "I'm assigning you to head the newest department in the agency. You'll work directly with HRT when necessary, but you'll answer directly to me. Alex will serve as advisor."

HRT, as in the Hostage Rescue Team, aka SWAT. Alex Stewart as in—*what the hell?*

By then, Tucker had sold his place. He'd moved Melissa out of her singles-only condo and into a comfortable home east of National Harbor with him and Deuce. It was a new start for the three of them, but from day one, she'd amaze him at the instant rapport she had with his son. Deuce hadn't called Melissa mom yet, but that's precisely what she was. His friend. His protector. His confidant. Everything he should've had all along.

Tucker was finally sleeping nights. He'd cut out the booze and slowed his response time to the demands from his office. He didn't need to be on-call twenty-four-seven. Not anymore. Let some younger agent take on that unrealistic challenge. Tucker was content to be caught up in the adventure of a lifetime—building his family. He was a winner again to the only two people who mattered, Melissa and Deuce. Everything and everyone else came in second place.

"Say I accept, what will my prime directive be? My mission?" Tucker asked his director.

Strong shrugged. "Counter-terrorism, both domestic and foreign. Protecting Americans. Basically, you and your team will do anything and everything you can to protect and serve. Just like you're doing today."

Alex never batted an eye.

Tucker swallowed hard, wishing he could see inside these two apex predators' hard heads. They weren't kidding anyone. There was a catch in the offer, a razor in the bait, a hook in this too-good-to-be-true proposition that blatantly promised an over-the-top federal salary no other agent that Tucker knew earned. It would be hard to turn down a raise like this one, and he was a family man now. He owed Melissa and Deuce a semi-normal, comfortable life.

Besides, he was tired. He'd just returned from an undisclosed trip to Vietnam to see if Vinnie had meant what he'd said when he'd promised he'd change. The man would've been smart if he had, but had he? *Not on your life*. And because he was still threatening children at his sweatshop, and because that mean old hag of his still used her rod on children, Tucker made sure the Vietnamese authorities received every single piece of the incriminating evidence Isaiah had gathered. By the time Tucker hit Tân Sơn Nhất International Airport to exfil out of there, Vinnie's place had been raided, and his sons were in the care of their Grandmama. Vinnie was on his way to join Nicole in jail. God, they deserved each other.

Alex cleared his throat, no doubt sensing Tucker's mind was a couple thousand miles from the decision point in front of him. Tucker shifted his gaze from one snake to the other. Stewart and Strong had also promised him his own budget and autonomy in selecting the agents he'd need. That part of the deal actually made sense. Tucker knew plenty of good men and women in need of employment, some from the Navy, some Marines or soldiers. But these two *gentlemen*, and he used the term loosely, were up to something. They had something up their crisply ironed cotton sleeves besides their hairy arms.

There *had* to be a catch.

Tucker kicked back in his seat, his elbow on his armrest, his index finger on his cheekbone while he studied Alex. "You haven't had much use for me before. Why now?"

As expected, Alex leaned into the question, his elbows to the table, his tough guy façade never wavering, his jaw tight. The guy didn't know the meaning of retreat. "I'm not here to play games, Chase. It's simple. You're the best man for the job. Take it or leave it, but hurry the hell up and decide. I've got work to do."

Tucker stared the hard man down. What he wouldn't have given for another chance to work with this straight arrow someday. Deep down, Alex was another legend, breath of King Leonidas from the Battle of Thermopylae. *Shit. Just shit.*

The last rule of negotiation tugged at Tucker's brain cells: *Always ask for one more concession.* "Fine," he breathed suspicion with his answer, "on one condition."

Zachary sent him the dare of a chin-lift.

Alex stared back, his eyes hooded. Calculating. "What now?"

"I want Ky Winchester and his wife, Eden." Tucker stuck out his chin, too. If a man was going to fight, he might as well throw in all the way. They were both psychics, Eden for sure, Ky a definite maybe. They'd be his ace-in-the-hole. Make that aces. "With them I can get this department up and running in no time. That's what you want, isn't it? Fast action? Results? Answers?"

Taking an asset from each Stewart and Strong sounded smart when Tucker said it. It sounded brash and pushy and professional—until a sneaky look passed between the two high-stakes power brokers. Why did Tucker have a sudden sinking sensation in the pit of his gut?

"I have no problem with that." Alex damned near smiled.

*Like that helped.*

Zachary extended a hand across the table. "Deal."

*Still not helping.*

Tucker's gut clenched tighter, but he shook his boss's hand to seal the negotiation. The first rule of a good SEAL: *Never let an opportunity for one-upmanship slide.* "Tate Higgins, too. I want... Tate." Now he just hoped Tate and Ky wanted to work with him. He might just have to develop some real, no-kidding people skills.

Alex never hesitated. "Done."

Damn, did he have ice water in his veins, willingly surrendering two of his best agents to the federal entity he'd battled for years? Tucker swallowed hard.

What the hell was really going on? That win should have sent him into a happy dance instead of a tailspin. *Shit. What am I not seeing?*

The thought of Melissa's pretty face spurred him to take his chances and double down. She owned him, heart and soul. She might as well have his ears and eyes, too. He went for broke. "And I'm done with this cochlear implant. I want it gone. The optical implant, too. I'm no guinea pig." There was only way this was going down—if he got every last perk he asked for. Melissa deserved that much, and by hell, for once, Tucker would come out ahead of his boss, even if it meant he'd let the rest of the world down. This was all about Melissa and he'd be sure to tell her about the surgery—beforehand. She deserved nothing but his best and he meant to give it to her. He only needed one person in his head anyway, and that person was Melissa. Maybe Isaiah.

Thankfully, this new position promised more pay, regular hours, and administrative work instead of fieldwork, all benefits. He wasn't that cocky ball-buster anymore. He wanted a job he could walk away from at the end of the day. He needed more time with his woman, with Deuce too. He wanted his life.

Zachary nodded indifferently. "It was always a voluntary choice. Consider it done."

Tucker fidgeted, the collar of his dress shirt all at once extra tight. Why couldn't he relax with these two guys? They didn't intimidate him. Who turned the thermostat up?

"So what's the new department? What's the new workload that's so important it gets its own budget?" he asked, ignoring the hairs lifting up on the back of his neck. Ignoring the warning pinging from his inner sniper that told him to run, duck, and cover his ass. Still meeting Alex eye-to-eye and toe-to-toe, though. Still an equal. *He thought.*

Alex finally smiled, if that was what you wanted to call that snide thing that crawled over his lips and coiled in those icy blue eyes. It looked more like a pet rattlesnake. "Congratulations, Agent Chase. You're now the first director of the Bureau's one and only paranormal unit. Good call negotiating for Ky, Eden, and Tate. They'll fit in perfectly."

Tucker jumped out of his seat. "The what? The paranormal unit? What's that?"

Zachary grinned. "We're expanding our one-person psychic unit, Director Chase. Glad to have you aboard."

Isaiah's steady voice crept through the backdoor in Tucker's mind. *"Hey, Boss."*

# The End

# About the Author

**Irish Winters** is an award-winning author who dabbles in poetry, grandchildren, and rarely (as in extremely rarely) the kitchen. More prone to be outdoors than in, she grew up the quintessential tomboy on a farm in rural Wisconsin, spent her teenage years in the Pacific Northwest, but calls the Wasatch Mountains of Northern Utah home. For now.

The wife of one handsome husband and mother of three perfect sons, Irish divides her time between writing at home, and traveling the country with her man while – writing. (Seriously, what else?)

She believes in making every day count for something, and follows the wise admonition of her mother to, "Look out the window and see something!"

To learn more about Irish and her books, please visit www.IrishWinters.com.

# In the Company of Sniper series

ALEX
MARK
ZACK
HARLEY
CONNOR
RORY
TAYLOR
GABE
MAVERICK
CASSIDY
ADAM
LEE
KY
Christmas Hearts

## Coming soon

Smoke, *Hearts and Ashes Trilogy*, Book 1 (January 2017)
Hunter, *In the Company of Snipers*, #14 (2017)
Eric, *In the Company of Snipers*, #15 (2017)
Jake, *In the Company of Snipers*, #16 (2017)